Philip Caveney, born ⟨...⟩ two-year spell at Manchester's Piccadilly Radio, writing and presenting a weekly film review programme. He is a professional writer and freelance journalist, and his previous novels include *Speak No Evil*, *Black Wolf*, *Strip Jack Naked*, *Slayground*, *Skin Flicks*, *Burn Down Easy* and *Bad to the Bone*. He lives with his wife and young daughter in Heaton Moor.

1999

Philip Caveney

 HEADLINE
FEATURE

First published in 1997 by
HEADLINE BOOK PUBLISHING

First published in paperback in 1998
by HEADLINE BOOK PUBLISHING

A HEADLINE FEATURE paperback

10 9 8 7 6 5 4 3 2 1

ISBN 0 7472 5661 6

Typeset by Avon Dataset Ltd, Bidford-on-Avon, Warks

Printed and bound in Great Britain by
Mackays of Chatham plc, Chatham, Kent

HEADLINE BOOK PUBLISHING
A division of Hodder Headline PLC
338 Euston Road
London NW1 3BH

This book is for everyone
at the Workshop –
past, present and future.
After fifteen years, you're still
my most valued critics.
And special thanks to
David Bradwell
for so much support
and encouragement.

Prologue

On the evening of October fourteenth, 1999, Martin Ambrose celebrated his seventeenth birthday. He also murdered his girlfriend, Sophie, though this part of his night out had not been planned.

It was early evening and Martin was feeling good. He and Sophie had met up with their friends Tim and Karen at a cyber-café on Oxford Road and now they were all heading into the city centre in search of some suitable birthday entertainment. Manchester was currently in the grip of feverish preparations for Metro 2000, the huge multi-faceted festival that would welcome in the new millennium.

There was an almost carnival atmosphere on the streets that even the rain and the ever-present legions of ragged beggars couldn't dispel. Martin and his friends sauntered along New Cross Street, now in the final stages of rebuilding after the big blast of '96. They were heading for Clubland Piccadilly.

On Oldham Street, they found a couple of lone cops who were amusing themselves by beating up a Rag Man they'd found begging in a shop doorway. Martin and his friends stopped to watch for a while. The Rag Man seemed to be off his head. He was singing a hymn as the heavy boots lashed into his face and ribs: and his long grey beard was spattered with blood. A crowd was gathering, most of the onlookers happy to cheer the cops on, but Martin felt sorry for the Rag Man. Still, he knew better than to intervene. The Greater Manchester Police were revelling in their new powers and they weren't too choosy about their targets: so he urged the others to move on, not wanting to let these events cast a pall over his big night out.

They headed down to Sodom and Gomorrah, a favourite mineral bar, where Martin dulled his misgivings by sampling the wide selection of alcoholic fruit juices, mineral waters and draught lemonade. An hour later, suitably oiled, they moved on to The Garden of Terrestrial Delights, currently the city's hottest nightclub.

On the way in, Martin noticed a bedraggled-looking Rag Man standing a discrete distance from the marble-columned, neon-lit entrance. He knew that these homeless people were often used as 'mules' by the city's dope dealers, so he approached the man with the intention of buying some genuine E's, something with a little more poke than the Herbal Highs on sale inside. The Rag Man smelled like wet cardboard and had a furtive air. Yes, he told Martin, he had some pretty good E.

'But if you're in the mood for some *real* fun, I can do you a special price on a couple of tabs of Warp,' he added.

Martin had heard about Warp, but he'd never tried it. He knew that it was the latest designer drug, a cocktail of ecstasy and amphetamines cut with a powerful hallucinogen. It was not for the faint hearted but several of his friends had told him that it was the chemical equivalent of a white knuckle ride and they'd urged him to try it. You got visions with Warp, they said, more vivid and more real than the VR machines in the city arcades. Sure, it wasn't all a bed of roses, there'd been a few fatalities reported in the tabloids, just as there had in the early days of E, before a safer version was manufactured under licence. But the figures were what, one in a million? And besides, it *was* his birthday.

At any rate, Martin was feeling reckless and his friends were impatiently calling to him to get his ass into the club before Happy Hour ended: so he handed the Rag Man a fifty-pound note and palmed the two tiny purple pills he was handed in return. Once inside the club, he slipped into the toilet and swallowed them down with a handful of water from the tap.

Twenty minutes later, he was buzzing, enjoying the ripples of pure euphoria that were jolting through his system. He got up to dance with Sophie and the others, deliciously aware of the coloured spotlights playing upon his skin like questing fingertips and he felt powerful, omnipotent, overwhelmed by sheer pleasure. He moved to the slamming four four rhythm of a vintage rap track, as though he was plugged into the mains, swinging his hips, wiggling his ass, his hands describing complicated patterns in the air in front of his face. And he was grinning, grinning like an idiot because he'd never felt so good before, never like this . . .

And then Sophie danced up close to him and he saw that her face was beginning to change. In the green glow of a spotlight, it appeared to be moving, rearranging itself, the cheekbones pushing against the skin, the nostrils widening, the eyes mutating into white reptilian spheres.

Take it easy, Martin warned himself. *It's just a hallucination* . . .

But he couldn't deny that he was beginning to feel afraid. Sophie's skin was taking on a tough, scaly quality: and when she raised a hand to place it on his shoulder, he saw that it had become a huge, misshapen club of rotting flesh, from which protruded a series of rusting hypodermics, each one filled with a scummy yellow liquid. The needles stabbed through the fabric of his shirt, sinking deep into the skin and there was nothing virtual about the pain it caused him. He yelped and stepped away from her.

Sophie spoke to him, but what came out was a series of snuffling grunts. Martin couldn't help staring at her tongue, which was long and black. It flopped out of her mouth onto the front of her T-shirt and it was hung with thick strings of saliva. Martin glanced wildly over his shoulder to where Tim and Karen had been dancing before but he saw that they too, had changed. Now two insect-like creatures had taken their place. Their bodies were metamorphosing as he watched, swelling into weird distended shapes that tore their clothing at the seams. Then the smell hit him, a vile stench of defecation and he had to catch his breath in order to stop himself from vomiting.

'That's enough now,' he said aloud, but he wasn't sure who he was talking to. God, maybe? He knew that he wanted to get off the dance floor though and he turned to make his exit: but Sophie's tongue shot out of her mouth like a long, sticky tentacle and wrapped around his neck, pulling him back against her. He cried out in revulsion and span back around, pushing her away from him with both hands: but as he pushed, his fingers tore through her clothing and sank deep into the flesh of her chest. When he withdrew his hands, he left two ragged holes from which cascades of writhing maggots began to fall.

It must have been around this point that he started screaming. He wasn't sure of anything now and his powers of reason had completely evaporated. He stood there on the brink of insanity and then, in that same instant, a jolt of hope went through him as he noticed that Sophie had a metal zip running in a rectangle around her face. It suddenly struck him that he'd been the victim of some bizarre practical joke: that the brutish face that was staring open-mouthed at him was just a latex mask, nothing more. He could easily remove it and reveal the real Sophie underneath.

So he threw himself at her, knocking her headlong to the ground. He grabbed the tab of the zip and wrenched it aside, revealing not a face but a huge, pulsing grub-like creature, curled up in the rectangular opening behind the mask. Martin swore viciously and plunged his fingers in to the soft folds of its flesh, releasing spurts of warm fluid that splashed onto his face.

The Tim and Karen creatures were clawing at him, trying to pull him off the Sophie-Lizard that was writhing and thrashing on the dance floor and he lashed out at them, screaming now, not with terror but with laughter, because he had just realized that this was funny, this was the funniest thing that had ever happened to him. Other creatures joined the fray. His knuckles flattened one of the insect's faces and his foot lashed into another's thorax, splitting it wide open, and this was great, this was the best, the best birthday ever, because . . .

He stopped fighting suddenly, surprised to find that there was a little black hole at the back of his eyes: and as he watched, it was growing rapidly bigger, eating into his vision, etching itself like a blob of acid on a sheet of acetate. First it appeared to be the size of a pea, then a fifty pence piece, now a saucer and . . .

Suddenly the broken and bleeding people surrounding him on the dancefloor didn't look like monsters any more. They looked scared and . . .

Martin turned around slowly, as the black saucer became a dinner plate. Around the edges of the circle of darkness he caught glimpses of something horrible . . .

Sophie lying on the floor, wearing a carnival mask of red raw meat, her head twisted over at an impossible angle. From the midst of the meat, her eyes stared up at Martin in dull surprise. Her splayed legs shuddered uncontrollably, her heels hammering out an urgent rhythm as she died, and . . .

'Fetch an ambulance,' whispered Martin.

That was all he could do because then the dinner plate became a round, black moon, spreading itself like an unfolding umbrella across his vision. The curve of it must have nudged against a switch in his brain, because he went out like a light and didn't even feel the dancefloor as it slammed against his shoulders.

By the time they got him to the hospital, he had slipped into a coma.

PART ONE
Warp

All books are either dreams or swords
You can cut, or you can drug, with words.

Amy Lowell, *Sword Blades and Poppy Seed*.

He hath awakened from the dream of life –
'Tis we, who lost in stormy visions, keep
With phantoms an unprofitable strife,
And in mad trance, strike with our spirit's knife
invulnerable nothings.

Percy Bysshe Shelley, 'Adonais'.

Chapter One

Somewhere at the back of his head, Will Ambrose was dimly aware of the telephone ringing. It rang again and again, cutting into his sleep-dulled senses, stinging like a paper cut and making him wince. He groaned, shrugged himself deeper under the covers. His brain was still fogged with whisky fumes and he had no inclination to thrust his naked body out into the chill October air of Roxy's badly heated apartment. Where was she anyway? Why didn't she answer the bloody thing?

The sound of the phone had interrupted a dream. He'd been back on the force, once again a Detective Sergeant with the Greater Manchester Police. He'd been chasing a suspect through what appeared to be a sewer, splashing through endless labyrinthine tunnels, clambering over railings, occasionally having to wade thigh-deep through the stinking water. He'd been holding his Police Issue 9mm Glock automatic out in front of him, but whenever he'd got a clear shot of the fleeing man, something had got in his way. Then finally he'd corralled the suspect in a dead end. The man had turned around and a shrill of terror went through Will as he saw his own anxious face staring back at him . . .

The phone continued to ring. Whoever was on the other end of the line wasn't going to give in easily. Will groaned again, but swung his legs out from under the duvet and twisted himself around into a sitting position. He sat for a moment holding his throbbing head in his hands, horribly aware that he'd downed the best part of a bottle of Whyte and Mackays the night before.

It hadn't been a celebration or anything, he'd got drunk on

his own, slumped in front of the television. Roxy had given up trying to talk him out of it and had opted for an early night. When asked about it later, his excuse would be that he was feeling depressed. It had been his son's seventeenth birthday and the kid hadn't even phoned to thank his old man for the card and the present he'd sent. Roxy had already pointed out to Will that really, it was up to him to phone Martin on such an occasion, but that kind of logic made little headway with Will when he was in the mood to drink: and since leaving the force a year and a half ago, he'd been in the mood for little else.

He reached out a hand and tentatively drew back the curtains an inch or so. It was raining heavily and the sea was a seething caldron of grey waves, crashing relentlessly against the harbour wall. He made a small sound of disgust and let the curtain fall back. Even in the summer, Southport was not the prettiest place in the world. Out of season, it could be positively grim.

He'd come here after the double whammy of losing his career and his marriage. An old friend, another ex-copper who happened to be based in the seaside resort, had come to his rescue, offering to get him a temporary job and a place to lay his head. The work was pretty menial, helping out on stalls, selling tickets, taking a turn at the controls of the waltzers or the big wheel. But it was easy work, the kind of thing you didn't have to think about too much and he liked the simplicity of that, so different from what he'd done before.

At the end of the season, the friend moved on, but Will stayed. He hooked up with Roxy, a Romany woman who fronted a small fortune-telling booth on the prom. Now he lived on the small amount of money he'd saved during the season and whatever Roxy could spare him. He knew that he was just treading water, but lacked the motivation to do anything about it . . .

That bloody phone! Still it clamoured, as shrill and persistent as a hungry baby. With a curse, Will got himself upright and stumbled out of the bedroom into the adjoining living area. He dropped into an armchair and picked up the handset.

'Yes,' he muttered irritably.

'Will? Oh, thank God you're there! I was about to give up.'

No such luck, he thought, uncharitably: he had instantly recognized the voice of his ex-wife, Suzanne. She must be phoning from Manchester, he thought, but the fibre-optic line sounded so clear, she could have been in the next room to him. A depressing thought.

'Will, it's about Martin . . .'

'Yeah, I know, I should have rung him. I was . . . kind of busy last night. Did he like the present?'

There was a long silence: then a sound that sent a chill of apprehension through him.

Suzanne was crying. She never did that. She was as hard as nails, that one.

Suddenly his hangover was gone. He was wide awake and uncomfortably aware of the grief being expended on the other end of the line.

'Suzanne, what is it?'

'It's Martin. Oh God, Will, I can hardly believe it. I'm phoning from the hospital . . .'

Will felt the blood rush to his face and his heart fluttered in his chest, leaving him breathless.

'Hospital?' he gasped. 'Suzanne, what's happened?'

'I should have called you earlier, I know. But it was ages before they got in touch with me and it was the early hours of the morning by the time . . .'

'Just tell me what's happened. Has Martin had an accident?'

'Yes, an accident. Or, I suppose, no, not an accident. They say he knew what he was doing. He's seventeen, you think these days that's a responsible age, don't you? So when he said he was going to a club, I didn't think anything of it. I actually gave him some money, told him to have a good time.' She gave a sharp little gasp. 'Oh, Will, they don't think he's going to wake up!' Again her voice dissolved into helpless tears. Will had to shout at her to get her attention.

'For God's sake, tell me! What the fuck happened?'

It took her a few moments to get control of herself. Then at last, haltingly, she told him what she could.

'He went out to this club with Sophie and some friends. You remember Sophie, don't you? Nice girl, I really thought they had something going. Martin . . . took some drug. Not

11

one of the legal ones. Something called *Warp*? He . . . he went crazy, they say. Attacked Sophie. She . . . Will, he killed her.'

'Killed her?' Will echoed the words and tried to picture them in connection with his son, but somehow he couldn't make them fit. 'No,' he said. 'Suzanne, there must be some mistake . . .'

'There's no fucking mistake!' she shrieked and now she was angry, the tone of her voice almost making him wince. 'Haven't I just been sitting by his bed for the last three hours? He's in a coma, Will. The doctors don't think he's going to make it.'

'No,' he whispered. Not because he didn't believe her. Because he didn't want this to be happening.

'It's true,' Suzanne told him, her voice quieter now, more composed. She sounded tired. 'I don't know what to do, Will. I'm losing it. There was really nobody else I could call.'

'Where are you?' Will heard his own voice asking the question. It sounded methodical, completely without emotion. He sounded, he thought, like a policeman.

'Manchester General. Ward D2.'

'I'll get there as quickly as I can,' he told her and he put down the phone. Suddenly he felt clear-headed and, for the first time in ages, in control of himself. He got up and went back to the bedroom, where he put on some clothes, jeans, sweatshirt, a battered pair of trainers. He pulled his suitcase down from the top of the wardrobe and began to throw shirts and underwear into it. It didn't take him long because he didn't have much to call his own, he'd left most of his baggage, both emotional and literal, with Suzanne and Martin. As he packed, his son's face drifted into his mind, the handsome, confident features, the big china-blue eyes. He tried once again to equate that face with the story he'd just heard and was unable to do it.

It would be all right, he told himself. He'd get to the hospital and Martin would be sitting up in bed, grinning at him. All a mistake, sure, it had to be. The stuff about Sophie, it couldn't be right, could it? The Martin he knew wasn't capable of violence. Will recalled an incident when the boy was about five years old. Martin's pet goldfish had somehow managed to jump out of its tank in the night and the boy had found it dead on the carpet, the next morning. He'd cried about it for hours, inconsolable, while Will held him and rocked him in his arms . . .

Will snapped the locks on the suitcase and carried it through to the living room. He phoned Railtrack enquiries and was told that a train bound for Manchester Piccadilly was leaving within the hour. That left him just enough time, he figured. The circumstances were urgent and he knew that Roxy wouldn't have blamed him: but even so, he felt he couldn't leave without saying goodbye.

He let himself out of the apartment building, into the cutting wind that swept in off the sea. Fine salt spray mingled with the rain and stung his cheeks, making him squint. He turned left and started walking, passing the rows of boarded up shops and stalls that patiently awaited the return of summer. There was something desperately sad about a seaside resort in the winter, Will thought. It had lost all reason for existence. Only when the sun came back would it rise again, a tawdry phoenix, conjured from the ashes.

He kept his head down and walked briskly the short distance to the pier head, where despite the awful weather, he suspected he'd find Roxy. She spent a lot of time sitting in the little wooden booth, even when business was virtually non-existent. Maybe it was just an excuse to get away from Will. After all, he certainly hadn't been much fun to live with, the last few months.

He rapped his knuckles against the plywood door and went inside, leaving his case out in the rain. Roxy was sitting in her folding chair, behind the square pine table. She had a copy of *Hello* magazine on her lap. She was small and dark, her face framed by layers of black curls. Her brown eyes flicked over him perfunctorily and her red cupid's bow lips curved into a tired smile.

'So, you're finally going,' she observed and he knew better than to be surprised by her perceptiveness. He had lived with her long enough to know that she was genuinely psychic. Leaving the case outside hadn't fooled her for a moment.

'I have to,' he told her. 'It's Martin. Something bad has happened. He's in the hospital, in some kind of a coma. They say he took illegal drugs . . .'

Telling somebody else about it made it seem real. Grief welled up in him, making him vaguely dizzy. He experienced a powerful urge to weep but refused to give in to it.

Roxy indicated the vacant chair on the other side of the table.

'Sit down a minute,' she told him.

He shook his head.

'I should be getting to the station. My train . . .'

'You've got time,' she persisted. 'Please, sit for just a minute, you can give me that much, can't you?'

He nodded, moved to the chair. They sat regarding each other for a moment, both aware that there was a lot to say, but not knowing where to begin.

'Sometimes it's best to say nothing,' Roxy told him, as though giving voice to his thoughts. She took hold of his right hand in both of hers and she bowed her head for a moment, concentrating. She closed her eyes and when she opened them again, her gaze was unfocussed, she seemed to be staring off into the middle distance at something only she could see. She didn't need to use props like tarot cards or a crystal ball, though she kept those things around for the tourists. Will knew that an outsider, watching this ritual, would probably find her actions laughable, but over the past year she had told him so many things about his life and she had been wrong about only one of them. She had said that they would always be happy together.

Now as he sat watching her, he saw that her eyes were slowly widening to gaze with a disquieting intensity.

'You won't come back to me,' she said, in a low, matter-of-fact tone.

'Sure I will,' he argued, but his voice lacked conviction.

'No. I see a change in your life. A change of direction. I see you . . . in rags. I see you with a young boy.'

'Martin?' ventured Will hopefully.

Roxy shook her head.

'Another boy. And a woman. They too are in rags. The three

of you are going down into a dark place and you are afraid . . .'

Will frowned impatiently.

'Martin. Is he going to be all right?'

She shrugged.

'I don't see anything about him. That part of your life is clouded. I see . . .' Her eyes narrowed, then widened again, as if in shock. For a long moment, she didn't say anything.

'Well?' he prompted her. 'It can't be that bad, surely?'

She frowned. 'Fire,' she said quietly. 'I see fire rolling across water. It's like a river of fire, flowing deep beneath the ground.'

He raised his eyebrows quizzically.

'Bit melodramatic,' he observed.

She seemed suddenly angry with him.

'It's what I *see*!' she snapped. 'I have no control over what I see, you know that!' She pushed his hand away and regarded him from beneath her long lashes. 'I won't ask you not to go,' she told him. 'I know you have to do this. I just hope . . .'

'What?' he prompted her.

'That you find what you need. I haven't been able to give you that. I tried and for a while, I thought I could succeed. But lately it's been impossible to reach you.'

He raised an eyebrow ironically.

'You should have seen it coming,' he told her.

The ghost of a smile played across her face.

'I did,' she said.

'But you told me we'd always be happy.'

She nodded.

'I know. Sometimes, I lie.'

He leaned across the table and pecked her gently on the cheek. They sat for a moment in silence, looking at each other. He had thought that saying goodbye would be hard but she had made it easy for him.

'I'll write,' he said, as he got up from the table.

She shook her head.

'No you won't. Good luck, Will.'

He nodded and went out of the booth. As he stepped into the rain, he saw that a late tourist, a plump woman in a multi-coloured anorak, was waiting patiently by the door.

'Is she any good?' the woman asked him.

He glanced back into the booth. Roxy was sitting at the table, gazing calmly out at him.

'She's the best,' he said. Then picking up the suitcase, he walked quickly away, without looking back.

Chapter Two

The train journey into Manchester was interminable. The ancient diesel engine seemed to keep breaking down every few miles, incurring maddening waits in the middle of nowhere, while unseen hands tinkered with the engine. The carriage in which Will sat was filthy, unheated and marked by layer upon layer of obscene graffiti. Some charmer had systematically razored all the seats and yellow foam spilled out of the rips like viscera seeping from flesh wounds.

As the train finally lurched into the outskirts of the city, it passed several huge hoardings announcing something called Metro 2000. They were hard to miss. Garish paintings in a primitive style, they all depicted variations on the same theme – happy, multi-racial Mancunians grinning inanely as they enjoyed a series of cultural events. Dancing in the streets to the strains of a calypso band. Seated in a theatre as they applauded a Shakespearian actor. Riding with their children on a neon-lit carousel as fireworks exploded in the sky above them. But the reality lay just behind the posters, the soot-blackened outlines of the abandoned factories and warehouses that flanked this part of the track, windows smashed, brickwork slowly crumbling into dereliction.

The train shuddered into Piccadilly station and there was a long wait while the driver attempted to deactivate the hydraulic doors. At last they creaked open with an asthmatic gasp of air and Will was able to step out onto the crowded platform. He stood for a moment, gazing around in dull surprise. It was even dirtier than he remembered but what had caught his attention were the large numbers of ragged men and women who sat wedged into every available corner, holding out their hands like Third-World beggars, to the disembarking passengers.

Will frowned. He'd heard that homelessness was bad here but he hadn't been prepared for the scale of it.

'Hey, mister!' Somebody tugged at the leg of his trousers and glancing down, he found himself looking at a teenage boy, crouched on his haunches against a wall. The kid was maybe thirteen/fourteen years old, Will thought, as skinny as a whippet, his thin face plastered with dirt. 'Spare us a couple of bob, mate.'

Will shrugged and instinctively reached for the loose change in his pocket. He held out his hand, palm uppermost and suddenly, there was a free-for-all. A couple of other, older kids seemed to appear out of nowhere and the coins were knocked from Will's hand. There was an undignified scuffle on the platform, the kids doing each other real damage in a desperate attempt to grab the lion's share of what amounted to about fifty pence.

Will made a sound of disgust and turning away, he headed for the exit. He followed the sign for the taxi rank, moving along a cheerless corridor and out into the open air, where a line of black cabs waited patiently in the drizzle. He climbed into the first of them and slammed the door shut, waking the driver who appeared to be having a snooze.

'Manchester General Hospital,' he said. 'And step on it, please, I'm in a hurry.'

On the drive through the congested city centre, the cabbie, a small but vociferous man with a Rochdale accent kept up a running commentary on the problems currently afflicting Manchester.

'I mean, this bloody government, who could have believed that they'd ever get in again?' he muttered. 'Did you vote for them? I know *I* didn't. And you try and find anybody who'll admit to it. Same old story. But the city council now, they want to get their priorities straight. I mean, how is it they've got millions to pour into this Metro 2000 rubbish, yet they can't do anything about the crime figures?'

The taxi chugged noisily around the one way system that encircled Albert Square and the driver blared his horn as he crossed a set of rails in front of an advancing tram, which appeared to have jumped a red light. The cabbie stamped on the accelerator and made it across with inches to spare, yet never faltered in his monologue.

'You take me for instance, I been held up at gunpoint three times in the last six months. Three times! And that's not in the rough areas, neither. Christ, we ain't even allowed to go into the Merton Estate anymore, it's considered a war zone. But I tell you what, I've had enough of it. Anybody tries anything else with me and they'll get this.' He brandished a baseball bat at Will through the metal grille that divided them. 'I don't care what the law says, there comes a time when you just got to make a stand. Next one even *looks* at me funny, I'll turn his head to cranberry sauce.'

Even if Will had wanted to contribute to the conversation, he couldn't have. The cabbie barely paused for breath before launching into his next tirade, a blistering verbal assault on various elements of society that didn't meet with his approval, including DSS scroungers, scousers, traffic wardens and people he would only refer to as 'shirt lifters.' Will had too much on his mind to pay him any more attention. He settled back into his seat, wrapped up in his own dark thoughts as the taxi clattered around a corner onto Oxford Road and began the short stop-start journey to the hospital.

He'll be all right, Will kept telling himself. *You'll see, You'll get there and he'll be fine*

But at the back of his mind, some doleful little voice kept nagging at him, telling him that this was just wishful thinking. He'd learned long ago, that in this brave new world, happy endings were in very short supply.

Scally left the station with thirty-four pence clutched tightly in one dirty little hand. He'd had to fight hard for it and his ribs ached where one of the other kids had landed him a good kick, but that was OK. He now had the down payment on one of the occasional little luxuries that made life more bearable – a bag of chips or a can of coke.

He went down the steps to Fairfield Street. On the walls you could still catch glimpses of an ancient mural, depicting various forms of transport, peeping out from beneath the layers of obscene graffiti. The city commuters moving up and down the steps gave him a wide berth as though afraid they might catch something. Maybe they figured poverty was infectious. He walked down three flights and out to the street. It was raining hard again and Scally shrugged his oversized coat tighter around his skinny frame, turning up the frayed collar to cover his ears. He'd found the coat in a charity bin he'd broken into the other week. It was meant for an adult, but he'd selected it because the thick tweed fabric would keep him warm through the winter.

The street was gridlocked with stationary traffic, yellow exhaust fumes rising in thick, choking clouds. Scally threaded his way between them, obliged to clamber over bumpers and bonnets, ignoring the outraged expressions of the motorists.

He made it to the other side, walked along a hundred yards and turned the corner onto the relative quiet of Sobriety Street, where his current shelter was located. No traffic came down here any more and a large band of Rag People, the Ardwick Tribe, had made it their home. They had pitched their shelters in a series of abandoned railway arches set into the crumbling viaduct that ran along the left hand side of the street. Only a couple of years ago, the arches had been the setting for several small businesses – garages, packaging companies, freight warehouses: but the big recession of '97 had put paid to those and now they were a logical place to make camp, relatively waterproof, with huge wooden doors that could be closed and barred against the dangers of the night.

Scally knew all about those. He'd been surviving on the streets for the best part of a year, ever since running away from the orphanage where he'd been incarcerated since the age of twelve. He'd gone there when his parents had totalled themselves in a motorway smash. They'd done it deliberately, it seemed, since witnesses had reported that their car had performed a U-turn on the M56 and had driven headlong into the vehicles behind. Scally had already been severely dysfunctional by then – indeed, there were some unkind souls who suggested that *he* was the reason for his parents' suicide pact – and none of his relatives had wanted the responsibility of picking up the wreckage he invariably left in his wake, so he'd been abandoned to the tender loving care of Manchester Social Services.

The orphanage was a grim, shabby hellhole, where he was brutalized at every opportunity, both by the staff and the other inmates. He vowed to escape and tried many times, but it was two long years before he was successful. Now at last, he had acquired the kind of family he could relate to.

He walked slowly along the cobbled street, nodding to the people that hailed him from the crowded archways, occasionally stopping to talk to a friend. He liked living among the Ardwick Tribe, because they asked very little from him and gave just as little in return. And he had stopped kicking against the traces. Here, you had to abide by the rules. If you didn't, they kicked your arse out onto the street and you were back to fending for yourself.

At one point, Scally passed a low brick wall which overlooked a stinking stretch of canal and he moved involuntarily into the middle of the road, giving it a wide berth. The canal passed under a culvert below the street and Scally knew that at some point, down there in the darkness, there was an opening that connected to the sewers. He was afraid of the people that lived in the sewers and he had good cause to be. A couple of months earlier, they had taken his best friend, Gyppo . . .

Now he had mixed feelings about Sobriety Street. The daylight hours were OK, it was a good place to stay, there was shelter from the wind and rain and some nights, when the weather allowed, the Rag People held big communal bonfires on the wasteland opposite the viaduct. But the short stretch of canal bothered him and most nights, he made damned sure that he was safely locked up inside one of the railway arches, surrounded by people he knew.

He reached the arch that was his home: some fifteen people lived in here, their own particular areas delineated by walls of cardboard and blankets hung on lengths of string. In the entrance, somebody had stoked the fire under the big tin bucket that was used as the communal cooking pot. As usual, it contained Pot Luck, a watery stew to which every occupant of the arch was obliged to contribute whatever they could forage. Peg was stirring the pot with a big wooden spoon. She glanced up and grinned as Scally approached, displaying rows of blackened teeth. She was the closest that he had to a mother figure, a short, stocky woman with prematurely greying hair and a sharp tongue. She'd had four children of her own, grown up now, and she had a tendency to look out for young loners like Scally, despite the disapproval of her husband, Frank, who was the tribe's Duke, or headman. Because of the unusual location of the tribe's shelter he was often jokingly referred to as the Arch Duke.

But Frank didn't seem to be about today. Scally reached into one of his voluminous pockets and withdrew a handful of carrots that he'd filched from a market stall earlier that day.

'Good lad.' Peg regarded them critically for a moment, as though she could afford to be choosy, but she must have decided that they were still edible. She reached for the kitchen knife that hung from a loop of string around her waist and sliced the carrots into the mixture. Scally could see that so far, the pot held mostly water but it was early yet and there were a few others to come in. Some of them might have had better luck with their foraging.

'Where you been?' Peg asked him.

'Took a turn begging up the station,' he told her. 'Didn't have no luck though. Too many others at the same game.' He did his best to keep a poker face as he reported this, but he sensed that Peg saw right through him. Officially, she had the right to demand that he put half of any money he collected into a communal fund, but she knew as well as Scally did, that such money was inevitably appropriated by Frank and his 'lieutenants' who invariably spent it at one of the few local off licences that wasn't too fussy about its clientele. Many a night they would come roaring home, their guts full of cheap wine and cider and then God help you if you didn't get out of the way quick enough.

'Got a bit of a treat for later on,' Peg announced confidentially. She indicated a small metal table in front of her and then, after glancing quickly left and right, she leaned over and lifted a teacloth, revealing a loaf of brown bread. As far as

Scally could tell, it hadn't so much as a single bite taken out of it. 'It's a few days old but it'll soften up nice in the stew,' Peg told him. 'It's amazing. I was down behind Asda and I opened up a skip and there it was, just sitting there, pretty as you please!'

'Great,' said Scally. He could already taste a chunk of it in his mouth, the wet bread dissolving against his teeth. His empty belly lurched sickeningly. He hadn't eaten anything since yesterday lunchtime. He thought about the coins in his pocket and wished he had enough to buy a packet of crisps. Ham and pickle were his favourite.

It seemed crazy having to buy them, it wasn't so very long ago, you could shoplift any amount of them, no problem. These days, every item in every shop, no matter how humble, was protected by TAG security. A microscopic code was impregnated into the packaging and had to be deactivated by a sensor at the checkout. Any attempt to get the product through the exit doors by other means resulted in a shrill alarm you could hear for miles. The nearest CCTV cameras would then pick you out and alert the police computer, which would simply scan the data banks for your ID. After all that, arrest was just a formality and the punishment for theft was harsh. It wasn't unheard of to do a year in the slammer for a first offence and under the current system of law, you got pretty much the same degree of punishment for nicking a packet of crisps as you did for stealing a car.

So Scally had reluctantly accepted that his shoplifting days were over and had resigned himself to getting his ham and pickle crisps by legal means. Just thinking about them made his stomach burble in protest and he had to take himself away from the appetising aroma of the Pot Luck. Maybe he'd get some shuteye, he told himself. It would stop him thinking about food. It would stop him thinking, full stop.

Sometimes thinking gave you a headache and just lately he'd spent too much time thinking, mostly about Gyppo: and about what might have happened to him down there in the darkness. It wasn't something he *wanted* to think about, but it was always there at the back of his mind, a jagged edge waiting to be brushed up against. From time to time, he forgot, he got careless. And then the razor edge cut into his skin, drawing blood. But he wasn't going to worry about anything just now. He was going to sleep and when he woke, please God, it would be time to eat.

He sighed, slicked back his wet hair with the fingers of one hand. Then he moved into the shelter of the railway arch, out of the rain.

Chapter Three

The taxi pulled in at the entrance of what had formerly been the Manchester Royal. The original name had been deemed inappropriate since the latest flux of Royal scandals. The last straw had been the appearance of the former Duchess of York in a soft porn movie and a widely circulated pirate video of a stag party held by one of the young princes. The dissolution of the monarchy was now under way and was expected to be fully achieved by 2010.

Will paid the driver what seemed like an exorbitant sum and went in at the hospital's main entrance. The 'automatic' doors were out of order and had been permanently propped open with a length of timber, which Will was obliged to step over.

The hospital was grubbier than he remembered, the walls in dire need of fresh paint, the tiled floors chipped and scuffed. Harassed-looking doctors and nurses ran about like headless chickens and as Will followed the signs to Ward D2, he passed several beds that had been set up in the corridors outside the wards. One elderly man had been obliged to use a bedpan in full view of every passing stranger and was doing so noisily, his head hung in shame.

Up on Ward D2, Will collared a young nurse and told her who he was. She made some dutifully sympathetic noises and told him she'd try to locate Dr Winston, who had been wanting to have a word with him. Then she led Will to what she called the 'High Dependency Unit', a small side ward containing eight beds.

'We're hoping to get your son into Intensive Care just as soon as a bed becomes available,' she explained. 'Mrs Ambrose is in with Martin at the moment.' She ushered him inside then hurried off to attend to other duties.

There were curtains drawn around all the beds, so Will could not, for the moment, see any of the occupants. Suzanne was sitting in a chair beneath one of the room's grimy windows. She straightened up as he entered and for an instant, a look of relief flickered across her face. A moment later, it was replaced by an expression of haughty detachment. Suzanne had never liked showing her feelings, something she had in common with Will, and probably one of the key factors in the breakup of their marriage.

She still looked great, he had to admit that. He didn't much like her hair which was cut in the latest 'severe' style, little more than a crewcut: and she'd shed a few pounds since he last saw her, her tall figure now dangerously close to the anorexic look favoured by the fashion conscious. But the large grey eyes, though tired and strained, still had the predatory gleam that had first attracted him to her. The wide, sensual mouth, so sexy when it smiled, was drawn into a tight horizontal line.

'You made it then,' she said and managed to make it sound like an accusation.

'I got here as quickly as I could,' he said defensively. 'I had to take the train. My car's in for servicing.' He was reluctant to tell her that these days, he didn't earn enough to keep a car on the road. He moved closer and leaned forward to give her the obligatory peck on the cheek. For a moment, he considered putting his arms around her, giving her a reassuring hug, but the tense set of her body did not encourage such an intimate act. 'How's Martin?' he asked. 'Is he still . . . asleep?'

Irritation flared in her eyes. 'He's not asleep, Will, he's in a fucking coma. Are you ever going to learn to say what you mean?'

He sensed the bottled-up rage in her and realized that she was angry with herself, that she was merely trying to project it onto somebody else. 'I didn't come here to fight,' he said quietly. He looked at the row of curtained beds, then glanced inquiringly at Suzanne. She indicated one of them with a nod of her head.

He moved across to it and reached up a hand to open the curtain. For a moment, he hesitated, his fingers brushing the garishly patterned fabric, unsure if he was properly prepared for what he was about to see. As a police officer, he'd witnessed the most hideous things: murders, mutilations and the aftermath of horrific accidents. He'd learned to take it all in his stride. But this was different. This was something that was going to affect him personally. He took a deep breath. Then pulling back the curtain, he gazed down at his son.

Martin looked so small in the bed. That was Will's first thought. The boy's eyes were closed and he lay there on his back, dwarfed by the hi-tech equipment all around him. There was a pipe going in to his open mouth from the ventilator, and Martin's chest was rising and falling steadily, accompanied by a kind of rhythmic hissing noise. The covers were pulled down to his waist and three monitors were attached to his chest. A saline drip was plugged directly into his neck. Apart from the regular movement of his chest, there was no sign of life at all. Martin might just as well be dead already. His face was as white as a fall of December snow.

Will felt a terrible dry heat blossoming like fire in his chest. It made him catch his breath in a loud sob. He found himself thinking about Martin as a little boy, the times he had found him asleep on the bedroom floor, cuddled up to a favourite soft toy. He thought how he used to pick Martin up and carry him back to his bed, settle him gently under the covers. How tiny he'd seemed then, how impossible it had been to imagine him grown, filling the whole length of the bed.

Then he thought how gradually it had happened, the slow, unseen process over the seventeen years of the boy's life, his limbs stretching as he acquired muscle, his body filling out as it approached adulthood.

And now, all of a sudden, here he was, somehow back to being small again, small and insubstantial in that big, big bed.

It was this thought, more than anything else, that brought the hot tears into Will's eyes. He felt his shoulders moving up and down and was unable to stop them. He lifted his hands and buried his face in them and he wanted so much for Suzanne to come over and hold him while he cried. But she remained where she sat, arms crossed defensively over her chest, her face expressionless. She had done most of her crying before Will got here, he thought, and she'd had nobody to comfort her. Suzanne had always believed in tit for tat.

Will let his tears run their course and after a few moments, he got a hold of himself and was able to ask questions.

'Can he hear us?' he asked hoarsely.

'They aren't sure. It's a very deep coma. Maybe.' Suzanne frowned and gestured for Will to follow her. She led him out of the room and into the corridor outside, closing the door behind them. It was pandemonium out there, people milling aimlessly about, looking for staff to give them directions. Suzanne turned to face Will, her expression grim.

'The doctors . . .' she said. 'They aren't holding out a lot of hope. Doctor Winston was in here a couple of hours ago. He told me . . . well, that we should be prepared for the worst.'

Will registered the words but refused to accept what they were saying.

'Martin's a scrapper,' he argued. 'I brought him up that way. He isn't going to give up without a fight.' He glanced inquiringly at Suzanne. 'How long has he been using drugs?'

'I didn't know he was. Not *real* drugs, anyway. I knew he'd had the herbal stuff a couple of times, like most kids, you know? But this Warp . . .'

'What is that? I've never heard of it.'

'It's new, I think. Tim told me it was what they call a cocktail.'

'Tim? Who's Tim?'

Suzanne gave him a scornful look. 'Martin's best friend. They were at school together.'

'Oh yeah, right. He was with Martin last night?'

'Yes. He told me Martin bought some of this stuff off one of the Rag Men . . .' She hesitated when she saw the look of puzzlement on his face. 'It's what they call the Manchester down-and-outs. Tim says that a lot of them sell drugs. The dealers use them as sort of middle men.'

Will nodded. 'There were a lot of beggars at the station, when I arrived. I had no idea things had gotten so bad. Where do they all come from?'

Suzanne shrugged. 'Ordinary people, like you and me, I suppose. They lose their jobs, their houses are repossessed, they find themselves out on the streets.' She shrugged. 'Next to London, we've got the biggest population of beggars in Europe.'

'And this Tim, he knew that Will had bought the stuff and he didn't try and stop him from taking it?'

Suzanne gave him a disparaging look. 'Come on, Will, think back to when you were a teenager. Would you have tried to stop your best friend from doing something he wanted to do?'

'I might, if I'd realized the danger.'

'Tim did at least try and pull Will off when he was attacking Sophie. He got very badly beaten up for his trouble, the boy had cuts and bruises all over his face.' She shook her head, glanced at the floor. 'He was too late to help her. They say . . . they say her neck was broken.'

A couple of porters pushed a trolley along the corridor, shouting at people to get out of the way. An elderly woman lay under a hospital blanket, gazing wild eyed at the ceiling in mute terror. She was babbling something about the end of the world.

'It won't end in fire, it won't end in deluge! But there will be a terrible reckoning on the day of judgement . . .'

The trolley moved on along the corridor.

'I don't believe this story about Martin killing Sophie,' said Will. 'Must be a mistake. He wouldn't do something like . . .'

'Believe it, Will! It happened on a crowded dancefloor in front of dozens of witnesses. It was the drug. Tim says it causes hallucinations. Martin had some kind of psychotic reaction. Doctor Winston told me there have been other cases like this.'

Will reached up a hand to trail his fingers through his hair in exasperation. 'Martin knew that could happen? And he *still* took the bloody stuff? Why, for God's sake? Why would anybody take such a risk?'

Suzanne shook her head. 'I guess he just thought it wouldn't happen to him.'

Will groaned. He stabbed a finger at the closed door. 'But it has happened, Suzanne. Jesus, why did I ever leave him? Why didn't I take him with me? If he'd been with me in Southport, this wouldn't have happened.'

'Don't blame me,' she warned him. 'I can't be expected to keep an eye on him every hour of every day. And it would have been no different if you *had* been there. In the end, they do what they want to do and if necessary, they do it behind your back.' She turned to open the door of the ward: then she hesitated, glowering at him over her shoulder. 'Besides, when did you ever spend time with him? He barely saw you. Out all hours, working on some bloody case ... that's when you should have thought about spending time with him, Will. When he really needed his father.'

Will felt his own resentment rising, old wounds beginning to open up. 'Oh sure, let's have it all out in the open, shall we? My job, the cause of everything.' He punched a fist into the palm of his left hand. 'Don't forget, Suzanne, you knew you were marrying a cop from the start and you had a good enough idea of what it entailed. I'll tell you something. I wish there'd been a cop around when Martin bought those drugs. At least then, he'd have just been in a cell, not a bloody hospital bed. I was out there on the front line trying to stop things like this. You can't do that kind of work on a nine-to-five basis.'

Suzanne laughed bitterly. 'But you could have had it easier, couldn't you? You were offered the chance for advancement, you could have been on easy street, delegating the donkey work to people further down the pole. But you wouldn't have it, oh no, you let your damned principles stand in the way. And where did that get you? You were treated as a piece of shit to be wiped off somebody's shoe. A lot of use that was to Martin.'

'That's not fair,' gasped Will. 'They wanted me to ...'

'Compromise, Will. They just wanted you to make a few compromises. But you stood firm, and they squeezed you out. And when that happened, there was no living with you, it was like you wanted to kick out at everyone and everything you ever cared about. Me and Martin, we had to come back to it every day. The anger, the disappointment, the drinking ... what do you suppose that did to Martin, eh? How d'you suppose that made him feel?'

'Look, Suzanne, I think you made your point. Can we just ...'

'The day you packed your bag and left, we all but opened a bottle of champagne, did you know that? We were virtually dancing in the street.'

Will closed his eyes. 'You bitch,' he said quietly. He glanced awkwardly around, aware that others in the corridor were taking more than a passing interest in the argument. 'Look, Suzanne, it's pointless to try and apportion blame. What's happened has happened. Now we have to try and . . .'

'Mr Ambrose?' A young doctor was approaching from up the corridor, a clipboard tucked under one arm. 'I'm Doctor Winston. I've already had a chat with Mrs Ambrose, but if you've a few minutes, I'd appreciate a word.'

Will turned to face the newcomer and shook the hand that was held out to him. The doctor was, he judged, in his early twenties, a pale, dark-haired young man with thick stubble on his chin. His eyes had the bleary, unfocussed look of somebody suffering from severe sleep deprivation. As if to enforce the point, he smothered a yawn.

'God, I'm sorry,' he muttered. 'Been a long shift. I'm supposed to be on holiday.' He laughed bitterly then glanced around and pointed along the corridor. 'There's a small office down the way, we can talk more privately.'

'I'll be in with Martin,' announced Suzanne, opening the door to the ward – but before she stepped inside, she shot Will a look of pure dislike. It was clear that she had not forgiven him for past mistakes.

Will sighed. Quite suddenly, he felt a familiar craving at the back of his throat, the sure sign that he needed a shot of whisky. But instead, he shook his head to clear the cobwebs and followed the doctor along the corridor to the office.

Scally approached the little curtained-off area of the arch that was his own tiny kingdom. He'd rigged it up himself, using lengths of twine, sheets of cardboard packaging and some opened-out polythene bags. He'd found an old mattress in a skip in a posh part of town and had gleefully carried it home on his shoulders, unperturbed by the large yellow stain on it. He'd rigged up a frame out on the wasteland and hung it in the sun for a few hours, avidly guarding it against other

Rag People and eventually, it had dried out a treat.

Scally lifted the flap of fabric that covered the entrance and nearly jumped out of his skin as a pale staring face smiled out at him. But he instantly relaxed. It was just the mad woman, come to share his space for a while.

'Hello, Marianne,' he said, clambering in beside her and settling himself on the mattress. 'How's it going?'

Marianne put her head on one side as though considering the question. Her blue eyes were wide and staring, she had that startled look she always had whenever you asked her a question, no matter how simple it was.

'OK, I think,' she replied: and Scally could smell the thick tang of booze on her breath.

She'd been hanging around the arch a couple of weeks now and seemed to be imposing on Scally's good nature. She was maybe in her late twenties, he thought, a thin, bedraggled creature in a poxy fur coat that was probably worth a lot of money once upon a time. Her hair was blonde and when the light shone on her a certain way, even under all the dirt, you could see that she must have been a looker once: probably still *was* if you gave her a good scrub. She had a taste for the booze and usually managed to get some one way or another, mostly because she didn't seem to be fussy about who she went with in return for a sup of the bottle.

Scally knew that Peg disapproved of Marianne, probably because Frank was one of the girl's most enthusiastic customers: but it was certainly true that she rarely came up with anything to add to the pot, she didn't spend time begging and seemed too fragile to be of much help when there was heavy work to be done.

Somehow, she had latched on to Scally. He knew he ought to tell her to sling her hook but there was something about the woman that moved him. She seemed such a tragic figure, a creature from an earlier time, unused to the dirt and squalor of modern life, feebly trying to make the best of things. She had told Scally that she used to be involved in the Manchester rock scene, that her boyfriend had played lead guitar with the Serial Messiahs.

He had scoffed at this, at first. After all, the Messiahs were a massively successful rock band, they'd recently performed a sell-out concert at Maine Road, the former football stadium from the days when Manchester had *two* teams. If her boyfriend, Steve, was the lead guitarist, how come . . . ?

But Marianne had explained that Steve was dead, that he'd died some six months back. The band had a new guitarist now and the other members had turned their back on Marianne. They'd never liked her because of the influence she'd had with Steve. That big hit they'd had a year or so back, *Midnight Dancer*. That had all been about Marianne. Scally kind of got the impression that the guys in the band somehow held her responsible for Steve's death, but he wasn't sure about that, because when he asked more questions, Marianne would just go off at a tangent and talk about some weird stuff that had nothing to do with the subject.

Everyone in the arch figured she was crazy, and called her 'the mad woman' to her face: but Scally wasn't convinced on that score. Once, when she'd had her coat off, he'd seen her bare arms and had noticed how the veins were scarred and pitted with needle marks. He thought that something terrible had happened to her a while back, something that had made her forget her reasons for being alive. Now she sold herself cheap for booze, so she could numb her brain and forget whatever it was that troubled her. But sometimes, when they talked, Scally thought he caught glimpses of the person she used to be. And maybe he was a little bit in love with that brighter, happier Marianne.

'You got anything to drink?' she asked him hopefully. 'I could do with something to keep out the cold.'

Scally shook his head. It had occurred to him that if he could get his hands on a bottle, he could pretty easily get her to put out for him: but on reflection, he was vaguely surprised to find that he didn't want that. He thought more of her. Perhaps he was beginning to care about her a little too much. It wasn't a good way to be. He'd cared about Gyppo and look what had happened to him . . .

'Cheer up,' said Marianne brightly. 'We don't have much longer according to Nostradamus.'

'Nostro-who?' muttered Scally.

33

'Nostradamus. He was this guy who lived in olden times. Made a lot of prophecies. He said the world would end in 1999.'

Scally frowned.

'Can't do that. What about Metro 2000? What about all the money they're spending?' He sneered. 'All those lovely adverts.'

'Waste of effort.' Marianne reached a hand in under the front of her coat and scratched abstractedly. 'I think you've got fleas in here,' she told him. 'We should teach 'em tricks and open a flea circus. They were big in Victorian times.'

He gave her a disbelieving look.

'Get away,' he said.

'No, really, Scally, it's true. They used to make them do all kinds of things. Tightrope walking, strong man acts, had them pulling little chariots. Maybe that's what Metro 2000 could do with. What do you think? Marianne and Scally's Fantastic Flea Circus.'

'Shouldn't that be Scally and Marianne's Flea Circus? They're *my* fleas. Anyway, if the world's going to end . . .'

'Oh yeah, I forgot.' Marianne laughed softly and her dirty face was briefly lit by an inner radiance. At times like this, Scally thought, you really could see that she was still pretty; but he wondered how much longer her looks would last, living in this shit hole.

'You should get out of this,' he told her. 'Couldn't you, like, you know, go and see the band? Ask them for some money. I mean, I'm sure if they knew you were living like this . . .'

'They'd laugh,' she told him. 'They'd dance a merry hornpipe. They never liked me, you see.'

'Yeah, but what about all the records Steve made? What about the money his songs must still be earning? How come you don't get any of that?'

'It all goes to his little white-haired mother in Alderly Edge. I wouldn't be entitled to anything, Scally. Steve and I didn't believe in marriage. And "common law" means nothing these days.' She made a gesture with one hand that put Scally in mind of some fancy Duchess or whatever. She should have been sitting in an open-topped carriage waving to a crowd of

34

admirers, not squatting in this dirty, dilapidated shelter on a Manchester back street.

Scally peered apprehensively through a gap in the curtains. The archway framed a miserable picture of grey acid rain.

'Winter's coming,' he said quietly. He'd spent one winter on the streets and wasn't looking forward to another one. 'You don't want to be here when that happens.'

But Marianne seemed to have slipped into a reverie. She was humming softly to herself, a slow, halting air. She was rocking gently to and fro and staring straight ahead at something only she could see. Scally knew better than to ask her any more questions. She would be like this for a while now, locked up inside her own head with the thoughts and visions she didn't want to share.

Scally's stomach rumbled. He glanced hopefully towards the arch, at the clouds of steam rising from the black iron bucket, but he knew he'd get nothing until Peg decided the stew was ready – and that wouldn't happen before Frank returned from wherever he was wandering. So Scally lay down on the mattress and pulled an old blanket over him, telling himself that the time would pass more quickly if he slept. Marianne reached out a hand and began to stroke his hair and the tune she was humming seemed to reshape itself into some half-remembered lullaby.

Scally sighed and closed his eyes.

Within minutes he was asleep.

Chapter Four

Doctor Winston found an empty office for them to talk in. Will noticed that Winston had to deactivate a heavy-duty electronic security lock first.

'Necessary precaution,' explained Winston. 'There's been a spate of thefts here lately. They'll take anything they can get their hands on.'

'They?' asked Will, raising his eyebrows.

'The patients,' said Winston. He moved to an ancient mahogany desk and took a seat behind it, ushering Will into a vacant one. For some reason, he was reminded of Roxy in the fortune-telling booth. Winston glanced at the notes on his clipboard and sighed deeply. 'You've had a chance to see your son?' he asked.

'Briefly. Suzanne says he's in a deep coma.'

Winston nodded. 'The forecast isn't good I'm afraid. Vital signs are negligible and I'd say at the very least, he's suffered severe brain damage. To be honest, it's only the ventilator that's keeping him alive.'

Will felt a numbness creeping through him. 'But there's a chance?' he reasoned.

Winston sighed again. He probably wanted to look sympathetic but was too exhausted to be bothered with the charade. 'I've dealt with these cases before,' he said. 'To be brutally honest, I've seen six of them now and in every instance, the patient died. This Warp stuff does massive neurological damage. It's as though the whole nervous system goes into overload. All the fuses blow. And of course, before that happens there's this . . . psychotic fit. That's the only way I can describe it.' He paused, as though considering his words, 'You're aware what happened before Martin went into the coma? What he did to that poor girl?'

'I'm aware of the allegations, yes.'

Winston gave a dry smile, then had to smother another yawn. 'Oh God, I'm sorry. I really can't help it. I had two hours sleep last night.'

Will nodded, made a dismissive gesture. 'So what are you telling me? That there's no hope at all?'

Winston nodded. 'Pretty much. Mr Ambrose, this is going to sound callous, but . . . well, I want you to consider giving me permission to turn off the ventilator.'

Will stared at him. For the moment, he couldn't find words. 'But . . . it's not even been twenty-four hours!' he protested.

'Yes, I know how it looks, but there are considerations. The hospital is hopelessly over subscribed and we are crying out for beds. I'm having to turn away people in quite desperate situations.'

'My son's situation is desperate,' retorted Will.

'Yes. Yes, of course. I'm not suggesting otherwise. But some of these others are people who we could actually *do* something for. People who through no fault of their own . . .'

'Stop right there,' growled Will. He could see where this was leading. 'What you're saying is that my son brought this on himself, aren't you?'

Winston looked uncomfortable. 'There are some who would suggest that,' he said.

'Well, they'd better not suggest it in my presence. Martin was just a kid out to celebrate his seventeenth birthday and have a good time. He made a stupid mistake. You never did that, Doctor, when you were a kid?' Will shook his head. 'What am I talking about, you still *are* a kid.'

Winston chose to ignore the taunt. 'The hospital operates a policy, Mr Ambrose. As you may or may not know, preference is given to certain patients, while others are discriminated against. Smokers and obese people are generally edged further down the waiting lists. There's a strong lobby demanding that drug abusers should be treated in the same way.'

'Martin's not a drug abuser,' snarled Will.

'Isn't he? I don't know what else you'd call it. He knew the risks of using Warp and now he's paying the price.'

'Oh really?' Will leaned across the desk and grabbed Winston by the wrist. He lifted the doctor's hand and indicated fingers yellowed by nicotine. 'And the hospital has a policy, you say? Bit fucking hypocritical, don't you think?'

Winston frowned down at his desk. 'I don't make the rules, Mr Ambrose. I just have to implement them.'

'You say you've already talked to my ex-wife about this. What did she say about it?'

'She told me that she couldn't make any decision until she'd consulted you – and naturally, we would have to obtain permission from both of you.'

'So I still have some use,' muttered Will.

'I beg your pardon?' Winston smothered another yawn.

'Nothing. Well, here's my answer, Doctor. While there's still hope for my son, no matter how slight, I want the ventilator left *on*. Do I make myself clear?'

'Perfectly,' murmured Winston. He was slumped back in his chair now and his eyelids were drooping as he gradually succumbed to sleep. 'But if we see no signs of improvement in . . . in the next twenty-four hours, I fear . . .'

The bleeper in his pocket sounded, a shrill, insistent tone and Winston sat up in his chair, a startled expression on his face. 'Here we go again,' he muttered. 'I'm sorry, we're going to have to leave.'

They got up from their seats and went out of the room. Will noticed that for all his urgency, Winston paused to secure the door behind him. They turned back into the crowded corridor, then were obliged to jump aside as a trolley hurtled towards them, propelled by a couple of frantic nurses. A third nurse sat astride the patient, an elderly man, pounding on his chest with her clenched fists. Winston span around to assist them, but he glanced back over his shoulder.

'Twenty-four hours, Mr Ambrose. Then we'll need a decision.'

The trolley careered on into the crowd, scattering people before it. Will watched until it turned a corner out of sight. He had never felt more helpless in his entire life.

He walked slowly back to Martin's ward, knowing that there

was nothing he could do now, but wait. And hope. At least they couldn't prevent him from doing that.

Scally woke abruptly to the sound of a gong, the signal announcing that at long last, the Pot Luck was about to be served. He shook off the last remains of sleep and nudged Marianne urgently in the ribs.

'Scran!' he said. 'Come on, let's get some before it goes.'

Marianne rubbed her eyes with her knuckles. She did not look enthusiastic.

'I don't know,' she said. 'Peg doesn't like me eating if I've brought nothing to the pot.'

'That's OK, you're with me,' he assured her. 'My guest.'

She smiled at this. 'You make it sound like we're staying at the Midland,' she said.

'What's that?'

'You know, the big hotel off Deansgate? Everybody calls it the Manchester Holiday Inn now, but when I was younger, it was still known as the Midland. You should have seen it, Scally. The crystal chandeliers, the beds, the way everybody bowed and scraped for you! And the food . . .' She rolled her eyes. 'Thing was, in those days, I didn't really appreciate it. You don't, do you, when it's right there on a plate? I used to leave most of what I was given, can you believe that?'

'You still do,' Scally reminded her.

'Yes, but then the food here isn't exactly *nouvelle cuisine*, is it?'

Scally shook his head. He couldn't understand a word she said, half the time. He grabbed a couple of empty tins which he used as dinner bowls. He always kept a spoon and fork in one pocket of his overcoat, for those occasions when he found something that was difficult to eat with his fingers.

'Come on, let's get moving,' he urged Marianne, and virtually had to drag her out through the shelter's flap. They took their place in the queue of people already lined up in front of the bucket. Peg was dispensing the food with a ladle while her friend, Liz, tore off small hunks from the loaf and handed them out. It was left to these two women to judge the size of the portions given to each person, though it had long ago been noticed that Frank's lieutenants and their immediate families tended to get more generous amounts than the others. Nobody questioned the system any more. Those who had tried it in the past had a tendency to go skinny dipping in the canal one dark night and that was generally the last anyone saw of them.

Scally noticed that Frank had returned from his day's scavenging. Needless to say, he had been served first and he was sitting on a packing case near the arch entrance, wolfing down the contents of his extra-large bowl. He was a messy eater and streams of thin gravy ran down his face and dripped from his stubbled chin.

Despite being better fed than his neighbours, Frank was tall and almost painfully thin. He was bald aside from a few scraps of dark hair around his ears and he had large, slightly bulging grey eyes and a sharp beak-like nose. His wide mouth contained only a few stumps of rotten teeth and consequently, he very rarely grinned. His habitual expression was the one he was wearing now, a lop-sided smirk.

He wore a black PVC raincoat which hung almost to his ankles and around his skinny waist, an ancient leather harness held his instruments of day-to-day survival: cutlery, tin opener, Swiss Army knife, screwdrivers, monkey wrench and a host of less easily identifiable tools and gadgets, scavenged from the waste tips of the city. It was also rumoured that Frank carried a hand gun, a real one with proper bullets and everything, though Scally had never seen it.

He didn't like Frank one little bit. As far as he was concerned, the man was a jumped-up thug, who was his own biggest fan. His knack for survival on the streets had made him the Duke of the Ardwick Tribe, but most of the time he was just a mean, nasty drunk who took the greatest delight in hurting or humiliating anybody who tried to oppose him. In a different world, Scally thought, a fair world where everyone had a home, a job and a wage, a man like Frank wouldn't last in a position of power for five minutes. He'd be sweeping the streets or cleaning out shit houses. Here in the arches, his power was total.

'See that,' he announced to the waiting queue, holding up

his spoon to display its contents. There was a chunk of pasty-looking meat lying amidst the vegetables and gravy. 'That's real chicken, that is. None of that soya shit. Had a bit of luck today.'

He hesitated, waiting for a reaction, and some of his supporters gave appropriate nods and chuckles of delight.

'Got this mate, see? Works on one of them there battery farms. He owed me a favour from a while back, wanted to give me money, but I said, "Hell no, give me one of them nice fat chickens you've got in there! I got a bunch of friends back at my arch who'll know just what to do with that." '

Now the murmurs of approval were more vociferous. Scally found himself doing it too. 'Good ol' Frank!' he heard himself say, and instantly felt annoyed. But it was just a reflex. It didn't do to get on the wrong side of Frank; and Scally remembered how hard life had been before he'd joined up with the Ardwick Tribe, when he'd had to survive alone on the unforgiving streets of the city.

At last it was Scally's turn in the queue. He held out his tin can and received his ladle full of hot glop, trying not to scowl when he registered the meagre amount of chunks in it. As he stood there, he was aware of Frank examining him, that mocking smirk on his thin face.

'Give 'im a bit more, Peg,' he said. 'Lad'll need to keep his strength up if he's to see to the mad woman.'

Scally felt his face reddening but he didn't dare offer a reply. He moved aside a step to receive his bread and Marianne stepped forlornly into the space he'd vacated. Peg looked at Marianne's proffered tin for a moment, an unpleasant scowl on her usually good-natured face.

'I don't know as if there's enough for them that hasn't earned it,' she said, loud enough for the others in the queue to hear. Marianne shrugged and began to move away, but Scally put out a hand to still her.

'She's with me,' he told Peg.

Peg stared back at him, an expression on her face that said, 'So?' Then she turned her head aside and looked inquiringly at Frank.

He was studying Marianne, studying her as a leopard might

41

appraise its prey before moving in for the kill. He continued to eat, more slowly now, pushing the heaped spoonfuls into his mouth with loud slurps. His bulging grey eyes examined Marianne intently as though she was some lesser life form that had crawled out from under a stone. She was compelled to lower her gaze to look at her feet. Scally felt like taking his own tin and dashing the scalding contents into Frank's face but he told himself to stay still and quiet. After what seemed an age, Frank gave a curt nod: and Peg reluctantly slopped a small amount of stew into Marianne's tin.

'No bread,' she warned Liz.

Scally began to walk back to his shelter and Marianne followed – but Frank stuck out a leg to obstruct their path. He didn't even acknowledge Scally, but kept his eyes fixed on Marianne as he spoke.

'Had a bit more luck with my friend, didn' I?' he muttered, speaking quietly so that Peg wouldn't overhear. 'He passed on some bottles of sherry to me. Decent stuff, not the sort they use for cookin' and that. Thought maybe you might like to try a taste of it one of these nights.'

Marianne didn't say anything. She didn't have to. Frank became aware that Peg was looking suspiciously at him and he moved his leg to let them pass.

'And next time, make sure you bring something for the pot!' he shouted after them.

Scally and Marianne crawled back into the shelter, moving carefully in case they spilled food. Scally adopted his habitual eating position, squatting down with his back against the brick wall. He began to spoon up mouthfuls of stew, telling himself that he should take his time over this, it was more satisfying if you did that: but his belly was an aching void it would take an avalanche of food to fill. He reached for the bread and was about to plunge it into his stew when he remembered that Marianne didn't have any.

'You can share my bread if you like,' he told her. 'I've got loads here.'

She shook her head. 'No, thank you, you're very kind, but they're right, Scally, I shouldn't be eating this. I didn't put anything into the pot.'

'That's OK,' he said. 'All I put in was a handful of carrots. And one day last week, I didn't come back with anything.'

'No, but at least you *tried*.' She sighed. 'I'm useless. I know I should be trying harder but somehow, it's all too much for me. I can't quite believe I'm here, that I'm living this way. It wasn't meant to happen to me, Scally. I always thought I had a charmed life, you know? I thought I could just go on dancing and drinking and having fun and there would always be money and a place to live until one day I turned around and everything had changed, everything had gone bad on me.' She pushed her spoon half-heartedly around in the contents of the tin can. 'God. It's like I really need to get my act together, you know? I don't know how you put up with me.'

'You're OK,' he told her. 'You're great, honest.'

She smiled. 'No, I'm not. I'm one of life's victims. Always have been. It's not something I'm proud of.' She put a small spoonful of food into her mouth and grimaced, had to swallow hard to get it down. 'I'll have to start being more like you, Scally. You get out there and do it, don't you? You're what they used to call a go-getter.'

'Yeah?' Scally beamed with pleasure. He hadn't realized that he was anything other than some homeless kid. 'A go-getter. I kind of like the sound of that.' He thought for a moment. 'What about Steve from the Messiahs? Was he a go-getter too?'

Marianne thought about it for a few moments, that sad serious look on her face again. 'I used to think so,' she said. 'But in the end, it turned out, he was just like me. Another victim.'

She sat there looking into her bowl and Scally didn't really know what to say to her after that. So he finished the stew, mopping up the last few bits of it with the remains of his bread. Afterwards, he felt better. The food had taken the edge off his hunger but it hadn't filled him up. He could barely remember what that felt like, the sensation of being really full. He supposed the last time was that pizza he'd shared with Gyppo. They hadn't expected that. It had been a great moment. And then afterwards . . .

He made a mental effort to thrust the memory aside. He

didn't want to think about that just now. Suddenly, he felt like getting out into the fresh air.

'Think I'll head back into town,' he told Marianne. 'Try and scare up some money on New Market Street. You want to come?'

'It's still pouring with rain,' she reminded him.

'Yeah, that can be good when you're begging. People feel sorry for you when you're wet.'

Marianne laughed at that.

'You see, Scally, you know all the angles! I would never have even thought of it.' She shook her head. 'No, you go on. If it's all right with you, I'll stay on here a while and dream my dreams. Maybe I'll come with you tomorrow.'

'Sure. Whatever.' He clambered out of the shelter and buttoned his overcoat. The other Rag People were sitting around, finishing their food and staring out at the rain. Frank watched Scally as he moved towards the arch.

'She's got you working hard,' he observed. 'Must be love!' He laughed unpleasantly and some of his cronies joined in. Scally felt his face grow hot again. He longed to turn around and say something witty, something that would make Frank look stupid, but he knew he didn't dare. Frank had all the power here in the arch and Scally was just a kid. It hurt sometimes to be reminded that he was nothing.

He pulled up the collar of his coat and stepped into the rain.

Chapter Five

Three days later, Will reluctantly agreed to let them turn off the respirator. By then, he and Suzanne had attended a meeting with the consultant, Dr Thomas, a tall ascetic-looking man in his fifties. He had shown them the results of a brain scan that had been performed on Martin.

'I'm sorry, but there's no doubt about it,' he told them bluntly. 'Your son is in a persistent vegetative state. There's not the slightest possibility of him waking from this.'

So, reluctantly, they signed the consent forms. The machine was turned off and Will and Suzanne sat on either side of Martin's bed, each of them holding one of his hands, until the cardiograph flatlined and they knew that their son was dead. It didn't take long, a little less than half an hour. Will felt numbed by the experience, detached from everything that was happening around him, as though he had used some kind of drug himself. He sat there looking at his son's blank features and he couldn't stop thinking about the people that had done this to him, the unknown faces who had manufactured Warp and had sold it on the street, knowing full well how dangerous it was. In that moment, Will knew something else: that he would have no rest until he found out who those people were and brought them to justice.

The nurses gave them ten minutes alone with their son. It couldn't be longer, they explained, as they had to make up the bed for its next occupant, a car crash victim. Will and Suzanne kissed Martin's cooling cheeks, then went to collect his personal belongings, a plastic bag containing his bloodstained clothing and a wallet, which held his ID papers, some credit cards but, suspiciously, no money. They walked out of the hospital into the grey light of another day. A heavy acid rain was still falling, drumming loudly on the roofs of parked cars. It had been coming down like this for days, a fact which made a mockery of the current drought emergency measures. They climbed into Suzanne's car, a Mitsubishi Shogun and she drove slowly back to her house in the suburbs.

'You'll be needing somewhere to stay,' Suzanne told him, her expression blank, her voice toneless. 'At least till the funeral. You can stay with . . . at my place.' Will realized that she'd been about to say 'us'. She'd have to get used to talking in the singular from now on.

Will nodded.

'Thanks. I appreciate it. Look, as regards the funeral expenses, I'll give you what I can, but I'm afraid it won't be very much.'

'Forget it,' she told him flatly. 'It's not a problem.'

Suzanne had a high-powered job with Delta, the city's leading property developers. They were currently in the final stages of a massive project, the brand new Millennium Stadium, a sports and leisure complex which was to be inaugurated with a prestigious concert on New Year's Eve. There had been the inevitable hitches and now teams of builders were working around the clock in order to have the place ready for the opening. Several times over the last couple of days, Will had overheard Suzanne out in the corridor, blathering about it into her mobile phone. Her constant apologies for her absence made him feel like punching her. She'd managed to make it sound as if Martin's condition was some irritating nuisance that was conspiring to keep her away from more important matters.

Perhaps, he'd reasoned, she was just dealing with the crisis in her own way. After all her career had always been so important to her and she had made a great success of it. When Will had walked out on the marriage there had never been any thought of him paying alimony: indeed there were some unkind souls who muttered that it ought to be the other way around. After all, by then, Will was unemployed with no real prospects and Suzanne was working as the company's Accounts Co-ordinator, bringing home a salary that made a policeman's wages look pretty sad by comparison. Nevertheless, he had turned over the family home to her, without a second's hesitation and had never once tried to press her for any settlement.

Since his departure, Suzanne had risen to the post of Co-Director. She had sold the modest semi that had been the family home and moved to a more spacious detached house in Heaton Moor. Will knew of the changes in her circumstances because they had kept in touch, Will phoning perhaps once a month, more to talk with Martin than with Suzanne. He didn't begrudge her success, because he knew that she'd worked damned hard for it. He also knew that she was quietly appalled by his lack of direction since losing his job.

'Where are you working now?' she asked him, as the car moved fitfully along the congested artery of Wilmslow Road. She kept her gaze fixed straight ahead, staring through the fan of clear glass made by the windscreen wipers.

'Same place,' he said non-comittally. He didn't feel much like talking, but realized that the alternative was a silence which he might be tempted to fill with a scream of mingled rage and grief. 'It isn't much but it pays the rent, buys me the odd bottle of whisky.' He saw her mouth draw down in an expression of displeasure and wondered at the little stab of satisfaction it afforded him.

'Isn't it time you got your life back on line, Will?' she asked him. 'I mean, it's been more than a year now. Slobbing around is OK for a teenager, but you're not getting any younger.'

He smiled thinly. 'Thanks for reminding me,' he said.

'You always take things the wrong way. All I'm saying is . . .'

'I know what you're saying. Thanks for the concern. But the trouble is, Suzanne, I'm trained for police work. That's what I do, it's all I really know how to do: and there's not a hope in hell of getting back on the force, not after what happened.'

'Granted. But there are other things you could try. A lot of ex-coppers become security guards, don't they?'

Will gave a grunt of disgust, picturing himself in some ill-fitting rent-a-cop uniform, trudging dejectedly around the

47

Westway Centre, on the lookout for the criminal masterminds who had just absconded with a Mars bar.

'Please, I'm not quite ready for that, yet. Maybe when I get to retirement age.'

'Well, a detective agency then? I'm sure you could make a go of that. And if it's a question of money, I could always loan you enough to get you started.'

'Thanks, but I really don't think so.' She had always tried to mould him into something he didn't want to be, it was one of the reasons why he had left her. But he didn't see why he had to suffer it now. 'You have to understand something,' he told her. 'I like having no responsibilities. The truth is, it suits me down to the ground. See, I did all that stuff years ago, caring about my work. Trying to advance my career. And look where it got me. Kicked into the gutter.'

'I appreciate that, Will. But perhaps it's time you climbed back out of it.'

Suzanne sounded her horn at a car in front of her that had braked too suddenly for comfort. Will shot her a venomous look. 'I don't want to talk about this right now, Suzanne. Our son just died back there, in case you'd forgotten.'

She grimaced and spoke through gritted teeth. 'That was a pretty cheap shot. Of course I haven't forgotten. I was just making conversation.'

'Yeah? Well if you must talk, let's talk about Martin, OK?' He looked at her for a moment before continuing. 'What else do you know about the night he died?'

She gave him a wary look. 'What do you mean? I've told you everything.'

'Not in detail. We never got the chance back at the hospital. You spoke to his friend, Tim, right? What else did *he* tell you?'

'God, I don't know. I was distressed, barely taking it in.'

He glared at her irritably. He felt like shouting at her but he realized that approach would get him nowhere.

'Just tell me what you remember. This club he was at, what was the name of it again?'

'Umm . . . The Garden of Eden? No, Delights. Terrestrial Delights, that was it. Apparently it's *the* place to be seen in now. You know, since the Hacienda burned down. It's one of Gary Flowers' clubs.'

Will remembered the name. Flowers was the city's best-known nightclub impresario. He'd been in the business for something like twenty years now and he ran a string of highly successful clubs in the city centre, plus a few smaller venues in several of the less salubrious suburbs. Will had visited them all at one time or another, usually in the line of duty, and though this new name was unfamiliar to him, he didn't doubt that it would turn out to be one of the same old venues decked out in the season's new colours.

'The drugs were bought there?'

Suzanne shook her head. 'No, on the street outside. The club operates a strict "No Hard Drugs" policy. Of course, they sell the legal highs. They all do now.'

Will scowled.

The policy of selling legal alternatives to hard drugs had been the government's misguided attempt to combat the growing problems of addiction, and to make up for the millions in revenue that was being lost because of declining cigarette sales. Implemented only a year ago, it had initially looked like it would succeed, as thousands of curious kids flocked to see what legal speed, cocaine and ecstasy was like. But just as quickly, it had become something to be sneered at. After all, for a large sector of society, the main attraction of drugs was the fact that they *were* illegal. These days it seemed, the main customers for legal highs were middle-class people in their forties, pining after the wild excesses of their youth, but too nervous to risk breaking the law.

'You said Martin bought this Warp from a down-and-out.'

Suzanne nodded. 'That's what Tim told me. A Rag Man. He said they often have it to sell.'

They had left the city behind now and were driving through the Asian quarter of Rusholme, the streets packed with sari-clad women sheltering from the rain beneath brightly coloured umbrellas. The countless curry houses and delicatessens were already open for business and the air was thick with pungent spices and the appetizing aroma of frying onions and garlic.

Will's stomach gurgled, reminding him that he hadn't eaten a square meal in days.

The car ground to a halt in the wake of a religious procession, dozens of people dressed in white dhotis, beating drums and banging cymbals as they marched in the pouring rain. In the middle of the procession, Will could see that several men were carrying an ornate wooden pallet containing the huge carved and painted figure of some many-armed mythical deity. Around this, danced several devotees in a trance-like euphoria. They were stripped to the waist and flailing at their own backs and shoulders with lengths of knotted rope. Blood mingled with the rain and ran copiously from their lacerated flesh. The Mitsubishi crawled along in the procession's wake.

'Have you talked to this Gary Flowers?'

Suzanne flashed him a wary look. 'No, why should I do that?'

'Because it happened in his club.'

Suzanne shook her head. 'He's one of Manchester's most respected celebrities.'

'I don't care if he's Great God Almighty, someone should ask him what he knows.'

Suzanne looked worried. 'Will, it's not as clear cut as that. Flowers has been a major investor in the Millennium Stadium, I've had to work with him in a professional capacity several times. I can hardly steam in there and start asking him embarrassing questions.'

Will shrugged. 'Fair enough. But I take it you don't mind if *I* do?'

Suzanne sighed, lowered her head. 'What would be the point? Martin is dead, nothing you do now is going to change that.'

'True. But there are other kids out there who might be tempted to try this stuff. What about them?'

Suzanne didn't answer. The procession had turned left now and the stalled traffic was able to speed up again. The mobile phone on the car's dashboard began to trill but Suzanne ignored it. Will slumped back in his seat and tried to gather his thoughts. He felt rough, weary, still not fully recovered from his last whisky bender. His face was covered with thick stubble and after several days spent waiting around at the hospital, he badly needed a bath and a change of clothes. Though Suzanne had driven back to her house in the suburbs every evening, Will had stubbornly refused to leave Martin's side and the only sleep he'd had during this time had been snatched on an uncomfortable chair beside his son's bed or on a hard wooden bench out in one of the corridors.

'What do you expect me to do?' Will asked at last. 'Just forget the whole thing? Act as if nothing has happened?'

'Of course not. But I would ask you to be discreet. Delta has a lot riding on Metro 2000 and the last thing we need is you going in there and stirring the shit.'

He glared at her for a moment. 'Fuck your precious company,' he snarled. 'And fuck Metro 2000. It's our son we're talking about here. Remember him?'

Suzanne had a pained expression on her face. 'There's no need to raise your voice, Will.'

'There's every bloody need! I can't believe you. Martin's dead and all you care about is appearances.'

'That's not true, you know it's not. But I just don't see what use it will do to go rocking the boat, simply because you're hurting and you want to hit out at something. It isn't going to bring Martin back.'

Suzanne's reticence was exasperating. As she always did in times of crisis, she'd retreated behind the cold veneer she liked to display to the world. Will wasn't fooled for a moment. He knew that beneath that businesslike surface, there was a frightened, wounded creature, whimpering with pain and grief. The veneer didn't crack for a moment. Her self-control was almost frightening. Will wasn't about to leave the matter alone. Watching Martin's quiet death in the hospital had only served to strengthen his resolve. Somebody had done this to his son. Will would track down the people responsible and make them pay, by fair means or foul, it didn't matter which. He was no longer a cop, no longer bound by the strict codes that had dictated his former life. He could play as dirty as he liked and he would do so, without a qualm. He wanted to hurt these people as they had hurt him. He wanted to have them at his mercy, begging to be spared, simply for the pleasure of denying that request.

But first there were other matters to attend to. He would see his son's remains laid to rest. Then the process of vengeance would begin.

Will and Suzanne didn't speak again until they had reached the quiet suburb where she lived. Three-storey Victorian houses flanked the road, exuding an air of affluence but Will noticed that many homes were surrounded by high fences topped with razor wire, and some windows were protected by steel bars or metal shutters.

Suzanne turned the car onto a quiet side street, reached into her pocket and took out a remote control. She pressed a six digit code into the handset and a pair of steel gates in a high brick wall up on their right began to swing slowly open. She drove inside, along a broad avenue flanked by naked poplars. The gates closed smoothly behind them.

They drove up to the house and parked on the gravel drive. The three-storey red brick towered imposingly over them. Will sat for a moment, gazing up at the expensive mirrored windows, wondering how much the place had cost. He couldn't imagine what Suzanne would think of the poky, dingy apartment he'd shared with Roxy in Southport. He turned to say something to her but she was already climbing out of the car so he opened the passenger door and followed her to the front porch. He watched as she deactivated the intruder alarm by punching in another six digit code.

She unlocked the door and they stepped into a neat and spacious hallway. Suzanne placed her thumb on a recognition panel on the answerphone on the hall table.

'Welcome back, Mrs Ambrose,' said a well-modulated female voice. 'You have sixteen messages recorded and there are four faxes in the tray. Would you care to hear the messages now?'

'Later,' said Suzanne impassively. She turned left and strolled through a luxurious living room into the large kitchen. Will followed. Through the metal bars on the picture window, there was a view of a large back garden. It must have been grand once when it was filled with flowers and shrubs: but now the naked, acid-scarred trees and empty flower beds looked very sorry for themselves. Beneath a scattering of rust-red leaves, the lawn was a rectangle of dead yellow chaff that the rain had arrived too late to revive.

'I'm having it all flagged over in the spring,' Suzanne told him. 'Following government guidelines. It's hopeless when they won't even let you use a hosepipe or a watering can. If only it would rain like this through the spring and summer.'

Will nodded, turned back to survey the kitchen.

'Still, this is quite a placc,' hc said. He felt like she'd been waiting for him to say it.

'Thanks. Would you like a coffee or something?'

'Maybe later. If it's all right, I'd like to have a look at Martin's room.'

She sighed, shrugged her narrow shoulders. 'Of course, it's on the first floor. Turn left at the top of the . . .' Her breath seemed to catch in her throat and she sat down heavily at the kitchen table.

'You all right?' he asked her. He took a hesitant step closer but she waved him away.

'Fine,' she gasped. 'You go. I'll be . . . all right.'

He sighed, walked through into the living room, then hesitated as he heard the sounds coming from the kitchen – a low, keening noise, the sound of an animal in pain. It trailed off into a series of ragged sobs. He glanced back through the doorway and saw that Suzanne was slumped over the table now, her face in her hands. She was crying her heart out.

He didn't go back in to her, he knew she wouldn't want that. So he retraced his steps to the hallway, climbed the steep staircase to the first-floor landing and stood for a moment, looking at the stripped pine door of Martin's room. A small plaque was affixed to it showing a cartoon cat seated in front of a huge computer. The cat had a look of intense concentration on its face and the caption read, *Quiet please. Genius at work!*

Will reached out and pushed open the door. The room within was surprisingly tidy. The yellow-painted walls were dominated by posters of rock stars but they were all neatly framed and carefully aligned. Will imagined that this was Suzanne's influence.

Over in one corner, there was a workstation with a flashy looking Apple Macintosh mounted on it. Will knew that his son had been an enthusiastic net surfer and it occurred to him that this was a potential source of information. He booted up the computer and tried to access the diary and address book icons but the system kept prompting him for a password and after several futile attempts to guess what it might be, he was obliged to abandon the idea.

For the time being, he restricted himself to a physical search of the room. He felt awkward doing it, as though he was violating his son's memory, but he told himself that it had to be done. He didn't come up with much. A notebook which Will found in the top drawer of the workstation had absolutely nothing in it apart from a series of weird, mildly pornographic doodles. Sandwiched into an innocuous-looking school textbook, he found an opened packet of condoms and in a decorative-looking box on the windowsill, there was a small block of hashish wrapped in cling film. It would require laboratory analysis to determine whether it was the genuine article or a Herbal High. Given Martin's age, none of these items seemed particularly unusual.

Will found something infinitely more worrying in a chest of drawers, lying underneath some shirts. It was a small unframed photograph, a picture of Will and Martin taken sometime in the 1980s on a rare family holiday in the Dordogne, the two of them wearing T-shirts and matching baseball caps. Martin would have been about ten or twelve, Will thought, the pair of them as thick as thieves in those days. They were grinning at the camera, their arms around each others' shoulders: but the picture had been vandalized. Will's face had been scratched repeatedly with a knife or a compass point, until it was just a series of jagged scars.

It made Will feel sick, finding that. It made him want to cry like a child. He slid the photograph back into the drawer and closed it, desperately trying to tell himself that at least Martin had kept the picture, that at least he hadn't completely destroyed it. It wasn't much consolation but it was something to hang on to, and right now he felt dangerously close to losing his grip.

He found himself wondering if Suzanne kept any alcohol in the house. The way he felt, he could just sit down with a bottle of whisky and drink and drink until he sank into oblivion. When he woke, he'd happily start all over again . . .

But he steeled himself, ground his teeth together, shook his head. He wasn't going to go back down that road, at least, not yet, not until he'd hunted down the answers to a few questions, questions that shuddered and jittered at the back of his mind like exposed nerves. There was a telephone beside the computer and reaching for the receiver, he dialled the number for Directory Enquiries. He was a bit out of touch but as far as he knew, he still had one friend who was clued in to what was happening in Manchester: and what's more, it was somebody who owed him a favour.

Maybe it was time to call that favour in . . .

Chapter Six

It's night time and Scally and Gyppo are wandering the backstreets of the city, looking for their supper. With practised skill they are searching through dumpsters and trash cans, rooting out the discarded treasures of another, more prosperous section of society.

The two boys have been a team now for something like three months. They are of a similar age and background and they get along pretty well together. They first met in a dark alley just like this one, both of them arriving on the scene as a kitchen worker pitches a bag of leftover food into the trash, the food still warm and aromatic.

From the start they were faced with a simple decision. They could fight for sole possession of the food or they could share it. Happily, they decided to share and they have carried on as they started, working together, watching each other's backs when trouble is around, dividing up whatever they can forage.

You wouldn't guess it is mid-June tonight, the sky is choked with thick clouds that promise, but never quite deliver, rain and the air is suffused with an unseasonable chill. They strike it lucky when the owner of an Italian restaurant spots them and brings out a big pizza that was destined for the trash. He chats with them as they eat, standing in the back doorway. He's a big, genial man who seems to want nothing from them in return. He's a rare creature in this city. There are many who offer favours, then seek to exact payment by a whole series of unsavoury methods.

The boys bid the man good night and go on their way. Their wanderings have brought them into the Castlefield area, a once-neglected part of the city, now redeveloped into an upmarket playground for the middle classes. Fashionable café bars nestle beside the canal and the police maintain a strong presence around here, making sure that the likes of Scally and Gyppo do not hang around to offend the eyes of the more privileged.

So the boys decide to sleep the night on the banks of the canal. They collect together enough cardboard to provide insulation and they go down the stone steps, walking along until the lights of the café bars have dwindled into the distance. They stop beneath the cover of an overhanging bridge and sit on the bank, their legs dangling, sharing a single cigarette that they've bummed off a stranger earlier that day.

Gyppo is staring down at the flat black stretch of polluted water that runs beneath their shoes. His long hair is hanging in his eyes and he seems thoughtful.

'Reckon it'll always be like this?' he asks Scally, as he passes him the cigarette.

'How d'you mean?'

'Living like this. You reckon there's any way out of it?'

Scally chuckles. 'Yeah. We could win the Lottery, couldn't we?'

Gyppo gives him a look, so Scally tries to be less giddy. That's the thing about Gyppo. You can piss him around a certain amount but then he gives you one of his looks and you know he's being serious and he expects you to act likewise. Scally shrugs, tries again.

'I dunno. I suppose not. The way I see it, the only chance is if you have family, someone with money who'll take you in. I ain't got nobody. But what about your mum and dad? They're still alive, aren't they?'

Gyppo frowns. 'Yeah, somewhere, I suppose.' He has never told Scally much about his parents, but tonight he seems ready to talk about them. 'They're travellers. They do drugs and drive around the country in an old camper van.'

'Sounds OK,' said Scally.

'Nah, they're full of shit. Always going on about peace and love but fighting like terriers every night. I couldn't take any more of it, know what I mean?'

Scally doesn't really, though he nods. His own parents are

just a vague memory to him, but none of those memories seem particularly unpleasant.

'When did you last see them?' he asks.

'I suppose about a year ago. We were going down to the Stonehenge Festival the next day. Rain took a lot of drugs and . . .'

'Rain?' echoed Scally, puzzled.

'Yeah, me mum. That was her name, see. Rain. And my old man called himself Sky.'

'Gerroff!'

'No, straight up. They all have names like that, the travellers. I mean, they didn't call me Gyppo neither, that was like a nickname I picked up later.'

'What's your real name then?'

There's a long silence. Gyppo is obviously reluctant to divulge this information.

'Go on,' Scally prompts him. 'Tell us.'

Gyppo sighs, takes a deep breath. 'They called me River.'

'River? You're kidding!' Scally throws back his head and laughs. The sound of it echoes strangely beneath the dark roof of the railway bridge and up in the metal struts, roosting pigeons flap and coo, their sleep disrupted. 'Why would they call you that?'

'Fuck knows. I think it's after some dead film star me mum fancied. Anyway, like I said, Rain took a lot of drugs. Magic mushrooms. She started giving me grief, you know, saying like how I'd ruined her life, how she was never able to do the stuff she wanted. And then she tells me that Sky ain't even my real dad, that it was some other guy she met at a rock festival.'

'Jesus,' murmurs Scally.

'Jesus is right. It was news to me. Trouble was, it was news to Sky too, 'cos he must have been listening at the door. He busts in there and starts laying into her, calling her a whore and all that. She's screaming at him, he's belting her . . .'

'So you stepped in to stop it, right?'

Gyppo sneers. 'Oh sure, like I'd do that for somebody who wasn't even a good mother.' He shakes his head and accepts the cigarette back from Scally. He takes a last deep drag on it and throws the butt into the canal. There is a brief hiss as the glowing tip hits the water. 'I just got out of there, didn't I? Hitched a lift in the first car that stopped for me and it was coming up to Manchester. Been here ever since.'

'And you never heard from them again?'

Gyppo shakes his head. 'They could have killed each other for all I know.'

There's a long silence. They sit there staring into the water.

'They might be worried about you,' ventures Scally at last. 'They could be looking for you.'

'Oh yeah.' Gyppo gives a sardonic laugh. 'And they could have gone to Stonehenge and had the best fucking time of their lives. Who cares?' He seems to grow suddenly tired of talking. He lifts his legs up from the canal bank and walks over to his cardboard bed. 'Time for some shuteye,' he announces: and Scally concludes that his friend's true confessions are over for the time being.

The two boys lie down and wrap themselves in layers of cardboard. They are tired and they quickly fall asleep . . .

Go on, Scally, you know what happens next. Tell them . . .

'I don't like to think about it, Gyppo. It scares me.'

Sure it does. But you can't stop thinking about it, can you? It sneaks into your head when you're sleeping, when you can't shut it out. And then . . .

'Please Gyppo, don't make me do this!'

Tell them. Scally. Tell them everything.

It seems like they've been asleep for only minutes, but it must be longer than that, maybe an hour or so, because the clouds have dispersed and moonlight is filtering in beneath the bridge.

Scally wakes suddenly to the awful sensation of rough hands pulling at his clothing. He scrambles upright, yelling in terror and sees that he is in the grip of two filthy, long-haired men. Their faces are horribly white in the moonlight, faces that seem never to have been exposed to the warmth of the sun. One of them is twisting Scally's arm up behind his back, causing flickering jolts of agony to dance along it: and Scally is horribly aware of their slimy hands on his wrists and the terrible smell of them filling his nostrils, almost making him gag. They smell like something that's been dead a long time.

He struggles desperately around to look for Gyppo and sees him fighting with two other men. They are trying to drag him towards something the two boys didn't notice earlier. There's a manhole set into the bank of the canal and it's open. Suddenly, Scally knows exactly who these people are.

Subs. He's heard other Rag Men talking about them. Old timers who claim that the Subs live down in the shit and stench of the sewers. They are always hungry and at night, they come up to the streets to scavenge for food. They aren't at all fussy about what they eat.

Scally has always dismissed the stories as bogey-man tales, fantasies used to scare kids into behaving themselves: but this is no fantasy, this is happening and if he doesn't use his wits, these people are going to drag him down there into the black maw of the sewer. He stops struggling and allows his body to go limp, as though he has fainted. The Subs relax their grip a little and begin to drag him towards the manhole. From beneath half-lowered eyelids, Scally can see Gyppo's face, pale and slack-jawed in terror. One Sub has climbed down the metal rungs below, keeping an arm tight around Gyppo's legs. The second man is lowering the boy by his arms, into the manhole. Gyppo struggles and curses and seems to be gaining control of the situation. Then, as Scally watches in mute horror, a man's arm rises up from the manhole wielding a big rusty steel hook. It rises above Gyppo's head and Scally wants to shout a warning, but he daren't because then his captors will tighten their grip, he'll be lost . . .

The hook curves over Gyppo's shoulder and comes down hard, the steel point biting deep into his neck. Gyppo throws back his head and screams in agony.

That's enough for Scally. He comes out of his 'faint' and jerks a knee upwards into the testicles of one of his captors. There's a sudden gasp of putrid, exhaled air beside his left ear. The Sub doubles over and drops to his knees. Scally whirls around, his free hand clawing in his pocket for the home-made blackjack he always carries with him, a large chunk of lead which he's painstakingly gaffa-taped to a length of flexible plastic hose. The other Sub draws back a fist to punch Scally but he's a fraction too late. Scally has the blackjack in his hand and he whips it hard into the Sub's bearded face. The lead connects with the man's forehead, making a dull thunking sound and leaving a bloody V-shaped dent in his cranium. His eyes roll up in their sockets and he drops at Scally's feet, lies there twitching violently.

Scally whirls back and looks for Gyppo, only to catch a glimpse of his friend's hands, gesticulating helplessly from the manhole as he is dragged down below the ground. There is a last despairing scream of terror and then Gyppo is gone. For a couple of seconds, Scally considers following him down there into the darkness, but the thought of it turns his bowels to ice, rooting him to the spot with terror. In that awful moment of indecision, the first Sub groans and begins to get up off his knees. One of the others, kneeling by the manhole, turns to look over his shoulder. Scally sees that he is salivating, thick strands of drool trailing from his open mouth into his matted beard.

Scally panics. He turns and runs for his life, back along the canal bank. The injured Sub limps in pursuit, muttering a string of unintelligible curses but Scally easily outruns him. He makes it to the lights of the café bars but the area is deserted now, all the revellers have gone home to their beds.

Scally scrambles up the flight of stone steps to street level and pauses to look back at his pursuer. The Sub has halted at the bottom of the steps and he is retching violently, his hands on his hips. As Scally watches, horrified, something long and glistening slides from the Sub's mouth and falls with a splat onto the stone steps. Then there's the pounding of feet and the other Sub comes racing along the canal bank, his long, filthy coat flapping behind him like a vampire's cloak.

Scally turns and runs and this time he doesn't stop until he has lost himself in the labyrinth of backstreets and alleys that criss-cross the city centre. In the days that follow the incident, his cowardice will come back to haunt him and he will make plan after plan to return to the manhole in search of Gyppo: but his terror of the place and of the people that live below ground is too powerful, too all-consuming to be challenged. He will never see Gyppo again, except in his dreams, struggling white-faced and desperate in the grip of those filthy stinking hands as the steel hook rises above his shoulder . . .

Scally, why did you leave me? Why didn't you help?

Now the questions come at him like they always do. He is sitting by the canal bank and Gyppo is lying on his back, just beneath the surface of the water. He looks dead, his face a horrible greenish-grey: but his eyes are open, his mouth is moving and the words emerge like cartoon bubbles from the dirty water.

Why didn't you use the blackjack? You could have taken care of the other guy, while he was still on his knees.

'Gyppo, I was scared. I just freaked. I *wanted* to help you, but I couldn't move!'

Oh, you moved all right. In the other direction. You had no problem running away.

'Please Gyppo, don't say that. Please . . .'

You want to know what it's like down here, Scally? You want to see how it feels?

Gyppo is reaching up from beneath the water. Scally tries to scramble away but Gyppo's arms are melting like rubber, they bend, elongate, claw up at him from beneath the surface. One hand clamps around Scally's wrist with a grip that makes him wince.

Come on, Scally. It's great down here. You'll love it!

He's pulling Scally headlong into the canal, pulling his head under the surface of the oily water and Scally is fighting him, thrashing his arms, kicking his legs; but Gyppo is dragging him inexorably down beneath the surface, down into the dark stinking depths. Scally opens his mouth to scream and it fills with muddy water.

He coughed, spluttered, closed his eyes. He opened them again and saw a pale, anxious face peering down at him. He was back. He was back in the reassuring surroundings of the railway arch. When his eyes filled with tears, Marianne thought he was frightened, but she didn't understand. These were tears of relief. He'd survived another of those awful dreams.

One night, soon, he was convinced, one of them would kill him.

'You all right now?' asked Marianne. She lit a candle and held it up to illuminate the inside of the shelter. Scally nodded, wiping his eyes on the back of his sleeve. He didn't want her to see him crying.

'I'm OK,' he said gruffly. 'Just a dream, that's all.'

'You were yelling,' she told him. 'Yelling your head off. I thought you'd wake everyone in the arch.'

He sat up. Marianne had come by earlier that evening and had shown no signs of moving on when night descended. It would have been bad manners to kick her out at such a late hour and besides, Scally didn't mind her being there, she was good company.

'What were you dreaming about?' she asked him.

He shrugged. 'I dunno. It was just a nightmare.'

'You poor baby. I hate nightmares. I used to get a lot of them when I—'

'Keep the noise down!' snapped a voice nearby.

Marianne made a face but dropped her voice to a whisper. 'Listen, I've got something that might make you feel better. I've been saving it for a special occasion.' He watched as she took a silk scarf from her pocket and unwrapped it carefully, revealing a half consumed bar of Cadbury's chocolate. 'I found it today,' she explained. 'Somebody must have dropped it. It's not even past the sell by date!'

Scally licked his lips. Marianne broke the bar into two equal portions and handed him his share. Four squares of pure pleasure. He began to eat the chocolate, breaking off one square and holding it in his mouth till it melted. Marianne did likewise but without as much enthusiasm.

'You know what I really fancy now?' she murmured. 'Scrambled eggs with smoked salmon. Ever eaten that?'

Scally shook his head. He didn't want to risk replying in case he swallowed the chocolate too quickly.

'It's more of a breakfast thing, really. Steve and I used to have that on Sunday mornings, when he wasn't on tour. The secret is a little fresh cream in the eggs. And plenty of black pepper. If we were feeling really decadent, we'd have a bottle of chilled Moet with it. Then we'd read the Sunday papers and listen to music . . .' She gazed at the squares of chocolate in her hand for a moment and her eyes filled with tears. 'I can't eat this,' she said.

'Sure you can.' Scally studied her for a moment in concern, remembering that she didn't eat any of the Pot Luck she'd been offered earlier that evening. 'You got to eat something, Marianne. You'll waste away.'

'Like a Pre-Raphaelite heroine,' she murmured.

'A what?'

'Never mind.' She looked quickly around as though seeking escape. 'I need a drink,' she concluded. 'I really could use a drink. Maybe Frank still has some of that sherry left. He might trade this chocolate for a taste of it.'

Scally frowned. He hated the thought of her making her way to Frank's shelter in the dark. He pictured Frank lying there beside the sleeping figure of Peg. Peg was a deep sleeper and Scally knew only too well what the charge for a drink would be at this time of night.

'Why not wait till tomorrow?' he urged her. 'We could go up to New Market Street and beg. I know somebody who'll lend us a puppy, you always get more that way.'

'Shut the fuck up!' growled the voice from the darkness, angrier this time. 'Or I'll come over there and shut you up.'

Marianne looked doubtful. 'I don't think I can last that long,' she hissed. 'I'm sure if I asked him, he'd let me have a mouthful.' She was already crawling towards the opening.

'Marianne, wait a minute!'

She paused and looked back at him. 'Take this,' he said. He found himself rooting in his pocket for the loose change he had begged at the station. *Fool!*, snapped a voice in his head, but he ignored it. 'It ain't much, but it's a start. Maybe Frank will sell you a swig.' He placed the coins into her hand. She stared at them doubtfully.

'Oh, Scally, it's good of you but I can't take this.'

'Sure you can.' He winked at her. 'Pay me back when your boat comes in, OK?'

She rewarded him with a bewitching smile and he felt a warmth inside that had nothing to do with the chocolate he'd swallowed.

'My hero,' she said. 'My young Lochinvar.' She leaned

forward and pecked him gratefully on the cheek. 'Oh, Scally, if you were just ten years older . . .'

He closed his eyes for a moment, savouring the thought. And when he opened them again, she was gone, taking the candle with her. He caught a glimpse of her in the flickering circle of light as she picked her way through the sleeping figures on the floor of the arch towards Frank's shelter.

Scally sighed. Sitting there in the darkness he put another chunk of chocolate into his mouth and waited for it to melt. OK, so his money was gone, he'd have to wait a little longer for the treat he'd promised himself, but not even a packet of ham and pickle crisps could make him feel as good as he had when Marianne had kissed him.

The memory of the dream was receding, held at bay by the grubby reality around him, but he knew it wasn't gone for good. It would be back the minute he relaxed his guard. Dreams were like that. The ones you wanted always eluded you and the ones you feared most kept coming back to haunt you, time after time.

But at least tonight there was chocolate in his mouth. The sweet taste of chocolate and a kiss from the woman he loved. On nights like this it still felt good to be alive.

Chapter Seven

When Will woke the following morning, the rain had stopped but the sky remained grey and overcast, threatening to resume hostilities at any moment. He showered, dressed in fresh clothes and went downstairs, only to find a note from Suzanne informing him that she had gone in to the office to 'sort out a few problems.' So after a perfunctory breakfast of tea and toast, Will left the house and caught a tram into the city centre.

He allowed himself a good two hours to make the short journey through the morning rush, not wanting to be late for his appointment, but even so he found himself in danger of missing his time slot because somebody decided to commit suicide under the wheels of the tram.

One moment they were trundling fitfully along the stretch of track on Wilmslow Road – the next there was a sudden jolt as the wheels briefly encountered an obstacle. Then the driver was slamming on the brakes and the passengers were all crowding to the windows to try and see what had happened.

Chaos ensued. Within what seemed like a few minutes, police cars and ambulances had appeared on the scene and the whole road was effectively brought to a standstill. Horns blared and policemen in fluorescent orange jackets began to set up incident tape and bollards. Everybody trooped off the tram and stood around waiting as the driver reversed to reveal the corpse. There was a concerted gasp of horror and a crowd seemed to appear out of nowhere, pushing and jostling to get a clearer look at the victim. Will found himself in the midst of them, craning his neck to peer over somebody's shoulder. He quickly wished he hadn't. The dead man appeared to be a hippy-type, his blonde hair styled into dirty dreadlocks. The wheels had neatly removed his head and feet and the separate sections were linked by copious streamers of blood.

'Another suicide,' muttered the man next to Will, a tall fellow in an ill-fitting suit. He gestured with a furled black umbrella. 'It's getting so you can't travel into town without some blockhead jumping under the wheels.'

'It's because they think the world's going to end,' said a woman in an anorak. 'People are scared.'

'So,' countered the man unsympathetically, 'if they want to kill themselves, why can't they do it quietly at home? I've got an important meeting this morning.' The man spotted the tram driver forcing his way through the crowd towards some waiting policemen. 'Hey you!' he shouted. 'When are you going to get that tram moving again?'

The driver turned to look at him in astonishment. He was a small runty looking fellow, his face pale and waxen beneath the peak of his oversized hat. He was clearly in a state of shock.

'How the hell do I know?' he croaked. 'Could be hours yet. I have to talk to the police.' He turned away.

'Oh, perfect. Perfect!' The tall man stared after the tram driver for a moment. 'And don't you walk away from me when I'm talking to you!' he snapped. 'Do you hear me? What about a refund, eh? What about an *apology*?' The tram driver ignored him. The tall man span around with an oath and began to march off along the track, towards the city centre. He was swinging his umbrella like a lethal weapon and muttering to himself.

Will decided to follow his example. There was less than half a mile to walk and it could be hours before things got moving here. He let the other man get a good distance ahead of him first not wanting to be drawn into conversation by somebody who was quite obviously deranged.

He made it to the offices of *The Manchester Evening Post* with five minutes to spare and pushed through the revolving doors into the foyer, where an elderly commissionaire wearing a creased uniform and an obvious ginger toupee, skulked sullenly behind a marble reception counter. He regarded Will doubtfully, an expression on his wizened face that suggested he was getting a bad smell from somewhere. Will recognized the old man, he'd been working here for years but he didn't seem to know Will.

'Yes, shur, can I help you?' He had ill-fitting dentures that made him pronounce his 'S's with a curious whistling sound.

'I've got an appointment with Clive Singleton, on the crime desk. My name's Will Ambrose, he's expecting me.'

The commissionaire peered at his computer terminal, the rows of digits reflected in his wire-rimmed spectacles.

'Very good, shur, Mr Shingleton. Oh yesh, you'll find him up on the . . .'

'Sixth floor,' said Will hastily. 'Yes, I know. Thanks.'

'If you would be sho good as to shine in?'

Will scribbled his name in the book and headed for the lifts. It was reassuring to note that apart from the odd computer terminal and the occasional framed print on a wall, the place hadn't changed much. He rode up to the sixth floor and walked across the large open-plan office where a dozen crime reporters were beavering away at their respective VDU's, drinking coffee from styrofoam cups and smoking cigarettes, in open defiance of the countless signs that designated this area a 'Smoke Free Zone.' Will could see Clive sitting at a desk that was littered with files, magazines and newspapers. A grubby VDU nestled amidst the debris with a huge, butt-filled ashtray balanced on top of it. Clive was inputing work on his keyboard but he glanced up as Will approached.

Clive looked ten years older, Will thought, his hair prematurely grey, his skin grizzled, the inevitable consequence of the hard-drinking, hard-smoking lifestyle of the professional journalist. He'd been Will's friend since school days, best man at his wedding, a useful ally and confidante all through those years on the Force: yet, since leaving Manchester, Will had not tried to contact his old friend once. He still wasn't sure why not. Perhaps he'd been too proud to admit his own failure.

Clive smiled warmly and, standing, shook Will's hand.

'Hello, stranger,' he said. He glanced quickly around, throwing a wary glance towards the glass-walled cubicle at the top of the room, the lair of editor Barry Summerby. Then he tucked a couple of manila folders under his arm and ushered Will into a vacant interview room, on the other side of the office. 'We can talk better in here,' he said, closing the door securely behind them. He seemed nervous, uncomfortable in Will's presence. His smile was replaced by a look of genuine bewilderment.

'Will, I don't know what to say to you, mate. I couldn't believe it when I heard about Martin. I just . . .' He shook his head. 'I read the report and at first, I didn't even link the name. Then we got the ID through and I started to put it together. I'm just so sorry. Situations like this, they beggar belief.'

'I know,' Will assured him. 'Thanks.'

Clive settled into a chair on the other side of the desk. He set down the folders carefully as if they contained something fragile.

'Of course, if there's anything I can do . . .' He smiled, rather wistfully, Will thought. 'But then, I suppose that's why you're here.'

Will frowned. 'It would be nice, wouldn't it, if after such a long break, I simply came to see you for old time's sake? No ulterior motive other than a couple of drinks and a bit of reminiscing.'

Clive made a dismissive gesture. 'Oh, look, don't worry about that. It doesn't matter.'

'Yes, it does. I should've got in touch with you, Clive. I should have phoned you, told you where I was, how I was getting along. I nearly did, several times, but, I don't know, I guess I just wanted to cut myself off from everything and everybody that linked me to this city. I wanted to start afresh.'

Clive nodded. 'I can understand that, Will, really I can. After what happened with Chalmers, nobody could blame you.'

'Yeah, well, I wanted you to know, I'm not proud of the way I acted. And I'm sorry the first thing I have to do on my return is ask for a favour.'

Clive spread his hands in an expansive gesture. 'Ask away,' he said.

'I need information, Clive. About what happened to Martin. This new drug. Warp? I need answers, even though I'm not sure of all the questions.'

Clive nodded. 'I anticipated as much,' he said. 'And of course, I'll tell you what I know.' He leaned back in his chair and considered for a moment, before continuing. 'Warp first came to our attention about nine months ago. It started as a word on the street, nothing more, but to have reached our ears it must have been around at least a couple of months before that.'

'Do you know anything about it? I mean, what it is, how it works?'

'As it happens, yes, I do know quite a bit. When the first deaths occurred, I planned to do a major feature on it. We managed to get hold of a sample and we had it analysed in an independent laboratory. I've got all the relevant paperwork here . . .' He reached for one of the folders and started to pull out a highly detailed lab report but Will waved it away.

'Just keep it simple, mate. Words of two syllables, if you can manage it.'

Clive allowed himself the ghost of a smile, then seemed to remember that this was a serious matter.

'Basically, somebody has taken the formula of ecstasy, and played around with it, synthesised it into something stronger and more devious. The lab found high concentrations of something called DOB, a powerful hallucinogenic amphetamine.'

'And how does this stuff work? I mean, what exactly causes the changes in personality?'

Clive frowned. 'That's a more difficult question. As I understand it, the drug reacts with a chemical in the brain, something called serotonin?'

'That's four syllables,' Will pointed out.

'Can't help that, mate. Anyway, this chemical holds a bunch of neurotransmitters and the drug excites them, gets them working overtime. The result is an initial euphoria, but unlike ecstasy, that's followed by a series of vivid, speedy hallucinations. Some people can't handle what they see and . . .'

Will nodded grimly. 'Yes, I know what can happen after that.' He sighed. 'So where does this charming drug originate from? What's the country of origin?'

Clive shook his head. 'Doesn't work like that, I'm afraid. Warp is totally synthetic. Unlike say, cocaine or heroin, it doesn't need an organic raw material. With the right equipment it could be manufactured just about anywhere, even here in Manchester.'

Will thought about that for a moment. 'But if that was the case, surely the force would be on to it, by now. They'd at least have busted some laboratories.'

'You'd think so, wouldn't you? Only they're having a disastrous success rate on this. Apart from a few small busts for possession, they seem to be no better informed than they were nine months ago. Whoever is running the operation is being very careful to cover their tracks. And they've found a clever way of doing it. Here, let me show you something.'

Clive opened another of the folders and removed a thick sheaf of papers and a few small photographs. He placed the papers on the desk in front of Will. They contained a list of typewritten names. Leafing through the pages, Will saw that there were dozens of them, mostly males. There was a column headed 'Address' but after every name, were the initials N/F/A – No Fixed Abode.

'Who are they?' asked Will.

'Missing persons,' said Clive. 'Or more specifically, missing Rag People. There's over fifty names there, all logged over the last six months: and you have to remember that most who go missing don't even get reported. That's probably just the tip of the iceberg.'

Will frowned. He looked through the photographs, most of them grubby cut-outs from *The Big Issue*, depicting sullen bearded men in anoraks and bobble hats.

'What about the highlighted names?' he asked.

'*Found* people. As in found floating in the ship canal. As you can see, there aren't many. The only assumption you can make is that the rest of them were more effectively weighted down.'

Will reached up a hand to scratch his head. 'What's your point, Clive? I know that the pushers are using these people to deal Warp. I was told that Martin bought the drug from a man just like this.'

'That's what I heard too. And where is he now, this man? The police scoured the streets for him after the incident and

71

came up with nothing. He probably went for a midnight dip in the Irwell. I expect I'll be adding his name to the list in a couple of weeks.'

'You're saying that he was got at?'

'Yes, that's exactly what I'm saying. You see, Will, it's a stroke of genius! The Rag People are a cheap, disposable work force. Yes, they'll deal class A drugs and what's more, they'll do it for the price of a square meal, simply because they can't afford not to. If they're arrested for dealing, they can't tell the cops anything, simply because they don't really *know* anything. And if it looks like their cover is blown, well, it's an easy matter for their employers to eliminate them.'

Will stared at the long list of names. 'You're telling me that *all* these people . . . ?'

'Think of it, Will! Nobody's going to make a fuss if they do a vanishing act: after all, they're transients, always moving on to new locations. In many cases, nobody even notices they've gone.' He spread his hands in a helpless gesture. 'So how are you supposed to make any headway?'

'I see what you're saying. How come you have this list of names?'

Clive rolled his eyes towards the ceiling. 'Because I was planning to include all this in the Warp article. I wanted to point out how the homeless were being exploited by the drug barons. Anyway, in the end, the piece never made it to print. Summerby spiked it.'

'Why would he do that?'

Clive shrugged. 'Maybe he just didn't like the story.'

Will felt a stab of irritation. 'Come on, Clive, there must be more to it!'

'Oh, I'm sure there *is*, but nothing I can prove. I'd say somebody got to him, wouldn't you?'

'Barry Summerby? You're kidding. I always had him down as one of the good guys.'

'Yes, but he can be got at. These days most people can be got at.' Clive pulled a packet of cigarettes from his pocket. 'Look, do you mind if I . . . ?'

'No, go ahead.' Will watched as Clive lit up a Marlboro. He'd given up the weed a year ago, mainly because he could no longer afford the habit but he understood Clive's awkwardness. These days, indulging in nicotine was liable to make you as popular as a leper in a public swimming pool. 'What about your contacts on the Force? They must know *something*?'

Clive laughed bitterly. 'What contacts? The days of the police being helpful to journalists are over, mate. A couple of my regular contacts were transferred to other divisions around the time I was planning my story on the disappearing Rag People.'

'Coincidence?' ventured Will.

'I doubt it. They were both replaced by hardline bastards who wouldn't give a journalist the time of day. What's more, I'm pretty sure your old friend DCI Chalmers, had a hand in it.'

This remark puzzled Will. 'But why? It doesn't make sense.'

Clive shrugged. 'Maybe he just doesn't like newspapermen. Or more likely, it's pressure from the city council. With this Metro 2000 thing looming on the horizon, they're desperate to promote an image of a squeaky clean, hunky-dory Manchester. The idea is to tempt lots of outside money into the city, big investors from abroad, America and Japan mostly. Drug wars and homelessness are two subjects that are not exactly designed to attract the buck and the yen. There are people on the city council, *powerful* people, who'd like to see all that sleaze swept under the carpet. As for Chalmers, he spends most of his time trying to lick every arse that's attached to a seat on the council.'

'No change there then,' muttered Will disdainfully. 'He always was a dab hand at that. When he's not wearing a blindfold and exposing his breast, that is.'

Clive grunted. He examined the end of his cigarette as though seeking some kind of answer in the tiny conflagration.

'I can appreciate you're no great fan of his,' he said quietly. 'After what happened . . .'

'Bit of an understatement, Clive! No great fan? I hate his guts. Bastard set me up for a fall and all because I didn't want to go along with all that secret handshake shit.'

Clive smiled sardonically. 'But Freemasonry doesn't exist in the Greater Manchester Police, Will! And that's official.

There was a full inquiry headed up by no less a figure than Chief Constable Arthur Bradly himself.'

'Don't make me laugh! Bradly? He practically walks around with his trousers rolled to the knee. You may as well send a psychopath to investigate a murder. Jesus!' Will gave a snort of disgust, then thought for a moment. 'What about Gary Flowers? You got any dirt on him?'

Clive shook his head. 'You are joking, I hope. Flowers is Mister Nice Guy, Manchester's favourite blue-eyed boy. He must be on the board of every charity going, including, I might add, the Police Benevolent Fund.'

'Hmm. I don't suppose there's any chance that *he* has an unusual way of shaking hands?'

'Not that I've ever heard.'

'OK, so what else is he into? What are the rumours?'

'Well, by all accounts, he was a bit of a lad in his day. Basically a lot of drinking and plenty of rumpy pumpy with Page Three bimbos. You'd expect that from a nightclub owner. But in recent years, he's cleaned up his act considerably. He's a married man now, with teenage kids. I know he's invested heavily in Metro 2000.'

'But does a leopard ever change his spots?'

Clive shrugged. 'I'm not sure what you're trying to say, Will. You think Flowers had something to do with Martin's death?'

Will made a sound of exasperation. 'I don't know what I'm saying. I'm like a dog worrying on an invisible bone. All I know is that Martin is dead and I can't just walk away and forget it ever happened.' He stared down at the photographs on the desk top, the glum, bearded faces staring helplessly up at him. 'These people are the key to it,' he said. 'They're the ones who are really being exploited in all this. Maybe if I hunt them out, start asking a few questions . . .'

Clive inhaled on his cigarette and blew out smoke. He looked doubtful.

'I don't think you'd get very far with that approach, Will. The Rag People have got an inherent mistrust of any authority. They're almost like a secret society themselves. I found that out when I was researching the article. As soon as I appeared and started asking questions, they just clammed up. Couldn't get diddly squat out of them, even when I offered them money.'

Will considered this information for a few moments. A crazy idea had just occurred to him and he wanted to sound it out on Clive.

'What if it was one of their own asking the questions?'

Clive narrowed his eyes. 'Come again?' he said.

'Supposing I went and lived among them for a while? Made out I was homeless myself?'

Clive flickcd his ash into a litter bin. 'Christ, they'd see through that in a minute! You can't just slap on some make-up, spend a couple of nights with them and expect them to accept you as one of them.'

'I appreciate that, Clive. But then, I'm not necessarily talking about a couple of nights. I'm talking about doing it, *really* doing it. Going into one of their communities and living with them for as long as it takes.'

Clive stared at him. 'Rather you than me, mate,' he said. He thought about it for a few moments. 'I don't know. You'd have to really go for it, you know. You couldn't take along a Gold card for when times got hard. They'd sniff that out in seconds.'

Will laughed mirthlessly. 'I don't possess a bloody Gold card,' he said. 'Or any other kind of card, for that matter. Unless you count my UB40.'

Clive looked appalled, then vaguely embarrassed. 'Will, I had no idea! Look, if I can help you out in any way . . .'

'Forget it. Money isn't a problem at the moment. Suzanne seems to have enough to take care of all the expenses. But if you really want to help me . . .'

'Yes?' Clive leaned forward across the desk.

'Well, if I decide to do this thing, if I really go for it, I'm going to need a contact, somebody I can meet on a regular basis to feed back whatever information I've picked up. It'll have to be fairly clandestine, of course, but if you wouldn't mind skulking around for a few hours every week . . .'

Clive smiled ruefully. 'Skulking is pretty much what I do best, Will. Of course, I'd be glad to help in any way I can.'

'Thanks, mate. I appreciate it.'

Clive leaned back in his seat and studied his old friend thoughtfully. 'So you're really set on doing this?'

'I don't know. I'll have to weigh it all up. And there's Martin's funeral to think about, I won't do anything until that's sorted. But you know, the more I think about it, the more it seems to make sense. If the Warp dealers employ Rag People, then maybe that's my best chance of getting close to them. I might even persuade one of them to employ me.'

Now Clive was looking decidedly wary.

'Hey look, you want to be careful, Will. Those people, whoever they are, do not play by the rules. I'd hate to add your name to my list of missing persons. Especially when you've turned up after an absence of two years.'

'I'll be all right,' Will assured him. He was looking at a small polaroid photograph on the desktop now, a strange-looking man with shoulder length red hair and intense grey eyes. He was wearing a Big Issue baseball cap and he had a crude black crucifix tattooed on his forehead.

'Don't know how *he* got in there,' muttered Clive. 'He went missing years ago.' He swept the photos up and replaced them in the manila folder. 'Maybe,' he said, 'we could have that drink now. For old times' sake.'

'I'm on the wagon,' announced Will and was almost as surprised as Clive to hear it. He hadn't realized it till this moment. He'd supposed he was just cutting down.

'Lunch then?' suggested Clive. 'The Crown still does a pretty good spread. My treat. What do you say?'

'Lunch would be good,' said Will.

'Great. And while we eat, you can tell me what you've been up to for the last two years.'

Clive returned the files to his desk and collected his jacket. They left the office and rode the lift down to the ground floor. As they stepped out onto the street, Will noticed an old woman crouched in the doorway of a vacant property, right next to *The Post*. She was covered with a filthy blanket and one arthritic hand was held out in supplication to the passers-by. She kept saying, 'God bless you, God bless you, sir,' but nobody seemed to be taking any notice of her. The expression on the woman's face suggested that she was in considerable pain and looking down, Will saw that her feet, where they stuck out from under the blanket, were covered with layers of bloody bandage. He stood there, looking at the woman thoughtfully, wondering what it must be like, how it must feel to be her.

Then Clive slapped him on the back and he came back to his senses.

'Come on,' said Clive. 'I'm starving!'

They crossed the street and had some lunch.

Chapter Eight

Scally lifted the heavy lid of the dumpster and standing on tiptoe, he peered inside. Smells rose up to envelop him in an invisible cloud, a heady mixture of the bad, and the inviting. His sensitive nostrils detected the presence of something dead, the awful gamey stench of decay, but it was far back in the mix and overridden by an appetising aroma that made his stomach lurch.

It was early evening, already dark and it was hard to see what was in there. No sense in mucking about, he decided. He vaulted up onto the rim of the dumpster and dropped down onto the precarious landscape of black bin-bags. His left foot burst through plastic and a gust of fetid air wafted up at him, but it would take more than that to put him off.

The dumpster was located halfway down a city-centre back alley that serviced several properties, one of them a Chinese restaurant of some repute where the staff habitually threw out perfectly good food simply because they'd had a slow night. It was a crime, Scally reckoned, on a par with rape or murder. The way he figured it, restaurant owners ought to be made by law to donate their leftovers to the mobile soup kitchens that performed nightly runs around some of the poorer city shelters. Of course, there were a few of them who did exactly that, but they were definitely in the minority. The sad fact was that most people would rather see leftover food go into the garbage than into the belly of a Rag Man. There were even some bastards who dumped coffee grounds or broken glass into the food to make sure that nobody but the rats could stomach it.

Scally examined the bins on which he was crouching, relying more on touch than on eyesight, running his hands questingly across the black plastic surfaces. After a few moments, his fingertips detected warmth and he knew that this particular bin had not lain here for long. He humped it upright, lifting it onto the edge of the dumpster to catch the light from the rear of one of the buildings. He unsnapped the plastic seal and examined the contents hopefully. Among empty tins and crumpled waste paper, he found another, smaller bag inside the first, this one transparent: and when he withdrew it, he saw to his delight that it contained a bewildering assortment of Chinese scran, all mixed together, the uneaten remains of a night's poor business.

Scally recognized fried and boiled rice, noodles, shreds of chicken and beef, some prawns, a dark splodge that was probably a spoonful of satay sauce and a few other things he couldn't identify, but which all looked to be perfectly edible.

Pleased with himself, he hefted his treasure down to the street. He clambered out of the bin and sought a quiet corner in which to dine. He settled himself on the back step of an office building, where there was an overhead light to see by, and where he was fairly hidden from the alley and any competitors who might happen by. Pulling a fork from his coat pocket, he wiped it on his sleeve and set about his meal. When he tore the inner bag open, a deliciously greasy and appetising smell rose up to greet him and he began to eat, cramming his mouth with the still slightly warm food, relishing the sticky texture of monosodium glutamate.

He was so intent on eating that it was some time before he realized he was no longer alone in the alley. A man was strolling towards the dumpster, a long-haired, bearded Rag Man in a shapeless grey raincoat. Scally instinctively shrank back into the shadow of the office building, but kept right on eating. He couldn't see the man too well but he was fairly sure that he didn't know him. He didn't look like anybody from the Ardwick tribe. The man paused beside the dumpster and stood there, glancing cautiously around. Scally's first thought was that he'd come looking for leftovers too, but the man made no move to look into the dumpster. He just stood there, hands in pockets, whistling tunelessly to himself. He seemed to be waiting for something or somebody.

Sure enough, only a few minutes later, a car appeared at the mouth of the alley and began to cruise along it, headlights blazing. It was a wide, low-slung American car with sharp tailfins. Its gleaming red flanks only cleared the walls of the alley by a few feet on each side. The Rag Man raised an arm to shield his eyes as the headlights illuminated him, and Scally instinctively ducked still deeper into shadow. The car came to a halt a short distance from the dumpster, the engine still running.

Thick clouds of exhaust coiled and drifted in the headlights. Scally kept expecting the lights to go off but they didn't. The Rag Man stood there, silhouetted, his back to Scally, one hand still raised above his eyes. Scally was suddenly aware of the deep rumble of the car's engine, resounding off the alley walls.

After what seemed an age, the driver's door opened and a man got out, a tall, heavy-set man wearing an expensive looking double-breasted suit. He had a fleshy, babylike face, his features no more than rudimentary bumps on the smooth sphere of his head. His straight brown hair was drawn back into a ponytail and Scally distrusted him instantly. In his experience, men with ponytails were generally bad news.

The newcomer was grinning at the Rag Man, his white teeth clenched in an expression of mirth, but Scally noted, the humour did not extend to his eyes which were small and suspicious and, so far as Scally could tell in the uncertain light, babyblue.

'Evenin' Mr Pinder. How's it goin'?'

It was the Rag Man who had spoken. Mr Pinder's grin vanished momentarily, replaced by a look of profound irritation, but the change was so fleeting, Scally barely had time to register it before that cheesy grin was back.

'Why, everything's just peachy keen, Tom. A1. Hunky dory. Top of the range.' Pinder had a creepy lah-di-dah accent. There was a smugness in it that seemed to announce that he was pretty damned pleased with himself. 'And how about your good self? Just come from a fitting with your tailor, I see. Who is it, Armani or Yamamoto? Or a little something you had tossed off in Savile Row?'

Scally forked a heap of rice into his mouth and chewed

instinctively. He was enjoying this, it was better than the telly, even if he didn't have the least idea what the big man was on about. Tom seemed to be having the same problem.

'Oh, er, very funny, Mr Pinder, very funny! You're a card you are, yes indeed.'

He was laughing dutifully but there was a hollow tone to his laughter which told you he wasn't really amused in the least, he was having to be like this because he worked for the other man and was obliged to be respectful.

'Glad you think so,' said Pinder. 'Perhaps I should try my hand at one of those comedy clubs that are all the rage these days. What do you think? Would it be a wizard wheeze, a jolly jape, a veritable feast of fun? I might work up a topical routine, something about the connection between hard drugs and home-lessness. Ought to bring the house down, don't you think?'

'I dare say,' muttered Tom. 'And when you look at some of the rubbish that passes for humour these days . . .'

Pinder seemed to suddenly tire of the subject. 'What say, Tommy my lad, that we cut the cackle and get down to business. Brass tacks. The nitty gritty. You're probably wondering why I've summoned you here a full two days before our regular appointment.'

'It, er, did cross my mind,' admitted Tom warily. 'But it's just as well, 'cos I've sold everything you gave me.'

'Really? You have been a busy bee, haven't you? Actually, Tom, that's sort of what I wanted to speak to you about. You see, it's come to my attention that somebody was selling Warp outside a club called The Garden Of Terrestrial Delights, the other night. And you may recall Tom, that amongst the various instructions I gave you when I first enlisted you, was a warning that certain places were out of bounds. That club being one of them.'

'Well, yeah, but you got to understand, that's a prime site. The kids that go in there, they're the ones who want this stuff. How do you think I got shot of so much so quickly? The pitch you gave me, well no offence, but business is kind of slow, see, so I thought . . .'

'You're not denying it was you?'

'No. See, Mr Pinder, I figured . . .'

Again the look of irritation flared in Pinder's eyes.

'Tom, I don't want to be wearisome, old *bean*, but would you kindly desist from shouting my name all over the place? After all, it's just possible that some vagrant is crouched in the shadows, overhearing our conversation.'

'What, here?' Tom looked slowly around the alley and Scally froze, the fork only inches from his mouth when he saw that the Rag Man appeared to be staring straight at him. 'Not much chance of that, Mr . . .' Tom caught himself, gave an apologetic shrug.

Pinder made an impatient gesture with one hand. 'I believe you have something for me?' he said.

Tom nodded and pulled a thick brown envelope from his coat pocket. The big man accepted it with an expression of slight distaste on his face, as though it contained something unpleasant. He reached in and extracted a thick bundle of money.

'Go ahead and count it if you like,' offered Tom.

'Oh, I intend to. I pride myself on never trusting a man because he has an honest face. Not that you have one, Tom. You don't even have a *pleasant* face.' Pinder turned away to examine the money in the full blaze of the headlights. He was silent for a long time as he counted the notes. Tom stood there fidgeting nervously.

Over in the cover of the stairs, Scally took the last mouthful of food and chewed it slowly. There was a long silence, during which he became aware, once again, of the low rumble of the car's engine. When Pinder spoke, his voice had acquired a sharper edge.

'Call me old-fashioned, Tom, but there seems to be rather less here than I was anticipating.' He turned back to smile at Tom. 'I'd say we're shy to the tune of twenty pounds.'

In the ensuing silence, Scally heard the Rag Man swallow. 'I can explain that,' he said quietly.

'Oh, I do hope so, Tom. Please proceed. I'm all ears. I hang on every syllable.'

'Somebody gave me a duff note. A forgery. The light wasn't good and by the time I realized it, the kid had gone.'

'I see. And where is this . . . duff note?'

'I threw it away.'

'You threw it away. Hmm.' Pinder replaced the other notes in the envelope and slid it into the pocket of his jacket.

'Well, I didn't see any point in keeping it. I mean, it was a poor fake, know what I mean? It would never . . .'

Tom stopped and Scally realized that he had done so because Pinder was looking at him in a funny way. Staring at him intently as a snake might study a potential victim.

'I'm awful sorry, Mr Pinder. Tell you the truth, I was dead nervous about tellin' you.'

'Nervous, Tom?' Pinder beamed, a big, magnaminous smile. 'Now why on earth should you be nervous?'

'Well . . .' began Tom but Pinder cut him off.

'Ah, I think I catch your drift. *You're* worried that I'll think that you pocketed that money.'

'Er, yeah and . . .'

'That you concocted some moronic story to fob me off in the pathetic hope that I'd just pat you on the back and tell you it wasn't your fault.'

Tom fidgeted uncomfortably.

'Well yeah,' he muttered. Scally couldn't see his face but he could picture the expression. 'I wouldn't want you to think . . .'

He stopped talking as Pinder slipped a hand into his pocket but when it emerged it was holding nothing more threatening than a pack of playing cards. Pinder began to shuffle them expertly as he continued.

'I'll tell you what I think, Tom. I think you're a double-dealing, back-stabbing little cockroach. I think you'd fellate a bull mastiff for the price of a drink and peddle your grandmother's pussy on the high street for the price of two. I think you're a slimy, filthy, money-grubbing turd freshly dropped from the arse end of society.'

'Yes, but listen . . .'

'No, you listen, Tom. I've got a little trick to show you. Watch closely.' He fanned out the cards, faces away from him and held them up for Tom's inspection. 'As you can see, they're a perfectly ordinary deck of cards. Take any one of them, but don't let me see it,' he commanded. Tom haltingly did as he

83

was told, holding the card to his chest. 'All right, slip it back into the deck there. Now, I give the cards a good shuffle. Are you watching closely?'

Tom nodded.

'Mr Pinder, if you'll just let me explain . . .'

'Hush. You'll spoil my concentration! Now . . . I take the cards again. I place the deck against my forehead, thus. And I'm forming a picture in my mind of the card you picked. I believe it was . . . the Jack of Diamonds. Am I correct?'

Tom nodded. 'That's very clever,' he observed. 'But how did you . . . ?'

'Very simple.' Pinder fanned the deck expertly with his left hand and held it up to Tom's face. 'As you can see, every card is now the Jack of Diamonds!'

Tom stared. 'That's amazing!' he said, with genuine enthusiasm.

'Wait. The trick isn't quite over. For behold . . .'

Scally watched intently. Now something was rising up from behind the fan of cards, a long bright sliver of metal that seemed to just float up into view . . .

'Jesus,' said Tom faintly. He began to laugh delightedly.

As the blade rose higher, Scally saw that the illusion was simplicity itself. The knife was actually held in Pinder's right hand.

'Jesus, indeed,' said Pinder. He made a brief passing motion across Tom's throat, then gave him a hard push with his shoulder. Tom's laughter ended abruptly. He reeled away a short distance and made a strange choking noise, lifting his hands to his throat. Something dark and wet sprayed in a viscous stream from between his fingers, splattering onto the cobbles. Tom staggered closer towards the light from the doorway and Scally saw his face quite clearly now, the look of surprise on it. His eyes were bulging white in their sockets and he appeared to have acquired a second mouth beneath the line of his beard, a deep scarlet mouth that was spraying a copious fountain of blood down the front of his coat.

'Of course, it's all done with mirrors,' said Pinder. He folded the long blade of the knife and slipped it into his pocket, along with the pack of cards.

Tom made a weird gurgling sound. He span clumsily around and lurched towards Pinder, his hands extended as claws in a desperate attempt to strangle his killer. Pinder moved gracefully for such a big man. He neatly sidestepped the lunge. Tom slammed against the dumpster with a grunt of surprise and Pinder grabbed him by the collar and the seat of his pants and heaved him upwards. Tom's head connected with the sharp edge of the open metal lid, emitting a dull crack that made Scally wince. Then the Rag Man's body folded and he tipped over the lip of the dumpster, falling onto his back on the garbage within.

Pinder reached into his pocket and pulled something out. He leaned over the edge of the dumpster.

'Big smile!' Scally heard him say. Then there was the flash of a camera, the buzz of a mechanism. Scally realized with a jolt of horror that Pinder had just taken a photograph.

Pinder slammed down the lid of the dumpster with a loud crash. He turned away, withdrawing the polaroid and pocketing the miniature camera.

'How tragic,' he observed to the empty alley. 'Society has consigned another lost soul to the trash can.' He laughed softly to himself and turned to walk back to his car. From inside the dumpster came a low, echoing moan, the sound of something stirring against the bin bags.

He's still alive in there, thought Scally; and the full horror of the situation suddenly hit him like an electric prod. His right hand, the one that still held the fork, twitched involuntarily. The fork fell from his fingers and clattered down the short flight of stone steps.

Pinder froze in his tracks. He turned slowly back to look in the direction from which the sound had issued.

'Hello?' he murmured. 'Could it be that we have a spy in our midst? A spanner in the works? A nigger in the woodpile?'

There was another groan from the dumpster and Pinder lifted a foot to aim a savage kick into the side of it. The crash reverberated around the alley.

'Shut it, Tom, I wasn't talking to *you*!' Pinder began to move towards the light above the doorway. Scally crouched in the shadow in a horrible indecision. If he moved forward, he would reveal himself. If he stayed here he'd be trapped. He flinched as he heard a sharp metallic click and a length of steel seemed to sprout magically from Pinder's hand.

'I'm not fond of eavesdroppers,' he announced to the pool of shadow at the top of the steps. He seemed to be looking straight at Scally. 'Me, I'm a great believer in the privacy of the individual. I tend to give nosy people very short shrift indeed.' There was now only a few yards between Pinder and the steps. Scally crouched there, sweating despite the cold, knowing that he couldn't just sit here and accept his fate. He had to do something, but what? What?

'Here pussy, pussy,' said Pinder, softly. 'I have something for you.'

Scally took the plunge. He jumped forward down the steps into the light, his hand groping for the dropped fork. Pinder grinned delightedly. He covered the short distance to the steps in a single stride.

'Well, well, what have we here?' he cooed. 'A mere stripling. A tender youth. A little chip off the old . . .'

And then he screamed and whirled away, the knife dropping from his hand. The handle of the fork still juddered from the force of Scally's blow, sticking out from the bridge of Pinder's nose like a misplaced aerial. Scally dashed by Pinder as he stood there, legs astride, frantically trying to pull the length of stainless steel out of his face. He kept screaming in a mixture of pain, shock and rage and the sound of his bellows seemed to fill Scally's head as he vaulted onto the bonnet of the American car, scrambled over the roof and slid down on the far side.

He hit the pavement running, trying not to hear the barrage of threats and curses that spilled from the mouth of the alley. He could only pray that he and Mr Pinder never ran into each other again.

Scally ran as fast as his legs would carry him and he didn't stop running till he reached the relative safety of the railway arch, which had never looked more inviting than it did tonight.

Chapter Nine

On the morning of Martin's funeral, the weather improved a little, as though making a half-hearted attempt to rise to the occasion. When Will pulled back the curtains in the third-floor guest room, he saw that a weak and watery sunshine was doing its level best to warm the rain-soaked earth.

Will had been sleeping in the spartan little room under the eaves for the past few nights or at least, he'd been *trying* to. But he'd too much on his mind to allow him any real chance of rest. The stuff in the papers had been particularly hard to deal with. Several tabloids had run stories of the 'Drug Death Teenager's Junky Father' variety. Will had known that this would all come out, sooner or later, but it had somehow been no less of a shock to him when Suzanne had shown him the morning papers. Since then, the press hadn't left them alone for a moment. There'd even been an invitation to appear on a television talkshow, an invitation that had been promptly declined.

Will could only attempt to get on with his life or at least those tatters that remained of it. He was still toying with the idea of going undercover on the street, but there was a part of him that kept backing away. He wasn't yet sure if he really had the guts to go for it.

He opened the wardrobe and found one of his old work suits, freshly pressed and dry cleaned, hanging on the rail. On the shelf above it there was a white shirt and a sober Marks and Spencer's silk tie, laid out where he couldn't miss them. This was Suzanne's work, of course, ensuring that he didn't show her up at the funeral, in front of the various aunts, uncles and cousins who were expected to be there. Will supposed that he should be indignant at such treatment, that he really ought to go downstairs defiantly dressed in sweatshirt and jeans; but there seemed little point in such an empty gesture.

Today was all about Martin, the last chance for Will to mourn his son officially. So he went meekly down to the bathroom to shave and shower and afterwards he dressed himself in the clothes that Suzanne had laid out for him. He had not worn a suit since leaving the force, two years ago and it felt strange to be wearing one again. It didn't feel as though he was going to his son's funeral, more as if he was setting out to interview a suspect.

As he came down the stairs, he heard Suzanne in the hall talking heatedly into the two-way microphone that connected to the front gates of the house.

' . . . and I'm telling you, sunshine, I have nothing to say to your newspaper, or any other paper for that matter. Today is a sad family occasion and I would very much appreciate it if you would respect that and keep away.' A pause, then the insect buzz of a compressed voice, babbling from the loudspeaker grille. Something about 'responsibility to the public'. Suzanne's reply was uncharacteristically caustic. 'Fuck public responsibility! If I see so much as one of you at St Cuthbert's today, I'll sue. Do I make myself clear?' She took her finger off the button and turned to face Will.

'Bastards won't give an inch,' she growled. 'They've been hanging around out there since first light.'

'Might not have been such a good idea to mention the church,' he chided her.

She gave him a superior look. 'I know what I'm doing,' she assured him. She prowled back into the kitchen and Will followed, watching her slip into a seat at the table where a half-finished cup of coffee waited. She was wearing a smart black dress and bolero jacket and on the table, there was a wide brimmed hat in black straw. In a strange way, mourning clothes brought out the best in her, accentuating her lean, leggy figure. The dress was cut to a length that hovered between modest and eye-catching. She looked, Will had to admit, quite stunning.

But it was more than just the look. Suzanne was now her

old self again. The few days that had elapsed since the hospital had given her the opportunity to get a firm grip on her emotions. As she always did in such situations, she had retreated into herself, burying her grief beneath layers of composure. The image she presented now was cool, detached, almost glacial.

'Help yourself to coffee,' she told Will. She was gazing thoughtfully out through the window at the dead garden. Will poured himself a cup and went to sit on the other side of the table. She eyed him critically, then gave a nod of approval. 'The suit still fits,' she told him, as though she had suspected otherwise. 'Can I fix you some toast or something?'

He shook his head.

'Not hungry,' he told her. 'Look, Suzanne, the shirt and tie, the dry cleaning and so forth, if you'll just make a note of what it all cost, I'll gladly . . .'

'It doesn't matter,' she assured him. 'It only amounts to a few pennies. What's that after everything that's happened?'

He frowned. He really didn't have an answer. He sipped his coffee and thought wistfully about adding a shot of something stronger to calm his nerves; but he had been on the wagon for several days now and though the cravings had never really stopped, he thought he had the measure of them.

'What are your plans after the funeral?' Suzanne asked him. 'You'll be going back to Southport, will you?'

'Not sure,' he told her. 'I'm still thinking about that. There may be a few things that need taking care of here, first.'

She studied him for a moment, clearly wondering what plans he was hatching. 'Well, if you need a little more time to get your act together. I mean, I don't want you to think that I'm trying to hurry you out or anything. Truth is, it's kind of quiet around here without Martin. Been nice to have some company.'

'I wondered about that. Look, I hope my being here hasn't cramped your style in any way.'

Suzanne's eyebrows arched slightly.

'Can't think what you mean.'

'Well, what I'm saying, I take it you would normally have . . . men friends around.'

'Friends, yes. And one or two of them are male. But nobody

special, you understand. No real commitment.'

Will suspected that she was being disingenuous, trying to give the impression that she was still the wronged wife living the life of a novitiate nun. But she was a good-looking, motivated and wealthy woman. Chances were that in the normal run of things, she'd be beating off prospective suitors with a baseball bat.

'I thought you and your partner from the agency . . . what's his name, Adam? I thought you had something going with him.'

'He's my business partner, Will. And I'm very fond of him. But a business partner isn't necessarily a bedroom partner.'

'No, of course not, but . . .'

The sound of the buzzer from the main gates saved Will from digging himself in any deeper.

'That should be the car,' announced Suzanne. 'If it's another reporter, I won't be held responsible for my actions.' She got up and went out into the hall. Will heard her talking briefly into the microphone and then there was the dull click as she pressed the button that opened the gates. She came back and picked up her hat.

'It's the car all right. We'd better not hang about. With the gates open we'll be invaded.'

They went outside and saw the car, a spacious black Daimler, hammering along the drive. It screeched to a halt and they climbed into the back of it. Several reporters and photographers were already running towards them across the lawn, waving microphones and television cameras.

'I'm really sorry,' said the uniformed driver, a plump ruddy-complexioned man. 'They came in when the gates opened, I couldn't stop them.'

'That's all right,' Suzanne assured him. 'Just get us out of here. Run the bastards over if you have to.'

The driver hit the accelerator and moved off, the rear wheels flinging up a spray of gravel. An instant later, the photographers were running alongside, crowding up around the windows and firing off their flashguns in a desperate attempt to get some kind of publishable picture. Will kept his gaze impassive, his eyes fixed straight ahead, not wanting to give them the satisfaction of capturing on film the anger he felt in his heart. The Daimler accelerated through the gates, scattering reporters to either side, and then it turned out onto the main road. Glancing back, Will saw that the reporters were all running for their own vehicles.

'They're going to follow us,' he said dismally.

'Let them,' said Suzanne. 'That's why I told the rest of the guests to meet us at the church. All we have to do is shake them off for a little while.'

'But you already let slip where we're going,' he reminded her. 'St Cuthbert's. That's way over in Failsworth, isn't it?'

'That's right. Only we're not going to St Cuthbert's. *We're* going to St Paul's in Alderly Edge.'

Will stared at her. He had always known his ex-wife was a control freak but he was astonished that she had not seen fit to share the details of this subterfuge with him. What had she been afraid of? That he would blab to somebody, give the game away?

'You might try trusting me a little more,' he said feistily.

But she was leaning forward, staring over the driver's shoulder, quite unaware of Will's anger.

'Now, if it all goes to plan . . .'

The Daimler swept around a tight bend in the road and took a sharp left, the driver sounding his horn as he did so. Will saw that an identical vehicle was waiting on the road they had just left. Two people sat in the rear of the car, a man and a woman, dressed in similar clothes to Will and Suzanne. The driver of the decoy car gave a brief wave and accelerated away from the kerb.

'Jesus!' exclaimed Will. 'You don't miss a trick, do you?'

Suzanne allowed herself a brief smile. 'With any luck,' she said, 'by the time that pack of vampires has trailed the other car to Failsworth and discovered they've been had, our service will be over and done with.'

Will shook his head in grudging admiration. Suzanne was pretty good, you had to hand it to her. Will would never have had the guile or the energy to dream up something like this.

'And the reception,' he prompted her. 'That's not really back at your house, is it?'

Suzanne shook her head.

'I've booked us into a quiet hotel in Cheshire. Only the drivers know where they're taking the guests and they've been paid handsomely to make sure it remains a secret.'

'Christ, Suzanne, this must have cost you an arm and a leg.'

She shrugged.

'I wasn't going to have those scum messing up Martin's funeral. Let's face it, it's the last thing I can do for him.'

Will reached out and took her hand, squeezed it gently. For the first time in years he felt a surge of genuine compassion for her and, for once, she didn't pull away from his touch. They drove on in contemplative silence to the funeral.

The service went as well as could be expected. Suzanne's ruse had worked and there were no reporters to make the day even more distressing than it already was. Will stood at the entrance of the small rural church beside Suzanne, greeting the carloads of sober-suited relatives as they arrived, people he hadn't seen or thought about in years. They were all polite enough but the looks they gave Will told him that they had seen the lies in the newspapers and had formed their own conclusions about him.

Martin's friends Tim and Karen arrived, both of them displaying the cuts and bruises of his violent assault on them. Will shook hands with them and thanked them for coming. They seemed distraught, displaying more real grief than any of the older guests. Will hoped that he'd get a chance to talk to them at the reception. There were still so many things he wanted to know about his son. The young couple moved on into the church.

Will was reminded of himself and Suzanne, nearly twenty years earlier, just married, standing on the steps of a church very like this one, and shaking hands with the same crowd of people as they emerged from the wedding ceremony; but then, of course, the mood had been optimistic, even joyful. He'd been so young then, so naive, newly embarked on a career in the police force and already convinced that this was an occupation that would see him through to his retirement.

Clive arrived, looking distinctly sheepish.

'And I thought we'd managed to give the papparazzi the slip,' joked Will, dutifully.

'Look,' murmured Clive. 'About that piece in the Post. I hope you don't think that I had anything to do with it.'

'Forget it. Thanks for coming.'

The two men stared at each other for a moment, aware of so much between them that remained unsaid. Then they hugged in a self-conscious British way, patting each other's backs. Clive broke away first and moved into the shadow of the church. Will took out a handkerchief and dabbed surreptitiously at his eyes.

'Thanks for inviting him,' he whispered to Suzanne.

'Well, I figured you needed at least one of the mourners on your side,' she told him.

When everyone was assembled, Will and Suzanne took their places in the front pew, where the coffin rested in front of the altar. Will sat there and listened to an elderly priest talk about his son. As far as he was aware, the old man had never met Martin, but he seemed to know quite a bit about him. Once again, Will put this down to Suzanne, who had doubtless acted in the role of script editor. It occurred to Will that he had done next to nothing with regard to the funeral and he felt vaguely ashamed.

The service was brief and moving. Several times Will felt that he was going to lose it, but glancing at his ex-wife, he saw a face so composed, so absolutely certain of itself, that some stubborn vestige of old-fashioned male pride prevented him from allowing such a weakness.

When it was over, he and Suzanne led the procession behind the coffin into the graveyard, where Martin Ambrose, aged seventeen years, was duly laid to rest. While the priest was intoning the burial service, Will heard the sound of a car engine intruding on the quiet of the graveyard. His first thought was that a reporter had managed to avoid Suzanne's carefully planned misdirection, but when he glanced up, he saw a midnight-blue Toyota gliding into a parking spot beside the church gates and he knew instantly that it was an unmarked police vehicle.

Sure enough, after a few moments, two men got out of the

car and leaned against the side of it, smiling in at the group of mourners as though they found the scene vaguely amusing. The taller of the two men lit up a cigarette and blew out contented clouds of smoke.

Will recognized him instantly. Don Bullen, a Detective Sergeant when Will had last had dealings with him. Bullen was a skinny, slippery streak of pelican shit with an eye to furthering his own career by performing as many unusual handshakes as was humanly possible. Needless to say, he'd been DCI Chalmers' right-hand-man when it came to fitting Will up, a task he'd accomplished with ease and considerable relish. Will suspected that Bullen had gained a promotion since then because his aggressive stance beside the car suggested that he was the superior officer of the two men.

His companion, a short, stocky individual with black curly hair and a thick stubble on his chin, was a stranger to Will, but he looked every bit as unpleasant as his partner, his pug-like features set in what appeared to be a permanent sneer.

Will felt a nudge in his ribs and realized that Suzanne had just surreptitiously elbowed him. Three other male relatives were waiting patiently for Will to help lower the coffin into the open grave which, cruelly, contained several inches of muddy yellow water. He stepped obediently forward and took hold of a length of canvas strapping. Flexing his muscles, he helped to lift the coffin clear of the grave. A couple of attendants stepped in to remove the wooden spars that bridged the gap. Then Will allowed the course fabric to slide slowly through his fingers and Martin descended to his last resting place.

There seemed such a terrible finality to this act, as though up till this point, there had still been some tiny possibility that it had all been a horrible mistake. But looking at the shiny lid of the coffin down there in the cold earth, Will knew that any last crazy hopes had gone. He felt like he was choking. He stooped, picked up a handful of moist earth and threw it down into the grave. The soil made a dull thud as it hit the roof of the coffin.

Stepping back to his original position, Will glanced quickly towards the church gates and saw that the two policemen were still waiting for him. An anger rose up in him, a dry heat that flared in his chest. Suzanne must have sensed his rage because she put out a hand and squeezed his arm in an attempt to calm him.

When it was all over, people began to drift back to the cars. Will and Suzanne lingered a while, gazing down into the grave.

'Who are they?' whispered Suzanne.

'Cops.'

'What do they want?'

'Your guess is as good as mine. They sure picked their time, didn't they? I ought to . . .'

'Don't make a scene, Will, not here. We'll just see what they want and we'll keep everything cool and calm, all right?'

He nodded. Suzanne slipped an arm through his and they walked down the path towards the church gates. Happily, most of the other cars were already moving away, the drivers taking the mourners on to the reception. As Will and Suzanne neared the gates, Bullen and his companion stepped away from the car and approached. Bullen was smiling insolently and Will felt a powerful urge to punch him in the teeth, but he held the desire in check.

'Hello, Will,' said Bullen, with forced cheerfulness. 'You got a nice day for it, anyway.'

'I don't recall seeing your name on the invitations,' said Will coldly. 'What do you want?'

Bullen looked hurt. 'Just paying my respects, old son. No need to get your knickers in a twist.' He nodded at the other man who was studying Will with a disdainful expression on his face. 'This is my partner, DS Lang. I'm an Inspector now, you know.'

'Bully for you. How did you find us, anyway?'

'Police Surveillance Helicopter,' said Bullen gleefully. 'Got thermal imaging on that baby, so they weren't fooled by the stunt you pulled with the second car. Worked on the journo's though, I got to hand it to you on that score.'

'Yes, well that's all fascinating, but as you can see I'm a little bit preoccupied at the moment, so if you'll excuse me . . .'

Will made to walk on but Bullen placed a hand on his chest, using a little more force than seemed strictly necessary.

'No, hold up, mate, I'm not exactly here on a social call. My Guv'nor has requested the pleasure of a quick word with you.'

'Chalmers?' Will made no attempt to hide his contempt. 'What does that arsehole want?'

'Now, now, no need to be unpleasant. Like I said, just a friendly word in your ear. He asked me to bring you down to the nick for a chinwag, just the two of you, all cosy like.'

Suzanne stared at him. 'What, *now*?' she cried. 'Don't you realize we've just buried our son? We're due to go on to a reception . . .'

'Calm down, lady,' said Lang. 'We'll make sure that hubby comes to no harm and we'll have him back to you before you've got stuck into your second glass of sherry, won't we, Don?'

Bullen sneered. 'Absolutely. Wouldn't want to spoil the knees up.'

Will flashed Bullen a warning look. 'This may come as a surprise, but an occasion like this doesn't lend itself to a dance party atmosphere.'

'No, 'course not. Tragic business. Tragic.' But Bullen's grin never faltered as he spoke and Will felt his temper rising again. He took a threatening step forward.

'Wipe that grin off your face,' he whispered, 'or they'll be sweeping your teeth off this path with a yard brush.'

Bullen scowled. 'Hey, there's no call for that kind of talk,' he protested. 'I'm just doing my job. Now, it's up to you, you can come quietly or you can be assisted, we don't mind either way, do we, Sid?'

Lang looked positively delighted at the prospect of a fight. He squared up to Will, his fists clenched.

'I hope he doesn't come *too* quietly,' he said. 'It's no fun when they do that.'

'Maybe you should go along with them,' said Suzanne nervously. She was uncomfortably aware that a few late leavers were taking notice of this little scenario. She glanced at Bullen. 'If you promise to have him back to the reception before too long.'

Bullen stood there appraising Suzanne for a moment, as though he'd only just noticed her. His mocking eyes roved across the curves of her body with unconcealed interest.

'For you darling, I'll have him gift-wrapped and delivered by Concorde. That be quick enough?'

Suzanne regarded him with a flat stare of disinterest. She reached into her bag and withdrew a card, which she handed to Will. 'This is where the reception is,' she told him. 'I'll stall things as long as I can. I'll tell anyone who asks that some of your former associates wanted to express their condolences in person. Try not to be too long, OK?'

Will nodded glumly. Bullen moved to the Toyota and held open the back door. 'Your carriage awaits, sir,' he announced, with a theatrical bow. Will moved across to the car and slid into the back seat. Bullen got in beside him. 'Good looking woman, your missus,' he observed. 'How does an ugly fucker like you pull a tasty slice like that?'

Will ignored him, realizing that Bullen would goad him like this all through the car journey into town, looking for an excuse to hit him.

Lang climbed in behind the wheel. He started up the engine and drove away from the curb, passing by Suzanne's Daimler. She was standing beside it, staring after the Toyota, a worried expression on her face. Beyond her, over the low wall of the church, Will caught a glimpse of the ranks of moss-encrusted tombstones stretching away up the incline of a gentle hill. Amongst them, Martin's open grave resembled a solitary cavity amidst rows of rotting teeth. A miniature bulldozer was already pushing the mound of muddy soil back into the hole.

Then the car accelerated and the church dwindled rapidly into the distance as they drove back into the city.

Chapter Ten

Pinder studied his reflection critically in the hall mirror, paying particular attention to his nose. Imposing at the best of times, it was now even more so because it had swollen to twice its previous size. The flesh had darkened to an evil-looking purple hue and at the centre of the bruising, a row of four angry red holes indicated where the tines of the fork had stabbed deep into cartilage.

Pinder reached up the fingers of one hand to prod experimentally at the wound but the pain this caused made him snatch them away again with an oath. He decided that there was a possible risk of infection and resolved to set up an appointment with his GP at his earliest opportunity. He'd almost certainly need an antibiotic.

That bloody kid! God help him if he ever fell into Pinder's clutches again . . .

He sighed. Control, that was the key. He removed his suit jacket from its hanger, put it on and took the pack of cards from his pocket. He studied his reflection again, this time concentrating on the hands as he went through his regular sequences, shuffling the pack one-handed, forcing a card to the top of the deck, sending it back to the middle again. He practised like this every day, sometimes for hours at a stretch. It was a discipline he'd followed ever since he'd done an eighteen month stretch for fraud in Strangeways when he was in his early twenties.

He'd been lucky enough to share a cell with an elderly lag called Arthur Pimlott, a former pro magician and a member of The Magic Circle. Under the stage name of The Great Arturo, he'd had a decent career in the seventies and eighties but had fallen on hard times and had found that it was actually easier to print large sums of money than it was to earn it. Arthur had showed him a few simple card tricks and Pinder had immediately been hooked. At Strangeways, boredom was the real enemy and he'd thrown himself into the task of acquiring new skills, offering Arthur sweets, cigarettes and sometimes even sexual favours in exchange for the secrets of the conjurer's art. Later, he'd become a trustee of the prison library and had ordered everything that he could find pertaining to the subject of magic. He studied avidly, reading each book several times over before he was satisfied that he'd gleaned all the information from it. Most of all, he had practised, practised, practised.

Despite his size, he was nimblefingered and had a natural aptitude for the sleight-of-hand moves that were an integral part of the more difficult tricks. After only a few months, he had learned everything that Arthur had to teach him and was mastering illusions that the old man, with his failing eyesight and shaky hands, would have no longer even attempted. When poor old Arthur died suddenly one cold January night, it was only natural that Pinder should inherit the battered leather case of props and implements that Arthur kept under his bunk. The old man had no surviving relatives and the arrangement was never questioned. Neither was the cause of Arthur's death but then Pinder had taken great care to ensure that it looked like a heart attack.

Towards the end of his sojourn at Strangeways, the Warden had requested the pleasure of Pinder's involvement in a prison talent show. He had been reluctant to do it, at first, but when the Warden intimated that Pinder's participation might incline the parole board to look more favourably upon an early release, he had grudgingly agreed to appear.

His debut performance was a disaster. Stepping out from behind a set of curtains onto the ramshackle stage to perform in front of several hundred listless inmates, Auberon Gerald Pinder, aged twenty-four, had experienced something unique in his young life. Sheer unadulterated terror. Caught in the merciless glare of a spotlight, he'd sweated and stuttered and fumbled his way through his familiar routine like Tommy Cooper, on a bad night. He'd actually dropped cards, for God's sake! The audience, already restless when he'd stepped out there, had been unforgiving, shouting out obscene abuse, laughing at him, even throwing empty drink cans and food wrappers at him. After what seemed a lifetime, he'd shuffled red faced into the wings with the sound of their derisive laughter ringing in his ears. The experience had convinced him of only one thing; that whatever his ambitions were, being the next Paul Daniels wasn't one of them.

These days he was disciplined enough to perform his magic in front of the most cynical crowd and occasionally, he did schedule appearances for invited audiences, close friends or other members of The Magic Circle. But he really had no interest in using his skills as a professional entertainer. The work he performed now required a whole different set of talents but there were similarities between the two disciplines, especially when it came down to what Pinder liked to think of as the ultimate magic trick – taking a man's life and making it disappear. Just like that.

He set aside the cards for a moment and practised instead with a gold sovereign, making it 'walk' across the back of his knuckles, 'vanish' in the palm of one hand and reappear in the other. His face was expressionless but inside, he was boiling, thinking about the boy, thinking about what he would do to him when he finally caught up with him. How he'd make him scream for mercy as he dealt out the pain slowly, one sweet spoonful at a time. He had always had a special way with kids . . .

The mobile phone in his pocket trilled loudly, breaking his concentration. He scowled, vanished the sovereign one last time, then took out the phone and pressed the receiver.

'Yes,' he said tonelessly. He couldn't get his mind off the boy. Down in the cellars of his semi-detached Victorian house, Pinder had a sizable room which he'd converted into a rehearsal space and storage area for his larger props. It had been professionally soundproofed, enough to ensure that screams, no matter how piercing, would never be heard above ground. He also kept his leather butcher's apron down there and a comprehensive selection of knives, saws and cleavers. Somebody was going to pay for the pain in his nose soon, and if not that one particular boy, then somebody very like him . . .

'I need to talk to you,' rasped a voice in his ear. 'In person.'

Pinder's employer, Gary Flowers, did not sound happy.

'Very good.' Pinder knew better than to mention Flowers' name on a cellular phone. 'Where?'

'In the garden. Say about half an hour.' The line went dead. Never one to waste words, Mr Flowers.

Pinder slipped the phone back in his pocket and headed for the door without further ado. He had attained his current position largely by virtue of his strict sense of discipline and he took his work every bit as seriously as he took his magic. He never allowed one thing to get in the way of the other.

The 'garden' Flowers had referred to was of course, one of his clubs, The Garden of Terrestrial Delights.

Pinder let himself out of the house, closed and locked the door behind him. His Pontiac, freshly cleaned and polished, stood on the tarmac outside his door. Pinder regarded it fondly for a moment. He knew that it was flashy and rather vulgar, but his taste in cars had always tended towards the flamboyant. Besides, he absolutely refused to drive anything Japanese, German or Korean and unfortunately all the famous 'British' makes were now owned by one or other of these countries.

He slid in behind the wheel, switched on the stereo and reversed out onto the street, accompanied by the glorious sounds of Wolfgang Amadeus Mozart's 6th Symphony. He drove briskly into town and on the way, indulged himself in a pleasant fantasy where he sawed a certain fork-wielding child in two, entirely without the aid of any magic tricks whatsoever.

Thirty minutes later, he pulled the Pontiac into the small parking lot behind the club. He got out of the car, approached the small rear door of 'The Garden' and rapped politely, turning his face to look directly into the lens of the ViewScan mounted on the wall above.

There was a brief wait, then a buzz, which prompted him to push the door open. He stepped into the gloomy corridor beyond and nodded to the skulking figure of Siggy, the doorman, a big heavy-set black man with a face like a Rottweiler and a disposition to match. Despite the gloom,

Siggy was sporting his wraparound shades.

'Hey, Hoodoo-Man, wha' 'appen?' he growled, in a near subsonic rumble. He had nicknamed Pinder 'Hoodoo-Man' the first time he had witnessed one of his card tricks. 'Mr Flowers is waitin' on you inside.'

Pinder nodded and, turning away, he pushed through the swing doors into the main part of the club. Vintage disco music assailed his ears, a shuffling wobbling rhythm overlaid by what sounded like three eunuchs wailing on about the trouble they had staying alive. Flowers was seated at a table a short distance away, wreathed in clouds of cigarette smoke. His back was turned to Pinder and he was studying a bunch of dancers who were moving backwards and forwards across the illuminated floor ahead of him.

Pinder shuffled forward and sat down beside his boss. Flowers glanced at him briefly, then returned his attention to the dancers. Pinder raised his own gaze and had a proper look at them.

It was hard not to register a wince of disgust. The dancers were all male, each of them stripped down to a pair of posing briefs, their bodies glistening beneath copious layers of baby oil. More unusually, every one of them had some kind of profound physical deformity. Pinder's astonished gaze registered a man whose hands protruded like appendages from his shoulders; another, whose face was covered with what looked like huge polyps; a third who had scaly flaps of multi-coloured skin hanging down from his shoulders like a flesh cape. There were other abnormalities, each more shocking than the last. Pinder frowned, glanced sideways at Flowers, who was studying the troupe intently as though watching a production of Swan Lake.

'What do you think?' he asked Pinder thoughtfully. 'They call themselves "Freak Show".'

Pinder studied Flowers for a moment before making a reply. The man had aged well, he decided. He must be pushing fifty now, but he still favoured the fashionable frock coats and regency shirts that were currently the vogue amongst the fashion-conscious. His long brown hair was worn loose over his shoulders. It was only when you were up really close that you noticed the worry lines around his eyes and mouth.

'It's enough to put you off your dinner,' said Pinder, disdainfully. 'You're surely not thinking of booking them here?'

'Christ, no. I thought maybe one of my less salubrious venues. The Carousel, maybe. They'd appeal to stag night audiences, that kind of thing. This lot have gone down a storm in The Smoke.'

'Which only confirms what I've long said about people in the capital. They're a bunch of decadent perverts.'

Flowers laughed at this, revealing a wide gap between his front teeth, which Pinder always thought made him look vaguely clownish.

'You're a fine one to talk!' he observed. For the first time, he turned his head to have a proper look at Pinder and his grin vanished.

'Christ,' he said. 'What happened to your nose?'

'Ah . . . a slight accident. I cut it shaving.'

'You were shaving your *nose*?'

'Of course not. I was just shaving and my hand slipped.'

'Yeah? What were you using, a cutlass?'

Pinder didn't answer that one. He took out his cards and began to shuffle them. Out on the dance floor, two of the handicapped performers were now bumping and grinding their slick bodies against each other in a ghastly parody of sexual arousal, while the rest of the troop circled them, wiggling their hips in encouragement.

'It's probably very important this,' said Flowers thoughtfully. 'You know, equal rights for the disabled and all that. OK, so maybe they ain't exactly oil paintings, but they have as much right to display their bodies as anybody else.'

Pinder smiled drily. 'And you don't think that the word "exploitation" enters into the equation, somewhere along the way?'

Flowers chuckled. 'Of *course* it does! Where would you and me be without exploitation? It's our bread and butter.' He looked suddenly alarmed as he noticed that a particularly odd-looking dancer had moved to the front of the stage and was starting to undo the strings on his posing pouch. 'Oh shit, here comes the gimmick,' he said.

'The gimmick?'

'Yeah, apparently one of them is a wotsit . . . hermaphrodite? Got AC *and* DC attachments, if you catch my drift. Dunno about you, but I'd be more than happy to take their word for it.'

'Amen,' muttered Pinder.

Flowers waved a hand towards the DJ's booth and the music stopped abruptly. Freak Show lumbered to an undignified halt. Flowers got to his feet, clapping his hands, and approached the dance floor.

'Very nice, gentlemen,' he enthused. 'Very . . . unusual.'

'But you missed the best bit,' complained the hermaphrodite. 'It's the most electrifying part of the act.'

'I'm sure it us! Unfortunately, business matters have intervened, but I'm sure we can find a spot for you in one of my clubs.'

'*Here*?' asked the armless dancer eagerly.

'Er, no, I don't think our audiences would er, fully appreciate what you boys have to offer. But you'd be perfect for one of my other clubs. Tell you what, why don't you go and change and I'll see you in my office in about fifteen minutes. We'll discuss the details then.'

Freak Show trooped off the stage, looking well pleased with themselves. Pinder reflected that they wouldn't be quite so perky when they arrived at The Carousel, a piss-smelling hellhole in darkest Ardwick, where the windows were permanently boarded up because they got smashed so often and where the regular punters ranged from the violent to the psychotic. Countless numbers of second-string musicians and comedians had met their nemesis on its blood and beer-stained stage but, Pinder reflected, with a name like Freak Show, this particular act ought to feel right at home there.

Flowers waited till the last of the dancers had clumped out of the door. Then he turned back to Pinder, his good-natured grin replaced by a stone-faced glare.

'Now,' he said. 'About this latest cock-up. I thought I made it plain enough that I don't want mules doing business outside any of my clubs. Especially this one.'

Pinder shrugged his big shoulders. 'It's like this, Mr F. You pay peanuts, you get monkeys. Everybody gets the same pep-talk when they're recruited but this one particular fellow seemed to have his own agenda. He won't be kicking against the traces again. I've dealt with the problem.'

Pinder placed the Ace of Spades face down on top of the pack, and rapped it gently with his knuckles. He turned the card back over and now it was the Two of Diamonds.

'Good.' Flowers came back to the table and filled a couple of glasses from a bottle of Chivas Regal on the tabletop. 'I'm sure I don't have to tell you how important it is to keep a tight lid on this. There mustn't be anything to link us with that kid.'

'I wouldn't worry.' Pinder set down the cards and took an experimental sip at his whisky. He was annoyed to discover that his nose injury had somehow affected his taste buds. The whisky didn't seem to have any flavour whatsoever. 'It was a hiccough, that's all.'

But Flowers didn't seem reassured. He didn't sit down, but continued to pace around, sipping at his whisky every so often.

'It's been all over the papers like a cheap suit. The kid's mother works for Delta, a big property developer in town. She's an influential woman. And the father is an ex-copper. We don't want him asking sticky questions, do we?'

Pinder went back to his cards, shuffling them expertly in the classic two-way method.

'You want me to take care of him?'

'Christ, no. How would that look?'

'It could look any way you want it to. A stroke, a heart attack, a car accident . . .'

'No. I don't think so, Auberon. Not this time.'

'Suit yourself. Actually, after the hatchet-job the papers did on him, I seriously doubt that anyone is going to take him seriously.'

'Let's hope not,' said Flowers, glumly. 'I've had about as much bad luck as I can use lately.'

Pinder studied Flowers, not without a certain amount of sympathy, knowing better than anyone how deeply in the shit he was. On paper, he appeared to be in clover. After all, he owned around half a dozen clubs in Greater Manchester, two of which were currently regarded as the hot places to be; but the reality was not quite so cosy. Currently on his third marriage to a former porn star, a woman half his age, Flowers was paying out a small fortune in alimony to his previous wives and their respective offspring. He was also handing out large sums in protection money to the various gangs that preyed on premises like his and, to add insult to injury, most of his staff spent all their spare time ripping him off at every opportunity.

He'd also invested heavily in Metro 2000, sponsoring events and offering large sums in prize money for many of the entertainment-based competitions. Oh yes, and one other thing. He had a coke habit of positively gargantuan proportions.

In short, he had been rapidly headed down the creek known as Shit when the manufacturers of Warp had moved in to recruit him as middle man for their operation. He'd had little option but to grab the offer with both hands and cling on tight. It was, after all, the only way to generate the kind of income Flowers needed to keep himself afloat.

Pinder didn't know who jerked Flowers' chain in this hierarchy; indeed, he didn't want to know. In this business, a little knowledge could be a very dangerous thing. His responsibility extended to the mules. Recruit them, police them, discipline them and when necessary, eradicate them. For this he was paid a handsome wage and of course, he carried out his work with the same diligence he applied to every other aspect of his life. He had no aspirations to rise any higher in the chain of command. If things went wrong, as they generally did, all he risked losing was his job. Flowers on the other hand, stood to lose everything.

Flowers downed the remains of his whisky and came back to the table. He sat in silence for a moment and watched as Pinder manipulated the deck, flicking through it to show that now every card was a heart. He turned it over, tapped twice with his knuckles and flicked again. This time they were all spades.

'That's pretty good,' observed Flowers. He topped up his glass with more whisky. 'Maybe I could find a spot for you at one of my clubs.'

Pinder smiled drily. 'Like the Carousel, for instance?'

'No, seriously. I've a half-share in a cabaret club in Piccadilly. Stand up comics, stuff like that. A good magic act might just do the business there.

Pinder shook his head. 'I don't do public performances,' he said. 'Only special shows for friends and so forth.'

'Don't see the point,' muttered Flowers. 'All that time and effort you put in. For what?'

'For me,' explained Pinder. 'You see, I *enjoy* what I'm doing, Mr F.' He looked his employer straight in the eyes. 'There's not many people that can claim that.'

Flowers averted his gaze and stared sullenly into his whisky glass, as if seeking the answer to a riddle in its amber depths.

'Listen, Auberon, we're going to need more people on the street. They're talking about stepping up production.'

'I see.' Pinder tapped the deck and changed the cards to diamonds. 'Yes, well there's plenty of detritus out there to work with. But it all takes time. I mean, I can hardly place an ad in the *Evening Post*, can I?'

'Course not.' Flowers smiled thinly. 'But do your best, eh? They're nervous about having too much stock piling up in the warehouse.'

'Consider it done. I'll start a little recruitment drive.'

'Good man. Oh, and Auberon?'

'Yes, Mr F?' Pinder tapped the cards a fourth time. Flowers had naturally expected clubs, but in fact, every card appeared to have turned into a blank. This threw him for a moment, he had to struggle to find words.

'Don't . . . don't take this as a criticism, but perhaps if you were less inclined to keep bumping them off . . .'

Pinder shook his head. 'I can assure you, that any disciplining I carry out is absolutely necessary. The chap who set up shop on your doorstep, for instance . . .'

'Well, yes, of course, he was in the wrong. But maybe a good telling off would have been just as effective.'

Pinder frowned. He detached a card from the top of the pack and turned it face-forward to show Flowers that it was a joker.

'You don't know the full story. He was trying to rip you off.'

'Why not?' murmured Flowers. 'Everybody else is.'

'I couldn't let it go. It was a matter of honour.'

Flowers sighed deeply. 'How much was he into me for?'

'Twenty pounds. Of course, I'll reimburse you for the loss.' Pinder blew on the card in his hand and it seemed to vanish into thin air.

'T-twenty pounds?' Flowers' jaw dropped. 'You . . . you're telling me, you killed a man. For twenty pounds?'

'A Rag Man,' Pinder reminded him. 'Hardly a man at all really. And besides, it's not the amount that matters, Mr Flowers. It's the principle.' He leaned forward and placed a hand briefly on his employer's shoulder. 'In business, you have to have principles. You can see that, surely?'

Flowers seemed to sag visibly in his chair. 'Auberon, I . . .' He shook his head, seemingly at a loss for words. 'Just . . . get onto the recruitment thing,' he concluded. 'And try to keep a sense of proportion, will you? I'll speak to you later.'

The meeting appeared to be at an end. Pinder gave the cards a last shuffle and slipped them back into his pocket. He lifted his prodigious bulk out of the chair and started for the swing doors.

'Left-hand waistcoat pocket,' he said over his shoulder and pushed through the exit into the corridor beyond.

Flowers stared after him, puzzled by the parting remark. He lifted a hand and felt in the pocket of his gold-brocaded waistcoat. His fingers emerged holding a plain brown envelope. He opened it, peered inside. The envelope contained a twenty pound note and a single playing card, the face turned away. Bemused, Flowers withdrew the card and dropped it face-up on to the table.

The joker lay there, smiling enigmatically back at him.

Chapter Eleven

The old place hasn't changed much, thought Will, as he followed Bullen along a grotty airless corridor, the walls painted a fetching shade of grey. The headquarters of 'C' Division still resembled a cross between a dole office and a morgue. People bustled back and forth, trying to give the impression that they were gainfully employed, but Will knew from years of experience that many of them would be busy working on their own scams. He'd rarely met a copper who didn't have some kind of lucrative sideline.

He recognized only a few of the faces that passed him by. This was a different crew to the one he'd worked with, predominantly hard-faced, sober-suited types, doubtless handpicked by Chalmers for their complete lack of compassion and their willingness to ride a pig around a room whilst wearing an apron and a pair of antlers.

Bullen glanced mockingly over his shoulder at Will. 'Must be like old times, eh?' he said.

'Old times,' murmured Will and had to restrain himself from going for Bullen's throat. He experienced a vivid flashback to a cold rainy morning, two years ago, when he'd been woken by the sound of the doorbell. He'd pulled on a bathrobe and stumbled blearily downstairs to find that same grinning face regarding him from the doorstep.

'Morning Will,' Bullen had said. 'Mind if me and the boys come in for a minute?' Will should have known that something like this was coming. He'd been rubbing Chalmers up the wrong way for a couple of months now, resisting every effort to recruit him into 'The Brotherhood', insisting on handling investigations his own way, kicking up a right royal stink when

109

his usual working partner, DS Jane Tennant was suddenly transferred to another division, with no hint of an explanation.

The crunch had come when Chalmers tried to press Will into accepting Don Bullen as Jane's replacement. Will had refused point blank. He didn't like Bullen or his working methods. More importantly, Will was aware that if he did agree to work with the man, everything he said or did would be reported back to Chalmers on a regular basis. Bullen was either already in the ranks of The Brotherhood or was desperately trying to gain admittance. At any rate, he was in Chalmers' pocket and couldn't be trusted. So Will had marched into the DCI's office and told him that he would prefer to work alone in future.

'But I don't understand, Will. What on earth have you got against Don Bullen?'

'I can't make out a word he says.'

'Whyever not?'

'Because it's hard for him to speak clearly when he's got his tongue stuck up your arse . . . *sir*.'

It had felt so good saying it, but only moments after leaving Chalmers' office, Will had begun to have qualms about the wisdom of it. And now, evidently, it was payback time.

Bullen had not come alone. He had been backed up by his current partner, a stone-faced Detective Constable called Wingrove, plus a squad of uniformed men. Will had stood there in the doorway, staring at them in dull surprise.

'What the fuck is this?' he'd demanded. 'April Fool's Day?'

'Got orders to search your gaff,' Bullen had said, with evident relish. He always styled his dialogue on naff television cop shows from the seventies, peppering his speech with words like 'Guv'nor', 'Manor' and 'Slag', all delivered in a phoney-sounding Cockney accent, a strange aberration in a man who originated from North Yorkshire.

'Are you trying to be funny?' Will had asked, knowing in his heart that this wasn't funny, not for one minute.

'No mate. And before you ask, yes, I've got a warrant.' Bullen had waved a slip of paper under Will's nose, then pushed past him into the hall.

'Hey, hang on a minute!' Will had gone after him, trying to

rationalize what was happening. 'Search the house for *what*?'

Bullen had turned back grinning and beckoned to the other men to enter. They had shouldered their way past Will as though he was some cheap little thug, whose house got turned over every other day.

'We've received information that you may be concealing illegal drugs on the premises.'

'What? Have you gone mad? Information from who?'

'A reliable source.' There had been a loud crash from the dining room as a uniformed constable upended one of the drawers of a cabinet, spilling cutlery all over the floor.

'Oi, go easy in there!' Will had snapped, taking a step forward. Bullen had placed a restraining arm on his shoulder.

'I do hope you're going to be co-operative,' he'd purred motioning to the constable to continue. 'Let's be nice and thorough, shall we,' he'd said. He had been enjoying it. Will had felt the urge to throw a punch into his face but made an effort to restrain himself. Starting a fight wouldn't have been the brightest idea under the circumstances.

'I've got nothing to hide,' he had said. 'Search away. But I want everything put back as you found it.'

'You're not really in a position to make demands,' Bullen had observed. 'Our information says you've been doing a bit more than just abusing the stuff. You've also been dealing it.'

'That's bollocks and you know it.' Will had tried to be dismissive but he was getting a sick feeling in his gut over this. He'd told himself that they wouldn't be so low as to fit him up; but then he'd thought about Chalmers' face when he'd made the remark the other day, how the little man's eyes had bulged with anger . . .'

'You look a bit peaky,' observed Bullen. 'You feeling all right? Anything you want to tell us?' Will had shaken Bullen's hand off his shoulder and turned away in disgust. Suzanne had appeared at the top of the stairs in her nightgown. Martin, thank God, had somehow managed to sleep through all the commotion. Suzanne had registered the uniforms down in the hallway and a look of apprehension etched itself into her pretty face.

'Will, what's wrong? What's happening down there?'

'Nothing, Darling. It's just a . . . it's some kind of mistake. Go back to bed, they'll be out of here in a few minutes.'

'Don't go on my account,' Bullen had said, leering up the staircase. 'I'm enjoying the view.'

Will glared at him. 'Listen, you,' he'd said. 'I've had about enough. If you don't . . .'

'Sarge.' Wingrove had appeared in the open doorway of the lounge, a triumphant smile on his normally expressionless face. 'I think you'd better come and look at what I've just found in here . . .'

And of course, there it had been, lying amidst the debris of the hifi unit, a big, incriminating kilo bag of cocaine, right where Wingrove had planted it. Useless for Will to scream and rave that he'd been fitted up. Everybody in the house had known that, but it wasn't going to change a thing. Not one jot.

Later, down at the nick, Chalmers had laid it all out for him, explaining how it worked in the soft, smug voice that Will had already learned to hate.

'Bit of an embarrassment for the force, Will, as I'm sure you'll appreciate. Going to cause an absolute stink if it all comes out.'

Will had glowered across the desk at him. 'What do you mean, "if"? Surely it's just a case of "when".'

'Not necessarily. In a normal situation, I'd be duty bound to report this all the way to the top . . . but there are occasions when the rules can be broken.'

'You ought to know that,' Will had sneered.

Chalmers' plump features had rearranged themselves into an expression of distaste. 'That kind of remark isn't going to help anybody. Now, you aren't the first copper to acquire a habit for the white stuff and I dare say you won't be the last . . .'

'Drop the pretence! You know as well as I do that stuff was planted. Just give me the deal and let me get out of here, where the air smells better.'

It had been simple enough. Chalmers had been prepared to 'lose' the report about the bust on two conditions: one, that Will signed a letter announcing his resignation from the police force (Chalmers had thoughtfully drafted a copy himself); and

112

two, that he never attempted to seek a career in law enforcement again.

There hadn't been much else he could do. He had considered going to court, fighting a long and expensive legal battle to clear his name, but had known that it would be his word against dozens of his fellow officers. No court in the land had been likely to uphold his case and besides, he'd felt so sickened by what had happened today, he'd seriously doubted that he would want to have any more involvement with the sick joke that currently masqueraded as a police force. So he had signed the letter, walked out of the building and straight into a pub, where he drank himself into a shit-faced stupor.

And the long slide downwards had begun . . .

Now, two years later, walking along the familiar corridor that led to Chalmers' office, he found himself wondering if anything had changed. He was still at the DCI's beck and call, dragged away from the worst tragedy of his life, as though it had been nothing more significant than a football match or his favourite soap opera. And what about 'the deal' he had struck with Chalmers? How effective had that been? Somebody had leaked the story of his former involvement with drugs to the newspapers and Will had a pretty good idea who it had been.

Bullen rapped his knuckles politely on Chalmers' door.

'Come.' The same smug little voice from out of the past, the sound of it making Will's skin crawl. Bullen opened the door and ushered Will into the DCI's presence.

Chalmers sat at his desk, making a big show of signing his name to a sheaf of papers. He had an expensive-looking fountain pen clutched in his pudgy hand and he made a theatrical flourish at the end of each signature. He was a short, plump man with a round pink face. His hair had dwindled away to a couple of tufted islands around his ears. An immaculately trimmed sandy-coloured moustache resided politely on his top lip. His blue eyes were bland and slightly magnified by the powerful horn-rimmed bifocals he wore. As Will approached the desk, his nostrils caught the powerful and cloying smell of Chalmers' familiar lavender-scented cologne.

'Sit.' Chalmers might have been talking to a dog. He indicated the vacant chair in front of his desk, without glancing up. Will did as he was told, while Bullen took up a position behind him, leaning against a filing cabinet. There was a short silence interspersed with the scratching of Chalmers' nib on paper. At last, he finished the final signature. He pushed the papers aside and lifting his head, he studied Will with apparent interest.

'So,' he said at last. 'The prodigal returns to the scene of former crimes. How are you, Will?'

'I'm pissed off if you want to know the truth. What's the idea of dragging me away from my son's funeral?'

Chalmers rearranged his face into an expression of sympathy. 'Regrettable, I know, but proof if it were ever needed, that we can summon you any time we like. It came to me on the grapevine that you'd been spotted back in Manchester and I just wanted to have a quick chat. For old times sake.'

'Don't give me that "old mates" routine. I've been back here a week and it just so happened you chose today to renew our acquaintance? I don't think so. Just another of your dirty tricks.'

'You watch your lip,' interjected Bullen. 'If you want to make it back to that reception.'

'Reception?' Chalmers raised his eyebrows inquisitively.

'Yes, that's where I was about to go when your gorillas picked me up. It's the usual thing after a funeral, believe it or not.'

Chalmers sighed. 'Indeed. And of course, it's completely understandable that you should be feeling . . . irritable at such a time. What happened to your son was most regrettable. But perhaps not entirely surprising under the circumstances. There is, after all, a tendency for children to make the same mistakes as their parents.'

Will laughed derisively at that. 'You kill me, d'you know that? All those years ago and still you insist on playing out this charade. You had Bullen and his stooge arrange all that, you know you did! And all because I didn't want to fit in with your idea of a responsible police force. All mates together, slamming each other's dicks in the door . . .'

Chalmers seemed to wince at this remark. He narrowed his eyes down to slits and pursed his pink lips, creating a little puckered, quivering hole that put Will in mind of a poodle's arse.

'Why so aggressive, Will? There are some people who would welcome the stability that comes from a united order, a brotherhood working together to quell society's ills. Just as there are so many who misunderstand our aims.'

Will gave a grunt of disgust. 'Skip the recruitment speech,' he said. 'I've had first-hand experience of what your little brotherhood is capable of.'

'You're wasting your time on that slag, Guv,' observed Bullen. 'He's a bad lot. You've only got to look what happened to his kid.'

Will turned in his chair and fixed Bullen with a warning look. 'Change the subject,' he snarled. 'Otherwise, cop or no cop, I'll put you in the fucking infirmary.'

'Yeah? You and whose army?' sneered Bullen.

'Come now, gentlemen, there's no need for any unpleasantness. Will, I fear you may have got the wrong impression about your little visit here today. It wasn't my intention to add friction to what must already be a very painful time. I simply thought it would be a good idea if we took the opportunity for a quiet chat.'

Will turned back to look at Chalmers suspiciously. 'About what, exactly?'

'Well, let's face it, we haven't had the opportunity to talk for, what . . . two years? How are things in . . .' He glanced at a sheet of paper in front of him, 'in Southport,' he concluded. 'I understand that you've gone into the entertainment business.'

Will stared at him. 'What do you know about Southport?' he demanded.

'Oh well, I've kept a friendly eye on you, naturally. And when I heard about what happened to your boy, it was on the cards that you'd be coming back to Manchester, at least for a little while.'

'Would you get to the point?' growled Will. 'I've got a bunch of guests waiting for me.'

'Yes, of course. Well, the point is simply this, old son. We're not going to make a fuss about you being here for such a . . . special occasion. That would be rather unreasonable. But we're confident that you'll be heading back to Southport in the next day or so . . .'

Will shrugged. 'I haven't decided on that, yet,' he said; then flinched as he felt Bullen's hand settle on his shoulder.

'Wrong answer, Willy-boy. Of *course* you're heading back, just as soon as they've cleared away the sherry glasses and the cucumber sandwiches.'

Will stared at Chalmers thoughtfully for a moment, then smiled thinly. 'Why, Derek, if I didn't know better, I'd say I wasn't exactly welcome in this city.'

Chalmers spread his hands as if to display that it was all beyond his control. 'Let's just say that I think you're better suited to a life fronting a coconut shy,' he said. 'We really don't want you hanging around here, sticking your nose into places it doesn't belong.'

Will considered this remark. What was Chalmers so scared about? After all, the frame-up was way back in the past, there was no way that Will was going to stir up any trouble on that score and leaking the story to the press had pretty much ensured that nobody would believe a word he said. So what else was there?

'There are certain questions to be answered first,' he argued, 'about my son's death.'

'There's no mystery,' said Bullen, coldly. 'Kid was a junkie who took one trip too many.'

Will bunched his hands into fists and told himself to wait until the time was right. 'Martin was no junkie,' he hissed. 'And I'm warning you, Bullen . . .'

'Whatever happened to your son,' interrupted Chalmers, 'is a matter for police investigation. Just leave it in the hands of the professionals.'

Will sniggered. 'From what I hear, the "professionals" aren't having much success where Warp is concerned.'

'Oh yeah, who you been talking to?' snapped Bullen.

Will stared at him for a moment, then allowed himself the

ghost of a smile, as he remembered something from two years earlier.

'Reliable sources,' he said.

Chalmers smirked. 'I'm afraid your sources are misinformed. We've been making substantial progress over the last couple of months, including video surveillance of some of the major suppliers.'

'Give me a break, Derek. You couldn't find your own arse with a forty-watt light bulb.'

Chalmers gave him an oily smile. 'Be careful, Will. It would be so easy to make you pay for that remark.'

'Like I paid for the last one, you mean? Let's face it, you already stole my career and fucked up my marriage. What else could you take from me?'

'Don't find out, Will. Just heed my advice. Go back to your reception, have a couple of drinks, say all the trite things that people say on these occasions . . . and then get on the first train back to Southport. I don't want to see hide nor hair of you in this city after midday tomorrow.'

'That sounds suspiciously like an ultimatum.'

Chalmers looked calmly at Will. 'Interpret it any way you like. Just do yourself a favour. Disappear.'

Will studied Chalmers for a few moments, savouring his own hatred of the man who had destroyed his life. And suddenly, he knew exactly what he had to do.

'Disappear?' he echoed. 'Oh, don't worry, Derek. I intend to.'

'Good.' Chalmers returned his attention to his papers, showing Will the pink, polished dome of his head. 'DI Bullen will drive you back to the reception,' he concluded.

Will got up from his seat and followed Bullen out of the office, leaving the sickly scent of lavender behind him. They strolled along the corridor beyond.

'Well, he hasn't changed,' muttered Will. 'Still all the charm of a rat in a nursery.'

Bullen chuckled. 'I'll pretend I didn't hear that,' he said. 'So, where do you want me to drop you?'

'Actually, I think I'll give the reception a miss. I've a few things to sort out before I . . . disappear.' They had reached the lift doors. Will punched the button. 'I'll make my own way.'

'Suit yourself,' said Bullen.

'I intend to. And I would like to take the opportunity to tell you something important.' He glanced cautiously around. 'In confidence, you understand.'

'Oh yeah, what's that?'

Will stepped closer as if to whisper a secret. Then he made his move. He backed Bullen up against the wall beside the lift doors.

'Number one,' he murmured. 'My son wasn't a junkie. Got that?' Bullen nodded eagerly.

'Number two, you are a low-down, arse-licking, slimy piece of shit. Isn't that correct?'

'Uh huh,' grunted Bullen.

'And last but not least, if I ever hear you make a remark about my son again, it will be more than just your balls on the line. Do I make myself clear?'

'Y . . . yes!' hissed Bullen urgently. Beads of sweat were popping on his brow.

'Good.' Will gave the man's testicles a last wrench and then released his hold. Bullen slid white-faced down the wall, his eyes streaming with tears, his hands cushioning his groin.

The lift doors pinged as they opened and Will stepped inside. He turned back to smile down at Bullen. A couple of secretaries had stopped to see what the problem was. They were bending over Bullen, cooing anxiously. He glared up at Will, his teeth clenched.

'You . . . are . . . dead!' he hissed.

'Not yet,' Will corrected him. 'But I'm working on it. Have a nice day.'

The lift doors closed and he rode down to the ground floor, feeling more motivated than he had in years.

Chapter Twelve

Scally trudged dejectedly back from the city centre after a long day spent unsuccessfully begging in a shop doorway. Crouched in a prime spot on New Market Street, trying to look his most pitiful, he had plied the passing trade with all the special skills he'd acquired over the last year and for his troubles, he'd earned the grand sum of fourteen pence. Finally, his efforts were curtailed when he'd spotted a sweep team of cops, making their way along the street, clearing out any beggars they encountered, with liberal use of their boots and electric batons.

Scally had taken the hint and legged it back in the direction of the arch. He was becoming increasingly nervous about the police and their new powers. When Scally first started living rough, the cops had been firm, but fair, always giving you the option of walking away before they started getting heavy. These days they were more likely to wade in without asking any questions and they didn't care how much damage they caused. On the contrary, they seemed to *enjoy* it.

Even more sinister was the organization that called itself the MLOD – the Manchester League Of Decency. They were a thriving organization of what could only be described as vigilantes, who seemed to have set themselves the task of aiding the police in ridding the city of 'undesirables'. This term didn't only apply to criminals; it also extended to drug addicts and alcoholics, prostitutes and of course, the homeless. Rumours abounded that the MLOD were responsible for a recent attack on a shelter in Wythenshawe where Rag People were brutally beaten and their shelters burned.

The MLOD dressed in khaki, military-style fatigues and

every one of them had a red bandana around his or her neck. They held regular rallies in Piccadilly Gardens, where they handed out leaflets condemning the 'evil tide of filth and depravity' that existed in their city. They urged followers to abstain from alcohol, tobacco and sexual activity outside of marriage, yet despite this, they were growing in popularity all the time. Meanwhile, the police seemed more than happy to turn a blind eye to their activities, seeing them as useful allies in what was increasingly becoming a moral crusade.

Scally turned on to Sobriety Street and began to walk along it, whistling some half-remembered tune to himself. He was thinking about something Marianne told him, about how the world was supposed to end in 1999. Maybe it wouldn't be such a bad thing, he told himself. Life was hard and with no prospect of it getting any easier, it was difficult to find a reason to struggle on.

An elderly Rag Man shuffled past Scally with a gap-toothed smile, his wizened body supported by stick-thin legs. *One more who won't see out the winter*, thought Scally gloomily. There weren't many elderly Rag People, because only the toughest of them survived into old age. Those that did often faced a bleak future of neglect and slow starvation.

But you had to keep telling yourself that there was some way out of this existence – that one day a miracle would happen – you'd make your escape.

Scally had this familiar daydream, a fantasy in which he rescued some rich old man from being mugged by a couple of villains. In the daydream, Scally fights with incredible skill and tenacity, half-killing the bad guys despite the fact that they are twice his size. Afterwards, the old man offers him a cash reward but Scally brushes it off, telling him he can't accept it. He's only done what any good person would do. Then he strolls back to the arch, to get on with his life.

But it turns out that the old man has recently lost his son in a tragic accident and has nobody to leave his money to. In the final scene of the fantasy, a big chauffeur-driven stretch limo turns up on Sobriety Street, the old man leaning out of the window, waving a set of adoption papers. Frank and the other Rag People look on in amazement as Scally saunters over to the car and the old man opens the door.

'You're *Lord* Scally now,' the old man tells him, smiling benevolently. 'You're one of the richest men in the city.' He indicates the pretty, dark-haired girl sitting beside him, 'and this is your step-sister, Kathy, who is going to take very good care of you . . .'

The daydream was rudely interrupted by the sound of a couple of young snappers, who'd come running towards him from the stretch of waste ground away to his right. They were laughing mischievously, but when they saw Scally, they hesitated, their expressions suddenly as guilty as hell.

'What's up?' he asked them.

'Nothing!' said the oldest of them, a boy of about seven with freckles and an unruly thatch of ginger hair, but he threw a glance over his shoulder to where a huddle of men were gathered some distance away beside an unlit bonfire stack.

'What's going on over there?' asked Scally suspiciously.

But the snappers just shrugged their shoulders and ran back towards their arch. Scally stood for a moment, feeling vaguely uneasy. From across the waste ground came the distant shouts of the men, sounding raucous and incoherent, the way people sounded when they'd been drinking heavily. Scally stepped off the street onto the grass and began to walk towards them.

As he got closer, he could see that there were maybe a dozen men, gathered in a half-circle, looking at something that was happening behind the cover of the bonfire stack. Several young snappers were running around the place, shouting delightedly. Scally frowned. A fight maybe? Tribal disputes were sometimes settled in this way, the two adversaries slugging it out with fists and baseball bats, in a no-holds-barred brawl.

As Scally drew closer, one man detached himself from the group and began to walk back to the arches. Scally saw that it was Frank. He was holding a sherry bottle and seemed decidedly unsteady on his feet. He noticed Scally approaching and gave him a weasly little grin as he passed by, reaching down to do up his flies as he did so.

'She's a good sport, your friend,' he slurred and he laughed unpleasantly.

Scally stared after him for a moment and he knew now that something was horribly wrong. Something bad was happening over behind the bonfire. He continued walking, quickening his pace, and now he could hear the shouts more clearly. They were shouts of encouragement.

'Go on, my son! Give it to her!'

Scally broke into a run. He reached the half-circle of men, pushing and jostling his way through them in order to get a better view. With an effort, he emerged at the front and then he stood there for a moment, staring down in mute horror.

Marianne was lying on her back on a soiled mattress that had been thrown down beside the bonfire. Her eyes gazed blankly up at the sky. Two men were holding her down, pinning her arms to the mattress, though she wasn't struggling. Her long dress had been pulled up around her waist and the front was torn open, exposing her small breasts. One of Frank's cronies, a solidly built fellow called Maxi, lay on top of her, his bare buttocks pumping up and down. One of the others had his face pressed against Marianne's breasts. He was licking them and slavering like a dog.

For a moment, Scally couldn't find his voice. The horror of the moment was too overpowering. Finally, he opened his mouth but all that came out was a feeble croak.

'Leave her alone,' he gasped.

'Push off kid,' said one of the onlookers. 'If she's not bothered, why should you be?'

Scally noticed the litter of empty bottles beside the mattress and he knew that Marianne was drunk. She'd have to be to endure this without screaming.

'Let her be!' yelled Scally, louder now. 'I'm warning you.'

There was laughter amongst the encircling men.

'Get lost, punk,' said another man. 'I'm next.' He aimed a punch at Scally's head, catching him a stinging blow on his ear.

Something seemed to snap at the back of the boy's skull. A red heat welled in his chest and exploded upwards into his head.

'Bastards!' he screamed. He ran to the bonfire, wrenched out a big wooden spar and turned back, swinging it like an

122

axe. The onlookers stopped laughing and scattered away from him but he wasn't so occupied with them. It was the three men on the ground who were the focus of his rage. The two holding Marianne down saw him coming and scrambled away in panic, yelling for Maxi to watch out, but he was somewhat slower to respond. As he got to his knees, Scally aimed a swing at him, catching him a heavy blow across the shoulders. Maxi howled and rolled away, his trousers still around his ankles.

'You fucking maniac!' he screamed. 'I'll pull your fucking head off!' He scrambled into a crouching position, unsure whether to fight back or run for his life.

'Yeah? Come on then. Come on! We'll see who loses their head first.' Scally squared up to Maxi, a mad light flickering in his eyes, the spar held above his head like a two-handed axe, ready to split the man's skull open.

Maxi muttered something and, standing, pulled up his trousers. His penis had shrunk to an insubstantial pink stub. He glanced around at his companions, seeking their support.

'Come on,' he said. 'He's just a kid. We'll deal with him and then go back for seconds.'

But the onlookers had been shamed by Scally's actions. Some of them were already turning away. Only Maxi's two partners-in-crime lingered and they were having trouble looking Scally in the eye.

'Well, come on,' Scully urged them. 'Who's first?' He swung the spar at them and they all retreated a couple of steps.

'Put the wood down,' suggested Maxi. 'We'll make it a fair fight, what do you say?'

'Like you were fair to Marianne?' yelled Scally. 'You filthy bastards. You're not men, you're animals!'

That did it for Maxi's friends. They turned sullenly away and began to follow the others towards the arches.

'You fucking wait,' snarled Maxi. 'I'll have you for this, boy, you just see if I don't. Nobody lays a hand on me and gets away with it.' He reached up a hand to rub at his injured shoulder and he winced. 'It doesn't have anything to do with you, anyway. We paid for it. We gave her booze . . .'

'She's my friend,' said Scally. 'You go near her again and I'll kill you. That's a promise.'

Maxi laughed scornfully, but it didn't sound too convincing. 'I'll have you,' he said again. 'You just wait and see.' He threw a last look at the woman stretched out on the mattress and then he made a dismissive gesture. 'Ah, who wants it anyway? She's nothing to write home about. She just lies there.'

He turned away and began to trail after the others but fearing a bluff, Scally waited until Maxi had moved off a considerable distance.

Then dropping the spar, he ran to Marianne and knelt beside her. Her eyes were open and she was gazing around as if surprised to find herself here. Blood was pulsing from a bite on her lips and her breasts and thighs were already mottled with dark bruises. Scally eased her dress back down over her knees and did his best to cover up her breasts.

'Scally?' She seemed to become suddenly aware of his presence. She reached out a hand to him and he helped her into a sitting position, cradling her head in his lap.

'I . . . I must have let go for a minute,' she whispered.

'Let go of what?' he asks her.

She looked confused. 'I had a couple of drinks . . . I remember that. And Frank was laughing. He said . . . we'd have a party. He said . . .'

'How could you have been so stupid?' he asked her. 'Didn't you realize . . . ?'

'Yes! Yes, of course. But you see, Scally, I didn't *care* any more. I didn't care what they did to me. I thought . . . *hoped* maybe, they'd kill me. I knew I deserved whatever happened to me. So I let go. I just let go . . .'

'Oh, Marianne, don't talk like that! You didn't kill Steve. You told me yourself, it was drugs.'

'Yes, but I turned him on to it. It was something he'd never tried. And because I had, it gave me the edge, do you see? I had one over on him. He felt he had to share it with me. We always shared everything. So I turned him on to it and he couldn't handle it. He just couldn't handle it . . .'

She began to cry, big wracking sobs that shook her frail body. She covered her face with her hands and wailed her grief into her palms, as though trying to confine it, smother it. Scally realized that it was the first time he'd ever seen Marianne cry. His sad, sweet princess who had never shed a tear. Till now.

His own eyes began to blur and he put his arms around her, held her close while he cried away his own misery.

'It's OK,' he told her. 'Honest. I'll look after you. They'll never come near you again, I promise. You don't have to hurt yourself any more.'

But it was a long time before she had calmed herself enough to allow him to help her to her feet; to lead her slowly back across the wasteland, to the cold, damp sanctuary of the arch and the sweet oblivion of sleep.

Chapter Thirteen

Will walked slowly into the city centre, taking the opportunity to have a good long look at his surroundings. After all, if he was going to be living on these streets for the foreseeable future, it made good sense to check them out.

He was somewhat surprised by the sheer numbers of Rag People that he saw. Of course, you generally noticed *some* of them whenever you were in town, but that was just the obvious ones, the ones sitting in shop doorways, holding out their begging bowls as you hurried by them. It was only when you started looking out for them that you quickly became aware of the true scale of the problem.

They were tucked away all over the place: every side street, every stairwell, every derelict building. They seemed to prowl the shady periphery of the urban landscape, hiding from the daylight like legions of shabby vampires awaiting the onset of night.

Will noticed the heavy police presence too, aggressive-looking young street cops strutting along in pairs as though they owned the place, which effectively, they did. They wore blue, American-style uniforms and their leather utility belts held a 9mm automatic, an electric prod baton and a can of Mace. Will noted the way they eyeballed everybody who looked in the least bit out of place and knew that it was only his respectable clothes that prevented him from being treated like a potential villain.

He noticed one other thing; that wherever the blue uniforms patrolled, the Rag People melted mysteriously away, hugging themselves deeper into shadow, running for cover until the coast was clear. Only one thing could cause them to act in such a way. Absolute and total fear. Will was quite certain that they had every reason to be afraid.

He found what he was looking for on Oldham Street, a small charity shop that specialized in second-hand clothing. He went inside and under the watchful gaze of the bespectacled middle-class lady who presided over the counter, he searched hopefully through the racks of clothing – but it was all freshly cleaned and laundered. He cast around and spotted a number of black bin bags piled up around the entrance to a store room. He opened the topmost bag and began to rummage through its contents.

The woman at the counter seemed horrified.

'Excuse me, sir, you can't do that,' she protested. 'That's a new delivery, it has to be cleaned and sorted yet.'

'That's OK,' he assured her, wrinkling his nose at the musty, mousey odours exuding from the bag. 'I'll risk it if you will.' After a short search, he'd found himself a suitable wardrobe – an oversized khaki raincoat, frayed and stained from years of abuse; a grubby red sweatshirt with a faded 'designer' logo on the chest; some shapeless green cord trousers, held up by an elastic belt; and a pair of ancient Reeboks, long past their sell-by date. To complete the picture, he dug out a battered felt hat which he figured would help keep off the rain.

Will took the clothing to the counter and watched impassively as the woman slipped on a pair of rubber gloves, before folding the garments into a carrier bag. She had a look of profound disgust on her face.

'It's very irregular,' she twittered. 'I'm sure items like *this* wouldn't have been considered salvageable. It would probably have ended up in the incinerator.'

Will forced a smile. 'I'm going to a theme party,' he explained. 'Tramps and Vicars. There's a prize for the most authentic costume.'

'Ah, I see.' The explanation seemed to reassure her. 'Gosh, I haven't been to a party like that in years. Nobody seems to bother these days, do they? I'd spray some cologne on them, before you go. We don't want to be *too* realistic, do we!' She thought for a moment. 'Well, shall we say five pounds for the lot?'

Will glanced at her sharply. He'd been thinking more in the region of fifty pence. Hadn't she just told him that the clothes were only fit for the incinerator? But he handed over the fiver without complaint, telling himself that it was all for a good cause. And besides, he wouldn't be needing any money after today. The woman took the five pound note and slipped it into her pocket. Will noticed that she didn't even bother to ring it up on the cash register, which made him wonder which particular charity his money would be going to.

He carried his purchases to the nearest tram stop and rode back to Suzanne's. He felt vaguely apprehensive about what he was getting into, but glad that he was finally doing something positive about Martin. He realized that attacking Don Bullen had been a stupid move. Satisfying but stupid. The man would undoubtedly come looking for him just as soon as he was able to walk without wincing – but this too would force Will's hand, make him appreciate that the only way he could stay in the city, would be to make himself invisible. And what better way to do that, than to join the faceless ranks of the dispossessed?

When he got back to Suzanne's he was relieved to find that there was no sign of the ladies and gentlemen of The Press. Presumably, they were still up in Failsworth, pursuing their phoney funeral. The gate stood slightly ajar as it had been left after their hasty exit earlier that day. Will strolled inside, punched in the six digit code that deactivated the alarm and let himself in with the spare key that Suzanne had lent him. He needed to talk to Clive Singleton and, glancing at his watch, he decided that there was no way he would still be hanging around Suzanne's reception when there were stories to be written. He dialled Clive's personal number at *The Post* to discover that he had been back in the office a good fifteen minutes.

'Will, what happened to you? I saw the cops pick you up at the church . . .'

'Chalmers wanted a little talk with me, basically a carefully worded invitation to fuck off out of Manchester.'

'Shit. What are you going to do?'

'What we talked about earlier. If you're still game, I'll meet up with you every Friday at one pm. Somewhere nice and public. Say, Piccadilly Gardens?'

'I'll be there, mate. I just hope you've thought this through carefully.'

'I've thought it through. Listen, in a week's time, I might not be so easy to recognize. Just take a seat on a park bench and I'll approach you.'

'Anything else you need?'

'Yeah. When you come, bring some butties with you. I might be glad of them, by then.'

He put down the phone, then went upstairs to change into his new clothes. In the third-floor bedroom, he stripped down to his underwear and socks. He folded his wedding suit and placed it in his suitcase. He also put in his wallet, his wrist watch and what little paper money he had left, leaving himself with the grand sum of seventy-four pence in change. Then he dressed himself in the filthy clothes and looked dubiously at his reflection in the mirror. It was astonishing but already he hardly recognized himself. For the moment though the effect wasn't quite right. His face, hands and hair looked too clean but it would only take a few nights of sleeping rough to take care of that little detail. He put on the hat, pulling the shapeless brim down to just above his eyes.

He heard the sound of the front door opening and slamming and then Suzanne's voice shouted up the stairs.

'Will, are you there?'

'Yes,' he called back. 'I'm in my room.'

Her footsteps came thudding up the staircase. She started talking before she was even in the room.

'Where the bloody hell did you get to? Everybody was asking where you were, I stalled as long as I could and then I had to pretend you—'

Her voice broke off as she came through the doorway and registered his new look. She gave a gasp as though somebody had punched her in the stomach. Then she just stood there staring at him, her mouth open in dismay.

'What . . . what's going on?' she demanded. 'Is it Hallowe'en or something? What's with the get-up?'

'It's the new me,' he told her. 'What do you think? From

now on, I'm joining the ranks of the Rag People.'

Her brow furrowed as she tried to fathom his reasoning. Then she laughed nervously. 'This is some kind of joke, right? Tell me this is a joke.'

He shook his head. 'No joke, Suzanne. It's a way to find out something about Martin. Maybe the *only* way, since Chalmers and his merry men seem intent on running me out of town.'

'They can't do that!'

'They can. They have. I'm to be gone by noon tomorrow.'

'I see.' Suzanne walked over to the bed and sat down on it. 'I knew it!' she hissed. 'I knew you were planning something, but I had no idea it would be anything as crazy as this. You don't change, do you Will?'

He spread his arms. 'But I have changed,' he said. 'And believe me, this clobber didn't come cheap. Five quid it cost me.'

'You know what I mean!' she snapped. 'Always with you there has to be some kind of half-assed masterplan, doesn't there? And you always end up in trouble.' She thought for a moment. When she spoke again her tone was careful, placatory. 'Don't you think . . . don't you think it would be more sensible to do what they want? Just go quietly back to Southport and pick up where you left off?'

Will laughed bitterly. 'Oh sure, more sensible, no question. But I'm not in the mood for being sensible, Suzanne. I'm in the mood for *revenge*. An old-fashioned word, I know, but one I can at least understand.' He glanced at her. 'I'll need your help.'

'Oh no, don't think I'm getting involved in this crackpot scheme. I don't want anything to do with it! Where will you sleep? What will you eat? For God's sake, Will, you won't last a week out there!'

'Well, that remains to be seen. And as for the help, all I want you to do is to hide this.' He indicated his suitcase. 'If anybody asks you where I am . . . particularly anybody from the force, I've gone back to Southport, OK?'

Suzanne shrugged. 'I suppose that can't hurt. When will I see you?'

'I honestly don't know. If you need to get a message to me,

something important, you can talk to Clive. I've arranged to meet up with him once a week. But don't mention my name over the phone or anything, you never know who might be listening in.' Reaching into his pocket he took out Suzanne's spare key and handed it to her. 'I won't be needing this any more,' he told her.

'Why don't you keep it?' she suggested. 'In case you need to get back in when I'm not here . . .'

He shook his head. 'That would give me an escape route. That's an advantage that the Rag People don't have. If I'm going to pull this off I have to be just like them.'

Now she looked incredulous. 'For God's sake, Will, I can't believe you're serious about this! I mean, aren't you getting a bit long in the tooth for all this cloak and dagger stuff? What do you hope to find out there?'

He glared at her and when he spoke, the venom in his voice made her flinch.

'The bastards who killed Martin.'

'But you're not a policeman any more. It's not your job to bring them to justice.'

He looked at her calmly. 'Who said anything about justice? If I find them, it won't be a court they answer to.'

He took a last look at himself in the mirror, then turned and started for the door.

'Just like that?' she shouted after him. 'You're just going to leave? Walk out of the door like you're going to the corner shop for a bottle of milk?'

He spread his hands in a shrug. 'How else would I do it?' He thought for a moment. 'It's pretty much what I did last time, isn't it?'

She frowned, nodded. 'I suppose so.' She looked up at him and he thought he glimpsed an unspeakable sadness in her eyes. It was only there for an instant but it shook him to the core. He'd always told himself that his leaving had brought her nothing but relief. She got up off the bed and came over to stand in front of him. 'Take care of yourself,' she told him. 'It's been . . . am I allowed to say that . . . that it's been good having you back? I just wish it hadn't been for such an awful, tragic reason.'

He stood there looking at her, once again torn between holding her in his arms and walking away without another word. He supposed it would always be like this between them now. They'd had their chance of making it work and had failed miserably. The rift between them would never be fully repaired.

'Well,' he said at last, with forced cheerfulness. 'Can't stand around chatting all day. I'm wasting good begging time.' He took off his hat and held it out to her with a pleading gesture on his face. 'Spare a couple of coppers, Guv?'

Quick as a flash, Suzanne reached into the pocket of her jacket and produced some coins. She threw them into the hat. He gazed down at them for a moment.

'Easier than I thought,' he said.

He pocketed the change, went out of the room and down the two flights of stairs. He let himself out of the front door and trudged towards the gate, his ancient Reeboks crunching on the gravel. Glancing back once, he saw Suzanne watching him from one of the upstairs windows. With a last wave he stepped out through the open gates and stood for a moment, gazing up and down the street. A young woman was approaching, pushing a baby carriage. He doffed his cap and nodded to her.

'Good afternoon,' he said.

She made an unnecessarily wide detour around him, a look on her face as though she had encountered a bad smell. Will smiled ruefully. It occurred to him that it was a six-mile walk into town, and that he could no longer afford to take public transport. To make matters worse, the darkening sky threatened more rain.

Better get used to it, he told himself. He pulled the hat down low over his eyes and whistling a merry tune, he started walking.

PART TWO
Rags

There is no scandal like rags. Nor any crime so shameful as poverty.

George Farquhar, The Beaux Stratagem.

It is not he who has many possessions that you should call blessed: he more rightly deserves that name who knows how to use the god's gifts wisely and to endure harsh poverty, and who fears dishonour more than death.

Horace (Quintus Horatius Flaccus.) Odes.

Chapter Fourteen

It had been six days.

Will acknowledged the fact with a shrug of weary resignation and told himself that it seemed longer. Much longer. He pulled his damp raincoat tighter around his shivering body and huddled back under cover.

He was crouching in the doorway of an abandoned shop on New Market Street. He figured it must be after six pm. It was already dark. For several hours he had been begging from the passing pedestrians and, so far, he had received absolutely nothing for his efforts.

He was so hungry, he thought he would die. He hadn't realized that hunger could be like this, because in his life so far, he had never experienced anything fiercer than the results of a few hours deprivation. Today, his belly was an aching, throbbing void that seemed to scream for food of any description.

A couple of people went by, heads bowed against the stinging flurries of rain that hammered the length of the street.

'Excuse me, sir!' Will held out his hat, uncomfortably aware of the desperation in his voice. 'Please, I haven't eaten for several days, I . . .'

'Fuck you,' snapped the man uncharitably, without altering his pace. 'Why don't you get a job?' he offered as a parting remark.

Will felt tears of humiliation welling in his eyes. 'Bastard!' he said. 'Lousy rotten bastard!'

How many times, he asked himself, had he seen down-and-outs muttering to themselves, just like this and dismissed them as mentally unstable? How many times had he shared a smile with some friend or drilled a forefinger into his head in the age-old gesture that signified that the object of derision had bats in the belfry? He knew now what made those people curse and gesticulate. It was the sheer injustice felt by anyone rendered incapable of buying their place in society. It was the callous indifference of their fellow man as he passed along the street.

A group of teenagers came swaggering from the other direction, young lads decked out in the current foppish Regency fashion, frock coats and brocade waistcoats. Ordinarily, Will wouldn't have gone near them but today, he was desperate.

'Please lads, could you spare a little change?'

The youths paused and stared down at him as though they'd been confronted by some lower life form. One of them smiled amiably and slipped a hand into his pocket, stirring his change; then as Will leaned forward gratefully, he hawked and let a big gob of spit fall into the hat. The youths moved on, laughing uproariously.

Will slumped back against the boarded-up door of the shop and closed his eyes. This was getting him nowhere. He told himself that he'd have to start looking in rubbish bins, something he'd resisted so far because he was afraid of poisoning himself. He'd seen plenty of others doing it over the last few days and he supposed it was just a case of being careful about what you ate. But hungry as he was, he knew that once he went down that road, he would not have the self-control to exercise any degree of selection.

Not for the first time, he asked himself if he wasn't wasting his time here. After all, what had he achieved? Nothing. A big fat zero. The other Rag People he'd approached had treated him with hostile suspicion. Most of them saw him as a potential rival, competing for food or shelter. He'd managed to get talking to one man a few days back, a strange, shabby little fellow in a plastic mac, dragging a battered shopping trolley full of junk along with him. He'd asked Will what tribe he was with. When Will explained that he was on his own, the man shook his head sadly.

'That's no use. You need to get in with a tribe, mate. Loners don't last long out here.'

'Well, how do I do that?' Will had asked him.

'Depends on the tribe,' the man told him. 'There's some as will let you barter your way in. Maybe you got something they want, know what I mean? Others, they'll let you fight for the right to join, but that's strictly for hard cases. Friend of mine got his head stove in, that way. He died 'cos no hospital would take him. But believe me, you want to find yourself a tribe and find one quick, before the winter comes.'

And with that, he'd gone on his way, dragging his worldly goods behind him.

'What tribe are *you* with?' Will had shouted after him, but the man hadn't even looked back at him. Will had become aware of heads turning to look at him in amusement and he'd walked quickly away in the other direction.

Will had spent his first night sleeping huddled up in a shop doorway, his second in a bus shelter on Chorlton Street, along with several dozen other people, but he'd been awakened in the small hours by the roar of engines as several Black Marias came into the street. As he struggled blearily to his feet, uniformed police officers, many of them with dogs, had spilled out of the vehicles and set about clearing out the station by brute force. Will's hip still ached where he'd taken a kick from a police issue boot when he'd failed to get out of the way in time. Some people tried to stand their ground and were either savaged by the dogs or struck down by electric prod batons. Will had spent the remainder of that night wandering around the city, trying desperately to keep warm. He didn't want to think about what it would be like on the streets come December.

On his third night, he had spent the last of his money on a portion of chips from a mobile snack bar, eating them slowly as though they were some exotic delicacy to be savoured like a vintage wine. Since then, no other food had passed his lips and he was becoming desperate.

'Please, sir, madam! If you could just spare me a few pence . . .'

The couple were middle-aged and respectable. The man gave Will a contemptuous glare, but his wife hesitated, began to reach for her purse.

'Oh, thank you,' murmured Will. 'God bless you . . .'

But the husband had taken his wife by the arm and was pulling her away.

'Leave it, Jane, he'll only spend it on drink.'

'I won't!' protested Will. 'Please, sir, don't . . .'

But they were moving on, the woman glancing back with an apologetic smile. Will stared after them for a moment, aware of anger welling up within him like a balloon filled with acid. In a moment it would pop and when it did . . .

He climbed to his feet, telling himself he had to get away from here. Pins and needles throbbed through his legs and he felt weak and light-headed. Afraid that he might faint, he weaved along New Market Street, moving amongst the crowds of late shoppers, not really sure where he was going, only sure that if food didn't pass his lips soon, he would be forced to mug somebody and take their money. He was meeting up with Clive tomorrow and hopefully he would remember to bring something edible but Will honestly doubted that he would last that long.

He reached the big branch of Burger Drome on New Market Street, the bright neon lights that spelled out its name spilling garish reflections on to the wet pavement. The tantalizing smell of chicken, ostrich and chilli-bean burgers wafted out through the swing doors. No beef of course, that had been off the menu since the Mad Cow epidemic of '97. Will had never been a fan of this kind of cuisine but right now, a Double Chicken Dromer with extra cheese sounded like the culinary equivalent of heaven. He pressed his face against the window and was treated to the mouth-watering sight of table upon table of diners, most of whom appeared to be virtually distending their jaws in order to cram great slabs of food into them. He turned away with a groan and looked doubtfully at the two solidly built bouncers who stood on either side of the entrance, imposing black men dressed in American World War Two flying jackets, complete with mirrored goggles and leather helmets. The men stood regarding him sullenly, their muscular arms crossed over their chests. Will realized that he had not a hope in hell of gaining admittance even if he had the money to pay for anything.

A teenage boy came out through the swing doors, munching

on an Ostrich burger but he seemed more interested in talking to the girl he was with, a crop-haired nymphette in a man's striped business suit and silk tie. As the couple walked on, the boy reached out a hand, the fingernails of which were painted with black lacquer and he casually dropped the remains of the burger into a litter bin.

Will saw it land, still wrapped in a napkin, amongst the piles of debris in the bin. Without thinking, he made a dash for the discarded food and he was just reaching into the bin when another Rag Man appeared, seemingly out of nowhere, a big, brutish looking fellow with an unkempt black beard and shoulder-length hair. He was a good six inches taller than Will, his ugly face decorated with crude tribal tattoos. To complete a very unattractive picture, he had a large silver ring hanging from his nostrils.

'What's the idea?' he growled, slapping Will's hand away. 'This is my pitch. You fuck off.' He gave Will a push in the chest that sent him staggering backwards. Will glanced towards the entrance of Burger Drome. The two bouncers were watching events with amused expressions on their faces.

'Yeah, that's the way Chilli Dog!' shouted one of them. 'Show the mother who's boss around here!'

The bearded man grinned with broken teeth, then reached into the bin and retrieved the burger, which seemed dwarfed in his huge hand. He brushed away a couple of cigarette stubs and raised it to his mouth.

'NO!' Something snapped in Will's head. The burger was his, and nobody was going to take it away from him! 'I saw it first!' he yelled. He felt ridiculous saying it but he knew that he wasn't going to let it go that easily. He lunged back at Chilli Dog, and pushed him in the chest, but hardly succeeded in rocking the big man on his feet.

'Hand it over,' he said. 'I'm starving.'

'Join the club,' observed Chilli Dog unsympathetically. 'Now get out of my face, I'm trying to have dinner here.' He opened his mouth to take a bite from the burger and Will, driven frantic by hunger, acted without a thought for the consequences. He reached up and grabbing the man's nose ring between thumb and forefinger, he jerked down hard. Chilli

Dog bellowed in pain and fell forward across the concrete bin, the hard rim driving the air out of him. Will prised the burger out of the man's grasp with one hand and gave the ring another fierce wrench with the other. The ring tore free in a gout of blood and Chilli Dog twisted away with a roar. He rolled off the litter bin and fell onto his back on the pavement, hands clawing at his torn nose.

Will saw that the Burger Drome bouncers were coming over to intervene, so he took off, cramming the food into his mouth as he ran, gulping the still-warm ostrich meat and melted cheese down in a couple of swallows. Glancing back, he saw that the bouncers were helping Chilli Dog back to his feet, not in order to assist him but merely to frogmarch him out of sight of the paying customers who might conceivably be put off their food by the sight of the fresh blood squirting down his face. Chilli Dog was looking wildly around for his adversary, doubtless stunned by the suddenness of the attack but Will was already moving deeper into the crowds that thronged the street. Looking down, he saw with a twinge of surprise, that he was still clutching the silver nose ring in his hand, complete with strings of bloody flesh. His first impulse was to throw it away in disgust but he hesitated, realizing that it might be worth something. What had the old Rag Man said about bartering your way into a tribe? With a sigh, Will wiped the ring on the sleeve of his raincoat and slipped it into his trouser pocket.

The few mouthfuls of food had helped a little but he was still a long way from being satisfied. He walked on towards Piccadilly. It was only now occurring to him what an incredibly violent thing he had just done. He had virtually torn a stranger's nose from his face and all over a mere handful of discarded food. He could hardly believe he'd done it and the only mitigating circumstance he could offer in his defence was the fact that he'd been desperate.

He remembered only a week or so back, coming out of the *Evening Post* offices with Clive and seeing the old woman begging in a shop doorway. He'd wondered then what it must be like to be her.

Now he knew. It was the most unspeakable, the most cruel

and terrible thing in the world. He felt as though he'd been living in a dream up till now, only glimpsing the bad things that lay on the other side of the wall behind which he had sheltered. Now he had awakened to find that he was in the midst of a nightmare but unlike the others that dwelled here, he could walk away from it any time he wanted. Thousands of others would never escape the misery, the poverty, the hunger. They would live it till the day they died.

Will thought wistfully about Suzanne's palatial home. He pictured himself sitting at a table with her, in her plush, centrally-heated dining room, eating coq au vin, drinking a rich red burgundy and telling her all about the wild adventures he'd had out on the street.

'You wouldn't believe it, Suzanne. A couple of mouthfuls of food and I was almost ready to kill for it!'

He could see Suzanne tilting back her pretty head and laughing out loud at the absurdity of it . . .

Will shook his head, gritted his teeth. No, he decided, he wasn't ready to give up on it yet. He'd stick at it a while longer and in the fullness of time, maybe he would make some progress.

Pulling up his collar against the chill wind of October, he carried on walking, looking for a suitable place to spend the night.

Pinder unlocked the door of the cellar and ushered the boy down the whitewashed stairs to the soundproofed room beneath his house.

'And down here,' he announced grandly, 'is where I store all my major illusions.'

The boy went slowly down the steps and stood for a moment, gazing around at the various props stored here. There was a large, glitter-painted saw-box; a fully working third-scale guillotine; and a whole assortment of boxes, hoops and cabinets.

'Wow,' said the boy. He sounded genuinely impressed.

Pinder placed a hand on the boy's skinny shoulder. He would be about fifteen, Pinder guessed, just a ragged teenage nobody picked at random from the ranks of human detritus that swarmed around Piccadilly station. Luring him into the car had been easy. Pinder had proffered a large bar of chocolate and had followed up with a few simple card tricks. It worked every time, kids adored magic. And when Pinder had mentioned some of the more elaborate stuff that he kept at home, well . . .

'What's your name, son?' Pinder asked him.

'Donny.' The boy smiled apologetically. 'I think it's a dumb name, don't you?'

He was thin, with a thatch of unkempt straw-coloured hair and large blue eyes. He was very dirty and he had a gamey smell about him that made Pinder's mouth water.

'Not at all. I think it's a delightful name. Quite charming.'

The boy's eyes narrowed suspiciously. Pinder could guess what Donny was thinking. He suspected he'd been lured here to be shown tricks of an entirely different sort and in that respect, he was correct – though surely not in the way he imagined. The boy was good looking, almost pretty, Pinder thought. He'd doubtless already be popular with the highly organized gangs of paedophiles that regularly preyed upon the Rag People and Pinder would be willing to bet that offered sufficient financial incentive, he'd know exactly what to do to earn his money.

But Pinder danced to a different drum. He had no intention of making sexual moves on the boy. At least, not conventional ones.

Donny broke off a couple more squares from the family-sized bar of chocolate and chewed happily, as he studied Pinder's damaged face.

'What happened to your nose?' he asked.

Pinder winced. He hated it when people mentioned the nose. Damn it, it ought to be getting better by now. He was taking the antibiotics the quack had given him, but they seemed to be making no impression at all. The wound had opened up into a large seeping pit, the centre of which was now a bilious yellowy-green.

'An accident,' he growled. 'If it's all the same to you, I'd rather we didn't talk about it.'

Donny shrugged. 'Suit yourself,' he said. 'You going to show us some more tricks then?'

Pinder beamed down at the boy.

'Why not?' he said. 'Let me see now . . . ah, yes!' He took a glittering silver top hat and a magic wand from a nearby table and held the hat so that Donny could peer into it.

'As you can see, it's quite empty. And yet . . .' He tapped the hat with his wand, laid it aside and began to pull multi-coloured silk scarves from the hat. 'Now how did they get in here?' He hung them around Donny's neck like a technicolour necklace, then looked into the hat again. 'Now, what else? Ah . . .' He reached in a second time and drew forth a large bunch of plastic flowers. He handed them to the boy and Donny's eyes sparkled delightedly.

'What else is there?' he asked.

'Hmm. Let's have a look shall we?'

Pinder's hand went into the hat a third time and emerged holding an electric prod. He pressed it gently, almost tenderly against a spot on Donny's left temple and pressed the trigger. There was a brief jolt of blue light and Donny's body jerked convulsively. The blue eyes rolled up in their sockets and he dropped like a stone, the half-eaten chocolate slipping from his twitching fingers and shattering on the floor.

Pinder set aside the top hat and stooped to pick the boy up in his arms. He carried him across to a metal table, laid him down on his back and began to remove his clothes. When Donny was naked, Pinder examined him thoughtfully, then shook his head. The boy was far too grimy, he decided. He preferred to work with clean flesh.

He strapped Donny into the arm and leg restraints and then went upstairs to fetch a basin of hot water, some soap and a flannel. On the way back, he switched the CD player through to the basement speakers and cued in a compilation album, which commenced with J S Bach's Mass in F Minor. Down-stairs again, he set the basin on the tabletop, squeezed out the flannel and began to wash Donny from head to foot, humming along to the music as he did so. He had learned long ago that the secret to all good magic was preparation. As he worked on the boy's thighs, Donny moaned and stirred. His eyelids fluttered and he came suddenly awake with a start.

He was shocked to discover that he couldn't move.

'What . . . what the fuck's going on?' he gasped.

'Relax,' Pinder chided him. 'I'm just getting you ready. There's really no need to be afraid.'

Donny struggled against the leather restraints. 'You better let me out of this!' he said. 'Otherwise I'll . . . I'll scream the fucking house down!'

'Oh, you'll scream,' Pinder admitted. 'But let me assure you, nobody will hear a thing. I spent several thousand pounds having this cellar sound-proofed.' He was scrubbing Donny's feet now, removing layer upon layer of ancient grime. 'We'll soon be ready to start,' he said.

Donny closed his eyes and screamed at the top of his lungs but the sound seemed to be absorbed by the acoustic panels set into the ceiling. Pinder smiled and set aside the flannel. He took a soft towel and some baby powder and began to dry the boy thoroughly. Donny screamed again and again, so loud that the muscles of his jaw creaked and the tendons of his neck stood out like strings. Pinder smiled like a proud parent attending a music recital. He reached out a hand and tousled the boy's hair fondly.

'That's the way,' he said. 'As loud as you like.'

He stood back and surveyed his handiwork. 'I think you'll do,' he observed.

Donny screamed again.

'I'd save your strength now if I was you,' murmured Pinder. He took off his jacket and hung it on the side of a metal cabinet. He rolled up the sleeves of his shirt. Then he touched a concealed button and the front of the cabinet tipped forward, wheeled legs dropped from the underside and snapped into position. He now had a metal trolley, laden with his stainless steel surgical instruments: rows of scalpels, cleavers, saws and pliers. There were also some power tools: a drill, a sander, a circular saw. He detached the trolley from its casing and rolled it smoothly up to the table.

Donny's eyes widened in terror. His mouth opened to scream again but no sound came. A pool of urine spread from beneath him, across the steel surface of the table.

Pinder hummed happily to himself as he strapped on his leather apron, the front of it nearly black with congealed blood.

'Let me tell you something about magic, Donny,' he said, as he tied the apron strings behind him. 'It's a constant search for new ideas. It's a marriage between the incredible and the meticulous. I practise every day, it takes hours and hours of intense concentration to perfect a new illusion. Consequently, those things that other people do for entertainment . . . watching television, reading, going to the theatre, dining out . . . those things are denied to me.' He opened a packet of surgical gloves, blew into them and began to pull them on.

Donny was sobbing now, his eyes wide and blank with terror. Pinder turned back to examine the trolley and after a lengthy deliberation, he selected a simple scalpel with which to make the first incision.

'I have learned to take pleasure in other ways,' he concluded. 'I have learned to pack everything into a few occasional short hours of joyful experimentation. And because opportunities are so limited, the pleasure I experience in that time must be intense, total, all-consuming. For me, nothing is as enjoyable as the partnership between hand and eye, working together for once, to effect something that has nothing to do with illusion. Something that is totally and utterly real.'

He turned back to the table. 'Think of this as research. Oh, and do feel free to scream just as much as you want. It won't bother me one little bit. I've grown rather used to it.'

He placed a hand on Donny's chest and probed one of the boy's nipples with an index finger as though unsure of where to begin. Then he seemed to come to a decision. He lifted the blade . . .

. . . and the new scream began to rise in Donny's throat . . .

. . . as Pinder leaned forward across the table . . .

. . . and J S Bach's inspirational music pumped from the stereo speakers . . .

. . . until the screams obliterated it.

Chapter Fifteen

It's getting late, thought Scally.

He was making his way wearily homewards through the darkness after a long day spent scavenging on the streets of the city. It was fully dark now and a thick pall of sulphurous fog had descended, turning the occasional working street lamp into a floating sphere of fuzzy yellow light.

In a sack over his shoulder Scally carried a selection of discarded fruit that he'd picked up from the weekly market. He'd had to stay late till the traders started packing up but he'd been anxious to try and nose out something special for Marianne, something that might tempt her to eat. He was worried about her.

After what had happened at the hands of Frank and the others, she'd been acting stranger than ever, hardly speaking to anyone, jumping at every shadow. She spent her days now crouching like a cornered animal in Scally's shelter, her back pressed to the crumbling brick wall of the arch. And sometimes she simply wept, burying her face in her hands and sobbing like a child, the way she'd done when Frank and his men had finished with her. That was the worst thing of all. It made Scally feel helpless.

And then this morning, when Scally woke, she'd been different again. She'd been squatting in her usual place, rocking herself backwards and forward and she'd seemed excited about something, a big grin on her face like she'd just had some good news. Concerned, Scally had crawled over to her.

'What is it?' he'd asked her.

She'd turned to look at him, her eyes wide and glittering with anticipation.

'He's coming back, Scally. Steve's coming back!'

It had frightened him, her talking like this. He'd begun to think that she really was as mad as everybody said.

'But how can that be?' he asked her. 'Steve is dead.'

'Yes, I know, but I had this dream. Steve came to me and told me . . . he told me that he'd be back soon! He won't look or sound like my Steve but it *will* be him . . .'

'Marianne, that was just a dream. Dreams aren't real.'

She laughed dismissively. 'You don't understand. Scally. Have you ever heard of reincarnation?'

He frowned. 'It's some kind of tinned milk, isn't it?'

Marianne threw back her head and laughed delightedly. People in neighbouring shelters started yelling at her to shut up and Scally had to clamp a hand over her mouth till she'd calmed down. Finally, she was able to continue in a quieter voice.

'Steve and I, *we* believed in it. Steve studied Buddhism. It's a religion. Buddhists believe that life is eternal, that after death, you come back in another form. Steve told me once that if anything ever happened to him, he'd do his best to come back to me. As a dog, or a bird, or a horse.'

'So . . . some *animal* is going to come here?' Scally considered the idea doubtfully. 'Christ, I hope not. Any animal that comes up Sobriety Street is going to get eaten.'

'No. In the dream Steve told me he'll be a man again. A stranger. He said that I'd know him when he arrived. Wherever I happened to be he'd come and find me. So you see, there's no need to be sad any more! All I have to do is wait for him!'

When Scally had left, she'd been rocking again and humming some half-remembered melody to herself. Scally had taken the blackjack from his pocket and pressed it into Marianne's hand.

'If any of them tries anything, you just use this, OK?' She hadn't even looked at the weapon, she seemed to be in some kind of a trance that only the arrival of Steve would dispel. He didn't have the heart to tell her that she was wishing for the impossible.

He'd left the shelter and walked out of the arch, only to

find Frank waiting for him, grinning his horrible shit-eating grin. Scally had been expecting something like this. The Arch Duke had been mumbling thinly veiled threats all week, warning Scally that if Marianne didn't pull herself together pretty soon, there'd have to be some kind of reckoning. Now he delivered his ultimatum.

'This is your last warning,' he said. 'I've had complaints about the girl again, crying and carrying on in the night, disrupting everybody. Either she shapes up and starts pulling her weight, or she's out.'

'She can't help it,' Scally protested. 'After what you did to her, it's no wonder she cries.'

'After what *I* did?' Frank seemed to find this amusing. 'Let me tell you something, kid, nothing happened to that girl that she didn't *want* to happen. Some women are like that. They can't get enough of it. But I bet she isn't giving you any. You should get wise and kick her arse out of your space.'

'I'll never do that,' Scally protested.

'Then feel free to go with her,' suggested Frank. 'Go back to sleeping on the streets in the middle of winter. It'll be no skin off my nose. You think on, lad. And remember what I said. If she's going to stay here any longer, she can learn to pitch in with the work and she can stop her bloody skriking.'

Now that he had shared her with his friends, he seemed to have lost all interest in Marianne. He talked about her as though she was some object that had outlived its usefulness. Scally had never liked Frank but now he hated and despised him. At night, he had dreams about fighting him, slamming Frank's bald head repeatedly against the concrete floor until his skull split open and horrible squirmy things came wriggling out of it. For the moment, it remained just a dream, but Scally had promised himself that if Frank ever laid a hand on Marianne again . . .

He stopped in his tracks as he thought he heard a noise up ahead of him, what sounded like the dull scraping of metal upon stone. He set down his sack for a moment and glanced nervously around, peering through the blanket of fog that surrounded him. He was in a lonely spot, lost in the labyrinth of alleyways and sidestreets behind Piccadilly station. His present route would take him through a long, narrow ginnel that cut between two buildings and connected to a main street a hundred yards ahead. There was a streetlamp a short distance from its entrance and in the unearthly glare, thick coils of yellow mist seemed to boil out from the mouth of the ginnel, making it look like the gates of hell.

Scally tried to laugh off the thought. It was just a ginnel, he told himself, one that he had walked along a thousand times before, morning, noon and night. It was the fog that was making him jumpy. Sure, he could choose another route home if he was *that* worried but it would mean going well out of his way and his young legs were already weary enough.

He shouldered the sack and began walking again, thinking that he'd lived on these streets too long to be frightened by mere shadows. He reached the mouth of the ginnel and once again, he hesitated.

Christ, it's dark in there!

He felt suddenly annoyed with himself. OK, so it was dark, but not so dark he couldn't see where he was going. At this rate, they'd be locking up the arch for the night and he'd be obliged to sleep out on the street, vulnerable to anything that might come clambering up from the banks of the canal.

The thought galvanised him, introducing as it did, the prospect of real fear. He snatched in a deep breath and stepped into the ginnel. The walls reared up on either side of him, cocooning him in a curious dead silence, broken only by the steady thud of his feet on the cobbles. A hundred yards further on, at the far end of the alley, there was another streetlamp and the yellow phosphorescent light seemed to beckon to him.

All right, he thought. *Let's step it out a bit.*

He lengthened his stride a little and pursed his lips to whistle a half-remembered melody, but the enveloping walls sent back a shrill, eerie parody of it that quickly put him off the idea of whistling. The last echo faded back into silence and then he heard the sound behind him. That same noise again, the dull scraping of steel on stone. He froze, glanced back over his shoulder.

He could only see the man in silhouette, a ragged scarecrow

with long hair and a flapping greatcoat. He was following Scally and as he walked, he was scraping something along the wall, something heavy. With the yellow light behind the man, Scally could see only too clearly what it was. A large metal meathook.

Fear ignited in the boy's chest like cold fire and suddenly, he was unable to catch his breath. The man was advancing slowly, almost sauntering and making no secret of the fact that he was there. Which meant . . .

Scally whipped around with a gasp of terror, just in time to see the second man appear at the top of the alley; a dirty dishevelled man bundled up in shapeless rags. At first, like his companion, he was no more than a silhouette but as he moved closer Scally could discern his unnaturally pale features, the festering sores around his mouth, the manic stare in his eyes. And one last terrible detail. The machete clutched in his hand.

The Sub was grinning now, aware of Scally's terror and clearly enjoying it. His teeth were jagged rows of yellow ivory.

'Well, well,' he said. 'Hello little egg. Thou art out a bit late, ain't thee?'

Scally slipped a hand instinctively into his pocket, his fingers searching for the blackjack; then he faltered as he remembered that he'd given the weapon to Marianne. He glanced desperately back over his shoulder. Meathook was still approaching. Sparks danced off the steel hook as it ground against brick.

'Please . . .' whispered Scally. He lifted his eyes to the walls above him, searching frantically for hand holds, a window, some chance of escape. But no, there was nothing. The Subs had chosen their spot well. 'Look,' he pleaded. 'I've got some food. It's yours if you let me go.' With shaking hands he clawed the sack off his shoulder and held it out for inspection. The men were very close now and he was almost gagging on the smell of them, the awful raw stench of the sewers. 'Food!' he yelled. 'I'll give you food.'

Machete smiled wistfully.

'Aye, little egg, that thou will!' he said. He opened his mouth to laugh and Scally saw something white and glistening, pulsing at the back of his throat. He lifted the machete and moved in for the kill.

Scally did the only thing he could do. He threw back his head and screamed for help.

Then they were on him like wolves.

Suzanne sat alone in her living room, staring blankly at the television screen.

It was currently transmitting something called *Feeling Lucky*, a game show in which husbands and wives were blindfolded, then invited to fondle the bodies of people of the opposite sex, the object of the exercise being to recognize the buttocks, breasts or elbows of their respective spouses. The winners were given expensive cosmetic surgery at an exclusive Harley Street clinic. Suzanne thought the programme was the most moronic exercise in self-abasement that she'd ever witnessed, but you couldn't argue with the viewing figures, which had virtually eclipsed everything else in the country.

Suzanne wasn't much interested in watching television tonight. She felt tense, edgy and decidedly lonely. This last week had been the first time she had spent more than a few hours alone in the house since Martin had died. She hadn't heard a word from Will since he'd walked out of the door six days ago and she had no way of knowing where he was staying, what he was up to. Though she'd tried telling herself that he doubtless deserved every discomfort he was experiencing, still she couldn't help worrying. Being back in his company after so long apart had made her realize how much she still cared about him.

Martin, she missed even more. When he approached his seventeenth birthday she'd resigned herself to the fact that soon she'd be losing him. But she couldn't have known how sudden and total that loss would be. Now every room in the house seemed to mourn his absence and Suzanne had begun to wonder if she shouldn't sell up and move somewhere smaller.

Thank God she had her work. She had thrown herself back into it with a vengeance, staying for extra hours, taking on extra responsibilities; but no matter how long she hung around the office, inventing duties for herself, the time came when she had to return to her big empty house, when she had to cook herself a meal and while away the last few hours till bedtime.

And that was the killer. Those hours weighed on her like a lead cloak. They creaked slowly by, every one of them seeming to last three times longer than its allotted span. And all she could find to do to ease them on their way was to sit in front of this brain-numbing goggle box with its garish images and its canned laughter.

So it was almost a welcome interruption when the buzzer at the main gate sounded.

She got up from her chair, went out to the security console in the hallway and flicked on the ViewScan at the gate. She frowned when she saw Don Bullen's weasel face staring up at the screen, a sardonic smile on his thin lips. He'd already phoned her, the day after Will had walked out, wanting to know where he'd gone. Suzanne had given him the arranged story. At the time, he'd seemed happy enough with the explanation.

Suzanne pressed in the 'talk' button. 'What do you want?' she demanded.

Bullen looked wounded by her abruptness. 'Oh now, come on, that's not very friendly, is it? I just wondered if we could have a little talk, Mrs Ambrose. About your husband.'

Suzanne shrugged at the screen, forgetting for the moment, that Bullen couldn't see her. 'Talk away,' she suggested.

He spread his hands in a helpless gesture. 'I can't talk properly like this, now can I? If I could just step inside for a moment?'

She didn't much care for that prospect. 'It's very late to come calling at the house, don't you think?'

Bullen made an exaggerated display of consulting his watch. 'Not that late,' he said. 'Come on, Mrs Ambrose. It won't take long. I mean, I'd prefer to do it this way than go through *official* channels. Of course, if you'd rather I came back with a warrant and some uniforms . . .'

Suzanne sighed. She knew only too well what that entailed. 'Ten minutes,' she told him. 'Then you leave. Understood?'

'Of course.' Bullen grinned cockily at the screen and turned back to his car. Suzanne hit the 'open' button and the gates slid back, admitting the Toyota. Suzanne was already having misgivings about allowing Bullen to visit at such a late hour, remembering the way he had looked at her the last time they'd met; but she also knew that she couldn't afford the embarrassment of a police raid and all the attendant publicity that would arouse. There'd been enough of that kind of thing already.

Still, she wasn't going to take any chances. She went into the kitchen and rooted through the cupboard where she kept the cleaning products. She located what she was looking for hidden away at the back, a can of Mace disguised as an ordinary can of cola. It was something that Adam had given her when she'd first split up with Will. When the ring tab was pulled, a button popped up and a cloud of blinding fumes could be directed into the face of an assailant.

Suzanne placed the can on the coffee table in front of the sofa, then went to answer the doorbell. Bullen was standing on the step, his legs crossed in a nonchalant pose, one arm raised and propped against the door jamb. He grinned at Suzanne oafishly.

'Evening, Mrs Ambrose. Got the kettle on, have you?'

Suzanne wrinkled her nose as she caught the smell of alcohol on his breath. She thought about asking him to come back tomorrow but he was already pushing past her into the hallway, gazing confidently about, as though he owned the place.

'Very nice,' he said approvingly. 'You've got good taste, Mrs Ambrose. At least in *most* things.'

Suzanne closed the door and turned to face him. 'It's late,' she reminded him. 'What can I do for you?'

'Coffee would be nice,' he told her, strolling through into the living room. 'Milk, one sugar. Instant will be fine.'

Suzanne gritted her teeth, then followed him. 'Now look,' she said. 'I was just about to . . .'

But Bullen had stopped in front of the TV and was staring at the screen. 'It's great this, isn't it? Did you see it last week? There were a couple of newlyweds who—'

But Suzanne had picked up the remote and turned the television off. 'What exactly is this about?' she asked him.

In reply, he walked through to the kitchen. He spotted the kettle, checked it had water in it, then switched it on. He turned to look at her, leaning back against the worktop.

'All alone then, Mrs Ambrose? Or can I call you Suzanne?'

'Mrs Ambrose will do fine,' she assured him. 'And yes, I'm alone. Not that it's any of your business.'

He chuckled gleefully. 'You're a cool one, you are. You should learn to relax a bit more. Stop taking everything so serious.'

'Look, is there a point to this?' she snapped. 'I've had a busy day and I'd like to go to bed.'

As soon as she'd said it, she regretted it. He was staring at her intently, like a dog reacting to a high pitched whistle. He probably interpreted the remark as some kind of come on.

'Don't flatter yourself,' she advised him.

He smiled thinly. 'Can't blame a bloke for trying. I mean, don't get me wrong, but you are a good-looking woman. Your old man must have been off his head to walk out on you.'

'Off his head?' Suzanne gave him a scornful look. 'Or devastated to learn that everything he believed in was a big fat lie? Because he was framed by colleagues who he'd thought he could trust. People like you, Inspector Bullen.'

Bullen smirked. 'Yeah, well he would tell you that, wouldn't he? 'Course he would. Devious people these druggies.'

Suzanne sighed. She knew it was pointless to argue the case. Bullen was like all the others, programmed to uphold the police version of the story, even when talking off the record. Perhaps these people lived in constant fear of concealed tape recorders. At any rate, the sooner she got him to cough up his reason for being there, the sooner he'd be out of here. She didn't much care for the way he was staring at her.

'You'll recall, I gave you ten minutes,' she reminded him. She lifted a wrist to glance at her watch. 'You're almost out of time.'

There was a silence interrupted only by the sound of the kettle coming to the boil.

'You're a hard woman,' observed Bullen, regretfully. 'What about that coffee?'

'You won't have time to drink it. Now if we can get to the point, *please*.'

Bullen's eyes narrowed down to slits. 'Well, if you must know, I was wondering if you could tell me the whereabouts of your husband.'

Suzanne gave a tut of annoyance. 'You know perfectly well where he is. As I've already told you, he went back to Southport.'

'Is that right? Well, it's very strange, Mrs Ambrose. You see, he hasn't returned to his previous address.' Bullen took an electronic notebook from his pocket and punched a few buttons. 'Let me see now. Ah yes, a Miss Molina. She claims she hasn't seen him since he left to visit his son.'

'Molina?' Suzanne raised her eyebrows inquisitively. It wasn't a name she was familiar with.

'Yeah. *Roxy* Molina,' said Bullen gleefully. 'Didn't you know? That's the woman he's been living with for the past year. I'm surprised he didn't mention it.'

Despite herself, Suzanne felt a stab of irrational jealousy. She told herself it shouldn't matter, but nonetheless it seemed to. Why hadn't Will told her that there was somebody else?

'It . . . it's really nothing to do with me,' she told Bullen. 'My husband and I are estranged. We've lived apart for two years. Our lives are our own.'

'Yeah, but who'd have figured it, eh? Leaving you for somebody like *that*. A bleedin' fortune teller.' He saw the reaction on Suzanne's face and went on trying to goad her. 'Oh yes, that's what she is, Mrs Ambrose. A gyppo. Sits in a little booth on the pier telling fortunes for a fiver a shot. Not much to look at either. Small, dark skinned, lots of cheap jewellery. You know the type. A bit . . . what's the word? Exotic. Mind you, looks like she's been about a bit, know what I mean? Looks like she'd know what to do with it . . .'

Suzanne turned away from him and gazed out of the window at the dark garden. She could see her own pale reflection staring sullenly back at her.

'Yes, well, this is all quite fascinating, Inspector, but as

I've already told you, I don't have the slightest idea where Will is. He certainly told me he was heading for Southport and I have no reason to doubt him. He left straight after the funeral and I haven't seen him since. Why are you so anxious to trace him?'

Bullen dropped a hand reflexively to his crutch, forgetting that Suzanne could see the gesture, reflected in the kitchen window.

'Something I wanted to discuss with him,' he muttered. 'And if he really is in Southport, he's keeping his head well down.'

Suzanne turned back to face Bullen. She felt a little more in control of her emotions now and she favoured him with a frosty smile.

'Must be a new skill he's acquired,' she said. 'He was never much good at that before.' She consulted her wristwatch again. 'And now, if you don't mind, it's time you were going.'

He stepped forward and laid a hand on her shoulder, setting alarm bells shrilling in her head.

'There's still time for that coffee,' he said quietly.

She twisted away, took his elbow and began to steer him through into the living room.

'Sorry. I'm fresh out.' She pointed to the can on the coffee table. 'A cola perhaps?' she ventured.

He shook his head, patted his stomach. 'Gives me gas,' he said.

She almost laughed at the unconscious irony of the remark. She kept him on the move towards the hall.

'If you should hear from him, you'll be sure and let me know?' he asked her.

'Oh naturally,' she lied. Anything to be rid of him. 'And you be sure and do the same.' She opened the door for him and nearly threw him out onto the porch. But he turned back, not quite ready to be dismissed.

''Scuse me, Mrs Ambrose, but you don't seem very concerned.'

'I beg your pardon?'

'About your husband. I mean, he isn't where he told you he'd be. To all intents and purposes, he's gone missing. Could

156

be floating in the ship canal for all you know. Could be lying in a shallow grave somewhere with his head smashed in.'

Suzanne smiled politely.

'He's well able to look after himself,' she assured him.

'And what about you?' he asked. 'Are you able to look after yourself?' He looked slowly around at the darkened gardens. 'Big place, Mrs Ambrose. Quiet. Must get very lonely stuck here all by yourself. You know, if you ever get worried or nervous about being alone, you just ring the station and ask for me. I'll come over and keep you company.'

'How very kind,' said Suzanne frostily.

'Not at all. It's like I said, an attractive woman like you can't hide her light under a bushel for ever. The time soon comes when you start wanting company. *Male* company.' He waggled his eyebrows meaningfully.

'That's very true,' she admitted. 'Unfortunately, I'd be looking for something a little higher up the food chain. No offence.'

He opened his mouth to reply and she slammed the door in his face, leaving him standing there on the porch, probably trying to absorb the insult she'd just dealt him. Suzanne went back to the ViewScan screen and watched as he climbed dejectedly into his car. She opened up the gates for him and stayed by the screen until she was sure that he was gone and the gates were secured behind him. Then she switched off the ViewScan, locked the front door and went upstairs to bed.

But sleep eluded her for a long time, that night. She lay there thinking about the mysterious Roxy, the lover that Will had lived with for more than a year and had neglected to mention to her. She wondered what the woman was really like and whether she was a lover or just a friend. More than anything else, she wondered why it mattered so much to her.

After all, Will was nothing to her now. So why was she beginning to worry about what he was doing tonight? Where he was sleeping. Whether he'd had enough to eat.

Then it came on her suddenly, a terrible sense of foreboding, a dark chill of premonition. Will was in danger. Somewhere out there on the cold streets of the city, bad things were happening to him. She knew it with the certainty that only comes when the night is long and weary and sleep seems so very far away.

Chapter Sixteen

The scream broke into Will's consciousness with all the delicacy of a brick smashing through a plate glass window. He opened his eyes and lay there blinking for a moment, unsure of where he was.

Then he remembered. Cold, hungry and exhausted after a long day spent trekking around the streets of the city, he'd finally lowered his aching body into the meagre shelter of a shop doorway on Oldham Street, where he'd fallen quickly into a shallow doze. Now something had woken him, the sound of somebody in trouble, somewhere close at hand . . .

The scream came again, a shrill cry of pure terror, echoing on the foggy night air. The sound of a young boy.

'Martin?' Will didn't know what made him think of his dead son, but an image of Martin's frightened face rose into his mind, like a ghost surfacing from a pool of still water. It galvanized Will into movement, making him claw himself upright and push himself out onto the street. He stood for a moment, trying to determine from which direction the cry had come.

'Help me!' The yell, so urgent, so desperate, came from somewhere to Will's left, amidst the warren of back streets and alleys that led down to Piccadilly station. It was the sound of somebody in a desperate plight and Will moved instinctively towards it, first at a trot, then quickening to a run as he fully registered the urgency of the plea.

He turned off the main street and ran along an intersection. Up ahead of him, he could see the mouth of a narrow ginnel, lit by the flat glare of a street lamp. A thick fog blanketed the ginnel but Will was aware of movement within it, a violent scuffle that he could hear but not see.

'Please!' The boy's voice implored him and he threw caution to the wind and sprinted into the ginnel. Ahead of him he saw a struggle taking place, a young boy pinned against a wall by two ragged assailants. One of them had a machete which he was trying to push down at the boy's throat; but the boy had hold of the man's wrists and was pushing back with all his might, his sheer terror lending him a strength that belied his tender years. The second attacker was standing slightly to one side. He had a big, double-handed meathook held ready to strike and appeared to be waiting for a clear shot at the boy's head, but for the moment, his partner kept getting in the way.

Will felt a shrill of fear go through him when he registered the weapons but his own impetus was too much to allow him to check his pace. As he ran up to the attackers, he let out a loud yell in the hope that the sound of it would be enough to put them to flight. But in that he was disappointed.

Meathook turned to face Will and he grinned malevolently, lifting the weapon above his head. Machete gave Will a cursory glance, then calmly carried on with what he was doing.

Will finally managed to check his pace, coming to a halt only a few feet from Meathook. He lifted his hands in a placatory gesture, but at the same time he was searching for an opening, knowing that he daren't take too long over it, that the boy was rapidly losing his one-sided struggle with his adversary.

'Do thyself a favour, Streeter,' growled Meathook, in a strange glottal sounding voice. 'Turn thee around and walk away.'

Up close, Will was suddenly aware of the smell of the man, an awful faecal stench of filth and decay that made his gorge rise.

'Sorry,' he muttered. 'My mistake.' He began to turn away and Meathook relaxed a little, returned his attention to the matter at hand. That was when Will made his move, utilizing skills he'd acquired on the force and had thought he'd forgotten. He leapt forward, lashing a kick into the back of the man's knee and grabbing a handful of greasy hair, he yanked back hard, tipping him off balance. As the man fell, Will drove his right fist hard into Meathook's face, feeling the nose flattening under his knuckles. Meathook went down hard, his shoulders slamming against cobbles. A grunt of exhaled air escaped him and he lay there, dazed.

Will didn't pay him any more attention. He advanced on Machete who, realizing what had happened, shouldered the boy roughly aside and span around to face Will. The boy slid down the wall momentarily exhausted. When he tried to scramble upright, Machete slammed a foot down onto his chest, pinning him to the ground.

'Stay where thou art, little egg!' he said. 'I'm not finished with thee yet!'

'Let him go,' said Will, with a calmness that surprised him.

Machete laughed derisively. 'This pup's mine,' he snarled, in a voice that seemed barely human. 'Go find thy own, Streeter!' He tightened his grip on the handle of the machete and the blade glinted wickedly in the glow of the streetlamp.

Will took a tentative step closer, then jumped back with an oath as Machete swung at him, the tip of the blade cleaving the air scant inches from Will's chest. Machete laughed wildly and a thick froth of spittle bubbled on his lips.

'Come on, Streeter,' he mocked. 'Nearly lost thy guts that time, didn't thee? Just give me one good thwack at thy pretty head . . .'

He swung again, directly overhead this time, aiming to split Will's skull open like a melon; but Will flung up his left hand, deflected the weapon to one side and slammed his right fist hard into the man's gut. Machete doubled over in agony and he dropped to his knees retching violently. He made a strange choking sound and then something long and glistening slid from his open mouth and fell with a loud slap on the cobbles.

Will shrank back in revulsion. It was a huge, flat-headed worm, some ten or twelve inches in length. It was pearly white, the body jointed in several sections and the head crowned with a purple orifice that must have been a mouth. It was wriggling frantically across the cobbles, like a stranded eel suddenly deprived of water.

Machete seemed to have forgotten all about the fight. He dropped his weapon and scrambled after the worm on hands and knees, making frantic little whimpering noises as he did

161

so. He tried to pick up the worm, but its slimy body slipped from his fingers and slithered away. It came to a drain cover, slid between the metal bars and fell into the blackness beneath.

Machete made a desperate keening sound. He kneeled beside the drain, his filthy fingers plucking at the metal cover as though trying to implore the worm to come back to him.

Will had watched the ghastly scene played out in a kind of dumbstruck trance. He'd never seen anything so disgusting in his life. Even when Machete got back to his feet and came menacingly towards him, Will remained rooted to the spot, staring in horrified fascination at the drain cover.

Once again, it was the boy's cry that woke him from his trance.

'Look out!'

Will sensed, rather than saw, a movement behind him, just as Machete was reaching out his hands to claw at Will's throat. He ducked sideways and the steel hook skimmed his left shoulder and buried itself in Machete's cheek. The bloody point erupted from the man's throat in a squirt of blood and he fell backwards from the impact, pulling a still-dazed Meathook with him. The two of them went sprawling onto the cobbles in a tangle of arms and legs. Suddenly, there was a hand tugging at Will's sleeve.

'Come on, let's get the fuck out of here!'

Glancing down, Will saw the young boy staring imploringly up at him. For the first time it occurred to him that he had seen the boy somewhere before but for the moment, he couldn't remember where.

Will gestured down at the fallen figures. Meathook was clumsily trying to disengage the weapon from Machete's face but it had got stuck and the man's head was bobbing up and down like some obscene marionette, the eyes staring up in dull surprise, not quite dead but well on the way. A huge puddle of blood was spreading outwards around his skull.

'That *thing* . . .' croaked Will. 'That . . . *worm*.'

'Come *on*!' the boy commanded him. He stooped, picked up a fallen sack and swung it onto his shoulder. Then he grabbed Will's arm and began to drag him away.

'But . . .' murmured Will. 'Who . . . what are they?'

'Subs,' the boy told him. 'They're Subs. Don't you know about them?'

Meathook had placed a foot on Machete's throat now and was pulling with all his strength, swearing rhythmically as he did so, the tip of the hook grinding against bone and ivory. Machete's chest was still feebly rising and falling, making wheezy gasping sounds like a ruptured accordion.

Will turned away in disgust, aware of a surge of nausea rising within him but also knowing that he had nothing in his stomach to vomit up. He followed the boy out of the ginnel.

From behind him, a long ullulating bellow of rage echoed off the walls, prompting Will and the boy to break into a run. The two of them raced in silence along the foggy street, into the unfamiliar night, both hoping against hope that nobody was following them.

Down in the cellar of his house, Pinder set about disposing of Donny's remains. Even opened up and bloodily eviscerated, Donny's face remained a picture of angelic contentment, his eyes closed as if in sleep, his blond hair tumbled about him like a golden halo.

He had been deceptively strong though, had gone on screaming lustily, even when his chest cavity had been opened and Pinder had felt the boy's heart, beating like a drum in the palm of his hand.

But all good times had to come to an end eventually and as ever, after one of his experiments, Pinder felt a powerful melancholy enveloping him. He found a flower, a single white lily and pressed it into one of the boy's lifeless hands. Then he reached forward and kissed him gently on his unresponsive lips.

This made him think of his mother. She was long dead now and Pinder rarely thought of her. When he did, it was with anger. Mother had never liked kissing and touching. She had always maintained that it was dirty, a way of passing diseases from one person to another. How she had ever given birth to a child in the first place was puzzling. There was no Father anywhere in evidence, not even any men friends. At Sunday School, Pinder had been told about the Immaculate Conception and had decided that his birth must have come about by a similar arrangement. The inevitable result of this was the firm conviction that he was the son of God, a state of affairs that gave him an incredible superiority complex which remained with him for the rest of his life.

When he was around six years old, Mother had discovered Pinder playing Postman's Knock with a little girl who lived down the street. She had taken him indoors and made him eat a large bar of carbolic soap. He had never forgotten it and he had always known that he would have his revenge. Many years later, his Mother became bedridden with rheumatism. Pinder had told her that he wouldn't dream of having her placed in a nursing home. He had assured the authorities that he would take care of her every need and had even prepared a bedroom for her on the top floor of his house.

That first evening, he had carried a tray of supper up to her room. Beside the plate was a saucer containing a bar of carbolic soap. He had explained to her calmly that she would have no food until every piece of the soap was eaten. Of course, that first night, she told him to go to hell and she held out for a very long time. Almost a week elapsed before hunger forced her finally to submit to his commands. She had probably thought that this was to be a one-off punishment but he soon put her straight on that notion. There were many nights over the remaining years of her life when he would sit there, watching the old woman gag and retch, knowing that the sweetest revenge was the one that had been a long time coming. And when his mother finally succumbed to a heart attack, some three years later, she must have been the proud possessor of the cleanest stomach in Britain.

On the CD player, the orchestra slipped into a silky version of Albinoni's Adagio for Strings and Pinder was aware of tears brimming in his eyes. One large drop ran along his ruined nose and fell with a plop onto Donny's forehead. Pinder reflected on the awful sadness and savagery of city life and thanked his lucky stars that he had somehow managed to rise above it. He thought too how unlucky Donny had been, appearing as he had, just as Pinder was contemplating what he wanted to do to the boy who had injured him.

Donny had simply been in the wrong place at the wrong time. Life could be a bitch sometimes.

Pinder went into the adjoining room and fired up the big gas incinerator, peering in through the observation window at the powerful jets of flame, rising up from the floor of the chamber. The incinerator had already been down here when he purchased the place, an ancient, rusting contraption that hadn't been used in decades. It had cost him a small fortune to restore it to full working order but it had been worth every penny. The flames were powerful enough to dispose of all his little indiscretions, reducing each of them to a couple of handfuls of clean white ash.

He went back to the rehearsal room, humming Albinoni's mournful melody as he did so. He slid his hands beneath Donny's lifeless body and gently lifted him onto a hospital trolley. He wheeled this through into the next room, then opened the door of the incinerator. He felt the fierce heat of it caressing his face. Donning padded gloves, he pulled out an extending platform of metal rollers, transferred the body onto it and pushed it feet-first up to the doorway. He paused for a moment for a final look at his handiwork.

'Goodnight sweet prince,' he murmured; and he kissed the unresponsive lips once again. Then he pushed the platform back into position. The body slid smoothly feet-first into the flames. Pinder slammed the door and moved to the observation window to watch. Donny's face gazed beatifically back at him, an upside-down Adonis, a bewitching smile on his lips. As Pinder watched, Donny's golden hair blackened and bubbled, erupted into orange flames. Pinder stayed at the window, watching until the boy's face began to pucker and melt like hot plastic. Then, turning away, he removed the leather apron and returned it to its hiding place in the concealed cabinet.

He felt tired after his efforts but very content. All he needed now, he decided, to bring the evening to a satisfactory conclusion, was a mug of hot cocoa and the Times crossword. He climbed wearily back upstairs, switching off the lights behind him.

Chapter Seventeen

Will's lungs felt as though they were going to explode. He'd been following the boy at top speed through the labyrinth of darkened streets for what he judged to be the past fifteen minutes, switching left, right, sometimes doubling back on themselves. But weak and hungry as he was, Will was rapidly nearing the point of total exhaustion.

'Hang on a minute!' he gasped. He stopped running and slumped down with his back against a wall, panting like a dog. The boy halted and came back to crouch beside his companion. He appeared to be breathing quite normally. He peered back the way they had come but after a few minutes, seemed satisfied that they were not being followed. He relaxed a little; then presumably remembering what had just happened, he held out a hand for Will to shake.

'Thanks,' he said. 'I owe you one. If you hadn't come along, they'd have finished me for sure.'

Will's breathing was gradually settling back to a more regular rhythm.

'But who . . . *what* were they?' he croaked.

'Subs,' said the boy, as if this were explanation enough. Then seeing the blank expression on Will's face, he added, 'They live in the sewers.'

Will stared at him. 'People live . . . in the sewers?' he said. The boy nodded.

'I know what you're thinking. I used to believe it was just a story too. Till I saw them.'

'And . . . that thing . . .' Will waved a hand towards his mouth. 'The thing that came out of him. What the fuck was that?'

The boy shrugged. 'I think they all have them,' he said. 'At least, all the ones I've seen. I've only bumped into them once before, mind.' He seemed to remember something and he stuck his hand out again. 'Scally,' he said. 'That's what they call me.'

Will smiled, did the handshake a second time. 'Will,' he said. 'Will Ambrose. Good to meet you.'

'Yeah, well, like I say. I owe you one. Anything I can do, you just let me know.'

Will eyed the boy hopefully. 'You . . . I don't suppose you've got any food? I . . . I haven't eaten properly for days.'

'No problem.' Scally unslung the sack from his shoulder and opened it for inspection. It contained several pounds of bruised fruit and vegetables, some of it bordering the state where 'ripe' became 'rotten'. But Will was too hungry to care about that. He grabbed an apple, ignoring the way his fingertips sank into it and began to devour it in a series of ravenous bites, swallowing it down, core and all. He reached for a black banana, peeled it and squashed it into his mouth in one swift movement.

Scally watched in quiet amusement. 'You weren't kidding!' he observed. 'You really ain't eaten for days, have you?'

'No,' said Will, through a mouthful of pulped banana. 'I'm . . . kind of new at this game.'

'What game?' muttered Scally, passing him another apple.

'At . . . living rough. Being homeless. I've only been on the streets about a week. I don't know where to go to get food.'

'There's plenty of places,' Scally told him. 'Like, today is market day, right? You got to get to know the market traders. They always have stuff they can't sell, but you got to give 'em a reason to give it to *you*. So I do a few jobs for 'em, you know, help 'em carry boxes and stuff. Then I get first pick at what they throw away.' He gestured dismissively at the bag. 'This is nothing,' he said. 'Most days I eat a lot better than this.' He handed Will a last pear, then closed up the bag. 'Can't let you have any more,' he said. 'Got to keep some to take back to The Arch.'

'The Arch? What's that?'

'It's my shelter. I'm with the Ardwick tribe.' He got to his feet and lifted the sack back onto his shoulder. 'I should be getting back there really. It's kind of late to be out. That's how I got into trouble. Maybe I'll see you round, some time . . .'

'Hey, wait! Hang on a moment. This Arch . . . would there be room for me?'

Scally looked doubtful. 'I dunno. It's kind of crowded in there just now. Frank's turned a lot of people away the last couple of weeks.' Scally began to walk on but Will fell into step beside him, still munching his pear and talking with a full mouth.

'Frank. Who's he?'

'Oh, he's the head man of the tribe. What we call the Duke.'

'Maybe I could talk to him.'

Scally frowned. 'I don't know,' he said. 'He ain't really the kind you want to talk to. I mean, don't get me wrong, I'd let you kip in my space for a day or so, if he said it was OK, but . . . well, there's Marianne staying with me, so it's already kind of crowded.'

'Marianne? She your sister?'

'No. She's sort of like . . .' Scally's face deepened a darker shade of red. 'She's sort of like my girlfriend, I guess.'

'Couldn't you squeeze me in?' Will begged him. 'Just for a night or two. I wouldn't take up much room.'

'Well, see, it ain't really up to me . . .'

'Last couple of nights I've slept in shop doorways, park benches. It gets so cold at night. See, I'm new to this Scally, I could do with someone to show me the ropes.' Will nudged him in the ribs. 'And you *did* say you owed me one. God knows what would have happened to you if I hadn't come along . . .'

Scally made an expression of disgust. 'I know what would have happened,' he said. 'They'd have taken me below.'

'Below?'

Scally closed his eyes for a moment, then nodded. 'Down into the sewers. They'd have dragged me down there in the dark. Like they did to my friend, Gyppo.'

Will stared at him aghast, forgetting his own worries for a moment.

'Those people . . . took your friend? By force?'

Scally rolled his eyes. 'Well he didn't go down there for the fun of it, did he!'

'What . . . what happened to him?'

'I don't know. But I never saw him again, I'll tell you that much. They took him down there and he never came out.'

'Christ.' Will reviewed some of the things that he'd seen and heard in the last few minutes and could hardly believe the evidence of his own eyes and ears. It was as though venturing into the world of the Rag People was like cutting through one level of reality into another alternate world, where all the rules were different. He thought about all those middle-class people living their quiet ordinary lives in their centrally heated homes, unaware of the horrors that existed out on the streets of their city. How could it all be so different now? Perhaps it was simply that living among the Rag People put you so much closer to the ugly truths of everyday life.

The Subs. He wondered if Clive knew anything about them. Could they be the explanation for some of those 'missing' Rag People? Had they simply given up walking the streets of the city and opted instead to live down in the filth and stench of the sewers, finding their sustenance amongst the detritus discarded by the people who lived above their heads? If he'd still been living with Suzanne in her grand house in the suburbs, he'd have dismissed the idea as unthinkable; but here on the streets, it was somehow much easier to accept. As there was a hierarchy amongst those who had homes, so perhaps there was one here.

Maybe the Subs were the ones who couldn't find anyone to take them in, who found it impossible to exist in the world of the Rag People. Dispossessed even at this level, had they quite literally descended even further, to the dark, wet labyrinths that ran beneath the city streets? But if all this was true, why did they occasionally return to the world above their heads? And why did they take children back with them?

Will shuddered. He didn't want to think about that just now. He made an effort to draw his mind back to the matter at hand. 'So Scally, you'll have a word with him, will you? This Frank.'

Scally looked apprehensive. 'He won't listen to what I say!' he protested. 'I'm just a kid. I'm just about hanging on myself.

He's been trying to get me to throw Marianne out for the last week.'

'Oh. Why's that?'

'He . . . says she's crazy. And she doesn't pull her weight. But . . . she's been through a bad time. I can't just ask her to leave, now can I?' Scally sighed. 'Anyway, look, the best I can do is take you to him and see what he says.'

'I've heard a man can barter his way in,' said Will.

'Yeah, well it depends what you've got to offer.'

Will reached into his pocket and pulled out the nose ring he'd taken from Chilli Dog.

'It's real silver,' he said. 'It's got a hallmark and everything.'

Scally looked impressed.

'It might buy you a few days,' he admitted. 'Frank could get a lot of booze in exchange for something like that.'

They had reached the side of Piccadilly station now – and suddenly, Will remembered where he'd seen the boy before. He'd been begging when Will got off the train from Southport. But if Scally remembered Will from that brief meeting, he wasn't letting on. He led him across the road and around the corner on to Sobriety Street. Will paused for a moment to take in the scene.

Along the wide stretch of the viaduct, he saw the open doors of a series of railway arches, each of them lit by the glare of kerosine lamps which were hung either side of the door. Around the arches, crowds of Rag People milled about, talking, trading, cooking food in large caldrons over open fires. To Will's astonished gaze, it resembled a medieval painting by Bosch or Breughel. He followed Scally through the crowds, gazing dumbly about at the various characters that surrounded him; here, a big tattooed man was bartering with a red-faced woman for a rusty axe; there, a group of young children were squabbling noisily for the possession of a broken, plastic toy. Will became aware of eyes appraising him: suspicious eyes, mocking eyes, friendly eyes.

He pushed past a voluptuous woman in a blonde wig, her face powdered and rouged into a parody of sexual allure. She was wearing a low cut blouse despite the cold and was lifting her skirts to every passer-by to reveal long legs covered with

170

tattered, laddered stockings. She crooked a finger at Will and rolled her tongue lasciviously around her mouth.

'Here's a new face,' she observed loudly. 'Would you like me to sit on it for a while?'

Will ignored her and followed Scally into the crowd. He noticed now that nearly everyone was wearing a green armband. They came to an improvised rostrum edging the wasteland to their right where a black man in a long grey raincoat was delivering an impassioned sermon to a crowd of jeering Rag People.

'Mark you, the time is at hand!' he roared, in a thick Rastafarian accent. 'Repent ye before the cataclysm overtakes us all! In nineteen ninety-nine the world will be plunged into a terrible conflagration. Not a one will survive. Jahwe plans to scourge the world of all his mistakes and start all over again . . .'

A chorus of laughs and catcalls drowned the man's words as Scally and Will passed by. At last they neared what had to be Scally's arch. He slowed to a halt and waited for Will to catch up with him. He nodded towards a crowd of men who were sitting around a packing crate, playing poker with a deck of grubby cards. There were a few coins on the improvised table and several other items as well: squares of chocolate, assorted vegetables, a keyring, a child's plastic toy. Most of the items resided in front of a tall, thin man with a bald head, a sharp nose and cruel grey eyes. He glanced up from his cards and fixed Will with a scowl of disapproval. Will knew instantly that this was the Duke, Frank, even before he registered the gold armband he was wearing.

'Leave the talking to me,' suggested Scally. He took a step closer.

'Who's the outsider?' muttered Frank, nodding curtly in Will's direction.

'Friend of mine,' Scally told him. 'I got into some bother tonight. I was jumped by a couple of Subs and he helped me out.'

'Oh yeah?' Frank examined Will for a moment, weighing him up. He didn't seem to care for what he saw. 'And I'm supposed to be grateful for that, am I?' He grinned crookedly

171

at Will. 'You should have left the kid to it and saved me a whole lot of trouble,' he said after a few minutes' deliberation. He jerked his thumb at a bubbling cooking pot just inside the entrance to the arch. 'Well, anyway, help yourself to a bowl of Pot Luck before you leave,' he concluded. He was about to go on with his card game but Will moved closer.

'I'd like to stay here,' he said. 'I'd like to be part of the tribe.'

Frank stared at him flatly for a moment. 'I bet you would,' he said. 'So would a lot of people. But we're already pretty crowded.' He lifted a hand to scratch at his thickly stubbled chin. 'Unless you could find someone who was willing to share his space . . .'

'He could kip with me,' offered Scally. 'Until he found a place of his own. Like I said, he helped me out tonight. I figure I owe him.'

This seemed to amuse Frank. He laid his cards face down on the table, glanced at his companions, then laughed derisively. 'I'd say you're crowded enough as it is,' he observed. 'Unless of course you're planning to tell the mad woman to take a hike?'

'I can't do that.'

Frank shrugged. 'And I can't ask this arch to find food for another mouth,' he said. He glanced at Will. 'Sorry friend, you'd best have some stew and be on your way.'

'Maybe you'll trade with me,' suggested Will desperately. Now he was here, within sight of light and shelter, the thought of going back to sleeping alone in shop doorways was more than he could bear.

Frank sighed. 'That would depend on what you've got to offer,' he said.

Will slipped a hand into his coat pocket and withdrew the nose-ring. He threw it down onto the packing crate.

'Real silver,' he said. 'Worth more than any of the stuff you're playing for.'

For a moment Frank didn't say anything. Then he picked up the ring between thumb and forefinger and examined it carefully. He nodded. 'Oh aye, it's silver all right,' he admitted. 'How did you come by it?'

'Just picked it up,' Will told him. 'Anyway, what do you reckon? Can we make a deal?'

Frank didn't answer that. He lifted his head and glanced back into the arch. A big man came out from the interior and stood just outside the light of the kerosine lamp, his face hidden in shadow. Frank turned back to Will with an oily smile.

'There *is* another way of joining,' he said. 'You might care to try your hand at that.'

Will stared at him suspiciously. 'What way?' he asked.

'You have to fight somebody. No holds barred. You win the fight, you get to stay. You take the place of the man you've beaten. Simple as that.'

Will swallowed uncomfortably. 'I've no intention of taking anyone's place,' he insisted. 'You heard Scally, here, he's willing to let me share, so . . .'

Frank grinned unpleasantly. 'I don't think it's such a good idea,' he said. 'Putting you in a confined space with a pretty young boy and a lusty young woman. You wouldn't know which way to turn next, would you?'

There was some coarse laughter from Frank's companions. Will felt his face colour up, but he did his best to dismiss the slur.

'Look, I thought we were going to trade,' he said.

Frank shook his head regretfully. 'A man can't barter with what don't belong to him.' He lifted a hand and flung the ring over his shoulder, into the arch. It was caught by a massive fist as the tall figure came striding out into the light of the torches.

'Oh shit,' said Will, under his breath.

It was the man called Chilli Dog, his nose bruised and swollen from Will's attack earlier that day. He stood there looking at Will, a sneer on his bearded face as though he was looking at an unfortunate insect that he was about to crush under his foot.

'This the man?' asked Frank quietly.

Chilli Dog nodded. 'That's him,' he said.

'Well, he's got some balls,' Frank admitted. 'Stealing from Chilli Dog. That must be a first. Fact is, friend, we were going to come looking for you tomorrow but you've kind of saved us the trouble.'

'Look,' said Will, 'I didn't exactly steal it, OK? Me and him, we had a dispute over some food. When it was finished, I realized I still had the ring in my hand. Well, I was hardly going to go looking for him to hand it back, was I?'

'A dispute, eh?' Frank glanced at Chilli Dog inquiringly. 'You never mentioned that.'

'He wad oudda line,' snorted Chilli Dog. 'Id wad my reg'lar pidge. He tore my fuggin' nose half off my face!'

'I was desperate!' protested Will. 'I hadn't eaten for . . .'

Frank held up his hands for silence. 'Enough!' he shouted. 'You'll each have a chance to make your claim, in the time-honoured fashion.' He glanced quickly around, then getting up from the card table, he grabbed what looked like a battery-operated karaoke machine and slung it across his shoulder. He strode across to the soap box preacher and yanked him rudely down off his rostrum, sending him sprawling into the mud behind him. Then, hopping up in his place, he activated the karaoke machine, lifted the microphone to his mouth and yelled a single word at the top of his lungs.

'DISPUTE!'

The reaction from the crowd was instant and unanimous, a full-throated roar of approval. People began to converge on the card table and the next thing Will knew, he was being swept up, he was being pushed, shoved, kicked in the direction of the wasteland across from the viaduct. Will looked down uncertainly to see Scally being pushed along beside him.

'What the fuck's happening?' he yelled.

'You're fighting,' said Scally apprehensively. 'You and Chilli Dog.'

'Supposing I don't want to fight him?'

'I don't think you have a choice.'

Will saw Chilli Dog a short distance away to his left. He too was being herded onto the wasteland by a crowd of cheering, backslapping admirers. He pointed a finger at Will and bellowed like a bull.

'Dis tibe I ready for you, boy,' he roared, his eyes blazing with hatred. 'I goada pull your fuggin' arms off and beat you to death wid 'em!'

Will glanced nervously down at Scally.

'What . . . what kind of a fight?' he gasped. 'I mean, what are the rules?'

Scally rolled his eyes at Will. 'I told you to let me do the talking,' he said.

Will glanced desperately around, looking for some avenue of escape, but there was none. He was completely immersed in a sea of shouting, running figures. He was being propelled towards the dark mound of an unlit bonfire. As he drew near it, there was a sudden whoosh and the stench of petrol. The bonfire erupted in a blaze of orange flame and Will could feel the heat of it on his face. Ahead of him, he saw that the crowd was forming itself into a circle. He winced as a hard hand came down with a clap on his shoulder. Glancing back, he saw Frank's ugly face grinning at him.

'Now, Outsider, we'll see if you've got the balls to join us after all. Here, grab hold of this.' Something was thrust into his hand and glancing down, he saw it was an ancient baseball bat, the hickory horribly dented and stained dark with what could only have been dried human blood.

'For fuck's sake,' he said. 'What are the rules here?'

'Rules?' Frank looked amused.

'There must be some rules. Or is the winner the man left standing?'

'Usually it's the man left *living*,' Frank corrected him. 'No offence but my money's on Chilli Dog.'

As Will stumbled onwards through the crowd, hands began to tear at his clothes, stripping off his raincoat, pulling his shirt up over his head. Stripped to the waist, he moved into the circle. Now a man was tying a length of thick rope tightly around his left wrist. Will saw that the rope was some ten feet in length and that the other end was being secured to Chilli Dog's wrist. In his right hand, Chilli Dog held an identical baseball bat. He was twirling it around as though it had no more substance than a drumstick while smiling malevolently at Will, eager to strike the first blow.

It was about this point in the proceedings that Will was struck by the terrible irony of it. He had come amongst these people in the hope that he would discover the answers to questions he had about his dead son. The way things were shaping up, it looked fairly certain that in the next few minutes, he'd have the answers he needed. He'd be able to ask Martin in person.

Chapter Eighteen

Gary Flowers was bored. He sat in his office on the floor above The Garden of Terrestrial Delights, watching the bank of monitors mounted on the wall above him, paying particular attention to the ones that were keeping tabs on the dance floor. From time to time, he dipped a silver spoon into a saucer of coke on the desk top and laid out a couple of lines for himself on a small rectangular mirror.

The kids on the floor seemed to get younger every time he watched them. He saw them whirling and twitching in the flicker of the strobes and mourned for his own youth, and the kind of music he'd grown up with in the sixties, when rebellion had meant smoking a joint and wearing a paisley shirt. He didn't like or understand the music kids were into now, soundbites of classical arias, industrial noise and animal mating calls, laid over a barrage of electronic drumming. To him, it sounded ugly and dissonant, a reflection no doubt of the violent times in which the musicians lived. Nobody seemed to bother with a melody any more and lyrics were considered passé.

Flowers felt kind of sorry for the kids, who had never experienced the freedom and optimism of the sixties. They'd grown up in the shadow of things that hadn't even been dreamed about when Gary was a teenager: AIDS, acid rain, the vanishing ozone layer, the Greenhouse effect, drive-by shootings, urban noise pollution . . . Jesus, you name it. Not that Gary had been some dewy-eyed hippy back in '67 but he had sensed the potential power of youth in those days, had actually believed that the world was his proverbial oyster, that everything he wanted was within his grasp.

In those days, everything had been about expanding your

awareness, soaking up the wonder of the world and enjoying life. Now, the kids just seemed to want to get numb as quickly as possible. Even Warp, that fabled bringer of visions, tended to conjure up images from the darkest reaches of hell. Where was the fun in that for God's sake?

Flowers had never tried the stuff he was helping to sell. He wasn't *that* stupid. Mind you, there'd been a time when he swore that he'd never try anything stronger than draw and now look at him. Hoovering up the Bolivian marching powder like there was going to be a famine. He leaned forward over the desk and snorted a couple of lines, just about registering the adrenalin charge through the fog of chemicals that already inhabited his brain. He fell back in his executive leather chair and studied the screens intently. Tonight he had an itch and he was looking for the right person to scratch it for him.

After fifteen minutes' search, he thought he'd found what he was looking for. She was in her teens, Flowers decided, but only just, a thin waif-like girl in a short black skirt from which her bare skinny legs protruded like a couple of white sticks. Her jet-black hair framed her face in an outmoded pageboy bob and her large eyes were thickly lined with kohl. She had a permanently startled expression that put Flowers in mind of a rabbit caught in the headlights of an oncoming car; and he could tell by the way her head twitched and by the way she kept clutching at her stomach, that she was hooked and hurting. It was just the way he liked them. She'd be so grateful for a hit from the saucer on Flower's desk, grateful enough to do whatever he asked of her.

He hit the intercom button and leaned forward to speak into the microphone.

'Siggy? There's a chicken on the floor. Over by the bar, she's wearing a black mini skirt. Bring her into my office, will you?'

'Sure boss.' Siggy's sleepy voice came back via his head mike. He was used to carrying out this kind of instruction. A few moments later, Flowers saw Siggy's hulking shape on the video screen, edging his way through the crowds on the dancefloor. Flowers spoke into the mike, offering directions.

'Go left, Siggy . . . no, not *her*. She must be eighteen if she's a day! Over by the bar. Now, go straight ahead. See her?'

'What, the skinny gal?'

'That's the one. She has a . . . hungry look.'

Siggy's reply was a low chuckle of amusement. His tastes were entirely different from that of his employer, he liked them big, black and preferably male but he knew well enough never to question his employer. Flowers saw him move forward and place a big hand on the girl's shoulder. Then he leaned forward to shout into her ear over the roar of the music.

Flowers snapped off the microphone and leaned back in his chair. He had no worries about what he was about to do. Here in the inner sanctum of 'The Garden' he was secure, all-powerful, the lord of all he surveyed, and nobody from the real world was ever going to breach these walls and find out what he really got up to in his leisure hours. He did, however, experience a nagging sensation that felt suspiciously like shame. Back in the sixties he would have expressed indignant outrage at the morals of a man who would do something like this. But it was amazing how passing time could erode and distort all those principles you nurtured in your youth, turning them into so much mush. So many things had gone by the wayside over the years.

When he was in his twenties, for instance, he'd once sworn that he would never marry. He'd recently married for the third time, church weddings all of them. He'd also said that he would never father children, but back at his luxurious home in Wilmslow, he had a whole clutch of offspring, ranging in age from seven years to just six months. Luckily, he had never sworn an oath not to fuck underage girls, otherwise it would have become a vow that was broken on countless occasions.

He didn't know why he was compelled to do it so often. It wasn't just the sex. If he wanted that there was no end of more mature women available at the snap of his fingers and his current wife, Bonnie, a former porn actress, was no slouch in the bedroom either. When it came to faking an orgasm there was nobody to touch her. But the young girls satisfied some deeper craving in him, a need to recapture his own lost youth. The simple truth of the matter was that when he fucked a teenager, just for a few fleeting seconds, he felt like one himself.

The door opened and Siggy ushered the young girl into the office. She looked frightened, apprehensive.

'Come in,' said Flowers brightly. 'Please, have a seat.' The girl was clutching a rubber handbag to her sparrow chest, clinging on to it as though it were some kind of lifebelt.

'What's this all about?' she demanded, her accent purest Salford. 'What am I supposed to have done? I ain't done nothing.'

'Calm down, there's no need to worry.' Flowers dismissed Siggy with a flick of his head and the big man went out smirking to himself, closing the door behind him. Flowers turned back to the girl, favoured her with his sweetest smile. 'Please, sit down. I just wanted to have a talk, that's all.'

The girl lowered her trembling body into the chair. 'A . . . about what?' she muttered. And then, more forcefully, 'Look, who *are* you?'

'My name's Gary Flowers. You've heard of me?'

She nodded. 'You own this club,' she said blankly. 'And some other clubs in Manchester.'

'That's right.' Gary got up and went to a small fridge on the other side of the room. He was aware that the girl was looking at the surface of the desk now. She couldn't have failed to notice the saucer of cocaine and the lines laid out on the mirror. He smiled to himself. He almost felt the jolt that ran through her body at the sight of the drugs.

'What's your name?' he asked her casually, as he opened the fridge. He took out a bottle of Bollinger.

'Chantelle,' she told him.

Flower's smile widened into a grin. It was perfect. Little Chantelle from some crummy council estate in Salford. He could almost picture the peeling wallpaper and the faded photographs on the mantlepiece. He could almost smell the odour of boiled cabbage wafting from the kitchen. His hormones juddered at the prospect of what lay ahead. It wouldn't take long. It never did with a girl like Chantelle.

He came back to the desk, located a couple of lead crystal glasses, then opened the bottle with a flourish. As he poured the drinks he noticed that Chantelle was unable to take her eyes off the cocaine.

'So, what do you think of my club?' he asked her.

'It's all right,' she told him.

'Just all right?'

'Yeah. Better than all right. It's . . . it's OK.'

'OK is better than all right?'

She shrugged, nodded. Flowers continued to embellish his mental picture of Chantelle. She didn't get on at school. Couldn't concentrate. She planned to leave just as soon as possible, get herself a job so she could earn money to support what was already a very expensive habit. She'd almost certainly get herself knocked up by some crackheaded lout on the estate before she was sixteen years old. She'd be dumb enough to believe she could look after the kid, but the boy wouldn't stick around. Flowers pictured her, a sad single parent in a grotty hostel, hopelessly trying to look after the kid until social services stepped in and took it away from her . . .

He was getting ahead of himself. He handed her the glass of champagne but she barely even registered it. She was still staring at the contents of the saucer.

'Is that like . . . is it legal stuff? You know, herbal?'

'This?' Gary acted surprised, as though he'd forgotten all about the cocaine. 'Oh no, Chantelle, that's the real McCoy. Pure Columbian. That stuff came through customs yesterday in the belly of a mule.'

'A mule?' She glanced up at him incredulously. 'You mean, like . . . a donkey?'

Flowers laughed delightedly. So many of the ones he talked to had not the slightest idea of what was entailed in securing their preferred recreational drug.

'A mule is a man,' he explained. 'About thirty-six hours ago, a guy in Columbia swallowed sixty packets of this stuff, each one of them packed in the finger of a surgical glove.'

'Gerr' away,' said Chantelle.

'Oh no, I'm deadly serious. The fingers are then wrapped in carbon paper and clingfilm, to avoid X-Ray detection. Think about that, Chantelle! How hard it must be to swallow just one package, let alone sixty. They have to train for weeks beforehand, swallowing sausages whole, things like that. When the time comes, they dip the packages in olive oil to help get them down. Then they have about thirty-six hours to make it through to their destination and shit them into a dealer's toilet. If they're held up for just a few hours, the gastric juices start to dissolve the packing. If just one finger bursts, it's *hasta la vista* baby.' He moved back around the desk and settled into his seat. 'Must take quite some balls to do that. And a man would have to be absolutely desperate to take the chance. But they do, because they get paid the equivalent of two years wages in their country.' He raised his glass to Chantelle. 'Cheers,' he said.

'Cheers.' She sipped dutifully at her drink but it might as well have been cola for all the enthusiasm she showed. 'I never knew all that stuff,' she said. 'I thought . . .'

'You thought what?' he asked her.

'That it was just . . . you know, brought through in boxes or something.' She thought about it for a moment. 'So that stuff has been like . . . swimming around in somebody's shit, right.'

'Right.' He swallowed some champagne. 'The thought tends to put you off, doesn't it?'

'Yes,' she said, unconvincingly. 'So er . . . whose is it? The Charlie?'

He studied her thoughtfully over the top of his glass. 'Mine,' he said quietly. 'All mine. But . . . I'm sure a young girl like you isn't interested in stuff like this.'

'I might be,' she said quickly, and took another mouthful of champagne. There were tiny beads of sweat on her forehead now and she could hardly hold her glass steady, her hands were shaking so badly.

Gary calmly spooned cocaine onto the mirror and began to arrange it into another line with a gold credit card.

'You . . . would like to *buy* some?' he asked her.

She bit her lip. 'I . . . ain't got no money,' she said. 'Leastways, only a few quid.' She ran the tip of her tongue around her dry lips. 'I don't suppose . . . I mean, maybe you could loan me a toot?'

'*Loan* you?' Gary kept chopping at the coke, drawing it out into two long fine lines. 'How could I loan you coke,

Chantelle? How would you ever give it back? It'd be inside your head, wouldn't it? Swimming around.'

Chantelle put her hands together to stop them from shaking. She looked down at the bitten nails on her fingers.

'There must be some way we can make a deal,' she murmured.

'I dare say there is,' purred Gary. He thought for a moment. 'What say we start with a blowjob and take it from there?'

Chantelle lifted her head to look at him, her eyes wide, more startled than ever. This was always the most interesting part, Flowers thought. Some girls just blew up at this point, started screaming stuff like 'how dare you?' and 'what kind of a girl do you think I am?' To which Flowers always wanted to give the classic reply, 'My dear, I *know* what kind of girl you are, now we're just haggling about the price!' But no matter how much fuss they made, they always came around in the end. It was simply a matter of application. Actually, he hoped that Chantelle wouldn't hold out for too long. He'd promised Bonnie he'd be home for some dinner party she was having tonight.

And sure enough, it was easy. The phoney look of shock was replaced by a sardonic smile. She'd known it would come to this, was probably thanking her lucky stars that it was going to be so easy. She got up, put down her handbag and came around the desk to Gary. She took his swivel chair by the arms, swung him around to face her and went down on her knees between his legs. She unzipped his fly, took his already erect penis in her hands, buried her face in his lap and went to work.

Flowers sighed contentedly. He reclined the chair and lay there, gazing blissfully at the ceiling, happy to be once again fleetingly in touch with his lost youth.

The red phone on his desk rang and he gave a tut of irritation, but knew he couldn't afford to ignore it. His personal number was given out only to a very few trusted people. He lifted the handset. 'Hello' he said tonelessly. As soon as he heard the familiar voice in his ear, he regretted picking up. It was Bonnie.

'Gary, I thought you'd be home by now.'

'Sorry darling, something just came up.'

Chantelle, alarmed by the word 'darling', tried to disengage herself from his penis but Gary placed a hand on her head and eased her gently back down again. He thumbed the 'silence' button with his other hand.

'Who told you to stop?' he asked Chantelle coldly. He waited until her head had resumed its rhythm, then released the button. 'Sorry darling, there's somebody with me. We'll have to make this quick, I'm afraid.'

He lay there being pleasured and listened calmly while Bonnie's disembodied voice reminded him that Johnny and Celine were coming round at nine o'clock, so could he make sure he was home for 9.30 at the latest? Oh yes, and if it wasn't too much trouble, would he pick up a jar of sun-dried tomatoes from the deli on his way home? He answered every question with a monosyllabic grunt and then, as Chantelle's head began to bob faster and faster between his thighs, he told Bonny that he really would have to go now.

'You won't be long will you?' she asked suspiciously.

'Not long,' he concluded. 'In fact . . . I'm almost . . . finished here.' He slammed down the handset just as he ejaculated into Chantelle's mouth. The years momentarily fell away from him as the hot blood engorged his brain and penis. Then he collapsed in the chair, spent.

He watched curiously as Chantelle swallowed his semen, stood up, straightened her dress and leaned over the desk to snort a couple of lines of coke. The effect on her was almost magical. All her awkwardness seemed to fall away in an instant and the girl who turned back to face him was much more confident than her predecessor.

'That's good toot,' she said.

Flowers smiled.

The best,' he assured her. 'Pure, uncut and very expensive. Now . . .' He glanced at his Rolex. 'You and me have got to work out exactly what you can do for me in the next . . . say, thirty-five minutes, that's good enough to earn you a whole gramme of that stuff.' He leaned forward expectantly, fluttering his eyelids at her in a parody of a romantic matinee idol. 'Any suggestions?'

As it happened, she had plenty, each one of them more inventive than the next and each one of them worthy of reward. Flowers got so caught up in it, he didn't keep an eye on the time and consequently, he didn't make it home till well after ten o'clock; but as he explained to a harassed-looking Bonnie, it could have been a lot lot worse.

At least he'd remembered to pick up the sun-dried tomatoes.

Chapter Nineteen

Will stood in the circle of cheering Rag People, their faces lit by the fierce glow of the bonfire, and he wondered how he'd managed to get himself into such a fix. An instant ago, it seemed, he'd merely been looking for a place to lay his head for the night. In a few moments' time, he'd be fighting to prevent it from being knocked clean off his shoulders.

He examined the heavy baseball bat in his hands, then glanced warily up at the massive sneering figure of Chilli Dog, who looked like he could hardly wait to spill blood. Will wondered dismally if it was possible to surrender before the fight actually began. But gazing around at the cheering, jostling crowd, he realized that after all this anticipation, they were going to want blood one way or another. It was either fight Chilli Dog or stand there and allow the man to bludgeon him to death.

His searching eyes found Scally standing in the circle, the sack of food still slung over his shoulder. The grim expression on the boy's face didn't do Will any favours. He looked like he was already in mourning for the loss of his new friend.

Frank shouldered his way into the circle with the karaoke machine over his shoulder and the crowd fell silent. He paced around, looking at the two men, held together by the short length of rope. He gave Will a gleeful wink, then lifted the microphone to his mouth.

'My friends!' he shouted. 'A great surprise for us all tonight. A sporting dispute which pitches our old friend Chilli Dog against . . .' He glanced uncertainly at Will. 'You got a name?'

Will glared back at him.

'Will Ambrose,' he said.

' . . . against an outsider who calls himself Will Ambrose. A man who has already attacked our brother and drawn first blood. A man who thinks he has the balls to be a member of this tribe!'

This last remark evoked a chorus of jeers and catcalls. Frank had to lift a hand for silence before he could continue.

'So we'll settle this dispute in the time-honoured fashion. With ropes and cudgels!'

A wild cheer went up and the crowd seemed to jostle each other again, vying for the best position to view the ensuing fight.

'As you all know, in a dispute there are no rules. The man who walks away, or who is carried away alive, is the winner. The other man . . . if he survives . . . is an outcast.' Again a roar of exaltation. Frank stuck the microphone into his belt. He came back to the two men, placed a hand on each of their chests and pushed them back from each other, until the rope was pulled taut between them.

'Begin!' he said and he retreated to the safety of the circle.

'Now hold on a minute,' began Will. 'Can't we just . . . ?'

Chilli Dog came at him, swinging the bat like a mad man. Will jumped instinctively backwards and felt the wind of the blow as it scythed past his face, missing by inches. He grunted in surprise as Chilli Dog pulled hard on the rope, dragging him into range.

Will sensed another blow an instant before it struck. He ducked his head and the bat glanced off his naked shoulders, throwing a jolt of agony into him and eliciting a bellow of delight from the crowd. Galvanized by the pain, Will danced in under Chilli Dog's reach and drove his own bat at the big man's belly. But Chilli Dog was faster than he had anticipated. He sidestepped the jab, threw out a leg and tripped Will up. As he went sprawling on his side, Chilli Dog followed up, heaving a vicious overhand blow at Will's head.

Will rolled aside and the bat thunked into the earth by his ear, leaving a deep round hole. Chilli Dog cursed, wrenched the bat up again and tried another downward stroke but this time, Will managed to get his own bat up to block the attack. The two weapons connected with a force that sent a shock wave juddering up the length of his right arm. He grunted, and rolled away as Chilli Dog rallied. Will was scrambling to his feet when Chilli Dog unleashed a powerful side swing at him. Will saw it coming and rolled again, in towards his adversary's legs, tripping him; then as the big man went sprawling over him, he jerked the length of rope up hard between his legs.

Chilli Dog's whoop of pain was echoed by the crowd as a concerted inhalation of breath. He went down face first and Will got to his feet, heaving upwards on the rope. Chilli Dog bellowed, rolled onto his back and kicked free of the rope. He too clambered upright, his face registering a mixture of rage and pain.

The two men began to circle each other warily and the crowd fell silent now, appraising them just as surely as the opponents appraised each other. Will told himself that if he didn't lose his nerve, he had a better chance than he'd initially thought. Chilli Dog was heavy and powerful, but his reactions were somewhat slower than Will's and he lacked the smaller man's speed. But, Will warned himself, Chilli Dog only needed to land one of those wild blows and it would all be over.

Now Chilli Dog tried to bluff Will, making a quick feint towards his head, then aiming a scything stroke at his legs. Will saw it coming and jumped the swing, bringing up a knee into the other man's face as he did so. Chilli Dog reeled back with a grunt of surprise, fresh blood squirting from his already tattered nose. Will followed through, aiming a blow at his opponent's kidney but Chilli Dog got a huge left hand there first and actually caught the end of Will's bat, holding it in a vice-like grip while he lashed a retaliatory blow into Will's ribs. Searing agony seemed to course through his entire body as the breath was driven out of him, and for an instant, he was dangerously close to passing out. But he gritted his teeth and hung on to his wits as Chilli Dog raised his bat for a killing stroke.

Will acted instinctively, releasing his hold on the bat in order to jump back out of reach. The crowd roared approval as Chilli Dog gave Will's bat a cursory inspection, before tossing it contemptuously aside, leaving his opponent defenceless. He raised his own bat above his head and ran at Will, roaring like a bull.

With nothing else to do, Will transferred both hands to the length of rope and began to retreat from Chilli Dog's attack, moving backwards towards the ring of onlookers and the bonfire beyond it. The crowd broke and scattered in all directions but Will kept retreating towards the bonfire, until he could feel the awful heat of it on his back. Chilli Dog was still swinging wildly, incensed by his opponent's refusal to stand still and meet his punishment. If Will could just get him close enough to the fire . . .

And then Chilli Dog seemed to guess what was in Will's mind, because he stopped advancing suddenly and planted his heavy feet wide apart, so that Will was jerked to a sudden halt, a puppet on a string.

'Oh do, by fred,' growled Chilli Dog. 'I'm nod *dat* stupid. C'mere.' He began to pull one-handed on the rope and though Will dug his heels in, he could not deny the prodigious strength of the bigger man. He was being pulled closer and closer to his own death . . .

'Tibe we ended dis,' said Chilli Dog matter-of-factly.

He lifted the bat above his head and brought it down at Will in a crushing blow. Will, however, anticipated the move. He threw up his hands to catch the bat, screamed as the hickory connected with his palms, but held on with the sheer force of desperation. Then he threw himself backwards, pulling the big man off-balance. As they fell, Will got his feet up into Chilli Dog's gut, thrusting upwards with all his strength, tipping him up and over in a somersault. Chilli Dog crashed onto his back with a grunt of surprise, that quickly turned into a scream of agony as he realized his legs were in the fire.

He tried to scramble madly upright but Will whipped around and clamped his hands onto Chilli Dog's shoulders, pinning him in position while the flames burned his shoes and trousers and ate greedily into the flesh beneath.

'Surrender!' yelled Will, aware of the awful heat burning his own face and shoulders. 'Surrender and I'll let you up!'

But Chilli Dog was kicking and thrashing like a mad bull. The bat slipped from his hands forgotten and Will grabbed it, then scrambled back from the fire, unable to take the intense heat any longer. He retreated to the end of the rope and turned back to await Chilli Dog, who was now rolling away from the fire, screaming like a wild animal. The trousers were all but burned from his legs and the flesh was red and flayed, the air filled with the rich stench of roasting meat.

Sobbing with pain, Chilli Dog somehow managed to get himself upright. He came staggering towards Will his huge hands outstretched like claws. The crowd had fallen into a shocked silence. Nobody had expected the favourite to lose the contest.

'Give it up,' Will advised him.

But Chilli Dog kept right on coming, a horror-film zombie stumbling along on smoking legs. Now Will became aware of a chant going up from the crowd, who had regrouped behind him, the chant soft at first but steadily growing louder and more urgent. Now Will could make out what they were saying.

'Take him down, take him down, take him down!'

Will shook his head and tried to walk away, then remembered that he was still roped to Chilli Dog. He began to fumble with the knot around his left wrist.

'Take him down! TAKE HIM DOWN!'

And then above that, another sound, a boy's voice yelling a warning.

'Will, look out, LOOK OUT!'

Will glanced up just in time to see the knife appearing in Chilli Dog's hand. As the big man launched himself in a final assault, Will spun away from the blow and came around in a hard, double-handed swing, catching Chilli Dog a ferocious blow on the side of the head, splitting his skull open like a watermelon and dropping him in his tracks.

Will stood there stunned, gazing down at the dying man, at the slow pool of red liquid spreading in a scarlet fan beneath his broken head.

It was suddenly silent again, so quiet that Will could hear the crackling of the bonfire, the rumble of a goods train moving along the viaduct behind him. He became aware of a warm wetness on his face and lifting a hand, he smeared the drops of Chilli Dog's blood that had spattered his face.

Then it started. The applause. Polite and restrained at first but growing louder and more heartfelt by the moment. Will felt a terrible weariness settling over him. His ribs and his shoulder throbbed with pain where Chilli Dog's bat had hit him. He went down on his knees, prised the knife from his opponent's nerveless fingers and cut through the length of rope.

As he stood up, Frank appeared at his side, a scowl on his thin face. He grabbed Will's right hand and reluctantly lifted it high above his head.

'You jammy bastard,' he muttered.

The crowd's applause swelled into a full-throated roar of approval and he was surrounded by Rag People, all wanting to offer him congratulations. Hands slapped his back and tousled his hair. He was being pushed and prodded back in the direction of the arches. Scally appeared at his side, carrying Will's clothes and beaming proudly up at him.

Will glanced back. Frank trailed the crowd, his hands in his pockets, a discontented sneer on his face. Behind him, Chilli Dog lay dead, an extrusion of grey brain leaking from the crack in his skull. A couple of women were gleefully stripping his body. One of them had found the nose ring in his pocket and for an instant, Will felt like turning around and demanding it for himself. But he was too shocked, too exhausted to do anything about it; and he was more than a little disgusted that he should have had such a thought in the first place.

He allowed his followers to escort him to the mouth of Frank's arch. Somebody pushed him into a tattered old armchair. Scally handed him his clothes and he pulled them on, aware now of the chill in the air. A bowl of hot stew was thrust into his hands and a canteen of water. He drank deeply and then began to eat, remembering how hungry he was and for the moment at least, he felt good. He'd been accepted by these people. He was one of them now. He'd proved he had the balls to join the tribe.

But then, one by one, they dropped away and went back to whatever it was they had been doing earlier, until finally, it was just Will and the boy sitting there; and Will was able to reflect on the cost of membership to this particular club.

'What's the matter?' Scally asked him, bemused by Will's expression of self-disgust.

'What do you suppose is the matter? I just killed somebody.'

Scally shrugged. 'He'd have done the same to you, no problem. Anyway, I didn't like him. He smelled bad and he stole a puppy off me once. He told everyone he traded it for whisky, but I reckon he ate it.'

'He was still a human being,' Will reminded him.

'I guess.' Scally looked doubtful on that score. Then he leaned in to confide a secret. 'Did you see Frank's face? He's mad. He thought you'd die for sure.'

'So did I,' admitted Will grimly.

'Oh, I knew you'd be OK. You're sneaky. That thing you did with the fire? That was so funny!' Scally grinned gleefully. 'Did you see Chilli Dog's legs? They were burning and he was screaming like a stuck pig. You could smell his legs cooking . . .'

Will held up a hand to silence the boy. He didn't want to think about those things just now. He couldn't afford to vomit up his food.

'Scally, I'm half-killed,' he announced. 'I have to sleep.'

'Sure, Will. You know, you can take Chilli Dog's space if you want. He's got a big space and quite a few things of his own . . . that's if it hasn't already been looted.'

Will shook his head. 'If it's all the same to you, I'd rather share your space.'

Scally smiled proudly. 'Whatever. Come on, I'll show you where.' He took Will's arm and helped him to his feet. The effort sent flickers of pain jolting through Will's ribs. Scally led him to the arch and, taking the stub of a candle from his pocket, lit it from one of the lamps at the entrance and led Will inside. They picked their way through the sleeping figures on the floor to the flap of plastic that was the entrance to Scally's space. Scally pulled it open and ushered Will inside.

Will paused. In the glow of the candle he saw the figure of a woman lying on a filthy mattress, covered by heaps of tumbled clothes and blankets. Her blonde hair was fanned around her on the makeshift pillow and beneath the layers of dirt that covered her face, it was apparent that she was appealingly pretty. Will jabbed Scally in the ribs with his elbow.

'That's . . . Marianne?' he whispered.

Scally nodded. He indicated a vacant corner, beside the

brick wall. 'You can stretch out here,' he said. 'Use some of this stuff to cover yourself. I've still got a few things to do before they lock up for the night.'

'Yeah, but wait a minute, I . . .'

But Scally was already gone, taking the candle with him and plunging Will into darkness. With a sigh, he settled his aching body down as best he could and dragged layers of whatever came to hand over himself. He lay there in this unfamiliar place and, when he closed his eyes, his head filled with ugly visions of a screaming bearded face. He told himself that he was a killer now. He had wanted to leave the society in which he lived and be accepted by another. That was just what he had done. But who could have guessed the price would be so high?

He told himself that he would never be able to sleep again, after what had just happened; but exhausted and battered as he was, the thought was hardly formed in his mind, when he fell into a deep dreamless sleep that held him tightly in its arms till morning.

Chapter Twenty

Don Bullen was in a foul mood this morning. He fed coins into the office vending machine and punched the buttons that would supply him with a paper cup of something that was amusingly listed as 'coffee, white, two sugars'. He took an exploratory sip of it and a foul mingling of chemicals seemed to dance a jig on his tongue.

It was a cold, wet October morning and the drive into work had taken far longer than it should have, mainly because of a horrific accident on Wilmslow Road. A uniformed man attending the scene had filled Bullen in on the details while he'd sat in his car waiting for the wreckage to be cleared.

A couple of joyriders had stolen an Astra GTI and had amused themselves for several hours by taunting police cars and leading them a merry chase around the low-spots of the city, including a lengthy excursion around the Merton Estate, a place where few police cars ever ventured these days. A crumbling hell-hole run by rival gangs of teenage crack dealers, the estate now resembled a war zone and police policy was to keep trouble corralled up in there and just let it happen. The pursuing cops had been pelted with bricks, bottles and other debris as they careered madly along the walkways and back alleys of the estate and all things considered it had been a relief when the Astra had headed back into the city centre.

On Wilmslow Road, the Astra's driver had made a fatal misjudgement approaching a crossing and had mown down a couple of luckless pedestrians, before mounting the pavement, overturning and smashing headlong into a coachload of pensioners on their way to a week's holiday in Bournemouth.

Incredibly, the thirteen-year-old driver and his two ten-year-old passengers had been pulled alive from the wreckage, but many of the pensioners had not been so lucky. Three were dead and more than a dozen had shattered their fragile old bones in the impact of the crash. The coach had ended up stretched right across the width of the road and it had taken hours to drag it to one side and get the traffic moving again – time which Bullen had spent listening morosely to some retard of a DJ babbling on about Metro 2000 and all the wild, fun things that were scheduled to coincide with the start of the new millennium.

Bullen took another sip of his coffee and reassured himself that the first sip hadn't been some kind of a fluke. How was it he wondered, they could put a man on Mars, yet they still couldn't invent a machine that made a half-decent cup of instant coffee? He still felt thick-headed from the drinking he'd done the night before and added to that was the sour taste of disappointment after he'd failed to get the Ambrose woman to put out for him. He'd felt strangely confident that she'd succumb to his charms, working on the assumption that what all these tight-arsed middle-class birds secretly wanted was a bit of rough. But no, she'd given him the elbow and afterwards he'd adjourned to the Police Social Club to sink more than a few pints of bitter with whisky chasers. Deep in his cups, he'd told some of his fellow drinkers about the woman's final remark, hoping that one of them might be able to explain it. To his disgust, they'd all pissed themselves laughing at him, which had not helped to improve his mood one little bit.

Sid Lang came out of the office for a refill. He studied his partner with evident glee.

'Christ, you look like shit,' he observed, uncharitably. 'What were you up to last night?'

'Mind your own fucking business,' snapped Bullen. 'And keep a civil tongue in your head when you address a superior officer.'

Lang rolled his eyes. 'Very sorry I'm sure . . . sir,' he added, almost as an afterthought. He fed coins into the vending machine and punched buttons. The machine spasmed into life and discharged powder and liquid into a cup. Lang withdrew it and eyed it dubiously. 'The Chief wants to see you,' he said. 'Came round looking for you first thing this morning.'

Bullen shot Lang an irritable glance. 'Why the fuck didn't you say so?' he snarled.

Lang looked bemused. 'I thought I just did,' he said.

'Sooner!'

'Christ, Boss, I only just saw you! What's up, you angling for promotion again? You seem to jump every time Chalmers breaks wind.'

'When I want your opinion, I'll ask for it,' said Bullen. He leaned closer to his partner. 'You want to shake your ideas up if you want to be accepted into The Brotherhood,' he concluded. He took his coffee and his bad mood in the direction of Chalmers' office and rapped politely on the door.

'Come,' said the high-pitched voice from within and this morning, even this was irritating. Why didn't the Chief just say 'come in' like any normal person?

Bullen took a deep breath, counted to ten and then opened the door. He stepped into the office. Chalmers was standing at the window, staring out over the rooftops of the city. His chubby hands were clasped behind his back and he seemed deep in thought. There was a long silence while Bullen waited patiently for Chalmers to speak. Nothing was forthcoming and eventually he felt obliged to do a little prompting.

'You wanted to see me, sir?'

'Hmm. Oh yes. Couple of things, Don.' Chalmers dragged himself away from the window with visible reluctance and sat down at his desk. He picked up his Mont Blanc pen and began to fiddle with it. 'I talked to my contact in Southport last night,' he announced. 'They still haven't managed to turn up hide nor hair of Ambrose.'

Bullen frowned. 'That's odd, sir. I spoke to his missus last night. Or I should say, his *ex*-missus. Unofficially, of course. She maintains that he went back to Southport the morning after his son's funeral. I've no reason to doubt her.'

Chalmers pursed his lips. 'If he was there, my contacts would have found him,' he insisted. 'Therefore, the logical conclusion is that he's still here in Manchester. That he's still sticking his nose into things that don't concern him.'

Bullen frowned. What was the old man so worried about? OK, so maybe Ambrose was a bit of a loose cannon but it would take more than one man to break the grip the force currently had on the city.

'I wouldn't lose any sleep over it,' Bullen advised him. 'Let him ask as many questions as he likes. He can't hurt us.'

'The hell he can't!' Chalmers regarded Bullen indignantly. 'That's the kind of sloppy attitude that might just get us into trouble. I run a tight ship, Don, I always have and I don't intend to change that policy now. Don't forget that Ambrose was a police officer and a bloody good one, too. I wish I had a few men of that calibre working for me today. If he hadn't been so bloody incorruptible . . .'

Bullen smiled sardonically. 'Excuse me, sir, but isn't that one of the things that made him a good police officer in the first place?'

Chalmers shrugged. 'Those are outmoded values, Don. The honest copper used to be something to be admired. But not any more. These days, a police officer needs to know how to adapt to the society in which he lives. Sticking stubbornly to the old ways doesn't make you a hero. It makes you a dinosaur. And we all know what happened to the dinosaurs, don't we?'

Bullen shrugged. He got the general idea. 'So what's our policy on this?'

'Simple. I want him found and I want him removed. Do I make myself clear?'

'Crystal,' said Bullen drily. 'Am I to take it this is a priority request, sir?'

'Top priority. We've farted about enough. Find him and deal with him.'

Bullen sipped at his coffee. He moved closer to the desk and lowered his voice, as if afraid of being overheard.

'And er . . . when you say, "deal with him" . . .'

Chalmers closed his eyes for a moment and sighed. When he opened them again, the expression in them was cold and businesslike. 'I'm giving you *carte blanche*. Don.'

'Eh?'

'I'm giving you a free hand to use whatever force you deem necessary to ensure that Ambrose is no longer a threat to us. He was given fair warning, a warning he apparently chose to ignore. Now he must pay the consequences.' Chalmers swivelled his chair back towards the window. 'Take care of the matter for me. When the time comes to reward those who've been of service, you won't be overlooked.'

Bullen smiled mirthlessly. 'Leave it to me sir,' he said. 'If he's in Manchester, I'll find him.'

He went out of the office and closed the door behind him. He drained the last of the foul-tasting coffee, crumpled the paper cup in his fist and tossed it into a waste bin as he strode down the corridor towards his own office. An idea was forming in his mind, an unusual occurrence so early in the morning. He spotted Lang, still leaning against the wall by the vending machine, chatting animatedly to a new blonde PWC who everyone had the hots for.

'Hey, Sid,' he shouted. 'I need a word.'

The PWC smiled apologetically and took off down the corridor. Lang trudged over to Bullen, looking none too pleased at the interruption. 'Thanks,' he muttered peevishly. 'I was nearly on a promise there. Anyway, I thought you were hacked off at me.'

Bullen waved a hand dismissively. 'Forget it. I was a little out of sorts, that's all. Listen, I've been thinking. When we picked Ambrose up at the funeral, last week. There was a journalist you recognized, amongst the mourners. Somebody from *The Post* wasn't it?'

Lang thought for a minute. 'Uh . . . yeah. Clive Singleton. He works on the crime desk.'

'And he and Ambrose go back a long way, don't they?'

'I believe so. What's this all about?'

'Surveillance, Sid. It's all about surveillance.' He slid an arm around Lang's shoulders and led him along the corridor. 'Come on, mate,' he said. 'I'll treat you to a proper breakfast in the canteen. And while we eat, I'll tell you all about it . . .'

When Will woke the next morning, he felt like he'd been hit

by a tram. He lay on his side in Scally's cramped living quarters, aware of the dull pain throbbing through his ribs and shoulder, where Chilli Dog's baseball bat had caught him a couple of good hits.

He clenched his teeth and moved around onto his back; then started violently, as he realized that somebody was sitting right next to him, watching him intently. It was the woman, Marianne, the one that everyone said was mad. Just at this moment, it was easy to believe. She sat cross-legged on the mattress, staring down into his face with big blue eyes that seemed half wild.

'Uh . . . good morning,' he muttered weakly. He glanced quickly around but there was no sign of Scally. 'You don't know me, I'm . . .'

But Marianne held one finger to her lips to silence him. 'It's OK,' she assured him. 'I've been expecting you.'

He stared at her, bemused. She was acting as though she already knew him. She placed a hand on his injured shoulder and he flinched involuntarily.

'You're in pain?' she asked him.

'Just a little,' he admitted. 'Mind you, you should see the other guy.' His attempt to be flippant only served to remind him of what had happened the night before. He had killed a man. Oh sure, it had been in self-defence, kill or be killed, but somehow this didn't make him feel any better about it. He had come here with the intention of doing harm to the people who had supplied his son with drugs, but as far as he knew Chilli Dog hadn't been one of them. 'Where's Scally?' he asked, dismally.

Marianne shrugged. 'Gone somewhere,' she told him. 'Probably out looking for food. That's Scally for you. A go-getter. I told him that once.'

Will struggled into a sitting position. He was feeling a powerful urge to empty his bladder. 'Look, I think I'll just go outside for a minute,' he announced.

'No, don't go!' Her tone was urgent, almost panicked. She put a hand on his chest, pushing him down again, making him groan. 'Sorry,' she said. 'But you only just got back. We've got so much to catch up on.'

Again that air of familiarity. 'What do you mean, "catch up on"?' he asked. 'We've never met.'

She laughed at that, a deep, throaty chuckle that inexplicably sent a shiver through him. 'Oh, Steve,' she said. 'Quit fooling around. I know you too well for that.'

'Steve?' He stared at her, bewildered. 'My name isn't Steve! It's Will. Will Ambrose.'

'Oh sure, *now*, of course. But names don't matter, Steve, not for a moment. You told me that, remember?' She reached out a hand to stroke his face gently with the tips of her fingers. 'The packaging might be different but I can sense that you're still the same inside. I've been waiting for you. Scally's been looking after me, just until you came back . . .'

'Now look, hang on a minute. I'm afraid you've got the wrong idea about me. I'm just looking for some people, that's all. I'm looking for some bad people who . . .'

'Deal drugs,' concluded Marianne. 'Yes, of course.'

Will sat there in open-mouthed astonishment. Maybe the woman wasn't so much mad as psychic. 'How . . . how did you know?' he asked her.

'Stands to reason,' she told him. 'After what happened. After what they did to you . . .' She bowed her head and gazed at her dirty hands which lay in her lap, the fingers interlaced as they twisted and turned nervously against each other. 'I thought maybe you'd want revenge on me too,' she whispered. 'After all, it was me who turned you on to it. It was me that said you should give it a try. See, the visions I had were so sweet, I never for a moment thought that . . .' Her voice trailed off and she looked at him gravely. 'If you want to punish me, I'll understand.'

Will stared at her. She was obviously upset, and he couldn't help feeling sorry for her. What's more, he was beginning to suspect that there might be more to her ramblings than met the eye. She'd just mentioned drugs and visions. Could she be talking about Warp? So far Will's inquiries had met with blank looks and denials. But this woman seemed all too willing to talk, and in the process she might just mention something of interest. Besides, weak and battered as he was, it was easier to play along with her than to protest that he wasn't who she thought he was.

'I don't want to punish you,' he assured her. 'I, I just want to find out who gave Steve . . . who gave *me* the drugs. We are talking about Warp here, aren't we?'

'Oh, Steve, you know we are! And you know who gave them to you. I did.' She was almost crying now, her large eyes wet and glistening. Will could see that she'd carried this guilt around with her for a long time.

'Uh, yes, but what I mean is, who gave them to you?'

'Marshall, of course. It was always Marshall, wasn't it?'

'Marshall.' Will shook his head. 'I'm sorry, I don't remember him.' He waved a hand at his head and gave an apologetic shrug, which almost made him cry out in pain. 'I'm . . . a little mixed up in my head.'

'I can understand that. Steve, what's it like? Being dead. Was it what you expected?'

'Well, er, it mixes you up,' he persisted. 'You can't always remember things that happened . . . earlier. Tell me about Marshall. I need to remember everything.'

'Well . . .' Marianne scratched her head absent-mindedly. 'Marshall Resnick works for Shed records. He's an A and R man. He's been the Messiah's representative for years and he also supplies them with their drugs . . .' She smiled self-consciously. 'I feel silly telling you all this stuff. You sure you don't remember any of it?'

He reached out a hand and placed it on her arm, gave it an encouraging squeeze. 'Bear with me,' he said. 'It's coming back gradually. Please, go on.'

'Well, let me think . . . about eighteen months ago, I met him at a launch party or something and he tells me about this great new drug that's just come on to the scene.'

'Warp?' ventured Will.

'Yeah, Warp, though I don't even think it had a name then. Anyway, Marshall slipped me a couple of tabs to try out. You were away on tour at the time, so I ended up taking mine with a friend. A *girl* friend,' she added, as though it mattered.

'Oh sure,' said Will. 'Go on.'

'We had this really intense trip, very vivid hallucinations. It was amazing. I started using it quite a lot after that.'

201

'You always had good trips?'

'Uh, yeah. Pretty much. Some were a little close to the edge, but I was always good with acid trips, remember?'

Will nodded, forced a smile. 'So then I came back from tour?' he ventured.

'And you wanted to try it too.' Marianne's eyes filled with tears again. 'I got some more from Marshall and I remember thinking, these aren't quite the same . . .'

'How did you know that?'

'Umm . . . well, they were a different colour. They were purple and they'd been blue before. Marshall said they'd improved the formula or something. Anyway, we had our trip together. We were in the Midland Hotel. We always used to go there when you came back from tour, do you remember?'

Will nodded uncomfortably. He hated deceiving her like this but knew that he couldn't miss the opportunity to learn more.

'Go on, Marianne. Tell me what happened.'

'We had a room on the top floor. A suite. We had food and some champagne. We dropped the tabs and then we made love.' She gazed into his eyes and it struck him once again what a beauty she must have been before she got so thin and bedraggled. 'You were so gentle, Steve. So loving. And then the trip came over us . . .' Her expression changed, became a mask of apprehension. 'It was beautiful at first. I was like, in a forest, you know some kind of fairy-tale place. I was lying in the grass and you were making love to me. And . . . and then you began to change. You became like an animal. Sort of like a wolf and sort of like a bear and, mostly, it was still you. The eyes. And the voice.' She was crying freely now, the tears making white streaks down her dirty face. 'And you were still inside me, but now you seemed bigger. Much bigger. The pain was awful. I started to scream. And you had your hands around my throat and you were laughing like a maniac. Laughing and drooling and telling me what you were going to do to me after I was dead. And I knew, from the sound of your voice, you would have done it too. You would have killed me. And I was screaming, trying to push you off, trying to pull away from you and . . . and then everything went black and I thought, this is death, this is what it's like. Nothingness. No heaven, no hell, just black.'

She pushed against him and obligingly, he put his arms around her so she could sob out the rest of it into the cushion of his chest. He had to grit his teeth against the pain this caused him. 'Then the next thing I knew . . . somebody was hammering on the door of the room and you were lying on top of me. I reached up and touched your face and you were cold. Stone cold.' She shook her head, unable to continue for the moment. He held her tighter and worried that holding her felt so good. That was a complication he didn't need right now.

'It's OK,' he whispered. 'It's all over with. You don't need to think about it any more.'

'And you don't blame me, Steve?'

'No, I don't blame you. But I need to find the people that make Warp. I want to punish them. Do you know where I can find them, Marianne?'

She shook her head. 'I only know Marshall,' she assured him.

'Well, it's a start. Where can I find him?'

'He used to have a Penthouse flat on the Salford Quays. He might still live there.'

'You remember the address?'

'Uh, yes, I think so.'

'Good girl. I want you to write it down for me so . . .'

Will broke off as the shelter's entrance flap opened and Scally stared in at him. He saw the way Will and Marianne were holding each other and his eyes widened in shocked surprise.

'What's going on?' he demanded coldly. He lifted a carrier bag into the shelter. 'I went for some breakfast,' he said. 'But maybe I should leave you two to eat it in peace.'

'Jesus, Scally, it's not how it looks!' protested Will.

'The hell it's not!' Scally turned on his heel and walked away in disgust.

'Shit!' Will detached himself from Marianne's arms. 'You wait here,' he told her. 'I'll be back in a minute. I'd better go and talk to him.' He got to his feet and went in pursuit of the boy, knowing that he couldn't afford to lose an ally as useful as Scally over a simple misunderstanding.

Why is life always so complicated? he asked himself, as he ran out of the arch into the chill of early morning.

Chapter Twenty-One

Will came out of the arch and saw Scally walking away along the street, his hands in his pockets. It was still early and there were few people up and about yet.

'Scally, wait!' Will trotted after the boy, the effort of jogging his body sending fresh ripples of pain through his ribs and shoulder. After a few moments, he caught up with the boy and fell into step beside him. 'Wait a minute,' he said.

'No thanks, I'm busy.' Scally kept walking, his head down, a fierce scowl on his face.

'Look, you've got it all wrong. Nothing happened back there. She was upset, I was just trying to comfort her.'

'Oh yeah, I could see that,' sneered Scally.

'You don't understand. She thinks I'm somebody called Steve.'

Scally stopped in his tracks. His eyes widened in realization. 'Oh God, yeah!' he said. 'I should have remembered. She *said* somebody was coming. She told me she'd had this dream and that he was coming back as a carnation or something. So she thinks *you* . . .' He lifted a hand to strike himself on the forehead. 'Christ, Will, I thought . . .'

'I was making a move on her? No, I swear. She was sitting there looking at me when I woke up. She . . . for some reason, she thinks I'm this guy she used to go out with.'

'Yeah, well . . .' Scally scratched his head. 'Everyone in the arch reckons she's crazy. And I suppose she has been worse since Frank and the others jumped her, so . . .'

'What do you mean, "jumped her"?'

Scally blushed. It was obvious he felt uncomfortable talking about this. 'Oh, you know. Frank and some of his cronies,

205

they . . . got her drunk and . . . they all took turns. By the time I got there, three or four of them had done it to her.'

Will stared at the boy in open-mouthed horror. He couldn't believe that anyone would speak so lightly of the matter, let alone a boy of fourteen; but then he reflected that rape was probably an everyday occurrence among the Rag People.

'My God,' he whispered. 'That poor girl. When did this happen?'

'About a week ago. She's been jumpy ever since. Crying a lot. She was never like that. She was always different, you know, and sad most of the time, but . . . she never cried before.'

'Scally, I don't know what to say. Shouldn't you report it to somebody? Call in the police maybe?'

Scally laughed bitterly. 'The Blues?' he said derisively. 'What, so they can take their turn as well? Nobody here would have anything to do with those bastards. But don't worry, I won't forget about it. First chance I get to pay Frank back, I'll do for him. Him and all the others that put their dirty hands on her.' Scally's expression was calm and unflinching. Young as he was, Will thought, he had already acquired a hunger for revenge. It was something the two of them had in common.

'Look,' said Scally. 'I was wrong to walk out on you like that. I guess I thought you were like Frank and the others. I'm sorry.'

'That's OK.' Will squeezed the boy's shoulder and was momentarily startled by the thinness of the body beneath the thick overcoat. 'Marianne means a lot to you, doesn't she?'

'I guess. It's not like she's my woman, or anything. I mean, she's too old for me really. I know that. But I worry about her, see. She's kind of . . .' He broke off, unable to articulate what he wanted to say, but Will thought he knew. The word Scally was looking for was 'vulnerable'. Now the boy was frowning as he remembered something. 'I didn't come right in, you know. I was listening at the door for a while. Why were you asking her all that stuff? About the drugs.'

Will glanced around. The arch doors were all open and people were starting to shuffle out into the grey light of early morning. He didn't want to risk being overheard. He took Scally's arm and drew him off the street onto the waste ground.

'Come on,' he said. 'I need to take a pee. I'll tell you all about it.'

They walked towards the large pile of ashes that was all that remained of last night's bonfire. Will unzipped himself and urinated into the ashes. Scally joined him. The twin streams of urine revealed a couple of pieces of scorched bone lying amidst some charred lengths of wood. Will raised his eyebrows and glanced at Scally. 'Chilli Dog?' he muttered.

Scally nodded.

'If somebody dies here they usually go into the fire. It's quick and clean and you don't have to worry about bringing in The Blues.'

Will thought about Clive's list of missing people. Another contribution to the numbers, he thought. Bodies turned to ash, scattered by the wind.

'The Rag People don't trust the police much, do they?' he observed.

'We don't trust anyone.'

'That's a pity. Because I'm going to have to ask you to trust me. Think you can?'

Scally thought about it. 'Maybe,' he said. 'I dunno. Those questions you were asking Marianne. What was that all about? You a dealer or something?'

'Far from it.' Will zipped himself up and stepped away from the ashes. He stood for a moment, gazing across the stretch of wasteland to the viaduct. 'Look, Scally, I'll level with you. I'm not quite what I seem. A couple of weeks ago I was living in a house in Southport. Not a palace, you understand, but I had a roof over my head and I was eating regular meals. And then Martin died.'

Scally looked at him inquiringly. 'Who's Martin?' he asked.

'He was my son. He was a few years older than you. A couple of weeks ago, his seventeenth birthday as a matter of fact, he went out to a nightclub and took a drug called Warp. He wasn't a big drug user or anything, I guess he just took it for the hell of it. At first, it was enjoyable. The drug gives you hallucinations . . .'

He saw the look of bemusement on the boy's face and attempted to make it simpler.

'It's like you're having crazy dreams only you're not asleep. They seem real to you, you understand? Anyway, suddenly, without any warning, Martin went berserk. He attacked some friends who were with him, including his girlfriend, Sophie. He broke her neck, killed her instantly. Then he collapsed and went into a coma. He died three days later without ever waking up.' Will closed his eyes for a moment. Relating it like that so calmly, so straight-forwardly, made it seem incredible, like something that couldn't possibly have happened. But it had, and even telling somebody about it served to rekindle all the pain of bereavement. He felt the sting of tears in his eyes and dashed them away on the sleeve of his coat. *None of that!* he told himself. He'd shed enough tears for Martin to last him a lifetime. He looked at Scally but the boy's face remained impassive, betraying no sign of what he might be thinking. Will cleared his throat, wanting to be sure he had his voice under control. 'From what Marianne just told me, something similar happened to her and her boyfriend.'

Scally nodded. 'Yeah, I knew about that,' he said.

'See, Scally, that's why I'm here. I thought if I came and lived as a Rag Man, I'd be able to learn more about the people that make and supply Warp. What I want . . . what I'm really looking for . . .'

'Is some payback,' concluded Scally.

Will stared at him for a moment. Then he sighed, nodded. 'Yeah. I guess that's pretty much it. I never thought I'd take the law into my own hands, but it seems the only way to stop the pain. To really lay Martin to rest. And Marianne, she just gave me my first lead. A name. An address. Something I can work on.'

Scally scratched his chin thoughtfully. 'Maybe I can give you another one,' he said.

'Oh?' Will raised his eyebrows.

'Yeah. There's this guy calls himself Mr Pinder. I don't know his first name, but he deals drugs. Maybe this Warp stuff, I ain't sure. But I know he gets Rag People to sell them for him. I saw him once, he . . .' Scally trailed off, shook his head. Evidently it was not a pleasant recollection.

'What?' Will prompted him. 'What did you see?'

'I saw him kill this guy who was dealing for him. A Rag Man, but not somebody from this tribe. Cut his throat. I thought for a minute there, he was going to do the same to me.'

Will frowned. 'He saw you?'

'Yeah. He came after me. If I hadn't stuck a fork in his nose, he'd have had me for sure.'

Will winced involuntarily. 'A fork?' he said.

'I was eating at the time,' Scally explained.

Will laughed at the matter-of-fact quality in the boy's voice. 'What else do you know about him?'

'Not much. He's a big bloke, wears his hair in a pony tail. And he does magic.'

'How do you mean, "magic"?'

'You know, card tricks and stuff. He was doing a trick for this guy and the next minute . . .' Scally drew an index finger across his throat. 'Jesus, it was scary.' He remembered something else. 'He rides around in a big red Yankee car, the kind you see in movies.'

'How long ago was this?'

'About two weeks?'

'Then I guess he still looks like Rudolph the red-nosed reindeer. He wouldn't be too thrilled about that.'

'No. I'd say he'd have killed me if I hadn't run so fast. And I sure hope I never bump into him again.' Scally's grave expression showed that he wasn't joking.

'You've no idea where this Mr Pinder lives?'

Scally shook his head. 'No, I only seen him the one time, standing in a back street.'

'Well, it's something to go on. I feel like I'm really making some progress here. It's men like him that I'm after, Scally. Men who are preying on the Rag People, exploiting them for their own greed.'

Scally pulled a face. 'But that ain't why you're here,' he said disparagingly. 'It's because of your son. If he hadn't died, you wouldn't have given us another thought. Would you?'

Will found it hard to look Scally in the eyes. Instead he gazed down at his own feet, shamed by the accuracy of the boy's observation. 'What you're saying is absolutely true,' he admitted. 'I won't pretend otherwise. But, Scally, being here has opened my eyes to a lot of things: things I previously never even dreamed of. So whatever my reasons for doing this . . . and yes, they are pretty selfish reasons, there's no two ways about that . . . I think the Rag People *will* benefit in the long run. At least, I hope they will. I'd like to think there's more to what I'm doing than just taking my revenge.'

'And when it's over?' Scally asked him. 'I guess you'll go back, won't you? Back to your nice house and your three meals a day.'

Will frowned. 'I don't even want to think about that for the moment,' he said. 'The truth is I don't know what will happen. These are dangerous people I'll be going up against. You said yourself you saw somebody get their throat cut. Could be they'll get to me before I get to them.' There was a long silence, punctuated by the clanging and rattling of an ancient freight train passing along the viaduct. Will gave Scally a playful punch in the ribs in an attempt to lighten the mood. 'Anyway, speaking of good food, what did you bring us for breakfast?'

Scally brightened. 'Doughnuts,' he said. 'They're a day old but they ain't bad.'

'Scally, you're a genius! Where the hell did you get hold of doughnuts?'

The boy grinned, proud of his artfulness. 'I've got contacts at a bakery in Levenshulme,' he said. 'They always have some left when they close for the night. But you got to be there real early in the morning if you want to get first pick.'

'Well, come on, what are we waiting for? I'm starving!' Will recalled Clive saying that only a couple of weeks ago, the day they'd gone for lunch together; but then 'starving' had merely meant 'hungry' or 'peckish.' Now Will could say it and really mean it. He and Scally started walking back towards the arch.

'Listen,' said Scally. 'I been thinkin' . . . about Marianne.'

'What about her?'

'Well, maybe she don't have to know that you ain't Steve. Not yet, anyway.'

'Gosh, Scally, I don't think that's such a great idea. I mean, OK, I let her think that just now to try and get the full story out of her. But I don't see the point in continuing the deception. What good would it do?'

'It might make her happier,' said Scally. 'I mean, it *would*, I'm sure of it. After what happened with Frank and the others she, well, she needs some good news, you know what I mean?'

Will sighed, shrugged. 'All right, I won't say anything for a while. But at some point, she's going to have to be told. We'll see how it goes.'

They moved in to the cover of the arch. More people were getting up off the floor now, throwing off their sleeping bags and covers and staggering out into the cold sunlight. Scally pulled open the flap and he and Will stepped into the shelter. They stood there bemused.

Marianne was sitting cross legged on the mattress. She had set out the doughnuts on makeshift plates and she'd put tin cans of drinking water beside each plate. In another tin can, placed centrally in the arrangement, there was a straggle of winter weeds that she must have dug up from somewhere. But this didn't surprise them half as much as what she had done to herself. She had combed out the knots and straggles in her long blonde hair and tied it back from her face with a piece of ribbon. She had even used some of the water to wash her face and hands. She smiled up at them and the smile seemed lit by some eerie inner radiance. Will and Scally exchanged puzzled glances. The change in her seemed so marked it was hard to believe this was the same person they had left behind only a few minutes earlier.

'There you are, boys!' she chided them. 'I was getting worried about you. Sit down and have your breakfast!'

Stunned, Will and Scally took their places on the mattress. Will grabbed a doughnut and was about to take a huge bite, when Marianne lifted her tin can in a toast.

'Here's to Steve's return,' she announced. 'It's really great to have him back.'

Scally raised his own can and slipped Will a sly wink. 'To Steve!' he echoed. He and Marianne drank while Will sat there feeling distinctly uncomfortable. Who knew where this charade would lead him? But for the moment, his own hunger overrode any worries he might have on that score. They all bit into their stale doughnuts which tasted simply wonderful. Scally remarked that it was great to see Marianne's appetite back again and she replied that it was all thanks to Steve. And Will meanwhile, reminded himself that he had to meet up with Clive later that day, to tell him what he had learned so far. He had anticipated having nothing to report, but in the last couple of days, a lot of pieces had fallen into place.

'A penny for your thoughts,' said Marianne.

'Oh, I'm just thinking how nice it is to be back,' said Will.

But really, he was thinking about the Warp salesman called Marshall Resnick; and about what he would do when he finally caught up with him.

He bit deep into his doughnut and the sweet red jam spurted onto his fingers, like the brief passing of a wasted life.

Chapter Twenty-Two

Suzanne got into Delta earlier than usual that morning, encouraged to do so by a restless night that had seen her awake by dawn, with no prospect of any further sleep. Laden with two large portfolios, she swept up the carrera marble steps at the entrance and pushed through the plate glass swing doors into the foyer.

With a brief nod to Zhandra, the skinny girl who sat at reception, she turned left along the corridor and made her way to her spacious office. She went inside, dropped the portfolios on her desk and turned to face the glass partition that adjoined the office of her co-director, Adam Fielding.

Adam was an American, originally from Washington DC, though he had spent most of his adult life in Manchester. She had known him for years and indeed, as Will had pointed out recently, there had been a time, a couple of years back, when he and Suzanne had been more than just business partners. But the passion had cooled and common sense had prevailed, warning them that to be tied up in a relationship, no matter how undemanding, was a problem when there was a business to run. So these days they were close friends, nothing more. And Suzanne, if asked, would have said that she knew Adam Fielding, inside out.

So it was something of a shock to see him standing in his office, a good half hour earlier than he generally came to work, deep in conversation with a small, tubby, bald-headed man, who was all-too familiar to Suzanne. They hadn't noticed her arrival and as she stood there looking at them, they extended their arms and shook hands warmly, *oddly*, Suzanne thought. They seemed to be clasping their hands in an awkward, rather unnatural way . . .

Then Adam glanced up and noticed her standing there. A look came into his eyes and his expression changed fleetingly to something that spoke eloquently of guilt. Chalmers looked up too. His piggy eyes narrowed, his already ruddy complexion darkened to a deeper shade. The two hands flew apart as though a powerful electric current had just been passed between them.

There was a long moment where nothing happened. The three of them stood like statues on their respective sides of the glass. Then Chalmers took the initiative. He walked over to the connecting door, speaking loudly as he opened it.

'Well, thanks for your help, Mr Fielding. The plans look marvellous, quite marvellous. I'm sure . . .' His voice trailed off as he pretended to recognize Suzanne for the first time. A better actor might have pulled it off but Chalmers' clumsy attempt did nothing but compound his guilt. 'Why, Mrs Ambrose!' he said. 'What a pleasure.' He stepped towards her, his hand extended for another shake but Suzanne made no attempt to take hold of it. After a few moments, he gave up and allowed the hand to fall to his side. 'Please allow me to convey my condolences regarding your son. Martin, wasn't it? How very tragic.'

Suzanne finally found her voice. 'What a surprise seeing *you* here, Chief Inspector. But then, I am somewhat earlier than usual.'

Adam had moved to the office door now.

'The Chief Inspector deliberately arranged to come in early,' he said. 'He didn't want to cause any embarrassment. With regard to Will and so forth.'

'How very thoughtful.' Suzanne made no attempt to mask the sarcasm in her tone. She gave Chalmers a frosty smile. 'And I wonder what you two were so deep in conversation about? My ex-husband, perhaps?'

Chalmers looked positively outraged at the suggestion. 'Good heavens, no, Mrs Ambrose. Not at all! No, I was simply discussing some points regarding the proposed new police headquarters in Wythenshawe. As I'm sure you're aware, Delta are going to be handling the internal design and there were a few points I wanted to talk through with Mr Fielding.'

'Such as where you'll store all those paperclips?' offered Suzanne caustically.

Chalmers smiled thinly. 'That kind of thing. At any rate, Mrs Ambrose, I must be going. A busy day ahead of me by all accounts. Good morning, Mr Fielding. Mrs Ambrose.' He went out of the office, closing the door behind him. Adam turned back to his own office.

'So,' he said, more in control now. 'Did you manage to get those cash projections sorted out? We've a presentation first thing with representatives from the Kendoshita corporation. Don't want everything to go all kung phooey on that one, do we? They . . .'

'Adam, what's going on?' Suzanne interrupted him.

He turned back to her, his face a picture of innocence. 'Come again?' he said.

'Don't play dumb with me! What was Chalmers doing here at this time of the morning?'

Adam spread his hands in a gesture of bemusement. 'I thought he already told you. The new headquarters . . .'

'Adam, I'm not completely stupid!' snapped Suzanne. 'Work won't commence on that project until the year 2004. And as if they'd send a Chief Inspector to discuss the placing of some filing cabinets!'

'Well, maybe he's just a "hands on" kind of guy. What can I tell you?'

'You can tell me the truth. That he was asking questions about Will. That *is* what was happening, right?'

'For goodness sake, Suzanne . . .'

'And what was with the special handshake? In case you've forgotten, it was stuff like that that got Will thrown out of the force in the first place. Don't tell me . . . *please*, don't tell me that you belong to the same club.'

Adam stared at her. 'Suzanne, you should hear yourself!' he exclaimed. 'What club? You've already been told what Derek was doing here, and . . .'

'Oh, so it's Derek now, is it? For God's sake, Adam, if you two get any chummier, you'll be in each other's pants!'

Now Adam looked distinctly annoyed. His face reddened and he bunched his hands into fists as he replied. 'Suzanne, I don't know what conclusion you've jumped to, but let me assure you it's the wrong one. It simply makes good business sense to keep the cops sweet. You know better than anyone how they can fuck you about if they decide they don't like the cut of your jib. Now, I can't blame you for being paranoid about the police after everything that's happened with Will but I have to say, I'm deeply offended by your suspicions. I mean, who stood by you when all that shit was going down about Will's past involvement with hard drugs? That kind of publicity could have seriously damaged our programme for the New Millennium theatre.'

Suzanne sighed. Now she thought about it, maybe she was being more than a little bit paranoid. 'I appreciate that,' she said. 'I'm sorry, Adam, I guess I over-reacted.' She moved across to her desk and sat down. 'I've been under a lot of stress lately. It's hard to keep a sense of proportion.'

'I hope you didn't come back to work too soon,' he told her. He sat himself on the edge of her desk and placed a comforting hand on her shoulder. 'God knows we need you here, but I'd feel a lot happier if I was sure you were up to it.'

'I'm fine on that score,' she assured him. 'Believe me. It's just that life at home is kind of weird right now.'

Adam made a sympathetic face. 'Still no word from Will?' he asked. His tone was so casual, so off-hand, she nearly told him the truth; she could even picture herself saying it. *Adam, you won't believe this but Will has only dressed himself up in a selection of Oxfam cast-offs and gone to live with the Rag People.*

But at the last instant, something in her nerves shrilled like a car alarm, warning her to keep quiet. She looked up into Adam's handsome face and his expression was somehow too calm, too unconcerned. *Oh look*, it seemed to scream at her, *I'm just making conversation, there's no hidden agenda here!*

Suzanne swallowed. 'Not a dicky-bird,' she replied. 'I'm sure he'll turn up in Southport before very much longer.'

'Umm, yeah, I guess. Still, it's kind of funny isn't it? Him heading off like that without a word. Without leaving a note or anything . . .'

He's definitely fishing, thought Suzanne indignantly. *Just what the hell is going on here?*

'I mean it's only common courtesy to leave a note. You'd have thought he'd have given you some idea of where he was going.'

She gave him a dismissive look. 'There was nothing, Adam. Not a word. Now, if you'll excuse me, I've got a mountain of paperwork to go through.'

'Yes. Yes, of course.' He got up off the desk and made for his own office door. 'I've quite a bit to work through myself.' He closed the door behind him and took a seat at his desk. After a few moments, he picked up his phone and punched in a number. When the call was answered, he swung his chair around so that his back was to the glass partition. He tried to give the impression that he was doing it aimlessly but Suzanne was convinced that he was worried about her picking up a clue from the movement of his lips.

She glanced at the phone on her own desk, a shared line with Adam and she experienced a powerful desire to pick it up and listen in to what he was saying; but she knew that he would hear the soft crackle as she picked up the handset.

She frowned. She didn't like secrets unless they were her own. And something odd was definitely going on here. Something that was beginning to frighten her.

She started to go through her papers, amending, correcting, signing them, but her mind was on automatic pilot. She was thinking about Will again and wishing that there was some way she could contact him.

Chapter Twenty-Three

It was an unexpectedly pleasant day, the sky clear and radiating some watery winter sunshine. Will crossed the street by the statue of Queen Victoria and peered over the metal railings into the large area of dead flower beds and blighted turf that was still known as Piccadilly Gardens.

As usual, the place was busy, the green-painted wooden benches peopled mostly by office workers on lunch breaks. Sandwiches, crisps and canned drinks were being consumed and scraps thrown to the few nervous pigeons that dared to visit the area. Up until a few years ago the city had had a real problem with pigeons but since they had become a regular menu item for the homeless they were in much shorter supply and a damn sight more wary than they used to be.

There were already a few Rag People wandering through the crowds begging off the workers, so Will told himself he wouldn't look out of place. He soon spotted Clive, sitting on a bench in the very centre of the gardens, but instead of going straight to him, Will strolled a few wary circuits of the area, wanting to ensure himself that no trap had been laid for him. At last, satisfied that all was above board, he wandered towards Clive's bench and took a seat beside him.

'Sorry, mate, that seat's reserved.' Clive's gaze flicked disapprovingly over Will's dirty face and clothes, moved away then came back for a second look. 'Bloody hell,' he whispered. 'Will? Jesus, I didn't recognize you!'

'That's all right.' Will eyed a plastic carrier bag that nestled on the bench between them. 'I hope that's what I think it is,' he said.

Clive nodded. 'Marks and Spencer's finest.' He slid the bag along the bench and Will grabbed it eagerly. He saw that it contained two plastic containers, each of them holding three sandwiches. There was also a can of cola. It was the kind of treat that he'd almost be ready to kill for and his eyes filled with involuntary tears. Clive was embarrassed by the reaction. He looked quickly away. 'I wasn't sure what you liked so I got a selection,' he said.

'It doesn't matter what's on them!' Will assured him. He lifted an arm to wipe the tears on his sleeve. 'I've gone well past the point of being picky about what I eat.' He tore open the first container with trembling hands and took a ravenous bite out of a cheese and pickle on granary bread. He chewed for a moment, relishing the tangy taste of mature cheese on his tongue. Then he pushed the rest of the sandwich into his mouth in a couple of big bites and grabbed the next one, which turned out to be prawn mayonnaise, something he wouldn't have dreamed of eating a week ago. He wolfed it down just the same.

Clive watched appalled from the corner of his eye. 'Christ, mate, you look *awful*,' he said. 'You must have lost a stone! And what are all those bruises on your face?'

Will shrugged. He tried to say that he hadn't been taking too much notice of his weight, but his mouth was still too full to speak clearly. He ate the third sandwich, chicken tikka and salad, without pausing to let the second one go down. The flavour was so intense he thought he'd died and gone to heaven. He was about to open the second pack, when he remembered Scally and Marianne, and how much they would enjoy a rare treat like this. So he crammed it into his raincoat pocket and opened the can of cola instead. He took a long swig from its contents and concluded with a loud belch, which he was quite unable to contain.

'Pardon me,' he said dutifully. 'Clive, you've no idea how wonderful that was.'

Clive smiled ruefully. 'I could see it was appreciated,' he said. 'Will, I hope this charade is worth all the grief you're putting yourself through. I hope you're making some progress.'

'I am *now*,' Will told him. 'Till yesterday, I was getting

nowhere fast. But I've made some useful contacts and I've been admitted into a tribe.'

'Really?' Clive seemed impressed. 'That's pretty good going. How did you manage it?'

Will frowned. 'It's a long story,' he said. 'Anyway, I've got a space in a shelter on Sobriety Street. You know, the old viaduct?'

'I know it well.' Clive frowned. 'Had a checkered career, that place. I seem to remember a few years back, there was a skinned body discovered in one of those arches. Feller who found it worked at *The Post*. A photographer, I believe . . .'

'Hmm.' Will interrupted Clive impatiently. 'Clive, you know anything about a man called Marshall Resnick?'

Clive considered for a moment. 'The name does ring a bell. He's something to do with the Manchester music scene, isn't he? The Messiahs, all that stuff.'

'So I'm told. I'm also told that he deals Warp.'

Clive raised his eyebrows. 'Well, drugs and rock music do tend to go hand in hand, I suppose. But somebody telling you he deals, isn't quite the same as having proof, is it?'

'I know that. But I've found out where he lives. I'm planning to go and see him, tonight.'

Clive grimaced. 'You think that's wise?'

'Not necessarily. But it's definitely what I want to do.'

'It wouldn't be better to tip off the cops, let them check him out?'

Will gave a snort of contempt. 'They're the last people I'd tell. The more I find out about the police, the more I think that they don't give a stuff how many people are dying from drugs. It almost makes me think . . .'

'What?'

'That they're involved, in some way.'

'Oh, come on Will, that's starting to sound a little bit paranoid, isn't it? OK, I'd be the first to admit that they aren't exactly Snow White these days, but . . .'

Will sighed. 'If you think that sounds loopy, I'm afraid there's worse to come.' Will glanced at his friend, unsure of how he would receive the next piece of information. 'You ever heard of people called Subs?'

Clive grinned. 'Sure. The Rag People's bogie-men, aren't they? Supposed to live in the sewers. I remember some old geezer jabbering on about them when I was trying to research the article. He told me that's where all the people kept disappearing to. The Subs came up and took 'em!' Clive laughed dismissively but when Will didn't join in, his expression grew serious. 'Will, it's a fairy story,' he said.

Will swallowed hard. 'What would you say if I told you I've seen them?'

'I'd say you'd been taking your disguise a mite too seriously, mate. You don't have to drink meths to convince the others, surely?'

Again Clive didn't get the laugh he'd anticipated. 'I was stone cold sober,' Will assured him.

Clive shrugged. 'Well, OK, but what do you mean, you've "seen them"? They were coming up out of a sewer, were they?'

'No, not exactly. But they certainly smelled like they'd come from one. The other night I helped out this kid, he was being attacked by these two weird-looking guys. You should have seen them, Clive. White faces that looked like they've never seen daylight. And the smell of them! Jesus, it almost made me hurl. And then, we had this fight. I punched one of them in the belly and . . .' He shook his head. 'You're going to think I've lost my mind.'

'Maybe, but tell me anyway.'

Will ran his fingers through his hair. 'This . . . this thing came out of his mouth. This big . . . worm or something. It was like, ten inches long, the body white and jointed. It was wriggling around all over the street and the Sub . . . he . . .' Will's voice trailed off. 'I've never seen anything like it,' he concluded.

Clive seemed unimpressed. 'Sounds like a tapeworm,' he said. 'There must be every opportunity to contract one when you're living rough, eating out of garbage bins and whatever. And believe me, ten inches is nothing. They can be several feet long.'

'Yeah? You ever seen somebody cough up a tapeworm and then spend the next few minutes trying to put it back where it came from? Anyway, Scally says they *all* have them.'

'Scally?'

'He's the kid I told you about. The Subs were trying to kill him when I arrived on the scene.'

Clive frowned. 'Kill him, why?'

'I don't know. Scally told me that Subs abducted a friend of his a while back. Took him down into the sewers. Scally never saw him again.'

Clive frowned. The expression on his face suggested that he really didn't want to have to take this seriously.

'You think it's a paedophile thing?' he ventured.

Will shook his head.

'Paedophiles can be scary enough but I don't recall them trying to murder kids before they took their pleasures with them; and I don't recall any of them lurking around in the sewers either, though I'd be the first to admit that it's probably their spiritual home.'

Clive smiled drily. 'Yeah, but you never actually saw them going into the sewers, did you?'

'No, but . . .'

'So you only have the kid's word for it, about what happened to his friend. And this kid is how old?'

'Fourteen, fifteen. Something like that. But Clive, I believe him! You weren't there, you didn't see those . . .'

'People?' ventured Clive.

'*Things*. That's how I thought of them, Clive. They seemed barely human.'

Clive let out a long exhalation of air. 'I don't know what to say to you, Will. As somebody whose whole career has been founded on the gathering of rational facts, I have to tell you that this all sounds pretty bloody hysterical.'

'I'm well aware of how it sounds,' snapped Will irritably. 'But before you go dismissing me as some kind of lunatic, let me tell you that being a Rag Man gives you an entirely different perspective on life. I've seen things this past week that I'd never dreamed of, things I couldn't believe would happen in the 20th Century. It's like when you put on the rags you step through some time warp into the middle ages. It's all still there. Every bad thing we thought we'd left behind for ever. It all goes on when you're asleep in your bed. Rape, murder, incest, starvation . . . they're all everyday occurrences for the Rag People.'

Clive picked up the discarded carrier bag and folded it neatly on his lap.

'I did try to warn you it wouldn't be a bed of roses,' he said. 'Try to remember, Will, those things needn't apply to you.'

'But they already do, Clive. I've already killed a man.'

'Jesus, Will!' Clive hunched closer on the bench as though afraid of being overheard. 'What are you telling me?'

'Just what I said. It's how I gained admission to the tribe. I killed a man in a fair fight. Split his head open with a baseball bat and spilled his brains on the ground.'

Clive's expression was grim. 'Maybe it's best you don't tell me any more,' Clive warned him. 'Remember what I do for a living.'

'Oh, I'm not worried. There's no evidence now. The body is gone, burned to ashes. And there's not a person in the tribe who would betray me to the police. It was a duel, Clive, a matter of honour. Simple as that. The Rag People understand honour.'

Clive was twisting the carrier bag in his hands now. 'But you mustn't become like them, Will. If you do, then you're lost. You must keep that in mind when you go to see this dealer, you mentioned. What you can't do is take the law into your own hands.'

'Maybe not in your society,' admitted Will. 'But in mine, I'll kill him without a second thought.'

'It's not your society!' insisted Clive. 'You're only visiting. Please try to remember that. You're an actor, playing a part. Don't lose yourself in the role.'

Will looked at his friend for a moment, then nodded. 'Sure,' he said. 'I'll try not to.' But in his heart, Will was already beginning to suspect that it was too late to worry on that score.

Up on the roof of the Metrosound Radio building, Don Bullen used a pair of powerful miniature binoculars to study the tiny figures far below him. He watched with a mixture of triumph and despair, the former because his hunch about Clive Singleton had paid dividends so promptly, the latter because

223

the state-of-the-art surveillance equipment with which they'd been issued was malfunctioning badly. Beside him, DS Lang was waving a foot-long directional microphone backwards and forwards at the gardens below them, in a futile attempt to pick up Singleton and Ambrose's conversation. What was emerging from the receiver was quite obviously Anthea Turner presenting an edition of *Desert Island Discs*.

'For fuck's sake,' growled Bullen. 'It would be nice if for once, they managed to issue us with equipment that actually worked, wouldn't it?'

'Probably something to do with atmospherics,' suggested Lang dismally.

'Oh yeah? Not something to do with ineptitude, then?'

Lang gave his partner an indignant look. 'I said we should have brought an expert with us. But no, you said we couldn't afford to have anyone else in on this.' Lang began to fiddle with the tuning dial. 'Wait a minute, I think I'm getting something else now . . .' *Desert Island Discs* faded out abruptly and was replaced by the sound of the artist formally known as Prince performing an old number called 1999, a song that seemed to be on the radio every five minutes these days.

'I love this,' observed Lang. 'Takes me right back to my college days . . .'

'Oh marvellous, I'm really pleased for you!' Bullen shot his partner a poisonous look, then turned his attention back to the tiny figures on the bench below. He hunched forward over the balustrade, as though hoping to overhear what they were saying. What was Ambrose playing at? He was dressed like a tramp. Indeed, when he'd first approached the bench, Bullen had thought it was just a Rag Man begging for food and sure enough, a few seconds later, Singleton had given him some sandwiches. Brand new, store bought. That had seemed suspicious and subsequent use of the binocular's powerful zoom facility had confirmed his suspicions. It was Will Ambrose all right, looking convincingly dirty and dishevelled as only a man who is living rough can look . . .

At last, Lang managed to lock on to the right signal.

'I'll try not to,' said Ambrose's voice. 'Anyway, I've got to run now, Clive. Things to do. I'll see you next week but not here. I'll contact you to arrange a time and place.' The tiny figures stood up, shook hands and then moved off in different directions.

'Shit!' yelled Bullen. 'They're leaving! The car, the car!' He turned and ran towards the blue Toyota, a short distance behind them on the rooftop car park.

'But the equipment,' mumbled Lang. 'We can't just . . .'

'Leave it!' snapped Bullen. 'We'll pick it up later!'

'Yeah, but somebody could . . .'

'Leave it!' Bullen was already strapping himself into the passenger seat. 'Come on, man, we're losing him!'

Lang sighed. He dropped the microphone and trotted across the roof to the car. He climbed in behind the wheel, started up the engine and accelerated towards the exit ramp with a shrill squeal of tyres.

'Which one do we follow?' he asked, as they descended the ramps to the street.

'Ambrose of course. We can get the other one any time. Looked like he was heading over towards the station . . .' The Toyota swung out of the exit and onto the main street, narrowly avoiding collision with an ancient red Metro. The driver blared his horn and jabbed two fingers at them in the time-honoured salute, but Bullen chose to ignore the man. Right now he had bigger fish to fry. The Toyota swept around the side of Piccadilly Gardens, the wheels thudding as they crossed the tram tracks. They drove along the street for a few moments before they spotted Ambrose strolling along the pavement, his hands in his pockets.

'Do we grab him now?' asked Lang.

'No. Slow down a bit. Let's see where he's headed, shall we?' Lang hit the brakes and car horns clamoured behind them as other drivers were obliged to adjust their speed. Happily, Ambrose didn't glance over his shoulder. He seemed to be deep in thought. He carried right on walking, unaware that he was being followed.

'Gotcha,' murmured Bullen, grinning like a Cheshire cat; and his bad start to the day was all but forgotten. He was back in control and Chalmers was going to owe him one for this.

'What are you looking so pleased about?' muttered Lang.

'I'm just a happy soldier,' Bullen told him. 'What's wrong with that?'

They kept creeping along behind their quarry, who was heading past the station now and walking briskly on in the direction of Ardwick.

Chapter Twenty-Four

Pinder spotted the group of Rag Men from his car as he drove around the back streets behind Piccadilly station. There were half a dozen of them, standing aimlessly around, hands in pockets, cigarettes in mouths. Their green arm bands identified them as belonging to the Ardwick tribe and one of them, a tall skinny individual in a black plastic raincoat, sported the accompanying gold band which identified him as a Duke. It was too good an opportunity to miss.

Pinder found a place to park up. He opened the leather holdall on the back seat and transferred some of its contents to a smaller nylon sports bag, packing enough supplies for six new hands. Then slinging the sports bag over his shoulder, he walked back to the Rag Men, whistling cheerfully to himself. He crossed the main street and entered the narrow back alley where he had seen them.

They glanced up as he approached, appraising him suspiciously, noting his expensive clothes, wondering perhaps what was in the sports bag and whether it might be something worth mugging him for; but they were doubtless thrown by his apparent confidence, the way he walked straight towards them, smiling benevolently like a man who was about to do them a massive favour.

'Morning, lads!' he said brightly. 'I don't suppose any of you would be interested in earning some money?' Asking the question matter-of-factly, as though they earned money all the time, like it was no big deal.

The Rag Men stared at him for a moment in slack-jawed surprise. Then one of them, the man wearing the Duke's insignia, laughed bitterly and his companions joined in.

'Oh aye,' he said. 'I suppose we wouldn't mind, would we lads? But don't think any of us are going to touch our toes for you, sunshine. You'll find people like that waiting up by the station.'

Pinder smiled. He studied the Duke for a moment. He was tall and thin, his hair receded to nothing on the top of his head. His hook nose and rotten teeth did nothing for his looks and it was evident that whatever had propelled this man to the top position in his tribe, it wasn't his personal charisma. Still, it was immaterial. Whatever Pinder thought of him, this was the man he had to win over. Get him and the others would follow on like sheep.

Pinder set down the holdall and cleared his throat. 'No, sir, you misunderstand my intentions. What I'm looking for today is a sales force.'

Again, the Rag Men laughed. 'Oh yeah, we'd make great salesmen us!' mocked the Duke. 'I can just see all those nice middle-class ladies letting *me* into their houses, dressed like this.'

'You'd be all right, Frank!' laughed another of the men, a squat, stubby man with a bristly ginger beard and a Scouse accent. 'Them posh tarts all like a bit of rough, now and then!'

Pinder smiled wearily. He imagined how refreshing it would be to cripple one of these imbeciles, instead of having to be Mr Reasonable the whole time. 'There's no door-to-door involved,' he assured them. 'Your customers would come to you and they wouldn't give a tinker's cuss how you were dressed.'

The man called Frank narrowed his eyes suspiciously. 'Then it's something illegal,' he observed.

'Oh yes, absolutely. Is that a problem?'

Frank glanced around at the others. He shrugged. 'Depends on what it is.'

Pinder gazed at him openly. 'Drugs,' he said. 'A charming little substance called Warp.' There were grunts of disapproval from several of the Rag Men. Frank made an expression of distaste.

'I don't want nothin' to do with that,' he said. 'I don't agree with drugs.'

'Really?' Pinder rearranged his babylike features into a look

228

of exaggerated astonishment. 'You surprise me . . . Frank. May I call you that? I understood you were all in favour of them.'

Frank laughed dismissively. 'What you talkin' about,' he growled.

'Well, excuse me, but . . . may I?' Pinder stepped closer and reached into one of the pockets of Frank's raincoat. His plump hand emerged carrying a small plastic package of white powder. 'What's this then?' he asked innocently. 'Castor sugar?'

Frank was astonished. He stood there, his mouth open. The others were looking at him doubtfully.

'How the hell did you—?'

But Pinder interrupted him by reaching out a hand and plunging his thumb and forefinger into Frank's open mouth.

'And what's this? Ah hah!' He pulled out another plastic bag this one containing a dozen purple tablets. He showed them to Frank.

'Now I understand your reticence,' he said. 'You've already set up in competition!'

'Here now, look!' protested Frank. 'I haven't got the first idea how . . .'

But now Pinder had reached into another pocket of Frank's raincoat. He pulled out a length of string. There were incriminating objects tied to it at intervals. A syringe. A coke spoon. A packet of extra large rolling papers. A crack pipe. A spliff. The men's initial astonishment had given way now to a kind of amused delight, like children at a magic show. Even Frank was grinning, displaying those cracked, stained teeth in an ugly grimace. And Pinder knew that he had them now. He had them in the palm of his hand.

'How did you *do* that?' asked Ginger Beard thoughtfully.

'It's a gift,' said Pinder dismissively. 'Now Gentlemen, if you will observe closely, I'll show you how my proposition can change your fortunes.' He showed them his empty right hand, made a quick gesture and clenched his fist. When he opened it again, there was a single purple tablet nestled in his palm. 'One tab of Warp,' he said. 'Cost to the punter . . .' He enclosed the tablet in his hand and when he reopened it, it had turned into a neatly folded twenty pound note. He opened it up to show it to them.

'Who'd give that much for one tablet?' muttered Frank.

'Oh, you'd be surprised, Frank. There are plenty of punters out there with a taste for this merchandise. People with more money than sense. People with money to burn. People looking for the fast road to oblivion. Believe me, you won't be short of customers. And for every twenty pounds you take . . .' He crumpled the note in his fist and opened his hand again, revealing a shiny new one pound coin. '. . . you get to keep one of these.'

Frank looked unimpressed. 'And you get to keep nineteen,' he observed. 'Not being overly generous, are you?'

'I didn't say it was a charity, did I?' murmured Pinder. 'But it's an opportunity to make some money of your own. On a good night, you might make twenty pounds. And Frank, if I could just have a word with you in private . . .' Pinder slipped an arm around Frank's shoulders, picked up the shoulder bag, and led him along the alley away from his companions, talking in a hushed tone so the others wouldn't hear. 'The deal I just mentioned, that only applies to a basic salesman. But the Duke of the tribe . . .'

'That's me,' said Frank, a little too quickly.

Pinder smiled, steeling himself against the awful smell that was emanating from the Rag Man.

'I should have guessed,' he purred. 'Well, this is how we work it. Your lads there, they would be your standard salesmen. You would be their coordinator. You would be responsible for collecting their money, ensuring that they stayed to their appointed pitches. And of course, you would liaise with me once a week to tally up the sales. Obviously, I couldn't be expected to meet with every Tom, Dick and Harry in the tribe.'

Frank shook his head. 'No, 'course not,' he agreed. 'But it sounds complicated.'

'It isn't,' Pinder assured him. 'It's really quite simple. But the post does carry special responsibilities and that's something that my employers wish to reward. So above and beyond the commission you make from selling the product, there would also be an additional weekly payment to you of twenty-five pounds.'

Frank's eyebrows arched in astonishment and Pinder had to

work hard not to burst out laughing. That was the beauty of using these scum-buckets. You mentioned a sum that would be considered an insulting pittance to most people and the poor bastards nearly wet themselves at the wonder of it. Pinder slipped a hand into his pocket. It was time to play the trump card.

'As coordinator, you also get one of these,' he said. He pulled out a disposable mobile phone and a compatible Smart Card. 'I'll give you a number where I can be contacted in the event of a problem,' said Pinder. 'The card allows you to make up to three local calls a week. Every time we meet up, I'll issue you with a new card.'

Now Frank was well and truly hooked, Pinder could tell. A mobile phone, even a cheap bit of disposable junk like this one, conferred prestige and an aura of respectability onto the owner. Frank took the phone and examined it curiously.

'The . . . other calls?' he murmured.

'Are yours to use as you please.' This was another laugh. Pinder reflected that Frank probably didn't know anybody he might call. But image was everything. He'd known one Duke who phoned the speaking clock a couple of times a week, just to give the impression that he was a big deal. Sad, sad, sad.

'So, what do you think?' he asked Frank. 'Interested?'

Frank was still admiring the phone. He glanced up, nodded. 'I reckon so,' he said. 'Sure, why not?'

'Good. Now mark me well, Frank, if I appoint you to the post, I need to be able to trust you. You have authority over your men? They'll do as you say?'

Frank grinned crookedly. 'They will,' he said.

'Excellent. And you realize that as their coordinator, you'll be responsible for them? If one of them tries to rip me off, you'll have to make good on the debt.'

'Don't worry. They won't step out of line.' Frank looked thoughtful. 'What, er, what happens if I get picked up by The Blues?'

'It's very unlikely. But if you do, don't say a word to anybody. When they give you your one phone call, ring my number and I'll arrange to get you out. But Frank, this is very, very important. Don't ever mention my name to anybody.'

Frank looked puzzled. 'I don't *know* your name,' he said.

'Good. Let's keep it that way, shall we? I had somebody working for me recently who picked it up from somewhere. Couldn't seem to stop mentioning it all over the place. So I had to stop him.' Pinder reached into his pocket and pulled out a polaroid photograph. He handed it to Frank.

'Jesus,' whispered Frank.

'Quite,' agreed Pinder. 'It's not a bad likeness of Tom. You probably knew him, he was the Duke of the Wythenshawe tribe. He's still alive in that picture but as you can see from the condition of his throat, not for very much longer.'

Frank swallowed hard. He tried to turn away but Pinder put a powerful hand on his shoulder, holding him in position. 'Don't misinterpret this, Frank. Old Tom here, he tried to fuck with me and naturally, I couldn't allow him to do that. But people who are straight with me, to them I'm as nice as pie. You catch my drift, old boy?'

Frank nodded. He kept his gaze fixed on the photograph until Pinder returned it to his pocket.

'Mutual trust,' continued Pinder. 'That's the only way for this thing to work. So if there's any problems at all, you ring me on this number, OK.' A card seemed to materialize in Pinder's hand and he gave it to Frank. It was a square of plain white card with a mobile telephone number printed on it. No name, no address, just a number. 'Now, Frank, I'm going to ask you one more time if you want to work for me – and if you say yes, we'll shake hands and I'll consider it a done deal.'

Frank hesitated for a long moment, a faraway expression in his eyes. Pinder knew he was thinking about the money, and knew also that there was really no way he could afford to turn down the offer. Not in his position.

'Yes,' said Frank at last.

'Good! Now, there's one last thing I must impress upon you. When you've collected the first week's money, it's going to be a lot of cash, probably more than you've ever seen; and the temptation to make a run with it will be very strong.'

'Don't worry about me,' Frank assured him.

'Oh, I don't. Because you see, if you did try something like that, I would find you, Frank, no matter where you tried to hide. I'd find you and I'd kill you and then I'd be using *your* photograph as a warning to my next mule. So I'm telling you now, be a good lad, eh?'

Frank stared at Pinder for a moment as though considering arguing the case. But it must have been evident that there was no arguing with somebody like this. So he simply lowered his gaze and nodded.

'Good.' Pinder gave Frank the sports bag. 'This is yours now. You'll find everything you need in there. Merchandise to be split six ways. Six envelopes detailing the sites where you will sell the merchandise, cash only. We don't accept cheques or credit cards, understood?'

'Yeah, whatever you say.'

'Another thing. You'll find a printed list in the bag. These are places where it is expressly forbidden to sell the merchandise. On no account must you or any of your men, disobey this order. Our mutual friend Tom didn't take much notice of that instruction and look what happened to him. Ring me in one week's time to arrange our next meeting. You should have no trouble getting rid of your stock by then.'

'What if we can't?'

Pinder spread his arms in a shrug. 'My dear chap, as I've already told you, just level with me and everything will be hunky dory. But I have the greatest faith in this merchandise. Believe me, it virtually sells itself! And your lads will have the great incentive of pure capitalism. The more they sell, the more they earn! Give them a few years and they could be doing my job. Now, go and get them organized.'

'What if others want to get involved in this?'

Pinder frowned. 'All that's for the future. For the moment, let's keep it as it is, OK? I'll tell you when the time is right to let others in on it. A word of advice though. People are naturally jealous. So tell your team to keep it to themselves, all right?'

'OK.' Frank shouldered the sports bag and began to walk back to the others. He paused, glanced over his shoulder and waggled the mobile phone in his hand. 'I'll be in touch,' he said, and he went on his way, looking for all the world like a man who had just had the biggest single stroke of luck in living memory.

Pinder watched him go not without a certain sense of regret. Oh, Frank would be as good as gold for a few months. He would work diligently, he would toe the line, he would perform every crummy task that was asked of him. But after a time, he would become restless, overambitious. He would want to know more, he would want to *earn* more. Then he would begin to take liberties, pocketing an extra pound here, an extra fiver there.

Pinder kept a large brown envelope in his study at home, containing dozens of polaroids, every one of them a portrait of a dead or dying Rag Man. These days he only carried the latest of them around to use as a deterrent but whenever he encountered a new face, he found himself viewing it with a photographer's dispassionate eye, imagining how it would look in the brief vivid flare of a camera flash . . .

He had little doubt that Frank's ugly mug would feature in his rogue's gallery before very much longer.

He turned and, hands in pockets, he strolled back to the Pontiac wondering where he might go for a decent spot of lunch.

Chapter Twenty-Five

When Scally got back to the arch around midday, there was no sign of Marianne in the shelter. He looked around and eventually spotted her sitting out on the waste ground beside the ashes of the bonfire. He went over to see what she was doing.

Despite the watery sunshine it was a cold day and Scally saw that she wasn't even wearing her coat. She was sitting cross-legged on the damp grass, her gaze fixed intently on the street up ahead, her breath clouding around her like a halo. She seemed to be waiting for somebody.

'Marianne?' He kneeled beside her and placed a hand on her arm. 'What are you doing out here? It's freezing. Come into the shelter and get warm.'

But she seemed hardly aware of his entreaties. 'I'm waiting for Steve,' she told him.

'Well, OK, but you could wait for him inside, couldn't you?'

She shook her head. 'No, I'll wait here,' she insisted. 'Then I'll see him when he turns onto the street.'

Scally thought for a moment about telling her the truth, that her new-found hero wasn't Steve at all, he was just some guy who'd happened along at the wrong time. But on reflection, he decided that he couldn't be that cruel. He couldn't bear to see her hurt as he knew she would be, by the honest truth. Sometimes it was better to let people have their dreams. He settled himself down beside her.

'How did you meet?' he asked her. 'You and Steve?'

Marianne smiled fondly. 'I was just a kid,' she told Scally. 'We both were really. I was sixteen, he was maybe a couple of years older. There was this club in town called . . .' She made an effort to remember. 'PJ Bells. One of those gloomy little downstairs rock clubs where you used to go on a Saturday night. I was there with some girlfriends and the Messiahs were playing.'

'The Messiahs, playing in a little club?' Scally raised his eyebrows. 'No way! They're massive!'

'Not then, they weren't! We're talking maybe 1991, '92 here. It was one of their first gigs, they were just the support band. To be honest, I wasn't that keen on what they were doing but I liked Steve right from the start. He looked so nervous, so unsure of himself, it kind of made you want to *mother* him, you know?'

'Not really,' said Scally.

'Anyway, they weren't going down at all well. Me and my mates, we'd had a few drinks, so we didn't care. We ended up bopping around at the front of the stage, you know, really getting into the music. Me and Steve started making with the eye contact. I knew he was interested, because he kept looking away, you know the way people do when they really like you?'

Scally frowned. 'I didn't know that,' he said. 'People look away when they like you?'

'Oh sure, like this.' Marianne demonstrated, glancing at Scally from the corner of her eye, then flicking her gaze away again. 'He kept doing that. Then, after they'd done their spot and the other band were on, he came over to the bar for a drink and we got talking.' She made a gesture of finality, smacking a clenched fist into the palm of her hand. 'That was it,' she said. 'Smitten, both of us. I went back to his flat that night and we made love . . .'

Scally blushed bright red and developed a sudden interest in examining his feet but Marianne didn't seem to notice. She carried on talking.

'Ah, it was the romance of the century, Scally! You know when you meet someone who is totally right for you? It was like that with me and Steve. As though we'd known each other for years. Maybe even in a previous life.' She leaned closer as if to confide a secret. 'That's how I recognized the *new* Steve! He looks different on the outside, but inside, he's just the same. I can sense that.'

Scally smiled at her uncomfortably. He didn't know what to say to her now.

A group of figures turned the corner at the top of the street and Marianne sat up hopefully; but she slumped back again when she recognized Frank and some of his cronies. Frank led the way along the street, walking with a jaunty spring in his step, the cock of the walk. As he drew closer to the arch, he noticed Scally and Marianne sitting over by the bonfire. He said something to his companions and stepping off the street, he strolled across the waste ground towards them, an unpleasant grin on his face. Scally noticed that he had a sports bag slung over his shoulder and that he was clutching in one hand what looked like a mobile phone. The phone would easily have fitted into one of his many pockets but Scally decided that he wanted others to see that he had a phone, even though it was only a cheap disposable.

Frank stopped a short distance away and stood, looking down at them with an air of superiority.

'Still here then?' he observed acidly. He waited a moment, as if expecting a reply. When he didn't get one, he continued, addressing his next remark to Scally.

'You had a word with her, did you? About pulling her weight.'

'Yeah,' said Scally, unconvincingly. 'Sure.'

'Only she doesn't look like she's doing very much at the moment, does she? And there's a bunch of people putting a meal together in the arch. Maybe she could go and help with that?'

'Maybe.' Scally glanced hopefully at Marianne but didn't get any reaction from her. He nudged her shoulder but she ignored him. He looked back at Frank and shrugged miserably.

Frank scowled. He took a step closer to Marianne and prodded her with the toe of his boot. She flinched but didn't even look up at him. She kept her gaze fixed resolutely on the opening at the top of the street.

'You heard,' said Frank. 'Shift your arse and go and help with the food.'

'No,' said Marianne quietly.

'What?' Frank looked incredulous. 'What did you say?'

'I said no.' Marianne still wouldn't look at him. 'I'm busy.'

'Busy? Busy doing what? You're just sitting there!'

'Look, why don't *I* help with the food?' offered Scally. He began to get to his feet but Frank stayed him with a hand to his chest.

'You stay where you are!' he barked. 'I told *her* to get up, not you.' He leaned over Marianne and prodded her in the chest with a dirty index finger. 'Maybe you didn't understand, lady, but I'm the Duke of this tribe and what I say goes. Now get the fuck up!' He reached out and grabbed a handful of her hair, pulling her roughly to her feet.

'Hey, leave her alone!' shouted Scally, scrambling up after her.

'Shut it!' Frank dealt the boy a vicious back-handed slap that sent him staggering backwards, little lights flaring in front of his eyes. 'I'm warning you,' he told Marianne. 'It's up to you. You can go and start work now or you can piss off out of the arch. Now what's it to be?'

'Steve!' Marianne twisted suddenly away from Frank, leaving him clutching nothing more than a clump of blonde hair. She ran across the waste ground and up along the street towards a figure that had just turned the corner. Frank stared after her in disbelief.

'Steve?' he echoed. He glanced accusingly at Scally. 'I thought his name was Will.'

Scally was rubbing his stinging cheek with the palm of his hand.

'Er . . . yeah. Steve's his *middle* name,' he muttered.

Frank scratched his head. He turned to look towards the approaching figures. Marianne had her arm around the newcomer's waist, her head resting on his shoulder.

'Looks like you lost your girlfriend, kid,' observed Frank gleefully.

'She never was my girlfriend,' muttered Scally; but he couldn't deny that he felt a powerful surge of jealousy, seeing Marianne and Will arm-in-arm like that. 'Anyway, they're just . . . mates, that's all.'

'Reckon so?' Frank laughed. 'Not for long, I'd say.'

Now Will and Marianne were coming into earshot. Will

looked at Scally and Frank, no doubt noticing the red patch on the boy's face.

'What's going on?' he asked.

'If you must know, I was having a word with your girlfriend,' said Frank. 'The lazy bitch was just sitting out here doing fuck all. I've told her already, if she doesn't get her act together, she's out of here . . . but does she take any notice of me?'

Will frowned. 'What exactly do you want her to do?' he asked.

'Peg and the others could use a hand in the arch, getting the food ready.'

'OK, I'm sure that's no problem.' Will turned to look at Marianne. 'What do you say? Will you help them out? Please?'

Marianne smiled. 'Of course,' she said. 'See you later.' She kissed Will gently on the cheek, then turned away and walked off towards the arch. Frank stared after her open-mouthed.

'Well, I'll be fucked!' he said.

'There's a way of asking,' Will told him. 'The trick is to make the person feel that they're being asked, not told.' He moved closer to Frank, until he was standing just a few inches away from him. 'Incidentally, I heard what you did to Marianne and it doesn't surprise me that she wants nothing to do with you.'

Frank sneered. 'Nothing happened that she didn't want to happen,' he said.

'Is that a fact? Well, I'm sorry, but I don't buy that. So I just want to tell you that if you ever lay so much as a finger on her again, you'll be very sorry.'

Frank stared at Will for a moment in utter disbelief. His reaction suggested that nobody had spoken to him like that in his entire life.

'Who do you think you're talking to?' he snarled. 'I'm the Duke of this tribe and I do as I please!'

'Not when it affects my friends,' Will corrected him.

'Your *friends*?' Frank laughed derisively. 'You've only been here five minutes! I wouldn't go overestimating your status if I was you. You're only here because I say it's OK.'

Will shook his head. 'I don't think so. I'm here because I won myself a place in a fair fight. As I understand it, nobody

239

can throw me out now unless somebody else challenges and beats me.'

Frank made a gesture of dismissal. 'I wouldn't set too much store by the rules, friend,' he said. 'I make the rules. And rules can be changed. If I decide I want you out, you're out, make no mistake about that. I only have to snap my fingers and I've got half a dozen boys who'll remove you, in pieces if necessary.'

Will didn't take his eyes from Frank's. 'But you don't have any boys with you now, do you? And how are you going to snap your fingers when I've broken them off and shoved them up your arse?'

Scally swallowed hard, watching the two men facing each other off. Amazingly it was Frank who glanced away first.

'Well, I can't stand around here all day,' he said. He patted his mobile phone. 'I've got business to attend to. And because I'm in a good mood, I'm going to overlook the way you just spoke to me. I believe in giving everybody one chance and you just had yours.' He began to walk away but then he paused, glanced back over his shoulder. 'You'd better keep your nose clean,' he said. 'One of these nights somebody might cut it off and make you eat it.'

Will didn't say anything. He just stood there staring at Frank until the Duke turned away again and walked off towards the arch. Scally moved over to stand beside Will. He felt decidedly apprehensive about what had just happened.

'You want to be careful,' he warned Will. 'He'll do it, you know. That stuff about the nose. It's happened to other people who got too lippy with him.'

Will shrugged. 'He doesn't scare me,' he said. 'I've dealt with his sort before. Cowards always hide behind other people. But get them out by themselves and they fold like paper bags.'

Scally frowned. He still felt worried and wondered if Will fully appreciated what Frank was capable of. Scally had witnessed some awful things over the time he'd been with the Ardwick tribe; people grabbed in the dead of night and beaten to a bloody pulp, or weighted down with stones and thrown into the canal. And always they were men who thought that they'd got the measure of Frank. Men who disputed his position as absolute ruler of the tribe.

He made a valiant effort to change the subject. 'So, where've you been today?' he asked.

'Out foraging,' Will told him. He took a plastic package from his pocket and showed it to Scally. 'A little something to go with our Pot Luck,' he said.

Scally brightened.

'Brilliant. Marks and Sparks!' He glanced at the label. 'They ain't even past their sell-by,' he observed.

Will grinned. 'I've got contacts too. Come on, let's see how Marianne's getting on with her chores.'

Forgetting their troubles for the moment, the two of them entered the arch. Neither of them noticed the blue Toyota that had just pulled to a stop at the top of Sobriety Street.

'Well, well, well,' said DCI Bullen, lowering the binoculars. 'Who'd have thought it, eh? A Rag Man!'

Lang was noisily munching his way through a packet of Coq-Au-Vin-flavoured corn snacks.

'What do we do now, Guv?' he asked. 'We're going to need some back up before we go in there. Rag Men are not renowned for their fondness of coppers.'

'Hmm.' Bullen looked thoughtful. 'We'd better get some advice before we make a move.'

Lang reached for the radio intercom but Bullen slapped his hand away.

'Don't be stupid!' He pulled a mobile phone from his pocket and punched some digits. 'It's the old man's personal line,' he explained. 'He asked me to be discreet on this one.' The phone rang a few times before it was answered by the familiar high-pitched voice.

'Boss? It's Don Bullen. I've managed to find our mutual friend, sir. And you were correct, he's right here in Manchester.'

'He is? That's marvellous. By golly, that was quick work!'

Bullen simpered. 'Oh, it was nothing really, sir. Had to do a bit of surveillance, but it payed off big time. It seems our friend has come down in the world, sir. He's living as a Rag Man.'

'You're kidding!'

'No, It's definitely him. There's a Rag community in Ardwick. The railway arches on Sobriety Street?'

'Ah yes, I've seen it from the train. He's there?'

'Appears to be living there, sir. Judging by the state of him, he must have been sleeping rough for some time. Can't imagine what he thinks he's doing . . .'

'He's *snooping*!' said Chalmers, a little too quickly. 'Put it together, man. The Rag People. Do I have to spell it out for you?'

'Er . . . no sir.' Bullen glanced self-consciously at Lang but he seemed to be taking little interest in the conversation. 'Thing is, what do you want me to do? It's a big community, it's going to take more than the two of us to walk in there and make an arrest.'

'No. Don't worry about that. I think we'll let somebody else take care of it for us.'

'Who, sir?'

'I'll er . . . call somebody who owes me a favour. Somebody who'd like to get on my good side.' Bullen realized that Chalmers didn't want to name names on an open line but it didn't take a genius to put it together. The headman of the Manchester League Of Decency was angling for membership of The Brotherhood: and the MLOD had already done the force a few Rag People-related favours in the past. 'Anyway, Bullen, great work,' concluded Chalmers. 'I shan't forget this.'

'Thank you, sir. Talk to you later.' Bullen switched off the phone and returned it to his pocket. He sat for a moment, gazing at the dark opening of the arch through which Ambrose had vanished. A pity, he thought. This was one collar he would have loved to have taken personally.

'What now?' asked Lang.

'A celebratory drink,' replied Bullen. 'At the Pig and Porcupine. My treat.'

'But what about Ambrose?'

'Don't worry. He's well taken care of. Come on, let's go, we're missing good drinking time here.'

Lang executed a speedy three-point turn and they drove out onto the main road. Turning left, they headed back into the city centre.

Chapter Twenty-Six

Clive Singleton sat at his desk in the *Evening Post* offices, staring at the screen of his computer. It was late and the office was deserted, but somehow he couldn't bring himself to go home yet. He kept thinking about Will, the way he'd looked, the way he'd talked, babbling on about things that no sane man would have talked about. And yet, the utter conviction with which he had spoken!

Clive sighed. He opened a new pack of cigarettes and lit one up, inhaling deeply, taking the smoke down deep into his lungs. On the screen in front of him, figures scrolled slowly upwards, the names of hundreds of lost persons. Clive didn't know what had impelled him to search out the relevant disc and he didn't know, either, what he expected to find that he hadn't discovered already. He'd been sitting here, looking through the database for the best part of an hour.

All those names, all those faceless people, all those empty columns displaying no address. What hope had anyone of finding out about these poor lost souls?

Of course, not all of them had been homeless. The database he was running was a complete list of everyone from the Greater Manchester area who had gone missing over the past five years. Naturally, a few of them were ordinary householders, people with respectable occupations who for one reason or another, had just dropped out of view.

There was one now, for instance. Roger Morse, aged thirty-six, a worker for the Water Utilities department. Clive clicked the mouse to stop the screen from scrolling. He selected the file on Morse and took a more detailed look. Morse had been a sewer worker who had gone missing on a routine inspection.

A co-worker had watched him descend through a manhole and had waited above ground for him to return, but he never had. The co-worker had even gone down to search but had found no trace of him. The official verdict had been that Morse must have fallen into the water and drowned; but no body was ever recovered.

Clive took a drag on his cigarette. He abandoned the document and returned to the list. He scrolled back several pages and found another man listed as working for Water Utilities. Trevor Dunstan had been forty-four years old when he'd gone missing. He and his team mate, Eric Robertson, thirty-two, had gone down into the sewers to carry out some routine repair work. When they failed to report in, a search was carried out around the area where they had been working. No trace was found of them, or the equipment they had been carrying – tools, flashlights, ropes, all had vanished. Again, no bodies were ever found. This time the deaths were blamed on a freak flood.

Clive stubbed out his cigarette. He felt a thrill of realization go through him. He'd been so intent on looking at the Rag People, he'd missed something that had been staring him in the face all this time. He punched up the search engine and tapped in the word 'Sewer'. After a few moments, it came back with six names from the database. Six men, over the past two years, all of them sewer workers, all of them missing without trace. No, that wasn't quite true. One body had been found some days later, floating in a culvert in Castlefield. The man was barely identifiable because so much of his body had been eaten, presumably by rats. A spokesman for Water Utilities, one Jonathan Hargrove, had expressed regret for the man's family and had pointed out the dangers of working in Manchester's dilapidated sewer system, which he claimed, had fallen into 'a disgraceful state of disrepair' and which now swarmed with vermin. Furthermore, recent tests on sewer rats had showed evidence of the presence of a hitherto unknown breed of parasitic worm, the eggs of which thrived in the host bodies of the rats. It didn't take a genius to work out that something had to be done about this situation and soon. Hargrove urged the City Council to try and find the money to fund some much-needed upgrading. Without it, he feared that more workers could die.

Clive sat back in his chair and massaged the bridge of his nose between thumb and forefinger. It was crazy, but he couldn't stop thinking back to what Will had told him earlier that day.

They live in the sewers. They have these worm things that come out of their mouths. They grab kids and take them down there . . .

Clive felt a cold shiver of foreboding go through him. He had just had a horrible thought and he began to wonder if it wasn't himself who was going insane. He suddenly wanted very much to be home in his warm flat, with the television blaring inanely away in front of him. He switched off the computer, stuffed his cigarettes into his pocket and headed for the exit. He rode down in the lift, thinking to himself, *You're going crazy! Things like this can't happen, it's 1999 for Christ's sake!*

The lift doors pinged open and he strode across the foyer, nodding to the guard on the reception counter. He pushed out through the revolving door onto the cold street. And he saw them, moving to and fro on the pavement. Dirty ragged people, their faces grey with hunger, their eyes the colour of lost hope.

An old woman pushing an ancient doll's pram, piled high with bin-bags full of what looked like old clothing. She turned her toothless face to him and held out a dirty, liver-spotted hand.

'Please, sir, spare an old woman a couple of coppers!'

A black paraplegic, sitting in a home-made wooden cart, propelled himself forwards with a push of his powerful arms. He wore a grubby canvas cap with fake sheepskin earmuffs and his eyes had the milky opalescence of advancing glaucoma.

'Please, Guv, just a couple of bob to get something to eat . . .'

A thin scarecrow of a man in a flapping raincoat ran at him, babbling incoherently. There was a thick froth of spittle on his lips and a badly healed cut on his forehead that seeped pus. He stank of urine and cheap booze.

'Please sir, God bless you sir, whatever you can spare sir, I missed my last bus home!'

Clive stood for a moment, and the beggars converged on him, taking his indecision as a sign that he might be persuaded to part with money. Hands groped at his sleeves and the smell of the Rag People engulfed him, settling around him like an oppressive cloud. He mumbled something and pushed past them, but they trailed after him, pleading with him, begging for his help.

He broke and ran along the dark street, not daring to look back at them, afraid that they might gaze into his eyes and recognize the fear in them.

Because he thought he knew now why the Subs took children into the dark stinking labyrinth of the sewers. Because they were hungry. And young flesh was more tender.

Will walked slowly along the banks of the canal, gazing up at the lights of the high-rise conurbation ahead of him. The rectangles of yellow light ascended into the heavens and were reflected in the oily waters of the canal.

The Salford Quays, once an area of crumbling dereliction, had been yuppiefied in the 1980s and was now one of the favoured addresses of the rich and relatively famous. Luxurious high-rise apartment complexes, a couple of five star hotels and a whole clutch of upmarket clubs and bistros hugged the waterfront, alongside a multi-screen cinema complex. A straggle of yachts rode listlessly at anchor in the stagnant waters of the harbour and the vehicles in the various car parks along the front bore testimony to the kind of money that residents here had to play with. Will noted BMWs, Porsches and Lamborghinis, nestling amidst the ubiquitous legions of four wheel drive jeeps.

Being in the presence of such affluence only served to make him more aware of his own bedraggled condition and he kept in the shadows whenever possible, aware that a man of his shabby appearance would stick out like a sore thumb.

He crossed the canal by a small footbridge and made his way to the brightly illuminated forecourt of Gallagher Towers, a ten-storey apartment complex named after one of the city's most celebrated musicians. Will hung back in the car park for a while, sizing the place up, noticing the ViewScan system that kept a close eye on all who came and went from the building. Telling himself that he would only attract more suspicion if he loitered, he made his way to the front entrance, trying to look as if he had every reason for being there. Resnick was in the music business after all, so maybe a large number of the great unwashed regularly beat a path to his door.

Will climbed the marble steps to the entrance door and he scanned the row of intercom buttons, each of them bearing a brass plate with a neatly printed name inscribed on it. Up on the very top floor, there was an M. Resnick in residence. Will reached up a hand and pressed the button.

He waited for what seemed an age and there was no answer. He imagined the ViewScan over the doorway conveying his image to a bank of video screens somewhere inside and he fought down an urge to turn and run. Steeling himself, he reached up to press the button a second time.

'Yes?' A deep voice rasped from the speaker grille, startling Will. He gazed up into the ViewScan, trying his best to keep his face impassive. 'What do you want?' Resnick sounded wary, suspicious.

'Mr Resnick?' Will allowed a smile to shape his mouth. 'I'm sorry to disturb you so late at night. I . . .'

'Who the fuck are you? Piss off, I'm busy!'

'No, Mr Resnick . . . sir.' Will leaned closer to the intercom and lowered his voice to a conspiratorial tone. 'This is important. Mr Pinder sent me.'

This was a gamble. Will didn't even know if the two men were aware of each other. But after working through the various possibilities in his head, he'd been left with this option as his only chance of getting to Resnick. He almost held his breath as he waited for a reply.

'Pinder? He didn't call me or anything.'

'Er . . . no, there seems to be something wrong with your phone. He's tried several times, but . . . look, it's a bit difficult to talk out here. Could I come up?'

Another long pause. Will could imagine Resnick considering the matter.

'Can't it wait till morning? I'm busy at the moment . . .'

Will shrugged into the ViewScan.

'Mr Pinder said it had to be sorted tonight. But of course, if you want to take responsibility for leaving it, I can always call him and . . .'

'No! No, it's all right. You'd better come up. All the way to the top, OK?'

Will nodded. The electronic lock on the doors opened with a harsh click and he was able to push them open. He stepped into the thickly carpeted foyer, decorated in the current Kitsch Baroque style. Harpsichord music tinkled from the speaker system and a couple of stone cherubs dispensed jets of water into a conch-shaped fountain. The lift doors were an incongruous smoked glass rectangle set in a rough plastered wall.

Will stepped inside and punched the topmost button labelled 'Penthouse'. He rode upwards, the sound of the harpsichord still all around him. He felt very calm, very cold inside. He was on his way up to meet a man who sold Warp and he didn't really know what he would do when he came face to face with him.

Resnick was waiting at the open door of his apartment when Will stepped out of the lift. He was a large man, his heavy frame running to fat. His plump features were liberally dusted with white face powder. He wore black horn rimmed glasses and like so many people in the music business these days, his hair was drawn into a tight bun at the back of his head. He had a neatly trimmed goatee beard which extended to both his chins and he was dressed in a full length red silk kimono. This, combined with the face powder gave him the look of an overweight geisha girl with hormone problems. Will was glad he looked so ridiculous. It would make it easier to hate him.

As Will approached, Resnick scowled at his visitor's unkempt appearance.

'There was no need to dress up on my account,' he quipped.

Will made a gesture of apology. 'Mr Pinder has me working undercover with the Rag People,' he improvised. 'There was no time to change.'

Resnick frowned at this information. 'Working undercover?' he echoed. 'Rather you than me, sunshine. Is there some kind of problem?'

248

'I'll say there is.' Will glanced around and noticed another ViewScan mounted in the corner of the landing. 'Look,' he said. 'Maybe we could . . .'

'Relax!' Resnick turned and walked back into the apartment, beckoning Will to follow him. 'I'll wind back the tape and erase you. I don't think Auberon will be too pleased at you shouting his name all over the place, do you?'

'I guess not.' Will closed the door behind him and felt a sense of triumph flood through him. He had reached his goal and now Resnick was offering to erase all evidence of their meeting. A thought struck him. 'But what about the other apartments? I'll still be on *their* cameras.'

Resnick chuckled. 'No you won't! This is my building, I keep the master controls up here.'

They were standing in a spacious lounge decorated in a severe Japanese style, with low, lacquered furniture. To their left, a series of panoramic picture windows gave onto a balcony, with a view of the brightly lit quayside stretching out below. Resnick picked up a remote control from a coffee table and gestured at a section of bamboo and paper screens set into one wall. The panels slid silently upwards revealing screens of a different sort; a bank of maybe twenty TV monitors, each of them displaying a different view of the exterior or interior of the building. Resnick called up the master control and hit the rewind button. After a few moments, Will saw himself walking backwards into the lift out on the landing. A few minutes later, he saw himself doing the same thing out through the swing door of the main entrance. Then there was some footage of him staring into the camera and jabbering at it, before he finally strode backwards across the car park and was lost in the shadows.

'There,' said Resnick. 'The wonders of technology!' He hit the 'record' and threw the remote down onto the table. 'I'll pause it for a few minutes before you leave,' he said. 'It'll be like you were never here.'

'That's quite a set-up,' observed Will.

'Yes, it's very useful,' Resnick agreed. 'As I'm sure you can imagine, I often have guests here that I'd rather not let the other residents know about.' He glanced slyly towards the closed door of an adjoining room and Will got the distinct impression that Resnick had somebody waiting for him in there. 'Anyway, it's like I told you, I'm kind of busy right now. What's so important it couldn't wait till tomorrow?'

Time for more improvisation.

'Mr Pinder's worried that there might be a problem with the . . . the latest batch. He wants me to check out your supply.'

'A problem? What kind of problem?'

'There's been some odd reactions. Even a couple of deaths.'

Resnick tittered unpleasantly. 'So what else is new? We've always had deaths, haven't we?'

Will was shocked to hear such an admission. He tried to keep the disgust out of his face as he went on.

'Oh, overdoses, sure. But these new deaths, they've happened after taking just one tablet.'

Resnick looked at him calmly. His eyes narrowed. 'Like I said . . . what else is new?'

'Uh . . . well, Mr Pinder, he wants me to pick up a sample from you. So we can check it out.'

'I see. And er . . . exactly how do you intend to do that?' asked Resnick, quietly.

'The . . . the usual way,' offered Will, desperately.

There was a long silence before Resnick spoke again. 'Oh, you mean the Anderson test?' he ventured.

Will nodded. 'Yes, of course.'

Resnick seemed reassured. 'OK,' he said. 'The stuff's in the bedroom. If you'd like to wait here . . .'

'Sure.' Resnick padded towards the doorway. He opened it and stepped through, but as he did so, Will thought he heard a low groan from inside the room, a woman's voice, he thought. It was followed by the sound of a slap and a brief inhalation of air. Will moved instinctively towards the door. He peered around the side of it.

Resnick was on his knees beside a large wardrobe, rummaging in a concealed draw which he had pulled out from the base of it. But it was the girl on the futon-style bed who drew Will's attention. She couldn't have been more than around fourteen or fifteen years old, he thought. She was naked and her wrists were tied to the bamboo headboard by a couple of silk scarves. Judging by the expression on her face, she was very badly stoned. Her eyes were glazed, the pupils shrunk down to tiny specks of black in the midst of whiteness. She was rolling her head from side to side and moaning softly. There was a smear of blood around her mouth and Will was horrified to note what looked like a couple of fresh cigarette burns around her nipples.

He stepped into the room.

'What the fuck is going on in here?' he demanded.

Resnick glared over his shoulder at Will.

'I thought I told you to wait outside,' he snapped.

'Yes, and no bloody wonder.' He pointed to the girl. 'What do you call this?'

'I call it recreation,' snarled Resnick. 'I also call it none of your bloody business. Now wait outside!'

'Get fucked!' Will moved towards the bed and began to pick at the knot on one of the scarves. 'You sick bastard,' he said. 'She's just a kid.'

'She's older than she looks,' Resnick told him. 'And you know the saying. "Old enough to bleed, old enough to butcher." Appearances can be deceptive. But then, you'd know that better than anyone, wouldn't you?'

Will stiffened, sensing a challenge. 'What do you mean?'

'I mean, you're some kind of phoney. Who do you work for?'

'I already told you. Pinder.'

'Really? Well, let me tell you something, my friend. There's no such thing as "The Anderson Test" . . . and you've made a big mistake coming here tonight.'

Resnick was coming up out of his crouch, he was lifting something up out of the drawer; not a package of drugs but a heavy pistol, a revolver, the barrel elongated by the heavy black snout of a silencer. Will registered it even as he moved, throwing himself away from the bed in a defensive forward roll. The gun spat flame with a harsh phut! phut! sound and Will heard but didn't see the bullets slam into the spot where he'd been standing an instant earlier.

His shoulders thudded against carpet and he rolled towards Resnick, the big man trying to bring the weapon around to

251

cover him. Resnick fired again, a bullet kicking up threads of wool from the carpet a few inches from Will's hand as he flipped over onto his side, got his feet back under him and launched himself at Resnick with a howl of fury. The gun went off inches from his face, the muzzle flash temporarily blinding him and he felt hot metal skim past his ear; but then his forehead connected with Resnick's making a satisfying clunk, knocking the big man backwards. He crashed up against the wardrobe with a grunt of surprise.

Will grabbed the wrist of the hand that held the gun and drove it back hard against the sharp edge of the wardrobe. Resnick screamed, a shrill girlish shriek of agony and the pistol dropped from his grasp, went spinning away across the carpet. With his other hand, Will grabbed a fist full of kimono and spun Resnick around.

'Wait!' gasped Resnick. 'Please, don't . . .'

Will hit him as hard as he could, putting all his weight behind the blow. He felt Resnick's jaw crack beneath the impact. The fat man went reeling backwards, his glasses flying off, his arms flailing in a hopeless attempt to restore his balance. Then his shoulders connected with the flimsy bamboo and rice paper wall and he crashed through it into the lounge, tearing it to pieces as he fell. He hit the floor with an impact that seemed to shake the whole apartment.

Will approached, his hands bunched into fists, but Resnick appeared to be out cold. Will kicked him in the ribs to make sure but got nothing more than a grunt out of him. He turned back to the bedroom, to prevent himself from launching a dozen more kicks into the man's prostrate form; and then he saw the girl.

'Oh no,' he whispered.

A stray bullet had hit her in the face, just below her left eye. It's exit had blown most of her brains across the pillows.

Will groaned, buried his face in his hands. His first impulse was to get the hell out of there but he fought down a sensation of panic, telling himself that he wasn't going to waste the opportunity of answering some questions. He noticed the gun lying on the carpet and went to pick it up, but snatched back his hand at the last minute, reminding himself that it would have Resnick's prints on it. Best to leave it where it was.

He transferred his attention to the drawer in the base of the wardrobe. He saw that it was a chemical treasure trove, packed full of drugs of various types. Amongst the contents, Will recognized packages containing the tiny purple pills that Clive had described to him. He crouched down and lifted out a package of Warp, studying it intently for a moment. Hard to believe that such little pills could be the cause of so much misery.

He carried the package through into the lounge, tore it open and sat down cross-legged on the floor beside the unconscious figure of Marshall Resnick. He waited.

After ten, fifteen minutes, Resnick began to stir. He groaned, tried to sit up, then fell back again with a grunt. He lay there for a moment, his eyelids flickering; and then full consciousness kicked in and he must have registered pain. His powdered face contorted into a mask of agony.

'Oh God,' he whimpered. 'My jaw . . . my fucking wrist!'

Will reached over and grabbed hold of his ear. He heaved upwards, jerking the man into a sitting position and held him there like a flabby marionette.

'Ahh, you're hurting me!' screeched Resnick.

'Not yet,' Will assured him. 'Or at least, not like I'm going to hurt you, you miserable shit-sucking lowlife.'

Resnick stared at him.

'Who are you?' he whispered.

'My name's Will Ambrose. My son, Martin, died from taking this filth.' Will lifted the pack of tablets and waved them in front of Resnick's face. 'Just one lousy tablet.'

'Oh Christ,' whispered Resnick. His voice was small and helpless, as he realized exactly what kind of shit he was in. 'Look, Mr Ambrose, that's nothing to do with me! I'm just a small time supplier. I don't manufacture the stuff.'

'No, but you're aware that people die from taking it. You virtually bragged to me about it earlier.'

Resnick attempted to shake his head, but stopped when it caused him too much pain.

'But I didn't mean . . . I didn't *know* . . .'

'Save your breath,' Will advised him. 'As far as I'm

concerned, Resnick, you're a worthless piece of shit that needs to be disinfected off the face of the planet. And that was before I discovered your unsavoury little pastime. The girl's dead, by the way. One of your bullets killed her.'

Resnick's eyes widened in shock.

'But . . . I never meant . . .'

Will was getting tired of the man's protestations. He slapped him hard across his bruised jaw. Resnick howled, began to cry.

'Please,' he blubbered. 'I beg you, stop hurting me! I can't bear it.'

'Then tell me what you know about Warp.'

'I don't know anything!'

'Of course you do. You know Pinder. Where can I find him?'

'I don't know where he lives!'

'Sure you do. Tell me.' Will raised his hand to hit Resnick again.

'No, please, you must understand. All I have is a mobile phone number.' He pointed frantically to an electronic filofax lying on the coffee table. 'It's in there under the name Pinto Management. Take it and go!'

Will shook his head. 'You've got to have met him in person.'

'Yes, but only at the club.'

'Club? What club?'

Resnick tried again to shake his head. 'I can't tell you. They'd kill me!'

'You're dead anyway,' Will told him. 'Do you honestly think I'm going to walk away from here and leave you alive?'

Resnick's eyes bulged. Fresh tears trickled down his face making pink trails in the white powder.

'But you can't . . . that's . . .'

'Against the law?' Will laughed derisively. He let go of Resnick's ear, took hold of his fractured wrist and began to apply pressure to it. Resnick screamed like a wounded animal and somewhere amidst the screams, Will registered words he recognized. *The Garden?* He stopped applying pressure and grabbed Resnick's ear before he could fall backwards.

'Did you say "The Garden"?' he hissed.

Resnick nodded weakly. 'Yes . . . Garden . . . of Terrestrial . . . Delights . . .'

'Flowers is involved in this after all? Gary Flowers?'

Resnick sighed, nodded. Thick beads of sweat had broken out on his forehead, further dissolving the white face powder. He seemed to be on the edge of collapse.

'He's my . . . my Governor. It's him I report to. I've seen Pinder there a couple of times. But I'm to tell nobody . . . they warned me.' He turned his face up to Will. 'That's all I know, I swear.'

'Where's the stuff made?' persisted Will. 'You must have some idea.'

'No, no. I swear to you.' Resnick began to cry again. 'I've heard Flowers refer to it as "The Warehouse". And I think it's somewhere in Manchester . . . but believe me, that's all I know.' He groaned. 'Oh God, my wrist,' he said. 'I need some pain killers. Please, for the love of God, could you get me some pain killers?'

'Why not?' conceded Will. He took a tab of Warp from the packet and lifted it to Resnick's mouth. 'Here,' he said. 'Try this.'

'Oh, thank you, thank you, I . . .'

Resnick's gratitude was short lived when he realized what Will was pushing into his mouth.

'Not that!' he gasped.

'But whyever not?' Will asked him. 'It's harmless, isn't it? It will make you feel better. Swallow it, you motherfucker!' He forced the pill in between Resnick's clenched teeth, then held his nose until he was forced to swallow. Then he reached down for the packet. 'Another one, I think . . .'

'No! Please, don't, don't!'

Will made him swallow five pills in all. Then he settled back to watch. Resnick was terrified, his eyes bulging with dread, a thick muck-sweat of fear staining his kimono. He lay there trembling.

'Dangerous,' he whimpered. 'So many. You shouldn't. You . . .'

And then the hallucinations must have started. First Resnick stared into the middle distance. Then he began to giggle, to point around the room at things only he could see.

'Look at that!' he exclaimed. 'Oh, God, just look!'

Will said nothing. He sat there watching. Now Resnick was looking down at his own arms in apparent delight.

'Feathers!' he exclaimed. 'So many beautiful colours.' He began to flap his chubby arms up and down, seemingly oblivious to his fractured wrist. 'I'm flying,' he gasped. 'I'm flying above the treetops and the sky is so blue. It's beautiful here. I want to live here forever.' Suddenly, a look of apprehension came to his face. 'But . . . what's that?' he whispered. 'It's like a cloud, only . . .' He craned his neck forward, peering intently into the distance. 'It's like . . .' He frowned, made an expression of revulsion. 'Oh God,' he said. 'There must be thousands of them! They . . . they're coming towards me. They're so big. And so dirty. I . . . I can smell them . . .'

Now his face contorted into an expression of absolute terror. He threw back his head and screamed, started beating his hands at the air in front of them, working himself up into an absolute frenzy. 'Get them off me!' he screamed. 'Get them off! They've got eyes in their nipples! They've got shit in their veins! They . . .' He scrambled to his feet and began to run around the room, frantically beating at something that seemed to be in the air all around him. He collided with a bamboo lacquered cabinet, splintering it and gashing his forehead. Blood squirted down his face but he seemed unaware of it. He was floundering around now, screaming like a banshee and Will realized it wouldn't be long before somebody came to investigate. He got up and went across to the picture windows. Using the sleeve of his coat, he unlatched a door and slid it open, revealing the balcony and the bright lights below.

'Escape them, Marshall,' he suggested. 'Just flap those pretty wings and fly away.'

'Yes, yes!' Resnick ran out onto the balcony. Will picked up the package of Warp and stuffed it into his pocket, telling himself that it might come in useful later. He also took Resnick's electronic filofax. Glancing back towards the balcony, he saw that Resnick was stripping off the kimono. He threw it over the edge and it flapped away in the wind like a big, red bird. As Will watched calmly, Resnick clambered up onto the wall of the balcony. He stood for a moment, flapping his arms madly, as though trying to build up some impetus. Then he stepped off and his pink, naked body fell without a sound.

Will didn't feel a moment's regret. On the way to the door, he remembered to hit the pause button on the master record; and riding down in the lift, for the first time in weeks, he felt a strange sense of peace settling over him. He had struck the first blow in his quest for revenge and it felt good to be alive. He had thought that he would have qualms about taking his revenge. On the contrary, he felt better than he had in weeks.

He went out through the front entrance and strode back across the car park into the shadows.

Chapter Twenty-Seven

As soon as Suzanne booted up her computer that morning, she knew that somebody had been snooping into her files. It was a tiny little giveaway, but nonetheless unmistakable. She was meticulous about maintaining order on her crowded hard disc and consequently, she always closed down a folder after she'd been working on it. But this morning, one of them had been left open, the contents unrolling for inspection as soon as the machine came online.

She studied the list of documents irritably, wondering what somebody might have been looking for; but then she noticed that one of the documents was entitled *Will: Let*. She remembered that some months ago, she had written a letter to Will in a spare moment, intending to mail it to his address in Southport. There had been nothing of importance in it, little more than a note asking how he was getting on, mentioning that Martin had been ill with flu, the kind of trivial letter that people wrote whenever they were feeling guilty about not having been in touch for ages. In the end, she hadn't even got around to sending it. Now she found herself wondering if the title had been of sufficient interest to prompt somebody to open and read the document.

She glanced up at the glass partition to Adam's office. She knew he was in there but for some reason, he had closed the Venetian blinds, preventing her from seeing inside, an unprecedented move that seemed to symbolize the change in their working relationship. Ever since Chalmers had paid his little visit, Adam seemed to have become a different person, a closed book. Whenever Suzanne challenged him, he would look at her in bemused innocence and suggest that she was being paranoid. But Suzanne knew now that something was terribly wrong.

She got up from her desk, walked over to his door and rapped politely with her knuckles. The very fact that she felt that she had to knock before entering seemed symptomatic of what was happening between them. There was a brief pause before Adam's voice told her to enter. She pushed open the door and stepped into his office.

Adam was sitting at his desk, studying a bunch of detail sheets and some large-scale maps. He glanced up and smiled at her but, she felt, the smile was mechanical, lacking any real warmth.

'Suzie,' he said. 'Didn't hear you come in. Problem?'

She studied him for a moment. 'Does there have to be a problem for me to come and see you?' she asked him.

He laughed uncomfortably. 'No, of course not. How's everything?'

'Fine.' She thought for a moment. *Best to come right out with it*, she decided. 'You er . . . wouldn't have been looking through my files, would you? On the computer.'

He frowned. 'Not that I remember,' he told her. 'Why? Something missing?'

'No, just . . . disturbed. Somebody left a folder open.'

He shrugged, held his hands up in a defensive gesture. 'Not guilty,' he said. 'Maybe you did it yourself. It's easily done.'

She shook her head. 'I don't think so.'

There was a long, uncomfortable silence. Adam clearly had nothing else to say on the matter and Suzanne was eventually compelled to change the subject. She decided to mention a business matter, see how that went down. After all, they were still in business together, weren't they?

'I had an enquiry from Mantissa Electronics, last night. They phoned just after you left the office. Seems they're still looking for suitable premises for that components factory. I was about to tell them we had nothing that would be suitable for their purposes . . . and then I remembered about the old grain warehouse in Castlefield. It might be perfect for them.'

Adam shook his head. 'No,' he said dismissively. 'I've got other plans for it.'

Suzanne stared at him in surprise. 'What plans? It's been empty for two years now. Mantissa could be a good move for us, a feather in our cap. They're planning on providing employment for several hundred people.'

'That's very commendable, Suzanne, but unfortunately, I've earmarked that site for something better. I'm just waiting for the right moment.'

'Really?' She stared at him expectantly. 'Would you care to share it with me?'

He smiled at her, rather patronizingly, she thought. 'When I'm ready,' he said, 'you'll be the first to know. So what did you say to Mantissa? I hope you didn't promise them anything . . .'

'No, I merely said I'd make some enquiries. But I'd love to know what you've got lined up that could be a sweeter deal than this one.' She considered for a moment. 'Come to think of it, this is the second time you've turned down an offer on that old warehouse. What have you got hidden away there?'

The question had been intended as nothing more than a flip remark, but its effect on Adam was dramatic. The colour drained from his face and he flinched in his chair, as though she'd just slapped him in the face.

'Nothing!' he said abruptly; and then, in a desperate attempt to lighten things up a little, he began to extemporize. 'OK, OK, you got me! Actually, I'm running a call girl service from in there. Rent-A-Hump. I've got hookers stacked up in crates, ready to go around the clock. You can get a piece of ass twenty-four hours a day, seven days a week!'

Suzanne sighed. 'All right, if you don't want to tell me, don't.'

He had recovered enough to give her his familiar wide-eyed look. 'Hey, what can I say? I have this long term plan for the place and if it comes off, you'll be amazed and dazzled by my business acumen. But you know me, I hate talking about a thing until it's in the bag. It's unlucky.'

'Funny, I don't recall it ever bothering you before,' she said. 'Seems to me we used to discuss everything. Isn't that what business partners are supposed to do?'

'Look, trust me on this one, OK? Just for a little while

longer. You won't be disappointed, I guarantee it.'

Suzanne scowled. 'Doesn't look like I have much choice,' she muttered. She turned back towards the door.

'Hey,' he called after her. 'You going to be available this afternoon? I've had an inside tip-off about some properties coming up for sale. Bunch of railway arches on Sobriety Street, going for a song. With a little intelligent redevelopment, I figure we could do ourselves some good there.'

'Sobriety Street?' Suzanne frowned. 'Wouldn't that be more trouble than it's worth? I understand there's a large community of Rag People living there.'

Adam smiled and gave her a sly wink. 'Not for very much longer,' he assured her. 'Let's get together after lunch and talk about it.' He went back to studying his papers, taking her agreement for granted.

Suzanne let herself back into her own office, her mind working overtime. What the hell was going on here? Adam's face when she'd mentioned the old grain warehouse had been the very picture of guilt . . . and then his attempts to obscure it with a half-arsed story about a call girl service were bizarre. Finally, there'd been the way he'd casually mentioned a tip-off about the railway arches. A tip-off from who?

She glanced back towards the partition and ensured that the blinds were still drawn. She went back to her desk, sat down at the computer and scrolled through the database until she found the folder that held the details about the grain warehouse. She attempted to open the folder and was prompted for a password. Another unprecedented occurrence. As far as she knew, none of the documents in the properties section had ever been assigned a password before.

She busied herself for a few minutes, trying variations on Adam's name and initials, but it quickly became apparent that it was something more complicated than that. She was left with two options. Abandon the idea or go and ask Adam for the password. Somehow, she was reluctant to try the latter approach. She didn't want Adam to be made any more suspicious of her than he already was.

Once again, she found herself wishing that there was somebody she could talk to about this. Somebody who might be able to advise her on what she might do next. Somebody, she thought wistfully, like Will.

It was the touch that woke him; the unaccustomed touch of a woman's warm body snuggling against him. He had just been dreaming of a fat, pink body stepping off a balcony and dropping into space and this was a welcome interruption.

Will opened his eyes to find that he was lying beneath the mounds of blankets and old clothing in Scally's shelter and that it was Marianne who was holding him, moving urgently against him, her hands exploring the flesh beneath his shirt, her mouth moving against his neck, his ear.

His first impulse was to push her away from him, but the feeling was short-lived, because he quickly registered how pleasurable it felt to be held, to be wanted. He could feel a stirring in his loins, a quickening of his pulse. He glanced guiltily over to Scally's corner and saw that the boy was still fast asleep, his tousled head pillowed in his arms.

Will returned his attention to Marianne. He was beginning to respond to her now, indeed, he was unable to stop himself. Some small voice at the back of his mind told him that it was wrong to take advantage of her, that if he did this, he wasn't behaving much better than Frank and his cronies; but another voice argued that they had taken Marianne by force, whereas now, she quite obviously knew what she wanted. So he allowed his mouth to search out hers and he let his tongue probe in between her teeth and then they were kissing hungrily, greedily, almost devouring each other in their haste to make love. Beneath the covers, their hands tugged frantically at each other's clothing, removing layer after layer to reveal the flesh beneath. And he was hard now, hard and eager to enter her. For the moment, nothing else mattered.

And it wasn't great sex, it was fast and fumbling and urgent, but it felt *real*, more real than anything he could remember in a long time. They had to be quieter than they would have liked for fear of waking Scally and, at the climax, Will had to clamp a hand over Marianne's mouth to prevent her from crying out. He was aware only of her beautiful eyes staring at him, inches from his own face, the naked, pleading expression in them and it occurred to him that he didn't want to go on lying to her any longer. He wanted her to want him for himself and not because she believed he was somebody else, miraculously come back from the dead.

It was over very quickly. They lay holding each other, her head on his chest. Will reached up a hand to stroke her hair. 'Listen,' he whispered. 'There's something I've got to tell you. I'm not who you think I am . . .'

But he got no response from her and he realized that she'd fallen asleep in his arms. He sighed. Later then, he thought. Now that he was finished, he felt a powerful urge to urinate, so he carefully disentangled himself from Marianne's arms and buttoning up his shirt and trousers, he crept to the exit and made his way outside. It was a bright, cold morning and for the first time in as long as he could remember, it felt really good to be alive. He walked for a short distance across the waste ground with his back to the arches. Then he unzipped himself and peed in a bright glittering arc onto the withered grass. Steam rose as the warm urine hit the frosted earth.

Will zipped himself up and turned back towards the arches. Then he noticed a figure up at the far end of the row of arches, where they joined the main street. He recognized the tall, skinny figure of Frank, leaning against the wall, as though waiting for something. As if on cue, a car pulled up alongside him, a sleek black BMW. The driver's electric window slid down and Frank leaned in to talk to the man behind the wheel. Curious, Will began to walk towards the car.

As he drew closer, he saw money change hands, a handful of paper notes. Frank pulled something out of his inside breast pocket and passed it in through the window, keeping whatever it was shielded by his hand. The secretive nature of the exchange led Will to an inevitable conclusion. The next moment, he was running up the street towards Frank.

The driver of the BMW must have seen him coming. He snatched the package and took off with a sudden shriek of tyres. Frank had been leaning in at the window and the sudden departure nearly pulled him over. He flailed his arms, managing to recover his balance. Then he turned to see Will advancing on him, a furious expression on his face.

'What the fuck are you doing?' Will demanded.

Frank glared at him. 'What's it got to do with you?' he retorted.

'It's got everything to do with me. What are you selling? Warp? Is it Warp?' He grabbed the lapels of Frank's coat and pulled him up close, until they were looking into each other's eyes.

'Hey, back off!' Frank hit Will in the chest, knocking him back a couple of steps. 'I'm getting a little fed up with your attitude, sunshine. What I choose to do with my time is none of your fucking business!' He pushed past Will and started to walk back along the row of arches.

Will came after him undeterred, trying to get his hands into Frank's pocket to see what he had hidden in there.

'Let's see what it is, shall we?' he said.

Frank swore and slapped his hands away. 'Are you out of your head?' he protested. 'Get your hands off me! I'm warning you, man, I'll have you dead and buried if you don't back off right now!'

But Will had managed to grab a small plastic package containing several purple tablets. He waved them in front of Frank's face.

'Warp!' he yelled. 'I knew it! How much are they paying you to sell this shit? You know what this is, Frank? It's poison. Kids die from taking this stuff. Did you know that? They go half-fucking crazy and they die!'

'So what? That's their problem.'

Will felt raw animal anger start to boil up within him. 'You dirty Motherfucker!' he snarled. 'I ought to . . .' But Frank was no longer taking any notice of him. He was staring off up the street, an expression of alarm on his ugly face. Will turned as he heard the sound of powerful motors advancing up the street behind him. He saw two heavy, canvas-covered lorries lumbering into view from around the corner. They were painted in khaki and green camouflage designs. They lurched to a halt outside the first arch and large numbers of men began to spill out of the back of it. They wore khaki uniforms, peaked caps and red bandanas around their necks. Will saw that they were armed with baseball bats and electric shock batons.

'Jesus Christ,' Will heard Frank mutter. Then he threw back his head and yelled at the top of his lungs. 'It's the God Squad! The fucking MLOD!'

More men disembarked from the lorries and came running along the row of arches waving baseball bats and what looked like petrol bombs. The four rearmost men peeled off and ran in through the doors of the first arch.

'For God's sake . . .' Will began to run back towards his own arch, expecting Frank to follow him. But when he glanced over his shoulder, he saw that Frank was running away across the waste ground. Will swore and kept on towards the arch. He saw four uniformed men run into it and a few moments later, an injured Rag Man came stumbling out of it, his hands clawing at his face. Blood pulsed from between his fingers. He dropped to his knees and another uniformed man, running past, lashed a kick into his ribs sending him sprawling onto the pavement. Then from within the arch there was a sudden flare of light and the four MLOD men came running out, laughing excitedly. Thick black smoke belched out behind them in an evil-looking cloud. They saw Will running towards them and the leading man, a big, evil-looking bruiser, paused for a moment, took what looked like a passport photograph from his pocket and examined it. He pointed at Will.

'That's him!' he yelled: and he reached behind his back to pull a long-bladed hunting knife from his belt. His companions did likewise.

Alarm bells started to shrill in Will's head as the four men came at him. He checked his pace, his feet skidding on the wet cobbles and he almost fell over. Regaining his balance, he abandoned the idea of going back to the arch and concentrated again on the simple act of self-preservation. It was quite obvious that if the men caught up with him they would kill him. He turned on his heel and began to run back the way he had come, intending to head up to the main road at the top of the street, but he hadn't gone half a dozen steps when he saw two more lorries pulling into position ahead of him. More uniformed figures scrambled out of the vehicles, cutting off his escape route. He glanced hopefully towards the wasteland but that too was swarming with uniformed figures. He stood for a moment, uncertain of what to do, glancing desperately around for an avenue of escape. Then he saw the short stretch of brick wall to his right, the section that overhung the canal culvert.

There was no time to think about his chances of surviving the drop. He veered right and ran for the wall, then flung himself up at it. His outstretched hands slapped against brick and then he was dragging himself up onto the top of it. He glanced over the edge and was momentarily shocked by the distance he would have to fall; but glancing over his shoulder, he saw the nearest knifeman closing on him, the sharp blade raised to strike.

There was no more time to think about the consequence of his actions. He took a deep breath and stepped off the wall . . .

Chapter Twenty-Eight

Scally woke suddenly to the sound of shouting. It was coming from the other side of the plastic bag wall that defined the boundaries of his shelter. He lay there for a moment, blinking, trying to figure out what was happening. His first thought was that some of his neighbours were having a dispute; but then there was a violent agitation by the entrance, the sound of an impact and someone came sprawling through the flap, tearing the plastic sheeting as he fell. An injured Rag Man crashed headlong into Scally's space, howling with pain and Scally caught a glimpse of a flattened nose, squirting blood. He sat bolt upright and saw a leering heavy in an MLOD uniform standing by the entrance. He was brandishing a baseball bat in one hand and a petrol bomb in the other. Behind him, the occupants of the arch were milling around like frightened sheep, yelling and screaming.

'Jesus!' Scally looked frantically around and saw that Marianne was awakening too, blinking at the injured man who was thrashing around at her feet. There was no sign of Will. Scally threw back the covers and scrambled across to Marianne on his hands and knees. 'It's the God Squad,' he told her. 'We've got to get out of here.'

She looked at him strangely, as though she didn't understand. 'But where's Steve?' she asked him.

'I don't know. He must be outside. Come on!' He grabbed her arm and tried to pull her to her feet; then saw to his embarrassment that her coat and shirt were hanging open, revealing her small white breasts. She fumbled with the buttons.

'He was here a minute ago,' she protested. 'Right here. We were . . .'

'There's no time,' he urged her. 'Come on, before . . .'

He was interrupted by a sudden crash off to his right. There was a stench of petrol and then a whoosh of air, a wave of heat that seemed to engulf him.

'FIRE!' he heard somebody scream; and then clouds of acrid smoke came drifting at him, making his eyes water. Fear swamped him, making his heart hammer in his chest. Desperately trying not to panic, he tightened his grip on Marianne's arm and pulled her towards the exit, but beyond his space there was a chaos of running, pushing, shouting people. A man went blundering by him, his coat and hair blazing, his arms thrashing madly in a desperate bid to extinguish the flames. He brushed against a woman and her hair caught alight too. Marianne began to scream and then Scally couldn't see anything, the smoke was too thick, it was in his lungs, in his eyes . . .

He stumbled in what he hoped was the right direction, keeping hold of Marianne's arm, pushing frantically against the backs of unseen people, tripping and stumbling over things that lay on the ground and then, suddenly, miraculously, he felt a rush of fresh air on his face. He dashed the tears from his eyes with his sleeve and found he was stumbling along behind Maxi, one of the men who had raped Marianne, but there was no time to think about that now because there were God Squaddies with baseball bats waiting for the Rag People as they came out of the arch. One of them gleefully slammed a bat into Maxi's stomach, dropping the big man to his knees.

Scally pulled Marianne hard to the left, ducked beneath a blow from another bat, aimed a wild kick at the Squaddie as he moved past him and then began to run for the waste ground, pulling Marianne after him.

'What about Steve?' she cried. 'We can't just leave him!'

'I haven't seen him!' he yelled back. 'Come on, before somebody sees us.' They ran on across the waste ground and when they reached the remains of the bonfire, they threw themselves down behind it. Lying there, panting, they were able to see what was going on back at the arches. All along the length of them, black smoke was pouring out from the homes of the Rag People. Uniformed men were waiting outside every arch, beating people as they staggered blindly into the open. Men, women, children, it didn't seem to matter to them. They laughed and joked as they swung the bats. Scally clenched his fists in impotent rage and beside him, he was aware of Marianne's shoulders shaking as she began to cry. He put an arm around her and they watched in silence as the beatings continued.

'Where's Steve?' whispered Marianne. 'I can't see him.'

Scally squeezed her hand. 'Maybe he got away before it all started,' he said. 'Don't worry, he knows how to look after himself . . .'

Then he saw the four MLOD men standing by the canal wall, peering down over the edge of it. One of them had a length of rope and was securing it to a metal stanchion sticking out from the wall.

Oh God, no, thought Scally. *Not down there, Will. Not down there . . .*

Will dropped like a stone to the canal bank twenty feet below. He seemed to hang in the air for an eternity and then quite suddenly, the bank came rushing up to meet him. He landed feet first, his trainers sinking into the soft mud, absorbing much of the impact, but it still jolted the breath out of him. He rolled forward and ended up lying on his back, gasping for breath. Above him, he had an upside-down view of the MLOD men, glaring down at him over the top of the wall. One of them threw a bat at him and it seemed to come whirling down with no more force than a toothpick. Then it buried itself in the mud a few inches from his head, with a thud that galvanized him into movement.

He got himself upright. He could hear the leader of the group above him yelling for somebody to fetch a rope and he realized he wasn't safe from them yet. It hadn't occurred to him that they'd follow him down here. He peered into the gloom of the culvert, the dirty black water flowing beneath the curve of a low brick arch. There was a narrow walkway on either side of the water and he started moving along the left hand side of it. He stepped beneath the shadow of the culvert, his shoulders hunched to prevent him from scraping his head on the brick roof. As he walked deeper into the gloom, he heard the sound of a coiled rope dropping onto the canal bank behind him.

He moved forward for about a hundred yards, the light fading all the time. Then, on his left, he saw a round opening in the brick wall, criss-crossed with a lattice of rusty metal bars; but when he looked closer, he could see that the bars had been sawed through on one side, leaving a gap through which a man might squeeze. He heard echoey shouts behind him and glancing back along the culvert, he saw the silhouettes of three men coming in pursuit. He swore viciously, then moved to the opening and squeezed himself through the gap. He had to wait a minute to allow his eyes to accustom themselves to the gloom.

Then he noticed a slab of stone beside the opening on which stood several ancient flashlights and a kerosine lamp, obviously left there by people venturing up through the culvert into the open. Will knew who must have left them there, but he didn't want to think about it right now. He had no matches with which to light the lamp, so he tried one of the flashlights. It didn't work, so he grabbed another one and when he pushed the switch, he was rewarded with a weak beam of light.

He could hear the clump of footsteps approaching along the culvert. To his right now, a short steep stretch of downward-sloping tunnel led into what must have been the sewers. He began to descend the slope but the stone was damp and slippery and he lost his footing. He went down on his rump and slid the twelve feet or so to the tunnel below. He just managed to stop himself before he continued onwards into the shallow stream of foul-smelling water that ran to left and right in front of him. He sat there for a moment, trying to decide which way to go. He shone the flashlight in both directions, but as far as he could tell in the weak light, the view was pretty much the same. He was in a seemingly endless black tunnel, lit only at occasional intervals by the rays of light that filtered in through manhole covers. Twenty yards up on his left, another tunnel intersected this one and he realized that it would be all too easy to get lost down here.

From behind him, he heard the sound of cursing, as the

leader of the uniformed men tried to squeeze his body through the narrow opening. There was no time to waste. Stooping forward to keep from banging his head, Will began to run along the tunnel, his feet splashing through the shallow, stinking water.

He reached the first intersection and scrambled over a low stone parapet into a slightly larger tunnel. His first objective was to lose the goons who were following him. He would have to worry about finding his way out of here when he had managed to shake them off.

He ran for what seemed ages, turning left or right at every opportunity. For a while he was occasionally aware of voices behind him as the MLOD men came in pursuit and once he caught a glimpse of a pool of light and realized that they must have lit the kerosine lamp. Soon their voices began to grow fainter and after a while, he couldn't hear them at all. He came to a place where a metal ladder led upwards to a manhole cover and he scrambled to the top, attempted to push it open. But the cover had been locked shut. No matter how hard he pushed, he could make no impression on it. He climbed down again and continued on his way.

Now that pursuit seemed to have tailed off, he slowed his pace and tried to keep some notion of direction in mind. But it was an impossible task. There were no landmarks down here, every tunnel looked identical and he had already lost track of which way he was heading. He was surprised to discover that it wasn't as cold down here as he might have expected. The smell would take some getting used to though.

Now that he had time to think about what had happened at the arches, it occurred to him that the MLOD men had quite specifically targeted him. Oh sure, Rag People were being beaten up back there and their homes were being burned – but the four heavies who had zeroed in on Will had made no attempt to disguise their intentions. One of them had even been carrying a photograph for the purposes of identification. It seemed that somebody had set up the raid as a cover for what amounted to an assassination attempt. But who would go to such trouble to get him? And why? He could only hope that Marianne and Scally were all right, that they had managed to get out of the arch before the petrol bomb went up.

A couple of sleek dark shapes skittered away from his advancing feet and Will gave an exclamation of disgust. Like most people, he had a profound dislike of rats. But, he reminded himself, from recent experience he had learned that there were worse things than them living down here . . .

Another intersection loomed in the beam of the torch, this one leading to an even wider tunnel. Will climbed over another stone parapet and began to advance along it. He was able to walk fully upright here without fear of bashing his head on the roof and when he directed the beam of the torch upwards, he saw that it was now quite high above him. Hopefully he'd find another manhole soon.

An unexpected sound came echoing out of the darkness ahead of him. The sound of voices . . .

He froze for a moment, thinking at first that he had come around in a circle, that he was closing back in on the MLOD men. But when he listened, he realized that this was a low hubbub of conversation, the sound of many people talking. The tunnel ahead of him began to curve around to the left and as he walked cautiously onwards, he could discern a glow of yellow light coming from somewhere up ahead. He slowed his pace right down, switched off his flashlight and began to edge forward, holding himself ready to run if necessary. As he came around the curve, he saw that the tunnel opened out into some kind of large, dimly perceived chamber. The water passed into a shallow pool here and, around the pool, some thirty or forty people were gathered in a semi-circle, several of them holding kerosine lamps suspended on long poles, which picked out their white faces. Most of them were men, but Will thought he could also see a few pathetic looking women and children.

His first instinct was to turn around and flee back where he had come from, but he realized that standing in the shadows as he was, he was in no imminent danger of being seen and he seemed to have stumbled upon some kind of meeting here. Rising up from the pool of water, there was a low concrete structure and several other Subs were standing on top of this, holding kerosine lamps and looking down on the crowd.

Will got onto his hands and knees and, keeping himself

272

pressed in against the curve of the wall, he crept closer until he was able to crouch behind a low parapet and observe the proceedings. Now he realized that he could smell something above the stench of the sewer, the appetising aroma of cooked meat. Beyond the crowd, there was an open fire over which a carcase was cooking on a spit. A big muscular Sub, stripped to the waist and sweating, was tending to the food.

Now the murmur of conversation amongst the crowd subsided as a new figure strode forward from the darkness at the top of the concrete plinth. He stepped into the glow of light from the torches. He was a tall thin man with white, shoulder-length hair and fierce, red-rimmed eyes. He spoke, his voice booming under the curved roof.

'Brothers and sisters!' he said. 'I bid thee welcome! Raise thy voices in appreciation for the sovereign lord of the underground. I give you, the Rat King!'

At this there was a loud cheer from the crowd. Another man stepped forward out of the darkness. He was dressed in a long green coat that Will saw had once been a Drizabone. He strutted to the edge of the podium and stood for a moment, his hands on his hips, grinning down at the crowd below. He was a giant of a man, heavy set and red bearded, with dark malevolent eyes and a crudely drawn crucifix tattooed on his forehead. This last detail seemed to ring a bell with Will. Hadn't he seen this man's face amongst Clive's collection of photographs? The man opened his mouth to speak and Will shuddered as in the glow of the lamps he saw something fat and white pulsing at the back of the man's throat. When he spoke his voice had a wet, glottal quality to it and, Will thought, an accent that could only have originated in darkest Yorkshire.

'Brothers, sisters, welcome! Today we celebrate another conversion to the faith. Another Streeter chooses to come and live amongst the people of the Underworld!' There were claps and whistles at this announcement and the white-haired man had to hold up his hands for some kind of silence. The man who called himself the Rat King gazed down upon his ragged subjects.

''Tis now four years since the good Lord guided my footsteps to the world beneath the streets,' he said. 'Four years since he showed me a safer place to live; a *better* place to live, away from the misery and violence of up above. In that time our numbers have grown beyond all my expectations. As I have told thee, the time of Armageddon is close at hand. When the terrible conflagration visits itself upon the surface world, 'tis we Underworlders who shall survive to repopulate this sick planet.' He strolled slowly across the front of the podium, looking for all the world like Rasputin in full flow, talking with a slow, practiced ease. 'Let me tell thee how it was. How the Lord came unto me and revealed unto me how we should turn our backs on the street and come to dwell in our new home.' He pointed a dirty hand up towards the dimly seen roof above his head.

'I had lived for many years in the world of the Streeters,' he said. 'And I had fallen upon evil ways. Oh yes, I was a thief. I was a fornicator. Yea, I was even a killer. And, hunted for my crimes, I chanced upon a path into the Underworld and lost myself in the passages and tunnels. I had thought that I would die here. But then the Lord appeared to me as if in a vision and spoke to me, just as clearly as I speak to you now, oh my brothers and sisters!'

'Amen!' yelled somebody in the crowd, and a couple of others clapped their hands and crossed themselves. Will was reminded of followers at an evangelical meeting. And just like a fire and brimstone preacher, the Rat King was working himself up into a frenzy.

'The Lord showed me how I could live in this place. How I could harvest our friend the rat for sustenance. And he sent me out to recruit others who would see this new world for the opportunities it presented. At first we were few but, in time, others came to join us.'

The Rat King paused and gave a couple of wet-sounding coughs. Blood spilled from his mouth but he seemed unconcerned. He wiped his lips on his sleeve before continuing. 'My worm brother is impatient for the ceremony,' he observed gleefully. 'And this makes me think of when the first Great parasite was born in me and my hunger began to rage. But the Lord calmed me and taught me to cherish the life he had placed within me; and it was then that he assured me that this new hunger was good. "Feed thy hunger," sayeth the Lord! "Claim the food that is thy right!" '

There were more whoops and whistles from the crowd. The Rat King's eyes were bulging manically as he paced up and down, waving his arms at his followers.

'The Lord explained to me that it was only just that we should prey upon the Streeters. After all, we were forging the new society that would replace them, it was only just that we should make use of them. But, the Lord warned me, "take only their whelps. Do not infect thyself with the sins of the fathers. Cull them young, before the rot sets in to their hearts!" ' The Rat King continued to pace agitatedly up and down as he spoke, slipping in and out of shadow, before returning to the front of the podium. To Will, it seemed patently obvious that the man was totally unhinged, but his followers seemed to be hanging on every word.

'Now the time of ascendancy draws near!' he roared. 'As it was written by the great prophet Nostradamus, so shall it be! But the Lord hath promised me that while those above perish in the flames, the fires of destruction will roll across our heads and we shall be spared. We shall continue to live here until the Lord tells me it is safe to venture above ground. And when that time comes, we of the Underworld shall inherit the earth!'

More cheers, whistles, wild applause. Clearly so long a time spent deprived of daylight had rendered the man's followers every bit as crazy as he was.

'Now!' he cried, 'bring unto me the Streeter who would join with us.'

A young Rag Man was hustled forward into the light by a couple of Subs. He looked apprehensive, but he went willingly enough. The Rat King reached out a massive hand and placed it on the man's shoulder.

'Now Streeter,' he said. 'Art thou ready to accept the ways of the underworld?'

The Rag Man glanced nervously around the dark chamber before nodding. 'I am,' he said.

'Then make ready. Hold him.' The two Subs standing either side of the Rag Man gripped his arms tightly.

The Rat King stepped forward and took the man in his

arms. Then he kissed him full on the lips and kept his mouth there. The other man stood rigid, offering no resistance.

Will couldn't suppress a low groan. Something was moving inside the Rat King's body, distending his throat. The Rag Man flinched violently and would have backed away if the other two Subs hadn't been holding on to him. Now his cheeks bulged as something filled them – and then whatever it was began to move down his throat, creating what looked like a huge, downward sliding Adam's apple. The Rat King pulled away, smiling and Will saw to his revulsion, the last few inches of the worm's slimy white body sliding into the Rag Man's mouth. His body began to shudder and shake uncontrollably and the two Subs let go of him. He slumped down onto the rostrum and began to roll around, retching and holding his stomach.

'Submit!' the Rat King urged him. 'Seek not to fight the new life in thee. Accept and learn to cherish, for he will guide thee to a new and better life!' The Rag Man gradually calmed himself. His writhings became less violent and he finally stopped retching. He shook his head and sat up, looking around at the crowd below him as though seeing them for the first time. Then he reached out an arm and one of the Subs helped him back to his feet. The Rat King stepped back up to him and anointed the man's forehead with his thumb, making a shape that looked suspiciously like the sign of the cross, mirroring the design that was tattooed to his own forehead.

'Now, Underworlder,' he said. 'How dost thou feel?'

The newly initiated Sub grinned malevolently. 'Hungry,' he said.

There were wild screams of delight at this. The Rat King embraced the young man and then held his right arm aloft in a gesture of triumph. 'Let the feast begin!' he roared.

The crowd converged eagerly on the spit. The cook moved around to the other side of it now and took a huge knife from a sheath on his belt. He began to cut large chunks of steaming, half-raw flesh from the carcase, tipping them onto a round platter on the ground. This was passed up to the Rat King and his new recruit. But Will hardly noticed that. For the first time, he was getting a clear look at the carcase on the spit. It was quite clearly human; and judging by the size, it was that of a child.

Will could bear it no longer. He was in very serious danger of vomiting. Ducking down out of sight, he turned away and retraced his steps back along the wider section of tunnel, keeping to his hands and knees until he was around the curve out of their sight. Behind him he could hear the sounds of conversation and wild laughter.

He switched on the flashlight and began to walk back down the tunnel, numbed with horror, hardly believing what he had just witnessed back there. Scally had been right. Even after what he had seen in that ginnel the night he met Scally, Will still had not allowed himself to believe . . . to *really* believe in the Subs. But now there could be no arguing with the evidence of his own eyes and ears. They were real. They had been living down in these stinking tunnels for years. *And they ate children.*

Will walked for what seemed hours, no longer caring which direction he was walking in. Whenever he came to a manhole, he climbed the ladder and tried to push it open, but every cover he found seemed to be locked tight. He splashed onwards, his feet and legs numb with cold and it occurred to him that the already weak beam from the flashlight was beginning to fail, soon he would be plunged into total darkness.

Finally, when he was almost dead with exhaustion, he found another ladder leading upwards and he climbed it, praying at every step that this time, the manhole cover would open for him. He got to the top and pushed his shoulders up against the cover and he thought that he felt it shift a little. He tried again, pushing with all his strength and he almost cried with joy when the heavy metal lid slid aside, revealing the light of late afternoon.

He clambered up and sprawled on the ground with a gasp of relief. Looking around, he saw that he was by the canal bank in an area that he didn't even recognize. He must have travelled for miles down there. He was tired enough to fall asleep right where he was but recent experiences had convinced him that hanging around in the proximity of an open manhole was probably not the best idea.

So, wearily, he climbed the stone steps to street level and set about making his way home.

PART THREE
Down Among The Dead Men

Easy is the way down to the Underworld: by night
and by day dark Hades' door stands open; but to
retrace one's steps and to make a way out to the
upper air, that's the task, that is the labour.

Virgil *Aeneid* Bk 6, 1. 126.

Chapter Twenty-Nine

Will had been searching for three days now. Three days spent wandering aimlessly around the city, scanning the faces of the crowds as they bustled by; three days spent begging for pennies, belly growling with hunger; and three nights trying to find sleep in cold shop doorways, all the time not knowing if Marianne and Scally were alive or dead.

When he'd finally escaped from the sewers and had got his bearings, he'd made his way straight back to the arches. The God Squad had gone but, it seemed, so had everybody else. The whole length of Sobriety Street was cordoned off behind high wire fencing and on the other side of it, a team of workmen were busy clearing out what remained of the Rag People's belongings, throwing combustible items onto a couple of big bonfires and the rest into a huge metal skip. The MLOD's petrol bombs had done no real damage to the brick railway arches but the heaps of smouldering clothing and blackened furniture that the Rag People had amassed over the time they'd lived here, was now good for nothing but disposal.

Will managed to get the attention of the foreman, a big, ruddy-faced man in hard hat and overalls. He wandered over to the wire and lit himself a cigarette, gazing at Will, not without sympathy.

'What's going on?' asked Will, doing his best to sound merely curious.

'Getting the place ready for redevelopment,' the man told him. 'The site's just been purchased. There's going to be some industrial units here.'

'Yeah? So what happened to the people that were living in the arches? You know, the Rag People?'

The foreman shrugged. 'Search me,' he said. 'I guess they must have moved on.'

'You've no idea where?'

The foreman smiled sadly. 'They didn't leave a forwarding address,' he said. He took another drag on his cigarette and then passed it through the wire to Will. He nodded and moved off towards the arches. Will stood there, looking at the stub clenched between his thumb and forefinger.

'I don't smoke,' he muttered; but nevertheless, he raised the stub to his mouth and inhaled deeply, taking the smoke down into his lungs. He kept toking on it until he felt dizzy and the ash was down to the filter. Then he flicked it aside and walked away.

And now here he was, three days later, stumbling along Market Street in the rain, footsore, hungry and aching in every bone. He had just about given up hope of ever seeing Scally and Marianne again and indeed, was beginning to think how nice it would be to just lie down in some deserted corner of the city, close his eyes and never have to get up again.

And then, quite suddenly, he saw them. They were standing in the rain outside Burger Drome, deep in conversation. Will stopped in his tracks and reached up a hand to rub at his sleep-deprived eyes. He saw them but for the moment, he didn't dare believe that it was really Scally and Marianne. He told himself that the image was just the product of wishful thinking.

Then Scally glanced up and saw him. The boy's eyes widened in surprise and a big grin stretched itself across his face. He nudged Marianne in the ribs and said something to her. She looked up at Will and her expression was one of delight. Will thought that she had never looked better than she did at that moment. She held out her arms and ran to him. Then they were embracing each other, oblivious to the amused stares of passers by. Will felt his eyes fill with tears and he knew that he never wanted to be separated from this woman again.

Now Scally approached, a sheepish smile on his face, as though he was reluctant to intervene. Will broke away a moment and held out an arm to him.

'Scally,' he said. 'We need to talk. Marianne and me, we . . .'

'I know,' Scally interrupted him. 'She told me. It's OK.'

Will hooked an arm around the boy's neck and pulled him in close. Now the three of them were hugging tightly and it occurred to Will that he was back where he belonged. With his family.

'I've been looking everywhere for you,' he told them.

'Same here,' said Marianne. 'We went back to the arches a couple of times, thinking you might go there . . .'

'I did,' he told her. 'It's all fenced off now.' He pulled away a little and looked at them both. 'I have to explain,' he said. 'I was outside when the MLOD came. I tried to get back to you but these four guys came after me with knives. They would have killed me if they'd . . .'

Marianne touched her fingers against his lips. 'You don't have to explain anything,' she said.

'Yes, I do! These men, they had a photograph of me, they'd come there to rub me out. To get away from them, I had to jump over the wall into the canal. I ended up going down into the sewers.' Will looked at Scally. 'I saw them,' he said. 'The Subs. There must have been thirty or forty of them. They . . .' He shook his head, remembering what Scally had told him about his friend, Gyppo. He wasn't about to tell him that the boy was almost certainly taken down there for food. He changed the subject. 'Where are you staying?' he asked.

'Frank has regrouped some of the tribe underneath Piccadilly station,' Marianne told him. 'There's only a few of us but more are coming in every day.'

'Frank!' Will scowled, remembering what the man had been doing the last time he'd seen him. Selling Warp. 'I've been wanting to have a word with him,' he said quietly.

'He got roughed up by the God Squad,' Scally told him. 'Three against one. He's got cuts and bruises everywhere.'

'Really?' Will's only recollection of Frank in that occasion was of him running away across the waste ground, as fast as his long legs would carry him. But, he reminded himself, he hadn't done much better. When it came down to survival, maybe it really was a case of every man for himself.

'Are you hungry, Will?' asked Marianne.

'Bloody starving,' he said. 'I haven't . . .' He broke off,

realizing that for the first time ever, she hadn't called him 'Steve'. He looked at her inquiringly and she shrugged.

'Scally and me, we . . . we've had time to talk these last few days,' she said. 'I don't know what I was thinking of, letting myself believe you were somebody else. I guess I must have wanted it too much. But I've thought it over and decided that it doesn't matter, not really. It's you I care about, whoever you are. And besides, I've always liked the name Will.'

He grinned. 'That's the best news yet,' he said. 'Well, come on you two, let's go and check out this new shelter,' he suggested. 'Maybe there'll be some Pot Luck on the go.'

'We can do better than that,' Scally told him. 'Why d'you think we're waiting here?' He nodded at the front entrance of Burger Drome, ignoring the scowls he was getting from the two muscular bouncers at the door. Will remembered them from his first encounter with Chilli Dog.

'I can't imagine,' he said.

'I got a connection in Burger Drome now. One of the kids in the kitchen used to be with the Ardwick Tribe. He got out of it, but he still remembers where he came from. Come on, let's check it out, he's had plenty of time.' Scally led the way along a narrow alley running up alongside the building. They walked along until they came to a fire door next to some dustbins. Scally lifted the lid off one of the bins to reveal a couple of wrapped paper packages sitting on top of the other rubbish. 'Ta daah!' said Scally. 'Two Ostrich Double Dromers with cheese, to go! If I'd known you'd be here, Will, he might have stretched to three, but we can divide these up, no problem!'

He handed one of the packages to Marianne but she passed it over to Will.

'You can have mine,' she said. 'I'm not that hungry.'

'Liar,' Will told her. He unfolded the package and broke the burger into two halves. 'From now on, we share everything, OK?'

Marianne smiled. 'OK,' she said.

Standing in the alleyway in the rain, they ate their burgers and to Will's food-deprived system, it seemed like the finest meal he'd ever eaten. Then, suitably fortified, they set off for their new lodgings.

Chief Inspector Derek Chalmers was frankly not in the best of moods. Indeed, he was fast approaching a state where he was going to start shouting at the top of his voice.

He stared across the wide expanse of his desk at Ralph McCandles, who sat squirming uncomfortably in the leather chair. McCandles was the Commander of the Manchester division of the MLOD.

He was a small, tubby man of late middle-age, who looked vaguely ridiculous in a tight-fitting khaki uniform and riding boots. His thinning hair was died an improbable shade of black and he wore round, wire-rimmed spectacles that gave him a distinctly owlish appearance. McCandles had just finished explaining how a couple of divisions of his best 'troops' had failed to locate Will Ambrose since he had eluded them three days earlier. They had, McCandles claimed, 'scoured the entire city' to no avail. Now Chalmers was digesting the information.

'I hope,' concluded McCandles, 'that all this isn't going to spoil my chances on the er . . . matter we discussed earlier.'

Chalmers sighed. He was well aware that Ralph McCandles' most devout wish was to become a member of The Brotherhood. However it must have been apparent to him that such a possibility was moving inexorably further and further away from him with every passing hour. Chalmers glanced over at Don Bullen who was lounging in his usual spot against the filing cabinet. Bullen rolled his eyes towards the ceiling in an expression that spoke eloquently of his feelings on the matter.

Chalmers cleared his throat before speaking, making an effort to keep his voice calm and precise.

'Ralph,' he said, 'at the moment, you have about as much chance as Jesse Jackson had of becoming president of the Ku Klux Klan.'

McCandles' plump face registered dismay. 'But it couldn't be helped, Derek. There was no way of knowing that culvert connected to the sewers. If we'd realized that, my men would have taken steps to ensure that it was covered. As it was, Ambrose had to make a twenty-foot jump down onto the canal bank. It's a wonder he didn't break his legs.'

'It's a pity he didn't,' growled Chalmers. 'Then he couldn't have led your lot such a merry dance, could he?'

McCandles frowned. 'To be fair to them, Derek, it's like a bloody labyrinth down there. They followed him for quite a distance, but they must have taken a wrong turning somewhere. Anyway, they got lost, it took them hours to find their way out.' McCandles thought for a moment. 'Of course, it's quite possible that your man is still down there. It would be all too easy to slip and break a limb . . . or simply to become lost, as my men did.'

'Hmm. What about the rest of the Rag People that you cleared out? Where are they now? If Ambrose escaped, he'd almost certainly try and team up with them again, wouldn't he?'

McCandles looked even more uncomfortable.

'Er . . . that's another problem. We can't seem to locate them.' Chalmers studied McCandles with increasing loathing. Now he really did feel like shouting.

'What are you telling me?' he growled. 'That you haven't managed to find a whole bloody tribe?'

McCandles looked defensive. 'It's really not that easy, Derek. There are literally hundreds of places in the city where they can hide out. And it's pointless trying to ask one homeless person for information on another. They seem to have undertaken a code of silence. It would have been different if we'd known you wanted us to keep tabs on the rest of them, but no, our orders were simply to throw them out of the arches and to eliminate Ambrose. Obviously, we'll keep looking but . . .' He broke off, studied Chalmers for a moment. 'I can tell you're annoyed,' he said.

'Annoyed?' Chalmers glared at McCandles. 'I'm not annoyed, Ralph, not a bit of it. I passed "annoyed" three days ago. Furious is what I am now. I cannot believe that Inspector Bullen here found the man I wanted and handed him to me on a plate; and then I, stupidly, entrusted you and your Mickey Mouse army to handle the matter for me. Why? Why did I do that? What made me think for one minute that you'd be up to the task?'

'I'll make it up to you,' McCandles promised him. 'I've instructed my lads to give this matter maximum priority. What we call a Code Red.'

'Oh well, that's all right then!' Chalmers looked at Bullen. 'You hear that, Don? Everything's sorted. Ralph has made this a Code Red.' Chalmers ran his fingers through the few wisps of hair that still clung tenaciously to the top of his skull. 'What do you think?' he asked. 'You reckon Ambrose is lying dead in a sewer somewhere, feeding the rats?'

Bullen shook his head. 'Sounds like wishful thinking to me, Guv. You won't get rid of Ambrose that easily. He's like one of those greasy turds you can't flush away, no matter how hard you try.'

McCandles drew his mouth into a tight dot of disapproval. Evidently, he didn't much appreciate Bullen's imagery. 'Don't worry, Derek,' he said. 'If he's in the city, we'll find him.'

'Now where have I heard that before?' murmured Chalmers. McCandles got to his feet. 'Well, must get on,' he said. 'Look, Derek, about what I said earlier. Surely if I find this man for you, we can reassess the situation, can't we?'

Chalmers was vaguely amused by the man's unfailing optimism.

'Membership of The Brotherhood is the reward for success,' he said. 'Not for incompetence. Find Ambrose and then perhaps we'll talk again.'

McCandles nodded. He looked somewhat reassured. He went out of the office, closing the door behind him. Chalmers sat there looking at the doodles on his desk blotter, as though hoping to divine some kind of answer from them.

Bullen came over and sat in the chair that McCandles had just vacated. 'So what do we do now, Guv?' he asked. 'Wait for the young Nazis to get their act together?'

Chalmers shook his head. 'No, we'll cut our losses and go back to what we were doing before. I want you and Lang to stake out the journalist again. What's his name, Singleton? Sooner or later, Ambrose, if he's still alive, is going to contact him. Oh yes and you'd better keep a close eye on the wife, too.'

Bullen smiled thinly. 'My pleasure,' he said.

Chalmers swivelled his chair and looked at a large-scale map of the city on the wall behind his desk. 'I made a mistake,' he said. 'I should have let you take care of it, Don. Bugger the consequences. I don't like Ambrose sniffing around our patch. It makes me decidedly nervous. Especially now, when we're so close to achieving what we set out to do. So if we get another chance, I want to be quite sure that we won't make the same mistake again. Agreed?'

Bullen grinned. 'Agreed,' he said. 'Next time I see Ambrose, he's a dead man.'

They sat there, looking at the map in silence.

Chapter Thirty

'This is the place,' said Scally, moving ahead of Will and Marianne. He indicated an ancient wooden doorway set into the crumbling brickwork of a wall at the back of Piccadilly station. They were barely a stone's throw from the arches. Will looked at the door dubiously, noting the stout padlock which secured the latch.

'Here?' he muttered. 'You've got a key?'

'Don't need one.' Scally glanced quickly up and down the street to make sure that they were not being observed. Then he reached up and pulled on the door. Magically, it opened. Will saw that the haft of the lock had been sawn through, the two clean edges of the cut fitting together so perfectly, it was impossible to detect the join. Scally held the heavy door ajar and motioned his companions through the opening with a flick of his head. He followed, closing the door carefully behind him.

They were in a low, brick-lined chamber, dimly lit by a wash of light coming in through an ancient, dust-grimed window above the door. To their left, there was a rectangular opening screened by a thick grey blanket. 'Through there,' said Scally.

Will reached out and pulled the blanket aside, revealing a glow of light from within. He stepped through the doorway and found himself in another, larger room, bare brick walls lit by the glare of a couple of kerosine lamps. Unlike the arches, there was no ventilation in the place, so there was a bad smell in there, an unsavoury mingling of the stench of unwashed clothes and bodies, kerosine fumes and a thick fog of cigarette smoke. There were maybe a dozen Rag People in residence, some of them standing around talking to each other, others lying in sleeping bags or on improvised beds made from cardboard boxes and items of old clothing. Looking around, Will could see that several people were badly injured, heads and limbs swathed in home-made bandages. He recognized one of them as Frank's wife, Peg. She lay under a filthy blanket, apparently asleep. The right side of her face was a mass of dried blood and bruises. Her friend Liz was on the other side of the room, filling a can with water from an ancient tap set in the wall. The scene put Will in mind of a tattered medieval army after a disastrous battle; and the mood in the place was certainly one of bitter defeat.

Will glanced at Scally. 'This is the pits,' he observed.

The boy shrugged. 'Beggars can't be choosers. Frank says it's just till we get something better sorted.'

The mention of Frank reminded Will that he still had a score to settle with the Duke. He looked around the room and soon spotted him, sitting on a packing case over in one corner. He was smoking a cigarette and talking with three of his lieutenants. The sight of the man rekindled Will's anger. He thought about what he had done to Marianne; and about what he had been selling a couple of days earlier, just before the MLOD intervened. He began to walk towards Frank. As he got closer, he noticed the dark bruises around the Duke's eyes and a badly cut upper lip; but Will told himself that the injuries were probably self-administered to back up his story about being beaten by the MLOD. Will glanced at Marianne and Scally who were still following him.

'Stay back,' he advised them. 'I've got a dispute to settle.'

They looked at him uneasily. 'Don't do anything stupid,' Marianne warned him.

'Don't worry.' He gave her a reassuring smile, then walked up to stand in front of Frank.

'That's quite a beating you gave yourself,' he observed.

Frank stopped talking and glanced up in surprise. A slow, lopsided grin spread across his ugly face. 'What are you doing here?' he asked. 'I thought we'd seen the last of you.'

'You mean you *hoped*, you had.'

'Where've you been anyway?' Frank inspected Will's filthy

clothes and he leaned forward to sniff ostentatiously at him. 'Smells like you've been in the shit,' he said.

'Yeah? Well, it's nothing to the shit you're in, believe me.'

Frank laughed. 'What are you talking about?'

'I'm talking about you, Frank. Do the others here know what you get up to in your spare time? What you sell?'

'That's nobody's business but mine. Anyway, you needn't get too comfortable. You're not staying here.'

'Oh, why's that? Worried that I'll tell the others about your little secret?'

He glanced around the room. All conversation had stopped and the Rag People were beginning to take notice.

Frank laughed nervously. 'I ain't got no secrets!' he said. He looked around at his followers. 'He's just trying to stir the shit, that's all.' He turned back to look at Will. 'No, my friend, the reason you ain't welcome is because of what happened back at the arches. It's a funny thing, ain't it? Just a couple of days after you arrived, the God Squad came down on us like a ton of bricks.'

Will kept staring insolently into the other man's eyes. 'Well, it didn't bother you, did it? The minute they showed their faces, you took off like a whippet. I didn't think you'd stop running till you reached the city limits.'

There was a murmur of agreement from the other Rag People. Clearly some of them had taken Frank's tale of being beaten up with a pinch of salt.

'Dunno what you're talking about,' protested Frank. 'I was in the thick of it, me. How d'you think I got these?' He indicated the bruises on his face.

Will shrugged. 'Trip over did you?' he ventured. 'When you were running away?'

There were some chuckles from the onlookers. Frank licked his lips anxiously. 'Funny fucker aren't you! No, I was trying to get back to Peg and my comrades in the arch. But before I could reach them, three heavies beat the shit out of me.'

'Really?' Will glanced around the room. 'Anybody here actually *see* this happen?'

There was an uncomfortable silence. Apparently, nobody had.

'As for myself,' Will said, 'I'd be the first to admit I ran away. Had to jump over the wall into the canal.'

'Yes, I seen him do that,' said an injured Rag Man, standing over by the entrance. 'There were four of the God Squad after him. They were tooled up, looked like they meant business.' He shifted his gaze to Frank. 'Didn't see *you* till the next day.'

Frank stared at the man. 'You keep out of this,' he said. 'I was there, I'm telling you.' He stared defiantly around the room. 'Besides, I'm Duke, I don't have to answer to any of you.' He glared at Will in open hatred. 'Now, I'm telling you for the last time, I want you out of here . . . and while you're at it, why don't you take those two with you?' He pointed a dirty index finger at Scally and Marianne.

'We're not going anywhere,' Will informed him. 'We belong to this tribe and we've every right to be here.'

'Is that so?' Frank seemed amused by this. He nodded to his three lieutenants. 'Throw them out,' he said.

The men moved to obey him and Will realized that he couldn't waste any time here. If he was going to establish control, he had to move quickly and decisively. He stepped forward and lashed a kick into the nearest man's testicles, before he was even up on his feet. The man screamed, doubled over and rolled onto his side, clutching at his groin. Will stooped over him, grabbed the handle of the baseball bat that stuck out from his belt and pulled it free. Then he turned as a second man came at him and swung the bat full into his face, swatting him back against the brick wall behind him. The man slid down it senseless, blood and teeth spraying from his mouth. Will turned to face the remaining lieutenant, the bat held ready to strike.

'Try your luck?' he offered. But the remaining man, the bearded scouser called Mike, lifted his hands in capitulation and sank back into his seat. Frank stared at Will in dismay, his mouth hanging open.

'Don't just sit there,' he hissed. 'Get him!' He looked around the room, appealing to the others for help, but nobody made a move. The silence in the place was palpable. Will noticed Scally and Marianne standing a short distance away, watching in shocked disbelief. They could have had no inkling that he was going to pull a stunt like this. Actually, he hadn't realized it himself until seconds before it happened. Will turned back to look at Frank.

'So, you're on your own,' he observed. 'What are you going to do, Frank? Show some of the fighting spirit you showed when those bully boys from the MLOD attacked you? Or are you just going to sit there and hope that somebody else will get you out of this?'

Frank got slowly to his feet, his hands raised. 'I'm not afraid of you,' he said. 'But this is hardly a fair fight, is it? You with the bat and me with my bare hands.'

'You want fair? OK.' Will turned to look at Scally. 'Hang on to this,' he told the boy, and threw him the baseball bat. Scally caught it in both hands. 'If anybody tries to take it from you, use it on them.' Will turned back and smiled at Frank. 'There you go,' he said. 'This fair enough for you?'

Frank smiled coldly. 'You really think you're something special, don't you?' he said. 'But you're nothing new. There've been plenty of others before you, think they can muscle in on my action, set themselves up as Duke of the tribe . . .'

'I'm not interested in that,' Will assured him. 'But I can recognize a piece of shit when I stand in it. It's time these people had somebody honest to lead them.'

Frank laughed, showing his rotting teeth. 'Yes, go on, keep talking,' he suggested. 'It just makes it all the more satisfying . . .' Frank stepped forward, sliding his hand under his coat as he did so.

'Will, look out!' shrieked Marianne.

But Will had seen the move coming. As the ancient handgun came out from Frank's shoulder holster, Will ducked inside the man's reach, swatted his right arm aside with an elbow and threw a short, hard punch into Frank's face. The gun went off with a roar in the enclosed space, the sound of it making Will's ears ring; and the bullet kicked a chunk of brick out of the ceiling. Then Will had Frank by the throat and was thrusting him back against the wall. His shoulder blades smashed against stone, driving the breath out of him. Will brought a knee up into Frank's groin, twisted him around and levered his right arm up behind his back. Frank yelped with pain as Will prised the gun from his fingers. It fell to the floor and Will kicked it away. Marianne stooped and picked it up.

'Now,' said Will, grinding Frank's face into the bricks. 'Let's talk shall we?'

'You crazy fucker! You'll break my arm!' Frank's voice was muffled where his mouth pressed against the wall.

'Tell me about the drug arrangement. You deal with a guy called Pinder, right?'

'Uh . . . I dunno. He wouldn't tell me his name. Uh . . . please, my arm! You'll break it.'

'If I have to. So how do you contact this man whose name you don't know? You must have to get in touch with him.'

Frank tried to nod but only managed to scrape his forehead on rough stone. He whimpered with the pain of it. 'Got a . . . mobile phone,' he gasped. 'In my harness. There's a . . . card with a number on it. Supposed to ring when I've . . . sold all the drugs . . . oh, please, man, let me up! My fucking arm!'

'Shut up, Frank, you're beginning to bore me.' Will took hold of Frank's collar and pulled him away from the wall. He dragged him to a clear space in the centre of the room and threw him backwards onto the floor. Then he kneeled beside him and started to open up the various compartments of the leather harness. He found the phone and the card with the number on it. In another compartment, he found a package of Warp. He held it up so the other Rag People could see it. 'There it is,' he said. 'Warp. He sells this stuff for twenty quid a pop.' He glanced at Mike who was still sitting sheepishly in the corner. 'You in on it too?' he asked.

There was a long silence, Mike glancing uncertainly around the room before he spoke. 'Yeah, we was in on it. Six of us all together. Frank collected all the money though. He just let us keep our commission.' He looked defensively around at the others. 'A quid for every twenty pounds we took, that's all! But I reckon Frank was getting a lot more than us.'

'You're dead,' Frank promised him. 'You hear me? You're fucking dead!' He tried to struggle upright, but Will pushed him over onto his back.

'So where's the money, Frank? Big money like that, you're sure to keep it on you somewhere, am I right?' He noticed a bulge under Frank's shirt and began to pull the hem of it out of his trousers.

'No!' screamed Frank. 'For fuck's sake, that money is owed. You can't just . . .'

'Shut up!' Will slapped him hard across the face. 'Now, let's have a look shall we?' Will had found a nylon money belt tied around Frank's skinny waist. 'So what's in here?' he asked. 'Your premium bonds?' He began to untie the belt and Frank came up into a sitting position, clawing at Will's face, bellowing for somebody to help him. He got his hands around Will's throat and began to throttle him, rocking him back on his knees.

'You fucker!' he screamed. 'Nobody lays a hand on me! I'm the Duke, nobody touches me without . . .'

And then his body jolted under a sudden impact and his voice dissolved into a scream of agony. He let go of Will's throat and rolled into a foetal position. He lay there whimpering, clutching at his shins. Will looked up in surprise. He realized that Scally had just stepped in and lashed the baseball bat hard across the back of Frank's shins, fracturing the bones. He was standing over Frank now, the baseball bat raised above his head, looking like he was debating finishing him off.

'That's enough,' said Will quietly.

The boy scowled, then nodded. He let a gob of spit fall onto Frank's head.

That's for Marianne,' he growled. 'You've had that coming a long time.'

Will went on with what he had been doing and Frank didn't resist any more. He got the money belt free and unzipped it, pulled out a thick wad of ten and twenty-pound notes. There was a concerted gasp of astonishment from everybody standing around the room. It was probably more money than they'd seen in their lives.

'Kind of ironic isn't it?' said Will. 'All of you living in this shit hole. Peg lying over there in need of a doctor. And Frank here has . . .' He did a rough count on the bundle he was holding. ' . . . around a thousand pounds on him. It's a wonder he isn't staying at a five-star hotel!'

'Give me that,' croaked Frank, feebly. 'That's all owed to somebody. I got to deliver it.'

'Oh, I bet you have! After taking your commission, of course. How much were they going to pay you, Frank?'

'That's my business.' Frank glared around the room at the others. 'I was going to let you all in on it,' he said. 'I was told we had to wait a while but you'd have all been making money from it in the end.'

'Oh yes,' said Will. 'And what a delightful way to earn it.' He stood up and held the package of Warp up so everybody could see it. 'This stuff is poison. It kills people. It killed my son, who wasn't much older than Scally there. One tablet and he was history.' He pointed to Marianne. 'It killed her boyfriend. A young man with everything to live for.' He pointed around the room. 'And you, you're just the means to an end. The people who manufacture this stuff, they see you . . . they see *us* as easy prey. They know we can't afford to have any qualms about selling their drugs. They know we'll go along like good little sheep because we're desperate, because we're hardly human, we can't afford to have scruples. But me, I'd like to think that just because we're down, doesn't necessarily mean that we're down-and-out.' He waved the package above his head. 'It's my ambition to see this stuff eradicated from the face of the planet, together with the people who created it. And I'm asking you . . . all of you, to help me.'

Frank lay there laughing at Will's speech. 'What the hell are you after?' he growled. 'A fucking sainthood? They ain't going to help you. The Rag People will do what they've always done; whatever it takes to survive. You think any of them care about your son? Nobody here gives a fuck about anybody but Number One!'

'That's your opinion,' Will told him. 'And maybe you've been making their minds up for them for too long. Now it's time they made their own minds up.' He looked at the wad of money in his other hand. 'As for this stuff . . . maybe we should put it to a worthwhile cause.'

'I've already told you,' protested Frank. 'That belongs to somebody else. It's their property.'

'But haven't you heard, Frank. All property is theft. So let's practice a little socialism here, shall we? Let's give this back to the people!'

'NO!' screamed Frank. But it was too late. Will flung the bundle of money into the air. It hit the ceiling, broke apart and then came floating down like oversized confetti. There was a long moment of silence while everyone stared at the falling money. Then there was a free-for-all as everybody rushed to claim their share.

Frank was sobbing in disbelief. 'You fucking idiot!' he screamed. 'You've just signed my death warrant! What am I going to tell my contact?'

Will picked up the telephone and handed it to Frank. 'Tell him you want to meet him tonight,' he said. 'Seven o'clock on Tib Street. Say there's a problem you need to discuss in person.'

Frank laughed bitterly. 'You must be joking,' he said. 'I'm not going anywhere near that guy without his money.'

'You won't need to,' Will told him. 'I'll keep the appointment for you.' He glanced up at Scally. 'I don't suppose you know how to hotwire a car?' he asked.

Scally was looking at the handful of ten-pound notes he had just scooped up from the floor.

'Is the Pope a Catholic?' he asked. But then he looked apprehensive. 'You're going to meet that Mr Pinder?' he asked.

Will nodded. 'Don't worry, Scally. I just want you to drive the car,' he said. 'You *can* drive, can't you?'

Scally frowned, shook his head. 'I can start 'em,' he said. 'But I ain't never driven one. Not properly.'

'I have,' said Marianne, stepping forward.

Will and Scally exchanged doubtful glances. 'I don't know,' murmured Will. 'It could be dangerous.'

'Hey, stuff that!' she warned him. 'It's exactly like the hamburger, OK?'

'The hamburger?' Will gave her a puzzled look.

'You said it yourself. From now on, we share everything.'

Will sighed, nodded. She was right, of course. And besides, he was going to need all the help he could get, before it was over. He smiled at her, then picked up the phone and pushed it at Frank.

'Make the call,' he said. 'And don't let him put you off. Tell him it has to be sorted tonight.'

297

Frank glared at him in cold contempt. 'I hope the fucker kills you,' he said.

Will shrugged. 'He's welcome to try,' he murmured. He picked up the white card and held it out so Frank could see it, noticing as he did so that it was the same number he'd got from Resnick's electronic filofax. 'Scally, come and stand behind Frank with that baseball bat,' he suggested. Scally did as he was told. Will smiled at Frank. 'Now dial the number,' he said. 'If it sounds to me like you're trying to tip him off that something's wrong, Scally here is going to see if he can knock your head clean off your shoulders.'

Frank glanced doubtfully up at Scally and saw the resolute look in the boy's eyes. He swallowed hard. Then turning back, he switched on the phone and with shaking hands, he dialled the number.

Chapter Thirty-One

It was Sunday and Suzanne had no legitimate excuse to go in to the office. Instead, she sat at home, not really knowing what to do with herself. She had intended to drive into town on the pretext of doing some shopping, but the idea wasn't really appealing. In the run up to Christmas, the city was as packed with shoppers as it was every other day of the week. And anyway, she had other things to worry about. The recent developments at Delta preyed heavily on her mind and she knew that she couldn't just pretend that everything was OK.

She felt, more than anything else, that she needed to talk to somebody. Will would naturally have been her first choice but she had no way of contacting him. So, after some deliberation, she opted to phone Clive Singleton.

She found two listings for him in her electronic address book; his personal number at *The Post* and his home phone number which he had given to her at Martin's funeral. She dialled and the line was picked up on the second ring.

'Hello?'

'Clive, it's Suzanne Ambrose.'

'Ah . . . Suzanne. How . . . how are you?'

He sounded hesitant, wary, as though he wasn't pleased to hear from her at all. Suzanne remembered Will's instructions before he had left. He'd warned her to be careful about what she said on a telephone line. *You never know who might be listening.*

'I'm fine. Look, Clive, I wondered if we could have a talk about . . . about a mutual friend.' She felt slightly ridiculous for having to be so cloak-and-daggerish. There was a brief pause before Clive's voice came back, curt and decisive.

'Meet me in Platt Fields at two o'clock. By the boating lake.' He didn't even wait to ascertain that she knew where this was, but simply put down the receiver.

Suzanne stood there for a moment, staring indignantly at the silent handset. She frowned, then glanced at her wristwatch. That only gave her about forty-five minutes to get to her destination. She grabbed a sheepskin jacket from the hall cupboard, armed the alarms and went out of the house, securing the door after her. She climbed into the Shogun and set off towards the city centre. The traffic wasn't much better than on a weekday, but at least it was on the move, a steady five-mile-an-hour crawl. In an attempt to occupy herself, she switched on the radio for the one thirty news bulletin and listened grimly as the newsreader recited a seemingly endless litany of doom and disaster.

The IRA had detonated their traditional pre-Christmas bomb in a department store in the West End, killing fourteen shoppers and injuring more than a hundred. Most of the countries of the world seemed to be at war, either with a rival power or with themselves. The Middle East. Angola, Rumania, Pakistan, Indonesia . . . the names unrolled in the rapid expressionless tone that typified independent radio presenters the world over. The world suicide rate was up by twenty per cent on the average. A learned professor came on to explain that this always happened towards the end of a century, blaming it on people being worried about the coming of Armageddon. He casually mentioned the fact that this time, there might actually be something to worry about, since the world's astronomers were becoming increasingly convinced that the earth might be on a collision course with a gigantic asteroid. Suzanne waited hopefully for the traditional 'light relief' item at the end, but they must have run out of time. Instead, the waggish DJ put on the old Barry McGuire hit, *Eve Of Destruction*. Comedy clearly wasn't what it used to be.

Suzanne made it to the huge municipal park on the edge of Rusholme with a few minutes to spare. She parked on the street, switched on the vehicle's alarm and walked in through the main gates, trying to remember where the boating lake was. It was years since she'd been here. This had once been a popular meeting place for courting couples, dog lovers and model boat enthusiasts but over the intervening years, neglected by city council funding, it had become the preferred haunt of crack dealers, child molesters and dossers. Now the acres of yellow litter-strewn grass and acid-scarred trees resembled some dead alien landscape. The few wooden benches that had escaped destruction at the hands of vandals had one or two Rag People in residence; and packs of feral dogs roamed over the open land, nosing amongst the heaps of illegally dumped bin-bags and other refuse.

Suzanne spotted Clive's tall thin figure standing beside the weed-choked boating lake, staring blankly down at the rotting hulls of a few old rowing boats that were gradually sinking into the stagnant water. She approached him and coughed politely. He turned with a start and nodded to her.

'Sorry to call you out of the blue,' she began. 'I was just . . .'

'Let's walk,' he suggested. He took her arm and began to lead her around the edge of the boating lake, aiming for the wide open spaces beyond. 'Forgive me for being so abrupt,' he murmured. 'It's just that I think I might be under surveillance.'

'You're kidding!' Her first impulse was to gaze around to see if anybody was watching them, but she resisted. Better not make it obvious, she thought. 'We're surely all right out here in the open,' she reasoned.

'I hope so. But surveillance systems are pretty sophisticated these days. They could be using a satellite or anything. So, we'll keep on the move . . .' He pulled a portable radio from his pocket and turned the volume up loud. '. . . and we'll have a little entertainment as we go.' The little radio was currently pumping out a jolly Eurotrash hit, extolling the virtues of tying your lover to the bed with ropes and beating her within an inch of her life.

'Who do you think is watching you?' asked Suzanne.

Clive shrugged. 'I wish I knew,' he said. 'I can't even be sure that I'm right about this. I know for a fact that the same car has been following me whenever I drive anywhere. And somebody's been in my apartment recently.'

Suzanne raised her eyebrows. 'Burglars?' she suggested.

'Funny kind of burglars who don't steal anything and put

everything back as they found it . . . only a *little too perfectly*. I've checked the place for bugs, but I haven't managed to find any. Of course that doesn't mean they aren't there. Meanwhile, my editor's been acting funny, asking strange questions, assigning me to stories he'd normally give to the kid who makes the coffee.' He glanced at her sympathetically. 'You probably think I'm just being paranoid,' he said.

Suzanne shook her head. 'If you are, then you're not the only one,' she assured him. 'It's one of the reasons I wanted to talk to you. Odd things have also been happening to me at work.'

Clive glanced at her sharply. 'What kind of things?' he asked her.

She frowned. 'Like you, there's nothing much I can put my finger on. Little incidents. Computer files left open, people acting oddly. It's all to do with Will of course. People seem to think I know where he is.'

'The police?' ventured Clive.

'Oh, of course, *them*,' said Suzanne. 'You'd expect that though, wouldn't you? But I'm talking about my business partner, a man who I've worked with for years. The other day I caught him in deep conversation with a certain DCI Chalmers . . . you're familiar with him, I take it?'

Clive nodded. 'Oh yes,' he said. 'I know Chalmers all right.'

'Well, I could be wrong but I'd swear I saw them doing this funny handshake business. And I remembered why Will hated Chalmers in the first place, how he swore he was ousted out of the force because he didn't want to join The Brotherhood.'

'You're saying that you think your partner's a member?'

'I'm saying it *looks* that way; and ever since Chalmers made his little visit, Adam's been acting fishy. Trying to worm stuff out of me, being all secretive about information we used to share. I think Chalmers asked him to try and find out what I know and to make damn sure I didn't learn anything else.'

They were veering left now across the broad expanse of yellow grass, picking their way through the debris and the dog shit. Suzanne scanned the horizon nervously. Now that Clive had tipped her off, everybody she saw looked suspicious. Those two Rag Men pulling a battered shopping trolley full of junk across the grass; wasn't there something phoney about them? And what about the two men in raincoats strolling along some distance behind them? What the hell were they up to?

'How much *do* you know?' asked Clive. 'About Will?'

'Next to nothing. Only that he's decided to go off and live with the Rag People. He hopes to find the people who sold those drugs to Martin. But I haven't seen or heard from him since he walked out of the door. What about you?'

'Yes, I've met with him once, about four days ago.' The scowl on Clive's face alerted Suzanne to the fact that something was wrong.

'How was he?' she asked.

'Well, let's just say that he seems to be taking his role-playing a little too seriously for his own good. I barely recognized him, he must have lost about a stone in weight. I took him some sandwiches and he wolfed them down like it was the first food he'd had in days.'

Suzanne shook her head. 'Why is he putting himself through this?' she asked. 'I mean, what does he hope to achieve? Did he say if he was getting anywhere?'

Clive didn't say anything for a little while. Suzanne thought he was deciding if he should trust her with more information. 'Oh, for God's sake, Clive! I hope you realize that I'm on Will's side in this. Whatever you tell me isn't going to go any further, I promise you!'

Clive sighed. 'I'm sorry,' he said. 'Maybe I really am getting paranoid. But I guess I've got to trust *somebody*, haven't I?' He ran the fingers of one hand through his hair and seemed to come to a decision. 'OK,' he said. 'Will told me some eye-opening stuff that day. There's one thing that sounds so crazy, I'm not even going to go into it right now, except to say that when you think about it, it isn't quite as crazy as it seems. But he also said that he'd just had a bit of a breakthrough. He was going to see a man called Marshall Resnick that same night.' Clive looked at her. 'Name mean anything to you?"

'Should it?'

'Well, not necessarily. Resnick was a major player on the Manchester music scene. PR, promotions, management, that kind of thing. But I thought you might have remembered the

303

name from reading about it in the newspapers.'

'The newspapers . . . ?'

Clive nodded grimly. 'The same night Will went to see him, Mr Resnick performed a swallow dive off the balcony of his penthouse flat in Salford Quays. Apparently, the ambulance crew that attended had a major problem separating his remains from the interior of the car he landed on. Went straight through the roof, I understand.'

Suzanne blanched. 'Good God,' she whispered. 'That's awful . . .' And then the implication hit her. 'You're not saying that Will had anything to do with his death . . . ?'

Clive raised his eyebrows. 'Given his motivation, I'd be surprised if he *didn't*. But don't worry, the police aren't looking for anyone else. There's a strong suspicion that Resnick was under the influence of narcotics. They found enough illegal substances in his bedroom to sink a battleship and witnesses saw him prancing about naked on his balcony just before he jumped. And yes, he did jump, he wasn't pushed. Apparently on the way down, he was laughing and flapping his arms like wings.'

'Warp?' Suzanne asked him.

'Possibly. But as far as I can ascertain, there wasn't enough of Mr Resnick left intact for the pathologists to draw a positive conclusion on that aspect of the case. They also found the body of a young girl in his apartment. She'd been shot and Resnick's prints were on the gun. She'd been tortured before she died.'

'My God,' said Suzanne. Reading between the lines, I'd say that a dealer was given a taste of his own medicine, wouldn't you?'

They walked on without speaking for a while. Suzanne noticed a gang of half a dozen youths on mountain bikes moving in slow single file across the grass to their right, the riders watching the two lone walkers intently. Suzanne felt intimidated by them but if Clive was worried, he didn't show it. He stared straight back at the leader of the gang and reaching into his pocket, he took out a hand-held electric prod. He pressed the trigger and the gadget emitted a sizzling spark of blue light that made Suzanne wince. The youths moved past and cycled off in the direction of the boating lake, looking for easier prey.

'You should get one of these,' Clive told Suzanne. '£24.99 from your friendly neighbourhood self-defence shop. I wouldn't go out of the door without one.'

Suzanne reached into her handbag and pulled out her own secret weapon, the Mace spray. She had kept it in her bag ever since Don Bullen had paid her a surprise visit.

'I know it looks like a can of coke,' she told Clive, 'but this really *is* the real thing!'

Clive smiled ruefully. They put their respective weapons back into their hiding places.

'So maybe it's all over,' reasoned Suzanne. 'If this Resnick was the man Will was after, maybe now he'll come home.'

Clive shook his head. 'It's not as clear cut as that,' he told her. 'Resnick was probably just the first rung on the ladder. Will is going to have to climb it right to the top, find the source of the drug. Somewhere there'll be a warehouse and . . .'

'A warehouse?' Suzanne stared at him. She was thinking of the old grain warehouse in Castlefield, the property that Adam had been so secretive about.

'Yes, the place where the drug is manufactured. What they call a laboratory. It needn't necessarily be a warehouse, of course, it could be anywhere large and relatively remote, maybe somewhere with a big cellar where there'd be room to store all the equipment. We don't know for sure that it's in Manchester but there's absolutely no reason why . . .' His voice trailed off as he became aware of the troubled expression on her face. 'What's wrong?' he asked her. 'Do you . . . know somewhere like that?'

She looked wary. 'Maybe your paranoia is catching,' she said. 'I mean, there is a property on our books. An old grain warehouse beside the river in Castlefield.'

Clive looked a bit doubtful. 'It's a bit upmarket there, isn't it?'

'No, not the redeveloped bit. Further down the river, maybe a mile from the clubs. It's been empty now for several years and Adam, my business partner . . . well, he's been evasive when I've asked him about the place. Keeps saying that he's got special plans for it, but won't tell me what they are.' She shook her head dismissively. 'No, it's ridiculous! It's all too much of a coincidence.'

'Why do you say that?'

'Well, think about it. If this *was* the place, it would mean that Adam is involved with Warp, that he's been a party to it for years. Now how is that likely when he's such close friends with the police? How would he ever conceal it from them? And think about everything that's happened to Will. The way he was framed for possession of drugs, the way it finished his career. And then for Martin to go and overdose on the very same drug that Adam is involved with? That's just one straw too many, don't you think?'

Clive was clearly pondering the matter. He took out his cigarettes, slipped one into his mouth and lit it with a battered-looking Zippo lighter. He inhaled smoke and blew it out in a thick cloud that momentarily wreathed his head like a dirty halo.

'But Suzanne, suppose Martin's death is the one, the only coincidence in all this? Supposing everything else you've mentioned is all part of a carefully constructed plan. You could accept one coincidence, couldn't you?'

'Yes, I suppose so . . . but . . .'

'Well, you said it yourself. Adam and Chalmers are pals. Let's just put Chalmers into the equation for a moment and see what kind of picture we get. Let's play a little game of "what if" shall we?'

Suzanne shrugged. 'OK,' she said.

'Now . . . what if . . . years ago, Chalmers came up with a way of making himself rich? And what if it wasn't legal. He can only pull it off if the rest of his department plays ball with him. Well, luckily, he has this secret organization called The Brotherhood. And one of the vows you have to take to join is that you will never, ever, inform on one of your brothers.'

Suzanne frowned.

'Is that a condition of entry?' she asked.

'I don't know. I'm just extemporizing here. OK, so one by one he's slipping the other members of the division into his back pocket, right where he wants them. But he comes up against a sticking point. An honest cop who won't be bought for love nor money. So Chalmers frames the cop, gets him fitted up with a phoney drug rap in order to take him out of the picture. At the same time, he targets the cop's wife's business partner, brings him into The Brotherhood.'

'Why do that?' asked Suzanne.

'Two reasons. One, Adam's in the property business and Chalmers is in the market for a nice, remote warehouse where he can start mixing up the medicine; and two, Adam will make a very useful contact if the honest cop should ever show his face again, because he's a direct line to the cop's ex-wife. Only of course, there's no worries on that score because Will has relocated to Southport and shows no sign of wanting to come back.' He paused, took a drag on his cigarette and sneaked a glance at Suzanne. 'How does it sound so far?' he asked her.

'Surprisingly convincing,' she admitted. 'Please continue.'

'Everything goes swimmingly for a while. Production gets underway, the local Rag People are employed as cost-effective mules and Chalmers and his team make big money. The whole shebang is kept under wraps, as tight as a duck's arse and that's waterproof. OK, people tend to die but nobody loses much sleep over that, that's an inevitable side-effect of the drugs market. And then, the coincidence happens. Martin dies. And instantly there are problems. Will comes back to Manchester and starts doing what he's always been good at, sniffing around. Chalmers gets worried and has to start calling in some favours, one of which is getting your business partner to snoop on you . . .'

'But . . .' Suzanne was shaking her head now, not because it didn't sound credible but because she didn't want to believe that such a monstrous allegation could be true. 'What you're saying, Clive, is that . . .'

'The police are the bad guys? Sure, why not? They haven't acted honourably in any of this so far, have they? Christ, Will told me he was beginning to wonder about it himself and I did just what you're doing, I passed it off as too absurd for consideration. You see, Suzanne, it is a frightening thought. If the forces that represent law and order are this corrupt, this

307

evil, then where does it leave the rest of us? Well and truly in the brown stuff, that's where. But just think about it for a moment. It's beautiful! Ever wondered why the force has had such little success in investigating the Warp epidemic? They don't exactly have a vested interest in arresting themselves, do they? There must be members of The Brotherhood working overtime to amend, misplace and generally destroy any evidence that gets handed in to them!'

Suzanne quickened her pace as though trying to distance herself from what Clive was suggesting. 'I can't accept it, Clive,' she told him. 'If what you're saying is true, then what we've got is . . . anarchy, total and utter fucking anarchy! If we can't trust the police, who can we trust?'

Clive lengthened his stride and caught up with her. He put a hand on her shoulder and turned her around to face him.

'Let's be optimistic and assume that it doesn't go any higher or further than Chalmers,' he said. 'That apart from a few civilian helpers, he's got it all sealed up in his division. If so, it's his superiors we have to go to. But Suzanne, we can't do that half-cocked. We're going to need some hard proof before we dare make a move.' He thought for a moment. 'And before we do anything, we need to talk to Will, tell him all about our suspicions. We have to be sure that what we do doesn't place him in danger.'

Suzanne nodded. She could see that was only sensible. 'When are you seeing him next?' she asked.

'It's supposed to be the day after tomorrow, but I don't know when and where. Will said he'd contact me to arrange our next meeting.' He shook his head, inhaled deeply on his cigarette. 'But I don't know if I dare risk it. If I am being followed, I could lead them straight to him.' He scowled. '*Them*,' he muttered. 'Funny, isn't it. Ten minutes ago I had no idea who they were. Now I'm pretty damned sure, it has to be Chalmers and his merry band. And if they think that Will is getting too close to the truth . . .' he thought for a moment. 'Maybe you could go in my place,' he suggested.

'Me? Oh Clive, I don't know . . .'

'Believe me, I wouldn't ask if there was anybody else I thought I could trust. Maybe . . . maybe I could go somewhere else that day, try and lead them off on a wild goose chase. What do you think? I hate involving you in this, but . . .'

Suzanne placed a hand on his shoulder.

'I'm already involved,' she said. She spread her hands in a 'so what' gesture. 'Of course, if you think I can help.'

'Thanks, I appreciate it.' Clive began to walk again and Suzanne fell into step with him. They had walked around in a big circle and were now heading back towards the park's main entrance. 'Obviously, when Will gets in touch with me, I'll have to find a way of directing him on to you without arousing suspicion. There's every reason to believe that they'll be listening in. And we'll need to come up with a few lines we can use if you need to contact me . . .'

They arranged a few code lines they might use if the situation arose. Suzanne felt rather foolish about this, creeping around like somebody in a Sixties spy movie, but then she thought about Chalmers and his division, how powerful they were. If Clive was right about them being behind the Warp operation, they both had every reason to feel afraid.

A helicopter clattered overhead, probably one from the police surveillance unit, monitoring movement in the park. They stepped under the cover of some trees and stood there waiting for it to move on.

'What happens,' Suzanne ventured, 'if they've got me under surveillance too?'

Clive scowled. 'In that case, we're fucked,' he said quietly. 'And they'll just be waiting to close the trap on us.' He glanced nervously around as though he suspected he might spot somebody lurking in the bushes. 'We'll leave separately,' he told her. 'You just carry on with your life and wait to be contacted, either by Will or by me. Meanwhile, try and learn what you can at Delta, but don't push it, OK? We don't want to risk letting them know that we've put it together.'

'OK.' She stood there, wishing there was something else she could say. She felt suddenly very nervous and extremely apprehensive about going back to her big, empty house. She realized that Clive was waiting for her to leave. 'Talk to you soon,' she told him, hopefully. She turned and began to walk towards the entrance. She glanced back once and saw him standing in the shadow of the trees, finishing his cigarette.

The Shogun was standing where she'd left it. She disarmed the alarm and climbed in behind the wheel. Turning off the street, she drove around the perimeter of the park and started for home.

She thought about everything that Clive had told her and asked herself once again if such a thing could be possible. She had been aware for a long time that the world was a deeply fucked-up place, but this was too much to comprehend. Then she thought about what Chalmers had done to Will and she realized that a man like that was capable of just about anything. She felt a black pool of despair welling up deep within her and she felt like weeping. Just what exactly had Will got her into here?

But then she thought about Martin and her resolve hardened. Whatever happened, she told herself, she would see this through to the end. She had put aside her natural desire for retribution for too long. Her son's death was an injustice that must be avenged.

She hoped and prayed it was a coincidence, but a couple of times on the way home, the police helicopter passed overhead, its tail lights blinking.

Chapter Thirty-Two

Will, Marianne and Scally sat in the stolen car, peering out towards the dark deserted stretch of Tib Street, a hundred yards ahead of them. The car was a battered rusting old Nissan that no self-respecting car thief would have looked at twice. They'd found it in one of the back street car parks a couple of hours earlier and had managed to get it to the meeting place without it breaking down on them.

Marianne sat behind the steering wheel, peering nervously out through the dust-grimed windscreen. 'Maybe we should get in a bit closer,' she suggested.

Will shook his head. He was sitting in the passenger seat fiddling with Frank's ancient pistol.

'This will be close enough,' he assured her. 'I want him to think I'm acting alone.' He glanced over his shoulder at Scally, who was hunched over the back of his seat. 'Remember what I told you,' he said. 'If anything happens to me, get the hell away and don't come back. If I go with Pinder, you follow, at a safe distance. On no account must either of you get out of the car, OK?'

Scally frowned, but reluctantly nodded his agreement.

Will cracked open the chamber of the pistol and held it up to the window to examine it. There were just two bullets left and Frank had carried no spare ammunition for the piece. Well, Will would have to make the best of it. He lifted his raincoat at the back and shoved the pistol into the waistband of his trousers.

'I'd better get down there,' he told them. Not for the first time, he wished he'd hung on to his wristwatch when he left Suzanne's. He'd taken a time check from the Town Hall clock as they swung around Albert Square some ten minutes ago, but the damned thing was notorious for being wrong. He opened the passenger door with the intention of getting out, but Marianne grabbed hold of his wrist and held on to him for a moment, gazing at him intently in the glow of the dashboard.

'Be careful,' she told him. 'Don't try anything heroic.'

'Don't worry about me.' He leaned over and kissed her gently on the mouth. Then he got out of the car, closed the door and began to walk down the road. He entered Tib Street and walked to a point halfway along it, where a working streetlamp offered some illumination. Glancing back, he saw that he must still be visible to the occupants of the car. He leaned his back up against the lamp post and settled down to wait.

Time passed. He found himself wondering what exactly he was trying to do here. It was a fair question. Well, hopefully Pinder would turn up and one option was to just rub him out, shoot him as he stepped out of his car, but Pinder was a bigger fish than Resnick had been and the chances were that he had a direct line to an even bigger catch, Gary Flowers. Knowing about Flowers was one thing but getting to him was quite another. There was no club in town that would admit Will looking the way he did now, especially not an upmarket joint like The Garden. But it had occurred to Will that Pinder might be able to get him past the door . . .

The sound of a car engine jolted him out of his thoughts. He looked up and saw a wide, low-slung American car approaching from along the street. It moved past Marianne and Scally's hiding place without checking its speed and approached Will, headlights blazing. It came to a halt a short distance away but for a while, the driver made no move to get out of the car. Will could imagine the man sitting in there, appraising this stranger, wondering where the hell Frank had got to. Will smiled into the glare of the lights and raised a hand in greeting.

After a long wait the driver's door opened and Pinder got cautiously out of the car, looking around him as he did so. Will's eyes narrowed. He hadn't known quite what to expect but it certainly hadn't been this great hulk of a man with a

312

vile, suppurating hole where his nose ought to be. Pinder closed the door and came slowly over to Will.

'Who the hell are you?' he growled. The hole in his face gave his voice a strangely hollow sound. 'I was expecting my man, Frank.'

Will nodded. 'Frank met with a bit of an accident,' he said. 'Broke his legs, I'm afraid.'

'I see.' Pinder digested the information for a moment. 'So . . . he appointed you to take his place, is that it?'

'Hardly, Mr Pinder.' Will smiled sweetly. 'You see, I'm the man who arranged to have them broken.'

Pinder's eyes widened in surprise, then narrowed suspiciously. He reached suddenly into his jacket and Will's body tensed; but Pinder's hand re-emerged holding nothing more menacing than a pack of playing cards. The big man began to shuffle them expertly.

'I admire plain speaking,' he said. 'I'm sorry, I seem to be at a bit of a loss here. You evidently know my name, but I don't believe I know yours?'

'The name's Williams. Peter Williams.'

'Very good. And would you mind telling me, Mr Williams, how you come to know my name?'

'My boss told me it.'

'Your boss?' Pinder was becoming more baffled by the moment but his big hands kept working through the cards with well-practised dexterity. 'And who is that, pray tell?'

Will snatched in a breath and offered up a silent prayer. 'Gary Flowers,' he said.

There was a silence so deep that Will became aware of the beating of his own heart. He stood there, trying to look composed. Pinder on the other hand looked like he was about to have a seizure. His hands however, kept right on shuffling.

'You're telling me . . . you work for Gary Flowers?' he said. 'In what capacity?'

'I'm selling merchandise for him. Special merchandise.' Will pulled his raincoat open and gestured to the pocket. 'May I?' he said.

Pinder frowned, nodded. 'Very slowly,' he warned.

Will did as he was told. He reached into his inside pocket and withdrew a package of Warp.

That did it. Several cards flew out of Pinder's grip and fluttered like dead birds to the pavement. He stood there, his mouth open, looking for all the world like someone who had just been punched very hard in the gut.

'But . . . I . . . nobody told me anything about this,' he gasped.

'Oh, I know. In fact, I was given strict orders not to let you know what was going on. But it seemed to me, you know, a bit stupid, the both of us trying to sell this stuff in the same areas.'

'The same . . .?'

'Yeah, I know. Crazy, right? We need to put our heads together, assign different tribes to each other, so we don't duplicate our efforts, if you see what I mean.'

Pinder gave up all pretence of working with the cards. He stuffed them back into his pocket and held up a hand as if appealing for silence. 'Let me just get this straight,' he said. 'And think very carefully before answering my questions, Mr Williams, because if I feel you're holding back on me, you might very well end up dead. Now, Mr Flowers enlisted you to sell Warp? Is that what you're saying?'

'Yeah, that's pretty much it. I'd been working for another club manager in Southport, guy called Bill Henderson. You know him, I suppose?'

'Afraid not.'

'Well, I'd been doing some pretty useful work for Bill, you know selling dope on the side. Speed, smack, whizz . . . the usual. Anyhow, Bill's an old friend of Gary's, he tells me that this guy up in Manchester wants some help on this big operation he's running. Bill owes him a favour, so he says he wants me to go up there and help him out.' Will spread his hands and grinned cockily. 'So here I am.'

Pinder nodded. 'Go on.'

'Well, not to put too fine a point on it, Flowers told me that the system he was using wasn't working any more. He said he had this guy who was running the operation, but that he didn't seem able to handle it. Said he had this injury that was . . . clouding his judgment. Making him act . . . funny. By the way, how did you do that to your nose? It looks bad.'

'Never mind that,' hissed Pinder irritably. 'Go on with your story.'

'OK, OK, I'm getting to it. I went in to see Flowers and gave him my pitch. Told him I figured the best way to bring more Rag People on board was to be one of them. Dress the part, look right, smell right. He liked the idea. Told me he figured that your way of doing it wasn't getting the results he wanted. He told me I could be responsible for a whole tribe initially and that if I did good, he'd maybe consider making me top hand.' Will shrugged, shook his head. 'But I'm not greedy, know what I mean? I think we can share the operation, work together, there'll be plenty for both of us. What do you say?'

Will waited in silent dread, aware now that he had pushed it as far as he dared. Pinder's ruined face was a mask of pure venom. You could almost hear the bottled-up rage hissing and bubbling like acid within him. Now he would act in one of two ways. He could choose to eradicate Will now, in which case it would simply be a matter of who was first to reach a suitable weapon. Or . . .

Pinder crooked a finger at Will and turned back to his car. 'Come with me,' he said. 'I think we'll see what Mr Flowers has to say about this.'

Will had to resist the impulse to shout 'Yes!'; instead, he put up the kind of resistance that a man like Williams would be expected to offer. 'Oh now, I don't know about that,' he muttered. 'Mr Flowers told me not to say anything to you. If he finds out I crossed him, I could get in serious trouble.'

'Don't worry on that score,' Pinder told him. 'If what you've told me is true, it's Flowers who's in trouble. Come on, get in, we haven't got all night.'

Will shrugged and climbed into the passenger seat beside Pinder. The car had white leather upholstery and stank of pine air freshener. Pinder took off with a screech of tyres and Will sneaked a look in the rear view mirror. Back up towards the top of the street, car headlights flicked on and Marianne and Scally moved in pursuit. But Pinder was too intent on the way ahead to notice. He was muttering to himself beneath his breath, clearly not a happy bunny. Will decided he'd risk pushing the envelope that little bit further.

'Nice car,' he said. 'I think I'll get me one like this when the money starts rolling in.'

Pinder shot him a look of profound irritation. In the lime-green glare of the dashboard, his face resembled something from a Hammer horror film.

'Shut up,' he snapped. 'I'm thinking.' Will didn't much like the sound of that. If Pinder was allowed to become too rational about this, he might notice how unlikely the whole thing was.

'Mr Flowers said that was your problem,' he ventured. 'Said that you think too much. "It's time for action", he told me. He reckons he ought to be shifting twice as many drugs as he is. Well, when you consider it, if we got together on this, there'd be no problem. I was thinking, you know, you take North Manchester and I'll take the South. Or vice versa if you like, I'm not fuss . . .'

He reeled against the passenger door with an oath as the back of Pinder's hand caught him a blow across the face.

'I told you to shut up!' roared Pinder.

Will sank submissively down in his seat, offering no reply but he saw that the barb had done the trick. Pinder was blazing now and they had almost reached their destination. Will risked another glance into the rear view mirror but couldn't see the headlights following. No matter. Marianne and Scally must have had a pretty good idea of where they were headed.

Pinder pulled into the car park at the back of the club and ordered Will to follow him. They got out of the car and Pinder led the way to a fire escape door. He rang a bell and glowered into the lens of a ViewScan mounted above the doorway. After a few moments, the door was opened by a muscular black man wearing a puffa jacket and a baseball cap.

'Hey, Hoodoo Man!' he said. 'Wasn't expecting to see yo' ass in here tonight.' He stared suspiciously at Will. 'Who's this?'

Pinder laughed bitterly. 'Oh, you mean you haven't already met?' he growled.

'Say what?' The black man stepped closer and examined Will for a moment. 'Uh uh, I don't think so.'

'It's OK,' said Will, patting the black man on the shoulder. 'I've told him everything.'

'Oh, you did, did you?' The man looked blankly at Pinder, then shrugged. 'I ain't got the first idea what he's talking about,' he said.

'Very convincing,' sneered Pinder. 'Is Flowers in?'

'Sure, he's up in his office. You want I should announce you?'

Pinder smiled drily. 'No, we'll just go up. I'd like to surprise him.'

The man shrugged. 'Suit yo'self,' he concluded. He threw a last mystified look at Will and moved away.

'Come on,' said Pinder. He led the way up a flight of stairs to the first floor of the building. It was Sunday and it was relatively early but already the music was pounding from the dancefloor below. They turned onto a scruffy-looking corridor and walked along it until they came to a solid oak door. Pinder reached out a big hand and rapped on it with his knuckles.

'Go away, I'm busy,' said a voice from within. Pinder glanced at Will then smiled with grim satisfaction. He turned the handle of the door and stepped inside. Will followed him into the room.

Gary Flowers was sitting at his desk, staring up at them in surprised indignation. In front of him there was a saucer of white powder. A matching smudge of the same substance on his top lip spoke all too clearly about what he'd been doing when they knocked. He pulled a silk handkerchief from his pocket and wiped his nose.

'Auberon,' he said. 'I wasn't expecting to see you tonight!'

'No, I'll wager you weren't. But something came up. I've brought a dear friend to visit you.' Pinder moved aside so that Flowers could get a good look at Will. Flowers stared at him blankly for a moment.

'A friend of *yours*?' he ventured.

'Oh, how strange,' observed Pinder coldly. 'Another man with a sudden loss of memory! First Siggy and now you. But I know all about it, Gary, Williams has told me everything.'

Flowers reached up a hand to scratch his head. 'Auberon, I'm sorry, I haven't got the slightest idea what you're on about.'

317

'No?' Pinder stepped closer to the desk. 'I'm talking about the operation, Gary. I'm talking about you recruiting this toerag here to take my place. Putting him out on the streets to sell for you without even having the common decency to speak to me about it first!'

Flowers' eyes bulged. He was clearly already stoned and maybe wondering if somebody had slipped a hallucinogen into his cocaine. 'What the fuck are you talking about?' he shrieked. 'I never saw this guy in my life before. He . . .' Flowers broke off as realization dawned. 'Just a minute,' he croaked. 'Maybe his face *is* familiar from somewhere . . .' He began to root amongst the litter of papers on his desktop.

'So you admit it?' cried Pinder triumphantly.

'No, you bloody idiot, I'm doing nothing of the kind. But I think . . . oh shit!' Flowers had found what he was looking for. A copy of a tabloid newspaper from the time of Martin's death, the cover headline blaring its familiar story. DRUG DEATH YOUTH'S EX-COP FATHER A DRUG DEALER! And underneath it a photograph of a younger, clean-shaven Will Ambrose. Even as Flowers was fumbling the paper around to show it to Pinder, Will was reaching for the pistol in his belt.

'You fucking arsehole!' Flowers was screaming at Pinder. 'He's tricked you! He's that kid's old man!'

Pinder turned to find himself looking down the barrel of Will's gun. His eyes widened in shocked surprise. He opened his mouth to say something but for the moment, nothing emerged.

'My apologies,' murmured Will. 'But I needed to get in here somehow.' He noticed Flowers' hands straying towards the handle of one of the desk drawers. 'I wouldn't if I were you,' he said and he cocked the trigger of the ancient pistol. Flowers stopped moving. Will surveyed the two men in silence for a moment. They were close enough together to make killing either of them an easy option.

'What the fuck do you want?' snarled Flowers, trying to play the hard man. 'You don't frighten us. All I've got to do is yell for help and there'll be back up coming through that door.'

'You can try,' Will told him. 'But I guarantee you'll be dead before anybody comes to your assistance. As you've already noticed, I'm the father of the boy you murdered . . .'

'That's a bit strong, isn't it?' countered Pinder. 'He wasn't murdered. As I understand it, he took an illegal substance and had a bad reaction to it. Death By Misadventure. You can hardly blame us for that, now can you? After all, we don't manufacture the stuff. We simply sell it.'

'Shut up, Auberon!' snapped Flowers. 'You're not helping matters, telling him that.' He tried to smile but drug-addled as he was, all that came across was a kind of grimace. 'Look, I'm really sorry about what happened to your kid. I really mean that. I've got kids myself and God forbid that anything like that should happen to them. So when I read about him in the paper, my heart went out to you . . .'

'Save the violins,' Will told him. 'It doesn't cut any slack with me. All I want from you are answers. Give me the right ones and who knows, I might let you live.'

'Big words,' observed Pinder. He began to edge away from the desk and Will fixed the gun on him.

'Stand still, or I swear I'll kill you.'

'Really?' Pinder smiled condescendingly at Will. 'I doubt it. I mean, you've had plenty of opportunities to shoot me if you really wanted to. It's one thing to say you'll do it and quite another to actually pull the trigger.'

'I wouldn't put me to the test if I was you,' Will warned him. 'Why don't we cut this short, gentlemen? I just want to know who's in overall charge of the Warp operation. Give me some names and I'll walk out of here.'

'That would be a mistake,' said Pinder calmly. 'After the little jape you just pulled on me, you must know that I intend to come after you and kill you if I can. And I dare say that I'm considerably more adept at it than you are. An ex-policeman, I believe.' Pinder took another step away from the desk. 'But I bet you haven't actually killed anybody, have you Mr Ambrose?'

'I told you to stay where you are,' snapped Will. 'And maybe you didn't hear about your old friend Marshall Resnick?'

Pinder and Flowers exchanged worried glances. 'The story is he committed suicide,' muttered Flowers.

'Sure. And the story on my son is that he just had a bad

night. But the story can be wrong, Mr Flowers. Or did you think that Resnick decided to go skinny dipping in a car park because it seemed like a good idea at the time?' He gestured with the pistol. 'This is taking far too long. One of you had better give me a name very soon, or one of you is going to be very dead.'

Flowers was now looking seriously worried. A thick sweat had broken out on his forehead. He glanced at Pinder. 'I think he means it, Auberon.'

'Does he hell! He's just talk.' Pinder was refusing to take the threat seriously. 'Tell you what, Mr Ambrose, are you fond of tricks? Here's one for you.' He lifted an arm in the air to display his hand, the finger's splayed. 'As you can see, nothing in my hand . . .'

'Just keep the fuck still!' Will warned him.

'Now, now, don't get excited. It's just a harmless little magic trick.'

Out of the corner of his eye, Will saw that Flowers' hands were moving back towards the handle of the desk drawer. He swivelled, aiming the gun.

'I told you to keep still!'

One second, Pinder's hand was empty. The next it seemed to sprout steel. His arm moved backwards and forwards and something flashed through the air towards Will's face. He threw up his left arm to cover his eyes and sharp metal thudded into his wrist, sending a jolt of agony flickering along the length of his arm. He span away with a yell and as he came around, he saw Flowers wrestling something black and heavy out of the desk drawer. Will jerked the gun up to eye level and fired. The pistol kicked hard and Flowers' face registered surprise as the front of his frilled shirt exploded in a gout of red. He was thrown back into his chair and he sat for a moment, staring at Will. Then he pitched sideways and fell behind the desk, out of sight.

Will was turning back to face Pinder when the big man charged into him, the impact lifting him clean off his feet and carrying his backwards across the room. His shoulders crashed into the plasterboard wall behind him and the gun discharged with a roar, sending the last bullet crashing uselessly into the ceiling.

'Now you little shit . . .' Pinder's huge hands closed around Will's throat with a power that seemed to snuff the strength right out of him. The pistol fell uselessly from his fingers and skittered away across the floorboards. Will got his hands up to Pinder's wrists and tried to lever them away from his throat but could make no impression on them. One hand seemed to have no strength at all. Then Will dimly registered the squat throwing knife protruding from his left wrist and he understood why. A high pitched noise shrilled like an alarm in his head and he realized that he only had a few minutes left to live. Through a red fog Pinder's ugly face grinned down at him in feral triumph, the obscene open wound only inches away.

Will knew that he had one chance left. He reshaped the fingers of his right hand, extending the index and forefingers into a pointing gesture; then summoning his last reserves of strength, he lifted his arm and thrust the fingers deep into the hole in Pinder's face. The fingertips pushed through membrane into something warm and pulpy and suddenly, magically, the throttling hands had lost their grip. Pinder was stumbling away, screaming at the top of his lungs, blood spurting down his face.

Will staggered towards the door. As he neared it, he became aware of footsteps thudding along the landing outside. He glanced desperately around for a weapon and grabbed a heavy trophy off the top of a filing cabinet. He ducked in behind the door and as he did so, he caught a glimpse of the engraving on the front of the trophy. *Gary Flowers, Entrepreneur Of The Year, 1996*. But there was no time to dwell on that because the door was crashing open and the muscular black man burst into the room, a heavy automatic in his hand. Will kicked the door away and brought the award crashing down on the back of his head, knocking him to the floor. Will didn't wait around to see if the man was capable of getting up again. As he headed for the door, he noticed that Pinder was getting control of the pain, was clawing himself upright by holding on to the desk. Behind it, Gary Flowers was lying sprawled on the carpet doing a very convincing impression of a dead man.

'Shit!' Will made it through the door and started running down the corridor beyond. He still felt groggy from Pinder's attack and his legs didn't seem to be obeying him properly. He made it to the staircase and as he turned to go down them, Pinder came running out of the office, with a gun in his hand. His face beneath its splattering of blood was chalk white and he seemed to be having trouble clinging on to consciousness. A thought flashed through Will's mind. *Is that Flowers' gun, or mine?*

Pinder's hand came up and he pulled the trigger. The harsh click confirmed what Will had been praying for. He carried on down the stairs, hoping his feet wouldn't slip out from under him. Pinder stared at the gun for a moment and then with a bellow of rage, he flung it down the stairs at Will. It caught him a glancing blow on the shoulder, nearly making him fall; but then he was down the stairs and running for the exit, the sound of rock music pounding up from the dancefloor below. Pinder came after him, yelling at the top of his lungs.

'You're dead, you fucker! D'you hear me? You are history!'

Will was getting some strength back now. He ran full tilt into the exit door and pushed, but nothing happened. He glanced back over his shoulder and saw that Pinder had just reached the bottom of the stairs. There was another knife in his hand now, a big-bladed hunting knife with a jagged edge, the illegal kind.

Will returned his attention to the door, trying to figure out the intricacies of the lock. It was a simple Yale. He tried to twist it open with his useless left hand and cried out at the pain it caused him. He glanced back. Pinder was close now, dangerously close. Will thought about turning back and making a stand. He thought about it for all of a millisecond and just as quickly abandoned the idea. Instead, he got his other hand up to the lock and turned the handle. The door swung open and he pushed through into the night air as . . .

Pinder came hurtling towards him, the knife blade poised to strike and . . .

Will saw the jalopy at the top end of the car park, the engine running, thick black smoke belching from the exhaust. He put his head down and began to run as fast as his aching legs would carry him. Pinder came after him, bellowing like a wounded beast and . . .

The rear door of the car opened and it started to move slowly away. Will ran alongside it for a moment and then threw himself in through the doorway. Scally grabbed hold of his arms and accidentally jarred the knife in his wrist. Will screamed with pain, almost fell back out of the car but Scally got a better grip on him as the Nissan accelerated towards the main road and . . .

Traffic coming at them, horns blaring, a blaze of headlights. Marianne had to brake to avoid a collision and . . .

Pinder came up level with the open door. He was staring in at the occupants, seeing Scally gazing wide-eyed back at him and . . .

'You!' gasped Pinder. Surprise stopped him momentarily in his tracks and Marianne stamped down on the accelerator. The rear wheels span around with a shriek of protest and then found purchase on the wet tarmac. The car moved away along the main road, picking up speed.

Scally leaned across Will and slammed the door. He glanced fearfully back through the rear window.

'He saw me,' he whispered. 'He saw me.'

It was a long time before either of them spoke again.

Chapter Thirty-Three

They dumped the Nissan on a deserted street and made their way back to the new shelter. On the short drive home, Will had managed to pull the knife out of his left arm. As far as he could ascertain, there wasn't any serious damage, but the wound hurt like hell and he was bleeding like a stuck pig. All he could do for now was to keep a firm pressure on the wound and hope that he hadn't lost too much blood.

Back in the grim sanctuary beneath the station, they found everybody crouched gloomily in the glow of the kerosine lamps. A caldron of Pot Luck was cooking and the air was thick with smoke and the smell of stewing vegetables. Frank lay beside the sleeping figure of Peg, an old blanket thrown over his injured legs. Will noticed that he was no longer wearing his leather harness of tools or his long boots, and he presumed that they must have been appropriated by other members of the tribe. Frank's bare feet stuck out from beneath the blanket and his toes were blue with cold.

Frank's position of power had ended abruptly and he must have been still dazed by the speed of his fall. In the space of a few hours, he had gone from being leader of the tribe to a pariah that nobody had any respect for. As Will, Marianne and Scally moved past him to their own space, Frank was feebly crying out for water but nobody was taking any notice of him. Will told Scally to go to the tap and get the ex-Duke a drink. The boy gave Will a disbelieving look but did as he was told.

Will took off his coat and Marianne picked out the cleanest rags she could find to bind the wound on his wrist. He clenched his teeth as she tied the knot, binding the wrist as tightly as she dared without risking loss of circulation.

'What happened in there?' Marianne asked him. They hadn't spoken about it on the ride home.

'I made a pig's ear of it, that's what happened,' muttered Will. 'I ended up shooting Flowers dead and I didn't learn anything from Pinder. Christ, I had them both right where I needed them and I let it all go down the pan.'

'Have a bit of trouble, did you?' snickered Frank. Scally had reluctantly handed him a tin of drinking water and he was gulping at it noisily. Beside him, Peg moaned but didn't wake. She looked as though she was in a bad way.

'You could say that,' admitted Will.

'What a shame!' Frank stared challengingly around at the other inhabitants of the shelter, seemingly amused by the situation. 'Maybe he ain't the superman you think he is,' he observed, to the room at large. 'Maybe he's all mouth and no trousers!' He waved a hand around the room and then looked back at Will. 'See, while you was gone, these idiots had themselves a little meeting. You'll never guess what they're planning to do . . .'

'Shut it,' said one of Frank's former lieutenants, the red-bearded scouser called Mike. 'When we want an opinion from you, dip-shit, we'll ask for one.'

There were general grunts of agreement from the other members of the tribe. Frank glared at Mike in undisguised hatred. 'You two-faced worm,' he snarled. 'When I think of all the times I helped you out. A week ago you'd have licked my arse, if . . .' Frank's words trailed off into a bellow of pain as Mike walked towards him and swung a savage kick into the former Duke's ribs.

'Times change,' said Mike coldly. 'Any more out of you and you'll be going for a midnight swim in the canal.'

Frank cowered like a whipped dog. He'd subjected enough people to the same fate in his time and knew just how horrible an end it was. Mike walked back to his own space. He stooped and pulled something from under his sleeping bag, then carried it across the room to Will. Will saw that it was the leather harness of equipment that had previously belonged to Frank.

'Like he just said, we've been talking,' said Mike. 'We liked what you did before. Throwing us the money and all

325

that. Most people would have kept quiet about it, tried to keep it for themselves. I noticed that you didn't take any of it.'

Will shrugged. 'Far as I'm concerned it's tainted,' he explained. 'For all I know twenty pounds of it could be the same money that bought my son's death.'

Mike frowned. 'Yeah, well, anyway, we've talked it through and we're all of the same mind. We want you to be the new Duke. What d'you reckon?'

Will studied Mike in quiet amusement for a moment. 'Just like that?' he asked.

'Sure. What else is there to say? We're not exactly in a position to hold a fookin' coronation, are we? The position's yours if you want it.' Mike glanced scornfully around at the tattered remnants of the tribe. 'It ain't exactly the big deal it used to be. We're on the skids, we ain't even got a decent shelter no more. But with the right man to lead us, maybe we can come back from this and . . . well, we figure you're our best bet. Will you do it?'

Will thought for a moment. He had mixed feelings about the idea. It seemed like a terrible responsibility to have thrust upon him, but on the other hand, in the days to come, it might be useful to have a small army of people prepared to follow his instructions.

'OK,' he said. 'You've got yourself a deal. But there's something I've got to sort out first. Remember what I was talking about before? Warp? I might need some help to take care of that.' Mike looked doubtful.

'That's a personal thing. It ain't really our business.'

Will looked at him for a moment, then shook his head. 'You couldn't be more wrong,' he said. 'Yes, it's personal, but it does relate to the tribe – to Rag People all over the city. It's because of this drug that we're being exploited. And why people like that,' he stabbed a finger in Frank's direction, 'are getting rich off our backs.' He gazed around the room. 'I'll make you all a deal,' he said. 'You help me to finish what I set out to do and I promise that I'll work to put this tribe back where it was, before the God Squad moved in on it. Does anybody have a problem with that?'

There were grunts of dismissal, a few people shook their heads.

'The Duke calls the shots,' concluded Mike matter-of-factly. He threw a contemptuous look at the prone figure of Frank. 'And anyway, look at the things we did for that piece of shit. You couldn't do a worse job than him.'

Will laughed bitterly. 'Thanks for the vote of confidence,' he said. 'I'll try and be worthy of your trust.'

Mike sneered. 'I wouldn't thank us yet, pal. It ain't no picnic we've invited you on.' He threw the harness down at Will's feet. 'Welcome aboard,' he said and turning away, he wandered back to his own space.

Scally came over and squatted down beside Will. He fingered the harness respectfully.

'You're the Duke,' he murmured, staring up at Will open-mouthed. 'Imagine that!'

Marianne smiled ruefully. She sat back on her bedroll and studied Will for a moment. 'What's the first thing you're going to do?' she asked him.

'That's a very good question,' he said. 'I thought I was making progress before but now I feel I've come to a full stop.' One of the women brought over an enamel bowl full of Pot Luck. Will thanked her and then indicated Marianne and Scally. 'What about some for my lieutenants here?' he asked. The woman went straight back to the pot and returned with two more bowls.

The three of them ate in silence for a while. The stew was mean and watery but the hot liquid helped to revive their failing spirits. As he was finishing up, Will became aware of a pair of eyes burning into the back of his skull. Glancing over his shoulder, he saw that Frank was lying there, gazing helplessly over at him. Evidently nobody had thought to provide him with any food.

Will thought about that for a moment. Then he got up, took his empty bowl back to the pot and refilled it, aware that the eyes of everyone in the room were upon him. He carried it over to Frank and kneeled beside him.

'Nice one!' whispered Frank, holding his hands out for the bowl but Will pulled it back out of his reach.

'This isn't charity,' he said. 'I'll trade you for your mobile phone. I believe there were two more calls left on the card.'

Frank glared at him indignantly. 'One lousy bowl of stew for a mobile phone!' he croaked.

'Suit yourself.' Will made as if to move away but Frank threw out a hand to stop him. 'No OK, you win,' he gasped. 'You can have it.' He pulled the phone from his pocket and set it down on the floor beside Will. Then he nearly spilled the stew in his haste to grab the bowl of Pot Luck. He lifted it to his mouth and began to wolf down the food, sucking and slurping noisily. Will watched him for a moment in silent disgust. He glanced over at Mike.

'Is this the only food he's had all day?' he asked.

Mike nodded. 'Too right. Why should we let the thieving bastard have anything? If it was up to me, he'd starve.'

Will shook his head. 'We're not savages,' he observed. 'And we don't have to live like them. From now on I want him fed when everyone else eats, OK?'

Mike shrugged. 'You're the Duke,' he observed. 'But you know the rules. If a man doesn't contribute to the pot, he ain't supposed to eat.'

'Those were Frank's rules,' Will told him. 'My rules are different. The first person who doesn't like them, feel free to come and discuss it with me.' He stared around the room for a moment, but there were no takers. Everyone had had the fight knocked out of them back at the arches. Will picked up the mobile and went back to sit with Marianne and Scally. He studied the phone for a moment, wanting to be sure that he remembered the number correctly. A world where people had nice houses with telephones in them seemed somehow surreal, a whole world away.

'Who are you going to call?' asked Marianne.

'A friend. Somebody who's been helping me with this Warp business. I need to fix up a time and a place to meet with him. Maybe he'll have made some progress. I just hope I don't get his answerphone . . .'

He punched in what he seemed to remember as Clive's home number and listened as it rang at the other end of the line. It sounded like a very long way away. On the fourth ring, it was picked up and Will smiled with relief at the familiar voice.

'Hello?'

'Clive, it's me, Will. I need to . . .'

'Sorry, wrong number! Phone Bobby. You understand? Bobby. From before you were married. He's talking to *you*.' The receiver was replaced and Will sat there, looking at the mobile in dismay. One of his only two calls wasted. And what the hell was Clive on about? Wrong number . . .

'That was a quick call,' observed Scally.

'Too bloody quick,' admitted Will. 'It was like he was afraid to speak to me. He told me to phone somebody called Bobby.'

'Bobby?' echoed Marianne. 'Who's that, a man or a woman?'

Will was about to say that it must be a man, because Clive had said something like, '*he's* talking to *you*', putting emphasis on the last word, when he said it . . . and then out of the blue a recollection came at him. A long, long time ago, when Will and Suzanne were first going steady, that name had meant something special to them. It was a nickname that Clive had attached to Suzanne. The three of them had been fans of the movies of Martin Scorcese, particularly *Taxi Driver*. One drunken night in Manchester, Suzanne had imbibed more than her usual ration of alcohol and had started to do the infamous 'mirror' monologue, slipping into her best approximation of a Robert De Niro accent and asking her drinking companions, 'Are you talkin' to me? Are you fuckin' talkin' to me?' From then on, Suzanne had always been 'Bobby' as far as Clive was concerned – he had even slipped a mention of it into his best man's speech at the wedding.

'Of course,' murmured Will. He glanced at the others. 'Cross your fingers,' he said. 'This is my last chance with this thing.'

He punched in Suzanne's number and listened to the trill at the far end of the line, picturing the sleek black answering console in the hallway of her huge house, waiting for the sterile tones of the mechanical voice to cut in and ask for his message. But thankfully it was Suzanne's voice that answered.

'Hello, Suzanne Ambrose?'

'Hi, it's me. Is it OK to talk?'

'Will? Oh, thank God! I'd just about given up hope. Are you all right?'

'I'm fine. And I hate to be abrupt but I really don't have much time. I just phoned Clive's number and in a roundabout way, he told me to call you.'

'Yes, that's right. Clive thinks he might be under surveillance. He's asked me to meet with you tomorrow instead. He's afraid that he might lead them to you.'

Will frowned. 'Them?'

'The people who are watching him.'

Will frowned. 'I don't know, Suzanne, I don't like getting you involved in this.' Out of the corner of his eye, Will noticed Marianne sit up and start taking notice, evidently surprised at the mention of another woman's name, but he couldn't allow himself to worry about that now.

'Too late, Will. As I told Clive, I already *am* involved. There are strange things happening out here. Listen, Will, how long do you have? Maybe I can ring you back.'

'No chance, it's a disposable. I've got a couple of minutes, no more.'

'OK. First, where and when shall we meet?'

'Tomorrow, twelve o'clock. Outside the City Art Gallery?'

'Got it. Now, listen carefully, I'll tell you as much as I know. You remember Adam at Delta?'

'Sure.'

'He's been acting strangely ever since you left. Had a meeting with our friend DCI Chalmers. Secret handshakes, all that stuff. I'm almost certain that he's a member of The Brotherhood . . .'

'Jesus, Suzanne!'

'I know. And that's not all. We have a property on our books. Cooper's grain warehouse beside the River Irwell in Castlefield? I can't be certain, but I think it could be a possible site for a drugs laboratory. Maybe the one where they manufacture Warp.'

'You're kidding! That's incredible . . .'

'Remember, it's only a suspicion. I could be way off.'

'Well, we'll soon know. I'll check it out first thing tomorrow. Look, we'll move our meeting back to three pm, just to be sure

I've had a chance for a proper recce. Castlefield, you say?'

'Yes, about a mile or two upriver from the Club Zone. Clive thinks ... well, he told me he reckons that the people behind the Warp operation are ...'

'Yes, go on!'

'It sounds crazy...'

'For God's sake, tell me, we're running out of time!'

There was the sound of Suzanne taking a deep breath. 'He thinks it's Chalmers and his whole division. Or at least, everyone that belongs to The Brotherhood.'

Will flinched as though somebody had just punched him. He opened his mouth to say something but for the moment, he was lost for words.

'Will, are you still there?'

'Yes. Yes, Jesus, Suzanne, what are you saying?'

'Will, I know how it sounds, but think about it! When you put them into the picture, it all finally begins to make a horrible kind of sense. Clive thinks it's been going on for a long time. That's why they framed you up and got you out of there ...'

'Oh, Jesus, Suzanne, no!' His eyes were filling with involuntary tears, because though he might have joked about such a thing in the past, though he might have made exasperated comments to this effect, he didn't want to believe that such a monstrous accusation could be true. A vision of Martin's blue eyes swam into his head and the thought of what had happened to his son made him want to cry out in despair.

'Maybe ...' he ventured. 'Maybe ... Clive's wrong.'

But the only reply was a drone as the smart card shut down.

'God damn it!' Will slammed the phone on to the stone floor with a force that cracked the plastic casing.

'What is it?' Marianne asked him. She saw the tears in his eyes and reached out to take his hands in hers. He just sat there staring at her.

'I just found something out,' he said. 'We know ... or at least, we think we know, who's behind Warp.'

'Well, that's great news, isn't it? I mean, that's what you wanted, right?'

Will shook his head. 'I wanted it to be somebody else,' he explained. 'I wanted it to be the bad guys, a corrupt organization, the Mafia, somebody like that. Somebody I could feel happy about hating. Instead of . . .'

Marianne cocked her head to one side in that slightly crazy way she had about her. 'Instead, of what?' she murmured.

'Oh, I don't know. Maybe we're wrong. I hope to God we are.'

'Who's we?' murmured Scally. 'I heard you say some woman's name. Suzanne?'

Will nodded. 'My ex-wife,' he said. 'She's been helping me. And another friend, Clive, a journalist.'

'You never mentioned a wife,' said Marianne, quietly.

'That's *ex*-wife,' he reminded her. 'Martin's mother. And she has every right to be involved in this if she wants to be.' He looked at them both thoughtfully. 'Tomorrow morning, I have to go and check out a warehouse in Castlefield. It could be the place where the drugs are being manufactured. You two can stay here if you like . . .'

'We'll come,' Scally assured him. 'We're your lieutenants now, remember?'

Will grinned. He reached out and tousled the boy's hair. 'Yeah, that's right. I nearly forgot.' He looked inquiringly at Marianne. 'What about you?' he asked.

'Count me in,' she said. 'Ex-wife or no ex-wife.'

'Good.' Will massaged his throbbing arm. 'That's settled then. We'll need to set off at first light, so I suggest we try and get some shuteye.' They rearranged the old clothing that currently served as their bedding and the three of them lay down in a corner of the room, trying to make themselves as comfortable as they could, huddling together in a vain attempt to keep warm. But exhausted as he was, Will couldn't sleep. A combination of the pain in his arm, the cold winter chill in his bones and a terrible anxiety at the back of his mind, denied him any rest that night. He was terribly afraid that Clive would be proved right. That the biggest villains in the city were the people who represented the forces of law and order. And whenever Will glanced over in Frank's direction, he was perturbed to see that the former Duke was lying there watching him and smiling coldly, as though he knew exactly how it felt to be afraid.

Chapter Thirty-Four

Pinder and Siggy sat rather sheepishly in a small room adjoining Gary Flowers' office, talking to the tall policeman who had introduced himself as Detective Inspector Bullen. Meanwhile, next door, a white-overalled forensic team was dusting for prints, taking photographs of the corpse and generally turning the place over in their search for evidence.

Pinder hadn't much liked the idea of calling in The Blues, but on reflection, he and Siggy had decided that there was little else they could do. They had briefly considered taking the body elsewhere and dumping it, but Flowers had been too prominent a figure to be swept under the carpet like that. A disappearance would probably cause more unwelcome attention than simply reporting his murder. So after putting their heads together on a suitable story about what had happened, they'd decided to break the habit of a lifetime and call in the cops.

The open wound on Pinder's face throbbed with pain and he chewed on a couple of aspirins to try and take the edge off it. He was still attempting to put the story together in his head. This character, Will Ambrose . . . how did he tie in with the kid who had stuck a fork in Pinder's nose? And more importantly, where could he find the pair of them?

'So, how exactly did the intruder get in?' asked Bullen. He sounded bored with the whole thing, as though he'd rather be somewhere else. Anywhere else. 'The place seems pretty secure . . .'

'Yes, but it's as I told you,' retorted Pinder. 'Siggy had just taken some trash out and sometimes the latch doesn't close properly. Obviously this fellow must have been waiting in the car park, watching for an opportunity . . .'

Bullen glanced through the notes in his electronic pad.

'And this is the best description you can give?' he muttered. 'A black man, about six feet tall, heavy build.' He looked at Siggy. 'You sure you didn't recognize him?'

Siggy shrugged. He was still holding a wet flannel against the gash on the back of his head. 'Hey man, they all look the same to me,' he muttered. 'What can I tell you? I heard a shot and came running up to the office. Next t'ing I know, the lights went out.'

'Hmm.' Bullen returned his attention to Pinder. 'And you reckon this guy was just after money, right?'

'It would appear so. Not that there was very much. Mr Flowers kept some petty cash on the premises, but that was all. A few hundred pounds at most. This fellow burst in and started shouting at us to get him some money. Mr Flowers went to open the drawer of his desk, where he kept the cash box and the man panicked and shot him. It was all over in a moment.'

Bullen glanced over at the desk drawer. Naturally Pinder and Siggy had got rid of Flowers' gun and his stash of drugs.

'So you worked for Mr Flowers, did you?'

'That's correct.'

'In what capacity?'

'I, er, was his personal assistant. A gopher. I took care of various little details on his behalf. I also entertained at the club occasionally. I'm an illusionist.'

'Yeah?' Bullen looked profoundly disinterested in this information. Pinder got the distinct impression that the detective was just filling in time, waiting for somebody else to arrive; and sure enough, a few moments later, another man entered the room, a small, tubby fellow dressed in a black crombie overcoat. Little blue eyes twinkled behind the lenses of his horn-rimmed spectacles. Bullen got up out of the chair as though royalty had just entered the room.

'Everything all right?' asked the newcomer, in a strangely high pitched voice.

'Yes sir, I think I've got most of the details.' Bullen pointed at Siggy. 'This gentleman has received a blow to the head. I think he may require medical assistance.'

'Very good, Don, see to it will you?'

'Yes sir.' Bullen crooked an index finger at Siggy. 'If you'd like to come with me . . .'

Siggy frowned and threw an uncertain glance in Pinder's direction; but he followed Bullen obediently out of the room. Pinder started to get up from his chair, but the plump man raised a gloved hand and ushered him back into his seat. He walked over and gently closed the office door. Then he turned back with an oily smile and came back to Pinder, one hand extended to shake.

'So you must be Auberon Pinder,' he said. 'We've never actually met but Mr Flowers has often spoken of you. I'm Detective Chief Inspector Chalmers.'

Pinder shook hands, vaguely bemused by the man's apparent friendliness.

'And what did . . . Mr Flowers . . . say about me, exactly?'

'Only good things, I can assure you.' Chalmers settled himself into the chair recently vacated by Bullen. 'It's a terrible tragedy,' he observed. 'Gary and I were very close.'

'Is that a fact?' Pinder was extremely surprised to hear this. He'd never known Flowers to express a good opinion about The Blues.

'Indeed. I realize it's not something he would have chosen to advertise. Our liaison was, by its very nature, clandestine. And I understand only too well that you have every reason to be distrustful of a man such as myself.'

'Well . . .' began Pinder, but Chalmers didn't let him go on.

'This is going to come as a shock to you, Auberon, but the fact is, Gary worked for me, just as you worked for Gary. We are, the two of us, on the same team.'

There was a long silence while Pinder tried to get a handle on this information. If he'd heard correctly, Chalmers was making an incredible admission.

'Excuse me, but . . . are you telling me that . . . are you saying . . . ?'

'That the Warp operation in this city is under my overall control. Yes, Auberon, that's exactly what I'm saying.'

'Then . . . you're not really a police officer at all?'

Chalmers seemed to find this amusing. He tilted back his head and tittered girlishly.

'Oh, but I am! I'm many things, Auberon, but above all else, I am a police officer and proud to be so. In the normal run of events, we might never have met, but the death of Gary Flowers has changed matters dramatically. And I do not have time to pussyfoot around this situation. So from now on, I think the two of us will be working together.'

'I see,' said Pinder, blankly. He didn't really but felt that he had to say something. It occurred to him that Chalmers might be bluffing him along, trying to get him to make an admission of some kind. But no, one look into those fiercely intelligent blue eyes was enough to convince Pinder that this was on the level.

'As I'm sure you can imagine, Gary was an important factor in the running of this operation. Not exactly irreplaceable, you understand, but a key figure. And his death has occurred at a particularly difficult time. So I will be looking to you, Auberon, to help keep us on track.'

Pinder laughed. He couldn't help it. There sat a Chief Inspector of the Greater Manchester Police, talking about a highly illegal operation as though it was the most natural thing in the world. Chalmers stopped talking and drew his mouth into a disapproving pout. 'Something amuses you?' he inquired.

'Forgive me. This whole incident seems . . . vaguely surreal. I mean, there I was lamenting my impending redundancy . . . only to discover that my life of crime will continue, aided and abetted by the forces of law and order. You must admit it's an unusual arrangement.'

Chalmers sat back in his chair. He brushed imaginary crumbs from his lap with a black-gloved hand. 'When I first came to my current post in the force, I took a good long look around me,' he said. 'I had already formed The Brotherhood and had inducted many of my most trusted colleagues into it. I saw us as a force for decency and righteousness in a city that seemed to be swimming around in a cesspit of filth and decadence. In particular, Auberon, I looked at the drug abusers and the crime associated with such abuse. It occurred to me that there was a small fortune being expended on the purchase of illegal substances, money that in turn went on to support

336

the criminal community. And it occurred to me that this money could easily be channelled in other, more useful directions . . . to support the fight *against* crime. Why not, I thought, create our own drug? Cut out the middle-man, so to speak.'

Pinder stared at Chalmers, thinking to himself that this little man was evidently quite mad; and doubtless capable of a level of evil that made Pinder's own transgressions seem like mere misdemeanours. 'So you started making your own drugs?'

'In a nutshell, that's exactly what we did. I enlisted the help of some of the drug-chemists we'd already arrested, offered to commute their sentences if they would synthesise a drug that would suit my purposes. When I offered them a percentage of all future profits, they were more than happy to oblige. After that, it took considerable investment on my part, allocating funds to the development of the merchandise. But I'm happy to say it very quickly paid for itself. It now makes a positively obscene profit.'

Pinder smiled suspiciously. 'And what happens to that profit, may I ask?'

'It's channelled into scores of worthy projects,' said Chalmers with apparent pride. 'We now have the best-equipped police division in the UK. You think the Met can afford to run ten surveillance helicopters? It cannot. But *we* can. We have the finest technology currently available in the fight against crime. Our DNA database is the envy of the country. Our surveillance equipment is second to none. You see, Auberon, to be victorious in the war on crime, it is necessary to have the right ammunition. Before Warp came along, we were just like all the other police forces across the country, struggling to exist on the pittance that Central Government allowed us, having to register as a charity in order to get the extra funding we needed. But now we have the edge; and we have the finances to ride out any crisis.'

Pinder frowned. 'But all that money; how do you explain it away?'

'The Brotherhood has some very inventive accountants . . . and of course, those who contribute to our charity fund are much more generous than they used to be! But we are unable to show the true size of our assets. All the cash that comes in on a daily basis has to be feathered away in a variety of secure locations. Mountains of money waiting for the time when we can assume absolute control.'

Pinder looked at Chalmers warily. He didn't much like the direction in which the conversation was heading.

'And . . . what time is that, exactly?'

'Why, the time of Armageddon, of course. It's close at hand. All informed sources agree that it will happen before the end of the century.'

Pinder made no attempt to mask an expression of contempt. 'You're talking about the end of the world?'

'Not the *end*, Auberon. A new beginning. We of The Brotherhood believe that Armageddon will be enacted in its true Biblical sense. It will be a savage battle between two armies. The forces of law and the forces of evil. A contest that we intend to win.'

'And you really believe this will happen?'

'We *know* it will. But surely it can be no surprise to you? Look around you, man. You must be aware of the sense of chaos and negativity that pervades every aspect of our lives. You know, don't you, that society is on the very brink of collapse? At such times, it is only the strong and the resolute who can hope to compete. When the conflict comes, it will be a case of survival of the fittest.'

Pinder looked doubtful. 'What if it happened right now?' he suggested. 'What good would all your accumulated wealth do you then?'

Chalmers smiled, shook his head. 'It *is* happening now,' he assured Pinder. 'The slide into chaos is a gradual process. There will be no nuclear devastation, no sudden collision with a meteorite. Only the steady erosion of everything we value.'

'Oh really?' muttered Pinder. 'Well, that's a relief, then.'

Chalmers studied him for a moment as though he suspected that Pinder wasn't treating this matter with the degree of seriousness it deserved.

'I hope you aren't making mock of my beliefs,' he said.

'No! No, no of course not. I'm just somewhat taken aback, that's all. I had no idea that so much foresight had been expended on this.'

Pinder was finding it difficult to look the little man in the eye. He had never gone in for any of this mystical bullshit. As far as he was concerned, magic was merely an illusion conjured by the speed of a man's hand. Pinder didn't believe in God or The Devil. He believed only in survival; and he relished the thought of how stupid Chalmers was going to look when he woke up on the morning of January first, 2000, to find that absolutely nothing had changed. But if he was anything, Pinder was a pragmatist, and right now, he needed to remain in gainful employment. So he leaned forward in his chair, affecting an air of intense concentration.

'So tell me,' he said. 'How can I be of assistance?'

Chalmers seemed reassured. He clasped his hands in his lap and crossed his plump legs at the knee.

'It's going to take some time to find a replacement for Gary Flowers,' he said. 'Unless of course, you'd be willing to take on his duties? I'm sure you'd make an ideal candidate.'

Pinder shook his head. 'Not really my forté. I've always dealt with the workforce. The mules. As I'm sure you know, we'd recently been stepping up on recruitment. I understood from Gary that a big new consignment was due soon.'

'Quite so! A very special consignment, as it happens.'

'Special? In what way?'

'A new formula. Much more powerful than previous versions. You see, rather than wait for the battle to ensue, I've decided to fire the opening salvo in this war of attrition. So now that we've hooked the enemy and milked them of most of their reserves, it's time to take them out of the equation. Cleanse ourselves of them and march forward into the new millennium, victorious.'

Pinder stared at Chalmers. 'You mean this new stuff is . . . ?'

'Deadly. They'll be dropping like flies when it hits the streets. And we'll take plenty of them down before people begin to catch on to what's happening, because you will instruct your sales force that everyone who expresses an interest is to be given a free sample.' He smiled coldly. 'A once only, never to be repeated, special offer. One to die for.'

Pinder had thought that he was through with being

astonished but nonetheless, he gasped. 'But that's, like, genocide!' he observed.

'Technically I suppose it is; but only of a sector of society that has relinquished its right to live alongside true human beings. We'll be striking a blow for all decent people and at the same time, initiating the decisive action that will culminate in us taking total control of this city.' Chalmers glared at Pinder as though challenging him to argue the point. 'I know how it sounds,' he said. 'But I can assure you that what you may perceive as the ramblings of a madman are nothing more than plain common sense.'

Oh yes, thought Pinder. *And I'm Catherine the Great.*

'You're taking quite a risk telling me all this,' he observed. 'Supposing I said to you that I didn't want to play ball. Supposing I said that I thought the whole thing was disgusting and that I intended to inform the media of what's been happening.'

Chalmers laughed softly. 'Oh come now, Auberon, I really don't think that a man who in his spare time likes to do surgical experiments on young boys, has any business going to the media, do you?'

That was a shock. Pinder gasped as though he'd just been slapped in the face. He stared at Chalmers, open-mouthed, as he tried to come up with a suitable reply. 'But how . . . how did you . . . ?'

'I've made it my business to find out about everyone that works for me. And while I cannot condone what you do for pleasure, it has to be said that all your victims have been mere streetbeggars, not members of decent society; so under the circumstances, I am prepared to offset these indiscretions against the bigger service you can do for this city. So may I take it that you will continue to work for me in this matter?'

Pinder swallowed hard. 'Of course,' he said. 'When is all this happening?'

'The day after tomorrow. But I'd like to meet with you at the warehouse tomorrow morning to discuss your duties. I take it you've been there before.'

Pinder nodded. He was still somewhat stunned by the recent turn of events. 'Yes. Yes, of course . . .'

'Good. Be there at ten o'clock sharp. I rarely like to be so directly involved in these matters, but this is a special case.' He looked thoughtful for a moment. 'Now, going back to events here at the club. This man who shot Flowers. I'll hazard a guess and say that he wasn't a black man at all. Am I right?'

Pinder nodded his head. 'Yes. It was somebody who called himself Peter Williams. But Flowers recognized him as Will Ambrose, the ex-cop whose kid died from taking Warp a few weeks back. I remember reading about him in the papers at the time, but I didn't recognize him tonight. He looked like a Rag Man.'

Chalmers scowled. 'So,' he said. 'It's as I thought. He's getting closer all the time. Have you any idea where we might look for him?'

Pinder considered the question. 'Well, he definitely knows a Rag Man called Frank, who I recently recruited. Frank's tribe was based in the railway arches on Sobriety Street in Ardwick. But I heard that those bloody idiots at the MLOD turfed them all out of there the other day, so I suppose they could be just about anywhere now.'

Chalmers coughed uncomfortably. 'Er, yes, I had the same information. Still, no matter. I have men looking for him, it's only a matter of time.'

'He had a kid with him,' murmured Pinder dreamily, gently tracing around the hole in his face with the tip of his index finger. 'And a woman. They were in a car, a White Nissan. I'm afraid I wasn't able to get the registration.'

'Pity. You recognized the people with him?'

'Hmm? Oh no, just street trash. But if you *do* find them, I'd very much like to be present at their interrogation. If possible.'

Chalmers smiled and nodded. 'I'm sure something could be arranged,' he said. 'Now, Auberon, I'm sure I don't have to tell you that I expect you to treat our little talk with the utmost discretion. Not a word to anyone, OK?'

'Naturally.' Pinder felt distinctly annoyed. Knowing what he knew about Pinder's hobby, Chalmers must have realized he had no need to ask the question. 'My lips are sealed.'

'Oh and naturally, this new responsibility will be rewarded by a substantial rise in pay.' Chalmers got to his feet. 'I'll see you at the warehouse tomorrow. We'll discuss the details then.'

'Wouldn't miss it for the world,' Pinder assured him.

'Good man.' Chalmers walked to the door and opened it a few inches. Through the gap, Pinder could see the room being lit at intervals by the glare of a flashgun. 'I'll speak to my men out here,' said Chalmers. 'There's absolutely no reason to detain you further.' He went out of the room, closing the door behind him.

Pinder reached into his pocket and took out a fresh pack of playing cards. He tore off the cellophane, removed the Jokers and began to shuffle the cards for a game of patience. It was a funny old world and no mistake, he told himself. In the space of a few hours he had gone from being a club-owner's assistant to a fully paid-up member of the Greater Manchester Police. The next thing he knew, Chalmers would be offering him membership of The Brotherhood. But he doubted that he would accept the offer. Not his style at all. And while Pinder was quite prepared to admit that he was far from perfect, at least he was still playing with a full deck.

Chapter Thirty-Five

Early the following morning Will, Marianne and Scally were crouched on the vantage point of an ancient metal bridge looking down at the old grain warehouse, a hundred yards upstream from them. Everything Will saw told him that this was the place where Warp was manufactured.

At first glance, it looked like many of the other derelict warehouses that dotted this part of the city, the brickwork crumbling, the windowpanes smashed. But on closer inspection, it became apparent that somebody had taken great pains to ensure that trespassers were kept out of the place. For one thing, the high wire fence that ringed the establishment was in very good repair and Will had spotted a couple of places where breaks in the wire had recently been patched. Closer inspection revealed that ViewScans had been installed at various points around the building and occasional flashing red lights on the casing of the surveillance equipment revealed that they were in perfect working order. Will judged that at this distance, they should be out of range of the cameras but he made his companions keep their heads below the parapet of the bridge, just to be on the safe side.

After they had been waiting a half hour or so, an ancient wooden door on the ground floor opened and two men stepped out, thick-set goons carrying Uzi's over their shoulders. One of them had a vicious looking Rottweiler on a leash. They began a leisurely stroll around the perimeter of the building; what must have been a regular patrol.

'Well, that about settles it,' muttered Will. 'There's something illegal going on in there.'

Marianne nodded. 'They've certainly got something they

want to protect,' she said. 'And I'd be willing to bet that it isn't the family silver.' She glanced at Will inquiringly. 'So what do we do now?'

Will sighed. 'I wish I knew,' he admitted. 'I thought once I found the place it would be a case of getting in there after dark and starting a fire or something. But look, it's virtually a fortress. There's a thirty-foot fence all around and cameras that will detect anything that comes within fifty yards of the place. I don't doubt that somewhere in there they'll have banks of video screens and God knows what other kinds of surveillance. We'd need an army to get into the place.'

'Maybe not,' said Marianne quietly. 'Look down there, set into the river bank.'

She pointed and Will saw that in line with the warehouse, there was a sewage outlet that drained into the river. The line of the pipe seemed to indicate that it ran back directly beneath the warehouse. The opening was easily big enough to admit a man.

'Christ, Marianne, you could be right! It must at least go *under* the place . . .'

'Sure. And if it does that, there are bound to be drains that lead up inside. Even if we couldn't get into the building, we could plant something in the drains. A bomb, maybe . . .'

Will laughed hollowly. 'I admire your thinking,' he said. 'But let's face it, where the hell are we going to get a bomb?'

Scally spoke for the first time. 'Maybe we could *make* one,' he said, matter-of-factly.

Will looked at him, amused by his casual air. 'What, you know now to make bombs do you?'

Scally shook his head. 'No, but I've got a friend who does.' He glanced up at Will and winked playfully. 'I'll take you to meet him, if you like.'

Will was about to answer when Marianne squeezed his arm. 'Looks like they've got visitors,' she said.

A black BMW was motoring sedately along the approach road to the warehouse gates. As it drew near, more armed men emerged from the building and hurried to unlock the gates. The ancient metal portals swung back and the car drove in to the cobbled courtyard towards a large brick outbuilding. Steel shutters rose and the car moved inside out of sight. As it drove in, Will caught a glimpse of other vehicles parked in there, big container lorries, painted an anonymous shade of grey. After a few moments, two familiar figures emerged from the garage and crossed the courtyard to the main building. Will's fists clenched involuntarily as he recognized Chalmers and Bullen. They wasted no time hanging around in the open, but strode quickly in through the main door of the warehouse. The door slammed shut behind them.

Marianne had noticed the expression of disgust on Will's face. 'Somebody you recognize?' she asked him.

He nodded. 'Old friends,' he said quietly.

'Yeah, and here comes an old friend of *mine*,' muttered Scally grimly.

'Another car was approaching the gates, a red Pontiac. As the three of them watched from the bridge, it drove into the compound and entered the outbuilding. Pinder got out and Will saw that he was wearing some kind of a prosthesis, a pink plastic nose protector on a length of elastic. Clearly he didn't want anybody else poking a finger into the hole in his face. Pinder too, hurried towards the main building. Behind him, the steel shutters closed. The armed guards followed Pinder through the main entrance, slamming the door behind them, and the place appeared once again to be deserted.

'They aren't taking any chances,' observed Will.

Marianne stroked his arm. 'You said you knew them. That they were friends . . .'

Will nodded. He looked at his two companions, realising that he had to be open with them.

'They're police officers,' he said. 'They're the men behind this whole operation.'

He'd expected some kind of a reaction from them, gasps of astonishment, expressions of disgust; but they simply accepted the fact without comment. 'You don't even seem surprised,' he observed.

Marianne shrugged. 'I've seen what the police are capable of,' she said. 'Nothing would surprise me now.'

Will sighed, realizing that this was perhaps the most searing indictment of all. He began to edge himself upright. 'Well, there's nothing more we can do here,' he said. 'Come on.' He led the way off the bridge, keeping his head down beneath the level of the rusting metal spars. They descended to the river bank and began to retrace their steps in the direction of home. Will slipped an arm around Scally's shoulders.

'Now,' he said. 'This friend of yours who makes bombs. Tell me all about him . . .'

Suzanne sat at her office desk pretending to work through a stack of correspondence, but her mind was elsewhere. Through the glass partition of Adam's office she could see him working at his computer, inputting data. She had already mentioned that she had to go out after lunch, something at home that needed sorting out and Adam had told her that there was no problem whatsoever. He hadn't even asked her what it was she needed to do and his very lack of curiosity, so unrepresentative of him these days, had served to make her suspicious.

She thought again about Clive's suggestion, about how she might try to gain access to the computer system and dig up what she could from those files that Adam had deemed worthy of protection. Why, she thought, didn't she come back to the office tonight, after Adam had gone home? OK, so she might be unsuccessful in finding the password, but at least she would feel she was contributing something, instead of leaving it all to Will. Clive had already supplied her with his ISDN number and it was simply a case of tipping him off, using the code words that they had already arranged between them. If she found anything of interest on the computer she could e–mail it direct to Clive's machine at home. And when she saw Will this afternoon, she could tell him what she planned to do. He'd be proud of her, he'd realize that she was no longer sitting on the fence, that she really was determined now to play a part in this . . .

Her mind made up, she picked up her phone, tapped 9 for an outside line and then punched in Clive's number at *The Evening Post*. After a few rings, his familiar voice answered.

'Hello, Clive Singleton, Crime Desk.'

'Tonight,' she said. 'From eight o'clock. Expect some e–mail.' She put down the phone again and glanced guiltily towards the glass partition. But Adam's gaze was still fixed on his computer screen.

Suzanne felt a little less anxious now she had settled on a course of action, but she was still unable to concentrate on the paperwork in front of her. She glanced at the clock above the door. Eleven ό'clock. She was meeting Will at three. Four hours that seemed a lifetime. With a sigh, she went back to her papers and reminded herself not to look at the clock again.

Back at the shelter, Scally introduced Will to an elderly Rag Man called Shaun, a stick-thin, bearded man in his fifties, with a hard Belfast accent and a shock of unruly white hair.

'Shaun used to make bombs for the IRA,' he announced, as casually as if he'd just said that Shaun used to work at Tescos.

Shaun threw a disparaging look at the boy. 'Jaysus, keep your voice down,' he snarled. 'You'll get me lynched, so you will!'

'This true?' asked Will doubtfully. He understood the old man's reticence. Since the big bomb of '96 the Republican cause had not been the most popular issue on Mancunian agendas. He studied the old man for a moment, noting the shaking hands and wizened features of an inveterate drinker and he wondered if Shaun hadn't just been mouthing off to a receptive audience when he was the worse for drink.

'Maybe, maybe not,' muttered Shaun irritably. 'Why exactly do you want to know?'

Will sighed. He sat down cross-legged in front of the old man. 'Because there's a building I want to blow up,' he said. 'And I wouldn't have the first idea about making a bomb.'

Shaun looked at Will incredulously for a moment then he threw back his head and cackled gleefully. Will noticed that he had only a couple of teeth left in his head.

'That's a good one! There's a place you want to blow up, is there? Well, I admire plain speaking, fair play to ya.' Shaun sighed, ran a tongue across his lips. 'Well now, I'll tell you the truth. I did fight for the Republican cause but that was a long time ago, back when it was just The Troubles and we were still all fighting like gentlemen. And yes, I built a bomb or two in me time. We all did.'

Will leaned closer. 'The thing is, do you think you could build one now?'

'Well, that would depend,' said Shaun evasively.

'On what?'

'The cause. This building you want to blow up. It could be many t'ings couldn't it? The House of Commons. The House of Lords. A JobCentre. A hospital. A school.' Shaun gestured with his thin, bony fingers. 'You can see, can't you, that it would make a difference? If it was a place that deserved to be blown up, well that's one t'ing. A place where innocent people will be hurt, that's something else entirely.'

Will nodded. 'Yes, I can see that. OK. The place I want to blow up is a warehouse where dangerous drugs are manufactured. Drugs that kill people. The same drug that killed my son. Oh yes, and it's run by a crooked police officer and his secret society.' He stared at Shaun calmly. 'Does that sound like the kind of place that deserves to be blown up?'

Shaun smiled, a tired, cracked smile. 'Oh yes, I'd say that would fit the bill nicely,' he said. He shrugged. 'Yes, well, I dare say I could fix you up with something. What kind of explosives have we got?'

Will frowned. 'That's just the problem. Whatever you build will have to be made from stuff that's relatively easy to get. Anything that can be bought across a counter, legitimately, I can get for you.'

Shaun looked puzzled. 'And what about the money?' he asked. 'Where would that be coming from?'

'Don't worry about that,' Will assured him. 'You just tell me what you need and I'll get it for you.'

'Strange kind of Rag Man, you are,' observed Shaun. 'Doesn't have to worry about money.'

'Let's just say I've got friends in high places.'

'Must be handy. Well, I'll make a list,' suggested Shaun. He rooted around amongst his possessions and after some searching came out with a tiny stub of a pencil and a scrap of paper. 'How big is this building, by the way?'

'It's big, all right. A four-storey Victorian warehouse.'

'Hmm.' Shaun scratched at his stubbled chin with the end of the pencil. 'Maybe I should go and have a look at it first.'

'I'm afraid there won't be time for that,' Will told him. 'I'm meeting my contact at three o'clock. We'll have to go and buy the stuff you need then. And if you can manage it, I'd like to be all primed and ready to go tonight.'

'Jaysus, you don't ask for much, do ya? What's the big hurry?'

'Because when I was there this morning, it looked like they were getting ready to do something. I saw container lorries waiting to be filled and there were people going in the place who, I suspect, wouldn't normally go within a mile of it. I'd hate to think that more kids died because I dragged my feet. But as far as that's concerned, I'm dependent on you.'

'Well, you're the Duke now,' observed Shaun. He considered his sheet of paper for a moment, as though seeking inspiration. Then he began to write in a slow laborious hand, the tip of his tongue protruding from his lips. 'You'll get most of this stuff from a DIY shop,' he said. 'A couple of t'ings you'll need a chemist for and the whiskey, you'll get from any off licence. But it must be Jamesons.'

Will frowned. 'You use whiskey to make a bomb?' he asked incredulously.

'No, you eejit. That's my fee! You don't t'ink I'm doing all this out of the goodness of me heart, do ya?'

Will leaned forward and slapped the old man on the shoulder. 'You build me something that does the job and I'll make sure you get a crate of Jamesons,' he said.

Shaun chuckled. 'As I said,' he muttered. 'A strange kind of Rag Man indeed.'

Will turned and smiled at Scally. 'Looks like we could be in business here,' he said cheerfully but the truth of it was he felt far from convinced by Shaun's prowess as a bombmaker. 'I've been thinking,' he said. 'About tonight. Maybe it's best if I go in on my own. I know how you feel about the sewers and . . .'

But Scally was shaking his head. 'I thought about it too,' he said. 'I'm coming in with you, Will. I'm small and wiry, I might be able to get in places you can't.' He glanced slyly across at Marianne who was sitting on the other side of the room, talking to Mike. 'Don't think *she* should come though.'

Will nodded. 'I agree. But how am I going to talk her out of it? I sometimes get the feeling that girl would jump off a cliff if I asked her to.'

'So *tell* her she ain't coming. Put your foot down.'

'Umm. Well, we'll see.' Will turned his attention back to Shaun. 'How's that list coming? We're a little pressed for time.'

'I'm about finished. The batteries we'll need are the big kind you'd put in an old transistor radio, you know? Get six of them. And it must be proper steel wool, not wire wool.'

Will perused the list, trying to decipher the old man's wobbly writing and horrendous spelling.

'What's this?' he asked. 'Weed killer? And a clock?'

'Yeah, not one of those digital t'ings, an old-fashioned wind-up alarm clock, you know the kind.'

'And here, something about soldiers?'

'A soldering iron. Remember, we've no electricity, so you'll have to get one of those new fangled battery powered t'ings. What are you laughing at, you eejit?'

'It's just the way you've spelled Jamesons.' Will folded the note and pushed in into his pocket. 'OK, thanks, Shaun, I'll be back with this stuff as soon as I can.' He got to his feet and slapped Scally on the shoulder. 'I'd better get moving,' he said. 'Hold the fort while I'm away.'

'Sure thing, boss.'

Will moved across the room to Marianne. 'I've got to go now,' he said.

'To meet your ex-wife.' Marianne smiled at him, and there was no malice in her eyes. 'Give her my regards, won't you? And tell her she's crazy.'

He looked at her sharply. 'Crazy?' he murmured.

'For ever letting you go.'

He reached out a hand and stroked her hair. 'Look, Marianne, about tonight . . .'

'I'm coming with you,' she said.

'No, but really, it could be dangerous. I've got a bomb maker over there who probably hasn't had his hands on a bunch of chemicals since Michael Collins cashed in his chips. We're going up a sewer pipe that we're not even sure connects to where we want to go to. And the place is crawling with armed men. We could be on a hiding to nowhere.'

'All the more reason for me to be with you. You're going to need as much help as you can get.' She reached up and kissed him on the cheek. 'Now scat, you'll be late for your shopping expedition.'

He sighed, shook his head. Pointless to waste any more time discussing it now. He pushed through the blanket-covered opening and let himself out, peeking cautiously up and down the street before he stepped into the open. Then he headed for the city centre and his meeting with Suzanne, offering up a silent prayer that she'd brought her credit cards with her.

Chapter Thirty-Six

Suzanne waited by the steps of the City Art Gallery, as nervous as a teenage girl on her first date. She had arrived fifteen minutes early for the meeting, which did nothing for her peace of mind, and as the seconds ticked inexorably away, and the minute hand of her watch moved past the appointed hour, she began to worry that something had gone wrong.

On the drive into town she had heard a news report about the death of Gary Flowers, shot dead when an armed robbery had gone horribly wrong. Her first thought had been that Will might have been responsible, but the newsreader wound up by saying that police were looking for a black man. Even so, it seemed a terrible coincidence.

And then at three fifteen, Will turned up and she almost burst into tears at the sight of him. He came shambling along the pavement towards her, a filthy, ragged, bearded figure that she barely recognized. Clive's assessment of his physical condition had, if anything, been underplayed. He was a mere shadow of his former self. His grubby clothes hung loosely on his skinny frame and the familiar eyes had a disquieting intensity about them, as though he had lost his mind along with the weight.

Suzanne couldn't think of what to say so she just stood there, forcing a smile as he came up to her. He acknowledged her with a curt nod, then took her arm, turned her around and started walking her along the street. He seemed agitated, nervous.

'Where are you parked?' he asked her.

She stared at him, unprepared for the question. 'I beg your pardon?'

'I said, where are you parked?'

'The multi-storey down the street. But . . .'

'Come on, we've got some shopping to do. I hope you've got money with you. Or plastic. Plastic will do fine.'

'Will, what's this all about?'

He glanced around before answering as though afraid of being overheard, though there was nobody standing anywhere near them. His movements were quick, jerky, uncoordinated and she began to fear, once again, that he was mentally unstable.

'You were right about the warehouse,' he croaked. 'It's where they're making the drugs. And I saw our friends Chalmers and Bullen going in there. A lot of activity. We're going to get some stuff I need and then I'm going to blow the place up.'

'Blow it up? Jesus, Will! What are you talking about? How will you do that?'

'I've got somebody who's going to make a bomb for me. Ex-IRA.' Will pulled a scrap of paper from his pocket and waved it at her. 'I've got a list of stuff here. We'll need to go to a DIY place.'

They moved in through the entrance of the car park, pushed through a swing door and began to climb the staircase beyond.

'Now just a minute,' protested Suzanne. 'Don't you think you should think this through before you go ahead? A bomb? You don't know anything about bombs.'

'No problem, I told you I've got this expert.' He laughed strangely. 'Well, not an expert exactly, but I suppose he knows what he's talking about . . .'

'But it's not your job to do this, Will. You've found the place, now you need to call in somebody else.'

He stared at her in the half-light of the stairwell. 'Oh yeah, like who? The police, maybe?'

Suzanne gestured at one of the numbered doorways and they pushed through it and walked across the concrete level to where the Shogun was parked. Suzanne deactivated the alarm and opened the driver's door. Will slid into the passenger seat. In the enclosed space, she was aware of the smell of him, a musty odour of unwashed flesh and clothing. She tried to ignore it and asked to look at the list. She scanned it for a moment, struggling to read the scrawl of ink on a piece of grubby, creased paper. It seemed to consist mostly of household cleaners, weed killers and electrical components.

'This is what you make a bomb with?' she muttered.

'Apparently.' Again he gave that strange little laugh, that inexplicably sent a shiver down her spine. 'There's other stuff we'll need, I was thinking about it on the way across town. Flashlights, waterproofs, things like that. We're going in by way of the sewer.'

Suzanne didn't know what to say to that. She reversed out of the parking space and drove down the three levels to the ground floor. At the barrier, she dropped coins into the slot and drove out onto the street.

'There's a big DIY superstore out on Oldham Road,' she said. 'I think we'll be able to get most of what you want there.' She glanced at him thoughtfully. He was sitting bolt upright, staring at the road ahead with those wide, staring eyes. 'How have you been keeping?' she asked him awkwardly. 'You look, well, I hope you won't mind me saying this, but you look awful.'

He turned and grinned at her. 'Thanks a lot,' he said. But he didn't seem in the least bit offended.

'Where are you staying at the moment?'

'We've got this delightful little spot underneath Piccadilly station,' he said. 'We had somewhere better but we were kicked out by the God Squad.' He glanced at her apologetically. 'The MLOD. In fact, three of them tried to kill me. Actually, thinking about it, I wouldn't be at all surprised if Chalmers had a hand in that. I reckon he knows I'm getting closer all the time and it's scared him shitless. He *should* be afraid. If I get my hands on him, I'll send him to hell along with Gary Flowers.'

Suzanne started so violently she almost lost control of the car. 'You heard about that?' she asked him.

'Heard about it?' he laughed harshly. 'I did more than hear about it. I shot the bastard. He was in on it, Suzanne. It's funny, isn't it? I asked you about him weeks ago, you remember, when we were leaving the hospital? But you said, oh no, it couldn't be Gary, he was Mr Fucking Wonderful! And all the time, he was involved right up to his neck.'

Suzanne shook her head.

'But that's not so! On the radio, they said they were looking for a black man . . .'

'Oh, sure they did! They can't risk telling the truth, can they? They don't want me blabbing to anyone who'll listen. Christ, I just might conceivably get to the one cop who hasn't yet been inducted into The Brotherhood. Oh no, what they want is to find me themselves and squeeze me out of the picture. That's what took me so long to get to you. The town is swarming with cops and MLOD men and you can bet that every one of them is looking for me. That's exactly why I've got to blow the warehouse tonight. I can't afford to waste any more time.'

Suzanne kept her gaze fixed on the busy road ahead. 'And the other man, Resnick? Did you have a hand in that too?'

'Sort of. I made him swallow some tabs of Warp and then he chose to go hang-gliding without the equipment. Don't shed any tears for him, Suzanne, that man was excrement in a suit.'

But she was crying, her eyes filling with tears. 'Oh, Will, what have you done?' she whispered.

He laughed dismissively. 'Nothing, according to the news reports. Resnick committed suicide and Flowers was murdered by a black man. Now I ask you, do I look like a black man? The police themselves have said as much and we all know what a reliable source they are.' He turned to glare at her and the expression in his eyes made her feel afraid for his sanity. 'I'm close, Suzanne! Close to finishing what I set out to do! I know where the bastards are making their poison and I can take them out in one fell swoop. I'll be performing a public service, don't you see?'

'I see only that you're getting in too deep,' she told him. 'Listen, there may be another way to do this. Tonight, I'm going in to Delta to snoop through the computer system. Adam has protected files in there and Clive and I are pretty sure they relate to the Warp operation. If I come up with anything, I'm going to ISDN them straight to Clive's home computer.'

Will was looking at her blankly.

'Well, don't you see?' she urged him. 'If we can come up with some evidence on Chalmers and his secret society, we can take them down through the proper channels. Clive could pass the information on to every newspaper, every television station in the country. At least give me a little time to do that before you go ahead with this crazy scheme of blowing up the warehouse.'

But Will was shaking his head. 'It's too iffy,' he told her. 'You don't know for sure that the evidence is there, do you?'

'No, but what's another twenty-four hours?'

'It could be everything! I could be picked up in twenty-four hours, executed and buried where nobody will ever find me. And a lot more drugs could be shipped out of that warehouse. Like I said, I saw a lot of activity going on there today. I think they're getting ready for something big. I don't want any more kids suffering the same fate that Martin suffered. By all means, Suzanne, go and search for your evidence and I hope to God you find something. But I'm through with farting around over this. I want to hit those bastards where it really hurts and I don't give a stuff about the consequences.'

They were approaching the huge shopping mall on Oldham Road where the DIY store was located.

'You got a pen and paper?' Will asked her.

'In my bag there.'

'Good. I've got some more things to add to the list, things we'll need for tonight. You're going to have to go and get this stuff for me. They'd never let a Rag Man in through the doors.' He found the pen and paper and hunched over the dashboard jotting down the list he'd been formulating in his head. 'It's going to cost you,' he warned her. 'I'll have to owe you.'

She shrugged. 'I'll live with that,' she told him. She turned the car in through the entrance to the car park and pulled to a halt outside the DIY superstore. She accepted the other scrap of paper from Will and studied it thoughtfully. A rucksack, flashlights, batteries, three sets of waterproof clothing, one of them for a woman, another for a boy aged fourteen. She raised an eyebrow and looked at him inquiringly.

'It's a long story,' he told her.

'Some other time then. There's an outdoor section in there, they should have waterproofs.' She went to get out of the vehicle but Will threw out a hand and grabbed her wrist.

'Did I say thank you?' he asked her.

She smiled, shook her head. 'I don't believe you did.'

'Well, I'm saying it now. I really couldn't do this without your help.'

She gazed back at him for a moment, her eyes still brimming with tears. 'I just hope to God I'm not helping you to do something really stupid,' she whispered. And then she was out of the vehicle and hurrying across the forecourt to the entrance of the store.

A couple of hours later, the shopping done, she dropped Will off on a quiet street behind Piccadilly station. She got out of the jeep and helped him unload the boxes of equipment. They set them down beside an ancient, paint-blistered door set into the crumbling red brick wall, but for the moment, Will made no move towards it.

'Home?' she asked him.

He nodded, but remained standing where he was, looking vaguely uncomfortable. She was reminded of an incident from her youth, when she'd been going out with a well-to-do boy and hadn't wanted him to see the modest terraced house that she and her parents lived in, so she'd had him drop her off outside one of the spacious semi-detached houses in a neighbouring suburb. Then she'd stood by the gate waving till the boy had driven away. She wasn't sure if Will had similar reasons for not inviting her in, or whether he had somebody waiting for him in there, somebody he didn't want Suzanne to meet. The woman who she had just bought a set of waterproofs for? She told herself it probably didn't matter. If Will went ahead with this crazy scheme of his, the chances were she wouldn't be seeing him ever again.

Impulsively, she reached out and hugged him. 'Please be careful,' she whispered.

He nodded. 'You too,' he said. 'This thing you're doing at the office later? Don't get caught.'

'I won't.' She stood there looking at him, knowing that there was so much more to say but horribly aware that this was not the time or place to say it. 'See you later,' she concluded.

She walked around to the driver's door, got in and slammed it shut behind her. She drove away along the deserted street and when she glanced in her rear-view mirror, she saw that the door was open now and that several ragged figures had emerged to help Will carry the boxes inside. She just had time to register that one of the figures had long blonde hair. Then the road turned to the left and she couldn't see them any more.

Will settled himself down in front of Shaun. The old man was contemplating the boxes of equipment in apparent awe. Maybe he hadn't really believed that Will could get everything that he'd asked for. He trailed one gnarled hand over the various containers and bottles stacked in the cardboard boxes and then his fingertips came to rest, shaking slightly, on the cap of the bottle of Jamesons.

Will frowned. He reached out and removed the bottle, slid it into the pocket of his overcoat. 'You can have the whiskey when the bomb is ready,' he said.

'Maybe one little shot to steady me hands?' ventured Shaun hopefully.

Will shook his head. 'Payment on delivery,' he said. 'Then you can drink yourself insensible as far as I'm concerned.' He indicated the rucksack. 'That's to carry the bomb in when it's ready. Now, time's against us and I've got some things to prepare myself. Let's see if you're all talk or if you really can make a bomb out of this stuff.'

Shaun licked his lips and reached for the metal screwtop container he'd asked for. 'Ah don't be worryin',' he said. 'Sure, you'll get your bomb. With what I have here, I can give you the biggest fuckin' bang in recent history. But I'm not used to bein' hurried. A t'ing like this takes time in the makin'.'

Will pulled back his sleeve and consulted the cheap digital wristwatch that Suzanne had bought him. 'You've got maybe three hours,' he told Shaun flatly. He got up and went over to his own space, where Scally and Marianne were unpacking the things he'd ordered. Scally had pulled out one of the expensive flashlights and was flicking it on and off. As Will came up to him, he lifted it to illuminate his own face with a ghoulish glow.

'This is like Christmas!' he observed.

Marianne was holding a navy-blue waterproof overall up against herself. She pouted like a supermodel.

'Not bad,' she said. 'But didn't they have it in red?'

Will laughed hollowly. Now that the time was drawing closer, he was having terrible doubts about taking these two into that sewer with him; but he knew only too well that they wouldn't let him go in there alone. Suddenly, he wanted very much for it to be over. Well, in a few hours it would be. One way or the other.

Chapter Thirty-Seven

As Suzanne pulled into the parking space at the rear of Delta, heavy drops of rain began to hit her windscreen. She glanced at her watch in the glow of the dashboard. It was eight pm and she was pretty sure that Adam would have been long gone from the premises. She climbed out of the Shogun and walked around the side of the building, climbing the steps to the front entrance. It was locked but Arthur, the elderly security man on reception, saw her waving to him and came over to unlock the door.

'Hello, Mrs Ambrose,' he said. 'I wasn't expecting to see you tonight.'

Suzanne smiled. 'Something came up at the last minute,' she explained. 'I've got a presentation to prepare for the morning.'

Arthur rolled his eyes towards the ceiling and swung the door back to admit her. She stepped into the reception area. 'Nobody else here?' she asked, trying to sound casual.

'No, Mr Fielding was the last one out, around six o'clock. I'm afraid it's just you and me, Mrs Ambrose. Would you like a coffee or something?'

'No, don't bother. I'll go and get on with my work. Hopefully it won't take more than an hour or so.'

'They work you too hard,' said Arthur, moving back to his desk. 'You should put your foot down, tell them you need a little time to yourself.'

'Maybe I will.' Suzanne went through the swing doors into the corridor beyond and walked down to her office. She went inside, switched on the lights and went straight to the door of Adam's office. She turned the handle, hoping that he hadn't

360

locked the door when he'd left. But no, it opened easily.

She went over to Adam's computer and switched it on, then took off her jacket and hung it over the back of the chair along with her handbag. She glanced at her watch again, knowing that Clive would be at home now, his computer switched on and ready to receive anything she could pluck from the files. The computer booted up and then prompted her for an introductory password, but this first one was easy. ADAM. She punched it in and the screen opened up, revealing an index of documents. The first one to catch her interest was entitled GRAIN.01. She clicked on it with the mouse and as she had expected, was prompted to supply another password. This was where she had to start getting inventive. She began to tap in a series of obvious possibilities. PASSWORD, PASS, OPEN, CODE, but none of these checked out. Next she tried various permutations on Adam's Christian and surnames. No luck there either. She frowned. OK, there were plenty of other possibilities and she had all the time she needed, she could sit here till morning if necessary.

She got out a pen and paper and began to note down other possibilities . . .

Will, Scally and Marianne stood on the bank of the river and looked at the dark outline of the warehouse up ahead of them. They could see no lights on in the place but that didn't mean that there was nobody in there. A few drops of rain spattered on Will's face and he looked up at the sky. There were no stars in evidence tonight, even the moon had been obscured by the thick cloak of dark grey clouds that had been massing overhead since late afternoon. Off in the distance, there was a low rumble of thunder.

The three of them descended the slope to the river bank, where Mike and Shaun were waiting for them.

'You sure you want to do this tonight?' Mike asked him. 'If this rain gets any heavier, a sewer might not be the most sensible place to be.'

'That's a risk we'll have to take,' Will told him. 'You just be ready with the blankets, when we come out. I imagine it's going to be pretty cold in there.' He glanced at Shaun who was holding the heavy rucksack with the bomb in it. He'd been making some last minute adjustments. 'Everything set?' he asked.

'Just about.' Shaun lowered the rucksack none too gently onto the ground and he cackled delightedly when he saw Will and the others wince.

'Relax!' he assured them. 'It's harmless till it's armed.'

'Show me again,' said Will, crouching down beside him. Shaun undid the leather straps and Will removed the powerful flashlight from the leather harness he wore around his torso and shone it into the interior. The face of the old-fashioned alarm clock registered the wrong time, one fifteen pm; it was actually eight twenty.

'Sure, it couldn't be easier,' Shaun told him. 'All you do is put the hands to the right time, move the alarm hand to the time you want the t'ing to go off, then give the key a few winds.' He indicated the various containers of powder and liquid gaffa-taped and wired to the metal chassis of the alarm clock. 'When this 'ould stuff goes up it'll be strong enough to punch a hole in sheet metal. If you can leave the bomb somewhere where there's combustible material, so much the better.'

Will frowned down at the jumble of wires and packages in the rucksack, thinking that it looked no more threatening than a pile of discarded rubbish. Not for the first time, Will was having serious doubts about Shaun's prowess as a bomb maker.

'This *is* going to work, isn't it?' he asked. 'I don't want to crawl all the way up that sewer pipe on a wild goose chase.'

Shaun reached out a hand to adjust the alarm. 'Only one way to find out,' he said.

'No, that's all right, I'll take your word for it.' Will sighed, retied the straps and lifted the rucksack onto his shoulders. Scally and Marianne were waiting, looking most unlike themselves in their navy-blue waterproofs.

'Ready?' he asked them.

They nodded and their faces were like two pale moons in the darkness.

'OK, let's go.'

They began to walk along the bank of the river towards the sewer outlet.

Clive sat at his desk in his study, chain-smoking and watching for the message on his computer screen that told him he had some incoming e–mail. He glanced at his watch. Nearly eight – thirty pm. What was taking Suzanne so long?

He felt particularly helpless now because everywhere he went, everything he did, he was aware that somebody was watching him. He had no doubt that it was Chalmers and the other members of The Brotherhood that had him under surveillance. And he was beginning to be very afraid of what they might do to him once they got tired of simply watching.

His one chance, he figured, was if Suzanne could dig something incriminating out of those files. Clive could then send copies of any documents she mailed him to every useful e–mail number in the phone book. But first she had to find the code word and that, of course, was something that might take the rest of the night . . .

Will saw it first – the round gaping hole in the wall of the river that led back in the direction of the warehouse. He stopped for a moment and the people behind him nearly walked into him in the darkness. The rain was heavier now, the rising wind driving it into their faces. He switched on his flashlight and moved closer to the outlet. He had expected to have to hacksaw his way through the metal bars that covered the opening but when he got up close, he saw that there was no need. Two sections of pipe had already been removed, resulting in an opening through which a man might pass.

Will glanced at Scally in the glare of the torch and saw the look of dread on the boy's face, knew that he was thinking the same thing that Will was. Subs had made this opening. Who else would have an interest in entering the dark icy maw of the sewer?

Will directed his torch beam along the seemingly endless brick sewer. It was virtually dry in there, only a trickle of liquid wending its way along the floor but it seemed to exhale a thick stench of decay at him and he suddenly felt very apprehensive about venturing in. He glanced at Scally and Marianne.

'Listen,' he said. 'There's really no need for you to come any further, not if you don't want to. What's the point of all of us risking our necks?'

'We wouldn't miss it for the world, would we, Scally?' said Marianne, with a cheerfulness that under the circumstances seemed positively weird.

Scally nodded grimly. 'All for one and one for all,' he said quietly. 'Come on, let's get this show on the road.'

Will shrugged. He glanced at Mike and Shaun, hoping perhaps that they would back up his case but they were too busy staring apprehensively into the sewer. He turned away, slipped the torch back into his harness alongside the baseball bat he had brought for insurance, and reached up to take a firm grip on the metal bars. He pulled himself up and squeezed through the gap, then turned back to help Marianne and then Scally to climb up after him.

'Everyone OK?' he asked and his voice seemed to echo along the length of the tunnel.

'Fine,' he heard Marianne say. He glanced back at Mike and Shaun, their open-mouthed faces framed in the circular opening.

'Good luck,' said Mike, glumly. 'See you in a bit.'

'Yes,' said Shaun. He raised his bottle of Jamesons and took a hearty swig from the contents. 'I'll save you some,' he said.

'Make sure you do.' Will pulled the flashlight out of his harness and directed a powerful beam along the sewer. Then, moving past the others, his head stooped to avoid hitting the roof, he began to walk . . .

Suzanne was about ready to bash her head on the desktop. She had tried virtually everything she could think of and still had failed to find the password. She stared at the long list of ticked-off suggestions on the scrap of paper in front of her, each of them more unlikely than the next. She sat there and racked her brains. What would it be? Something simple, easy to remember, something that related to a secret that Adam might want to keep from her.

Well, she told herself, be logical. Take it straight to the core of what this whole thing is about. Adam has a secret, a terrible secret and it concerns the warehouse. What is the single most obvious thing it could be?

And then it occurred to her. Could Adam be cynical enough to use that?

She tapped in the short, four-letter word. WARP.

Again, the password was refused.

OK, so not that, but maybe she reasoned, something very like it. She tried a variation. WARPED.

Code accepted! She was so thrilled as the document opened up, she almost cried out in delight. And there it was, filtering down the screen in front of her. Information about the old grain warehouse in Castlefield. Dates, names, lists of equipment. She scrolled through the various pages with mounting excitement. There was more here. Pages of accounts, the minutes of meetings held between Adam and a certain Chief Inspector Chalmers of the Greater Manchester Police Force. Enough here, she was certain, to convince the most cynical mind that something really rotten was happening in Manchester. OK.

She exited the document, clicked her e–mail application and keyed in Clive's ISDN number. She'd send him this first one straight away and then search through for anything more of interest.

And then the door of the office opened and Adam and Chief Inspector Chalmers stepped into the room, both of them smiling at her as though she was a dear friend. She froze, staring back at them in open-mouthed horror; then remembered that Clive's number was on the screen. She tried to delete it but Adam stepped forward and caught her by the wrist.

'Oh no, Suzie, don't do that,' he told her. 'Mr Singleton will be expecting a message from you. Let's give him one, shall we?' He reached over her shoulder, created a new document and tapped a short message into it. She saw what he had written and made a move to wrest the mouse from his hand. Adam hit her, a hard back-handed slap across the face that pitched her out of the chair and sent her sprawling onto the floor. She lay there stunned for a moment, while Adam completed the message and clicked on *send*. Then she struggled to her knees and started to get back to her feet. Chalmers was standing there, watching her with some amusement.

'My dear Mrs Ambrose,' he murmured. 'What an awful mess you've got yourself into. Whatever did you think you were doing?'

'I was just . . . I was just . . .'

'Snooping,' said Adam flatly. 'Unfortunately, Suzanne, we've been monitoring all your calls to Clive Singleton for the last few days. We knew you were going to try something tonight, we just weren't sure what it was. I had a shrewd idea it would be something like this.' He turned the swivel chair around and smiled at her. She found herself wondering how she could ever have thought this man was handsome. His eyes were like dead stars, black holes in the hard white pallor of his face.

'You've been leading us a merry dance, Suzanne,' he said. 'We had a car following you today after you left the office but unfortunately, you managed to shake them off at the first set of lights. They didn't catch up with you until you got back to your house. The thing is, Suzanne, I'd be willing to bet you met with your ex-husband today. And we are very anxious to talk to him.'

Chalmers stepped closer to her now. He took hold of her by the back of the neck and wrenched her to her feet, but he was still smiling as he did it.

'Where is he, Mrs Ambrose? Where is your husband? Where can we find him? I really think you should answer my questions. You see, I don't have time to fool around with this any more. I'm tired of fooling around. Get the picture?'

Then he punched her, very hard in the stomach, driving all the breath out of her body. She dropped to her knees, retching, gasping for breath. She was terrified but some stubborn part of her would not submit to their violence. Even as Chalmers dragged her to her feet for another punch, she told herself that they would have to beat her insensible before she would tell them anything about Will. Maybe they would even have to kill her.

Clive saw the 'You have e–mail' message winking in the corner of his screen. 'At last!' he said. He stubbed out his cigarette and moved his chair in closer to the computer.

'All right,' he murmured, 'Let's see what you've got for me.' He moved the mouse to click on the icon and the screen opened up to reveal a brief, one-line message. Clive sat there staring at it in bemused silence.

GOODBYE MR SINGLETON

He sat there, trying to figure out what the hell that was supposed to mean and then registered the sound of a movement right behind him but before he could move a muscle, something brushed past his throat and he felt a brief stinging sensation against his jugular. There was a hiss of escaping air and then the message on the screen was obliterated by a vivid splash of crimson liquid. He sat there for a moment, staring at it. It took him a couple of seconds to realize that the spray was escaping from him; that it was his life's blood spurting from a cut in his throat.

Panic flickered through him and he lifted his hands to try and staunch the flow. But the blood ran through his fingers and dripped onto the keyboard in front of him. He struggled up from his chair, his heart pounding and he saw somebody standing there, calmly cleaning the blade of a knife on a handkerchief, a big, heavy-set man wearing what looked like a novelty plastic nose. The man grinned at Clive, displaying yellow teeth. He folded the knife and placed it in the pocket of his jacket.

'It's just like they've always said,' he observed sardonically. 'Spending too much time in front of a computer can be bad for your health.' Clive tried to take a step towards the man, but he felt weak, uncoordinated. The blood was pumping down the front of his shirt now and when he examined his hands they appeared to be encased in skintight red PVC gloves. He tried to cry out but all that issued from his mouth was a soft sigh of exhaled air. A large red bubble swelled on his lips and popped. He couldn't catch his breath, it wheezed and rattled in his lungs, as his system began to shut down. He tried to take another step forward and his leg gave way beneath him, pitching him face down onto the carpet.

The killer gave him a sympathetic look, then turned away and headed for the open door of the room. He moved quietly for such a big man, it was little wonder that Clive hadn't heard him coming up the stairs. Clive lifted a hand as though to wave his killer goodbye. It was all he had the strength left to do. He was dimly aware of the grey carpet against his cheek and the slow dark stain that was spreading out beneath his head like a halo. But everything else was turning grey, the colour draining out of it.

Darkness hovered on the periphery of his vision, then closed in around him, cutting him off from the light forever.

Suzanne clung tenaciously on to consciousness as Chalmers' boot crashed into her ribs once again.

'Tell me, damn you!' he shrieked. 'Where's he hiding? What is he up to?'

Suzanne ground her teeth, shook her head. She lay sprawled on the carpet of Adam's office, her whole body aching from punches and kicks. She had lost count of the times he had hit her. 'Go and fuck yourself,' she whispered; then steeled herself as he drew his foot back again.

'This is stupid,' she heard Adam say. 'Maybe she doesn't even know where he is.'

'She knows. And what worries me is that she might have tipped off Ambrose about the warehouse.'

'What are you talking about? She didn't even know about it.'

'Really? Well what do you suppose she was looking for here, eh? Just give me a few more minutes and . . .'

Then the trilling of a mobile phone. Chalmers cursed and turned away, fumbling in his pocket. 'Yes? Oh really?' Chalmers glanced at Adam contemptuously. 'It's HQ. Somebody's got a report on one of Mrs Ambrose's credit cards. Seems she's been spending a lot of money today . . .' He lifted the phone to his mouth again. 'You got any idea what she spent it on? Hmm. You have a printout? Read it to me. Yes, all of it!' He listened in silence for a moment, his face grim. 'What?' he said. 'Flashlights? Waterproofs?' He listened again. 'And the chemicals, what does that suggest to you? Yes, that's what I thought. No, no, that's all right, carry on.' He switched off the phone and moved back to stand over Suzanne. 'So she doesn't know anything, eh?' He glared at Adam. 'So why is it, do you suppose, that she's just purchased all the chemicals you'd need to make a pretty effective home-made bomb?'

'Jesus, you're kidding!' cried Adam.

'Oh no, not for a moment.' Chalmers' eyes widened in realization. 'That's what she bought them for. The warehouse. She must have known, damn it! She must have told Ambrose. Get her up on her feet!' Now Chalmers was punching another number into the phone and pacing around the room in high agitation. After a few moments, the call was answered.

'Ah, Pinder, you've taken care of the matter? Good. Well that's one loose end we don't have to worry about. We have the other one here.' He stared down at Suzanne in contempt for a moment. 'No, she hasn't told us anything. Look, I want you to proceed to the warehouse, without delay. I'm going to bring everything forward by twenty-four hours, we'll start shipping the goods tonight. Why? Because I said so, that's why! Everything's ready to go isn't it? Good, well let's not waste any more time. I'll meet you there. Oh and we'll bring the woman with us. Perhaps you'll have more success in making her talk than we did.'

Adam had got his hands around Suzanne's waist and was lifting her to her feet. He found her jacket and made her put it on.

'My handbag,' she moaned. She made a grab for it but Chalmers snatched it away and went quickly through the contents, suspecting perhaps that she was carrying a weapon. But he seemed reassured. He thrust the bag back at her. Then he pulled a pistol from his pocket and waved it in her face.

'All right, we're walking out of here and getting into my car,' he told her. 'One word to the nightwatchman that anything is wrong and I'll shoot him dead, do you understand? First I'll shoot him and then I'll shoot you.'

'Did you have to beat her so badly?' grumbled Adam. 'She can barely stand up.'

'She's lucky I haven't killed her,' sneered Chalmers. '*Yet.* Come on, we've got to get to the warehouse.'

'You don't really think that Ambrose would try anything,

do you?' said Adam. 'I mean, a bomb! He wouldn't get within a hundred yards of the place.'

'You obviously don't know him like I do,' said Chalmers. 'He's planning something that involves the use of torches and waterproofs, so he obviously doesn't intend to use the main entrance.' Chalmers was pacing up and down now, trying to work it out. 'Somewhere that's dark and wet, now where in the hell could that be? Somewhere . . . my God, isn't there a sewer outlet to the river? You don't think he could get in that way, do you? Come on, let's get moving!'

Suzanne was half pushed, half carried out of the office and along the corridor to reception.

'Mrs Ambrose isn't feeling well,' she heard Adam telling Arthur. 'We're going to drive her home.'

'Oh dear, I was just saying she's been overdoing it . . .'

Now she was tripping and stumbling down the steps to the street, the cold air reviving her a little. A car door opened and she was bundled onto a plush leather interior. Adam wedged himself in beside her and slammed the door.

'Hello, hello,' said the driver. She glanced up and saw that it was Don Bullen. He was grinning at her, seemingly amused by her condition. 'Looks like you've been in the wars, Mrs Ambrose.'

'Drive,' snapped Chalmers, sliding into the passenger seat. 'We're going to the warehouse.'

'Yes sir.' Bullen started the car and it accelerated smoothly away from the pavement. Chalmers had his mobile out and was punching in another number.

'Gibbons? DCI Chalmers speaking. I want you to take a detachment of armed men and go and investigate the sewer outlet on the bank of the river. The one that runs beneath the warehouse? Yes, I *do* mean now, this is a Code Red situation!' A lengthy pause while somebody jabbered on the other end of the line. 'You must have torches there, surely to God. Well then, find some! I have reason to believe that somebody might be trying to make their way to the warehouse by way of that sewer. Yes, if you find anybody down there, eliminate them. They may be armed, so shoot on sight.'

He switched off the phone and then looked over his shoulder at Suzanne.

'You know, Mrs Ambrose, I almost hope he *is* down in that sewer. It's the most fitting place for a rat to die, don't you think?'

Suzanne didn't answer him. She just lay slumped against Adam, as the black BMW sped through the city towards Castlefield.

Chapter Thirty-Eight

Will kept following the powerful beam of the flashlight. It was impossible to tell how far they had walked but he began to think that they must by now be somewhere beneath the warehouse.

They came to an intersection, a larger tunnel leading off to the right and Will hesitated, wondering which way to go. He listened intently and thought he heard sounds emanating from further along the new tunnel, a deep constant hum of machinery. He glanced at the others and indicated that he thought they should try in that direction. They nodded, their faces pale and grim in the torchlight. They were able to stand fully upright in the new tunnel and there was considerably more water here, sloshing a couple of inches deep around their ankles, the movement releasing powerful smells all around them. The noise grew steadily louder as they advanced along the tunnel and then, up ahead of him, Will saw a wash of electrical light filtering down from a metal grille overhead. A rusty steel ladder led upwards to the grille.

Will switched off his torch and positioned it back in his harness. He glanced at the others and lifted a finger to his lips, then approached the ladder. When he reached it, he stood for a while, gazing up at the grille which was some ten feet above his head. He was aware now of other sounds up there. People moving about, voices shouting instructions. He took a firm grip on the ladder and began to climb, moving cautiously upwards until his head was just a few inches below the grille. He peered through the rusting grid, trying to get a handle on what was above him.

He decided that he was looking at the laboratory itself,

which had been set up in the basement of the warehouse. There didn't seem to be anybody close to the grille so after a few moments, he reached up a hand and tentatively pushed. The thing creaked but gave a little beneath his hand. He was fairly sure that it wasn't secured down. He climbed up another rung and put both his hands to the task. This time the grille lifted a few inches clear of the ground and he was able to peep out through the gap and get his bearings.

The grille seemed to be located in a dark corner of a huge underground chamber. It was lit by overhead fluorescent light but the grid was cloaked in the shadows cast by a stack of steel shelving. A short distance away, there was a lot of machinery set up, great big plastic drums, hose pipes, containers of chemicals. There was a powerful portable generator beside which cans of petrol were stacked one on top of the other. Beyond this, there were men in white overalls moving around on the ground floor and above their heads, a metal gantry ran around the four sides of the room. Will could see a couple of armed men up there, the two of them chatting and smoking cigarettes.

The cans of petrol looked like a good place to plant the bomb; assuming some of them were full of fuel, the resulting fire should ensure that maximum destruction was achieved. But the problem was getting the rucksack over there without being spotted. Still, no point in beating about the bush, he decided. The sooner the device was set and planted, the sooner he and his companions could be on their way out of here . . .

He reached behind him and unslung the rucksack. Then bringing it around in front of him, he fumbled open the straps. He set the time with the digital watch on his wrist, a few minutes before nine pm. Then he pushed the alarm hand to fifteen minutes past the present time. As he was doing this he felt movement on the ladder and Scally pushed himself into position beside him, so that he too could peep out through the gap.

'What's happening?' he whispered.

'I'm setting the bomb. You'd better get back down the ladder.'

'Where are you going to leave it?'

373

'Over by those petrol cans.' Will pointed them out. 'I'm only giving us fifteen minutes to get clear, so you and Marianne had better start back now.'

Scally frowned. 'How are you going to get it over there?' he whispered. 'They'll see you!'

'No they won't. Now come on, move back down the ladder and let me . . .'

'I'll take it.' Scally grabbed hold of the straps of the rucksack. 'I'll be quicker than you, and I'm a smaller target.'

'No,' said Will firmly. 'I want you to head back.'

Again Scally shook his head. 'Give me the rucksack,' he insisted. 'You know I'm right. Just hold the grid open for me.'

'Scally, for Christ's sake . . .'

'Come on, let's do it before somebody comes over here.' The boy was glaring at him insistently and Will had no option but to capitulate it was either that or risk having the argument overheard.

'All right,' he said reluctantly. 'Try and place it in the middle of the cans, where it won't be seen. And for God's sake, be careful.' Will snatched a deep breath and reaching gingerly beneath the clock he gave the action a couple of twists, his skin crawling at the thought of it simply detonating as he held it; but nothing happened. The clock began to tick at what seemed a ridiculously loud volume. Will let his breath out and quickly retied the straps. He handed the rucksack to Scally, then with a quick look to left and right, he lifted the grille wide enough for the boy to climb through.

Scally eased himself up the ladder and crouched behind the cover of the shelving. He lifted the rucksack to his shoulder and paused for a minute, gazing calmly up at the two men on the gantry. They were still deep in conversation. Scally dropped onto his hands and knees and hugging the cover of some empty packing cases, he started off across the warehouse floor . . .

The steel gates swung back and Pinder pulled the red Pontiac to a halt in the courtyard of the warehouse, not even bothering to park out of sight in the outbuilding. On the way back he'd had another call from Chalmers, the little man all in a panic about a possible attack on the warehouse. He was on his way here now but in the meantime, he'd sent a division of men to check out a sewer outlet on the bank of the river and he wanted Pinder to get down to the laboratory and make sure everything was OK down there. What the hell was he expecting, a raid by the SAS?

Pinder switched off the engine and climbed out. With a nod to the two armed guards who regularly patrolled the perimeter, he crossed the courtyard to the main entrance and went in through the big oak doors. He walked along the empty corridor beyond, his footsteps clumping on stone. Turning left, he pushed through another door and descended the ancient stone steps to the basement . . .

Scally approached the petrol cans in a series of zig-zag movements, keeping low to the ground and using whatever cover was available. Now he was about twenty feet from the cans which were stacked up in the very centre of the warehouse floor. From the corner of his eye, he saw a white-coated worker moving towards him and he hunkered down behind a filing cabinet. The man walked right by him without noticing him and disappeared behind some big plastic canisters away to Scally's right. The boy took a deep breath and snatched a glance up towards the gantry. The two men were still leaning on the rail, smoking their cigarettes.

Scally began to move forward again, reminding himself that he only had about fifteen minutes on the clock and that he couldn't afford to waste any of it. One of the guards was moving his gaze in Scally's direction now and the boy froze where he was, completely out of cover this time, but the man's eyes swept on without seeming to register the small huddled figure.

Scally took his chance and scrambled the last of the distance to the petrol cans. He dropped down beside them, temporarily shielded from the sight of the men on the gantry. He unslung the rucksack, located a gap between two of the cans and pushed it into darkness, out of sight. He gazed back across the warehouse. Away in the shadows on the other side of the room, he could see the raised grid, Will's eyes staring at him imploringly. Will's hand came up in a beckoning gesture and he tapped his wristwatch.

OK, thought Scally, all he had to do now was get back again. Piece of cake.

The boy took another deep breath and started back on his hands and knees . . .

Pinder pushed through the swing door and stepped onto the gantry. He saw to his displeasure that the two guards, Wilson and Tetlow, were lounging on the rail, smoking cigarettes. They straightened up when they saw him approaching and nipped out their fags behind their backs, like a couple of guilty children caught smoking behind the bicycle sheds.

'Everything all right down here?' Pinder asked them.

'Yeah, no problems,' muttered Tetlow. 'We heard there was some kind of panic on. Some of the others were sent off to the river a little while ago. What's going on?'

Pinder frowned. 'Damned if I know. Somebody's got their knickers in a twist about something.' He began to pace along the gantry, staring down at the warehouse floor. 'Seems to think somebody might try and make their way in here.'

Wilson laughed. 'I'd like to see 'em try,' he said.

Pinder kept moving, attempting to observe the laboratory from every angle. The two guards trailed unenthusiastically after him.

'I was told there's a way in here via the sewers,' Pinder told them. 'Could there be?'

Tetlow shrugged. 'Well, I seem to remember there's a drain over in that corner . . .' He pointed and Pinder tried to look in the direction he was indicating, but there was a stack of steel shelving in the way. He walked further along the gantry, freeing his line of sight. And then he saw the small, ragged figure, moving on hands and knees past the plastic drums of chemicals. He stared for a moment, hardly believing his eyes. Then he shouted at the top of his lungs.

'Hey, you! What are you doing down there?'

The boy froze, glanced guiltily back over his shoulder, a look of pure shock on his pale face. Pinder's heart jumped into his throat. For a moment, he was literally rooted to the spot.

The same boy, again! The white face seemed to glow against a background of darkness. Then Pinder was moving to the metal staircase, waving to Wilson and Tetlow to follow him . . .

Suzanne peered out through the rain-battered window of the black BMW as it moved in through the entrance of the grain warehouse. Bullen pulled it to a halt alongside a red Pontiac.

'I see our friend with the holey face is here,' he observed gleefully.

Suzanne was feeling a lot stronger now but didn't want to let her captors know that. Chalmers seemed to be in a real panic. He had spent the short journey dictating order after order into his mobile phone. The sight of the American car seemed to reassure him a little.

'Good,' he observed. 'At least there's one man we can trust to do the right thing.' He glanced over his shoulder at Suzanne. 'Perhaps we'll introduce you to him, Mrs Ambrose. He's a resourceful fellow, I'm sure he'll think of various ways to entertain you.'

Suzanne gave a weak groan and fluttered her eyelids.

'You overdid it,' complained Adam. 'She's barely conscious.'

'Oh, I think she's made of sterner stuff than that,' Chalmers assured him. 'She's only . . .'

He broke off in surprise at the sudden, shrill wail of an alarm, coming from the warehouse.

'What the bloody hell?' snapped Adam. 'That means an emergency.'

'Let's get in there,' Chalmers urged him. 'Don, you stay here and keep an eye on Mrs Ambrose.' He threw open the door and stumbled out into the pouring rain, went running across the courtyard. Adam followed him, hunching his jacket up around his ears and slamming the door behind him.

It was quiet in the car then aside from the drumming of rain on the roof and the distant howling of the siren. Suzanne became aware that somebody was watching her. She groaned, opened her eyes. Bullen was staring at her from the driver's seat, a horribly lascivious smile on his face.

'Alone at last,' he said. 'You've no idea how much I've longed for this moment, Mrs Ambrose.'

Will waved his hand at Scally but the boy seemed frozen in shock. He kneeled where he was, staring back towards the gantry as Pinder and the two men descended the staircase.

'Come on!' yelled Will, hoping that the sound of his voice would do the trick; but Scally seemed to be in a fear-induced trance. 'Come on, Scally move, move!'

Then behind him, Will heard Marianne shouting up to him. 'Will, there's somebody coming! I can hear them!'

Will clung to the rail in an agony of indecision. What the hell was he supposed to do now?

Then the alarm started, a shrill ear-splitting shriek, and that seemed to do the trick as far as Scally was concerned. The boy jerked like he'd been hit with a cattle prod and then he got to his feet and began to run back across the warehouse floor, all attempts at concealment abandoned now. A man in a white coat stepped out from behind a large plastic drum and made a lunge at Scally, but the boy ducked under his arm and ran on. Will threw back the grid completely and began to descend the ladder. An instant later, Scally came sprawling through the opening in a tangle of arms and legs. He slammed feet first into Will, making him lose his footing and the two of them fell down the ladder into the water below. Will felt hands under his arms and he realized that Marianne was helping him back to his feet. He flailed upright and registered with a sense of surprise how much deeper and faster flowing the water was. The rain, he concluded, flooding through the tunnels.

'Come on, let's move,' he said, and pointed back the way they had come.

'We can't!' Marianne wailed. 'I told you, there are people back there!'

She was right. Up near the opening of the larger sewer, the beams of several flashlights were cutting through the darkness as somebody approached along the river outlet. Over the sound of running water, they could hear hostile, echoey voices shouting orders.

'Shit!' Will looked up to the opening above his head and realized it would be mere moments before somebody was framed in that rectangle of electric light. Only one way left to go, he decided. On along the new sewer, deeper into the system.

'This way,' he told them, and began to splash along the tunnel, having to push hard against the force of the current which was flowing against them. He realized with a sense of misgiving that the water was almost up to his knees now. Scally and Marianne blundered after him and as they left the only source of illumination behind, they switched on their flashlights. The tunnel lay ahead of them, seeming to go on forever, a dark forbidding labyrinth deep beneath the earth . . .

Pinder stared into the open sewer, his disbelieving gaze taking in the rusty metal ladder leading down to the fast flowing water. He swore under his breath, then turned to look at Wilson and Tetlow.

'Follow me,' he said. They stared at him in open-mouthed surprise.

'Down there?' muttered Tetlow weakly.

'Of course, down there. Come on, they're getting away.' Pinder turned around and began to lower his considerable bulk in through the rectangular opening. For several long moments, he seemed to stick fast in it. But with an effort, he wriggled through and his feet found the rungs of the ladder. He went down and lowered his legs into the ice-cold, stinking water. Then, turning his head to the left, he saw the the beams of three flashlights leading away into pitch darkness.

Glancing up, he saw Wilson's face peering apprehensively down at him.

'We'll need torches,' he shouted up. 'We won't see a damned thing without them. Hurry, man!'

Tetlow ran off to find something suitable. Wilson stayed where he was, peering down at Pinder.

'Get down here,' Pinder told him. 'And bring your gun.'

'There could be rats down there,' said Wilson.

'Of course there are rats, you idiot, it's a sewer. Come on, man, we haven't got all day!'

Wilson turned obediently around and lowered himself through the opening. He came down the ladder and lowered his legs gingerly into the water. The expression on his face was one of absolute revulsion. 'It stinks down here,' he complained, bitterly.

Pinder took the Uzi from the man's shoulder and pushed him aside to get a better shot at the three tiny points of light perhaps a hundred yards ahead of him. The Uzi wasn't much use with that kind of range but if he unleashed a whole magazine into the tunnel, the chances were he'd hit something. But even as he raised the weapon to his shoulder, the lights went out as though they'd been suddenly extinguished. Pinder cursed, realising that the fleeing people had turned a corner into another intersection.

Tetlow came down the ladder carrying three torches. He seemed as overjoyed to be down here as his companion was.

'Your suit's going to be ruined,' he observed, as he handed Pinder a flashlight.

'Shut up and follow me,' Pinder told him.

'Maybe we should wait for the others.' Wilson indicated the beams of more flashlights issuing from somewhere behind them.

'No time. They'll give us the slip. Come on, let's go!'

The three men headed down the sewer into the unknown, leaving the lights of the laboratory behind them.

Chapter Thirty-Nine

Chalmers descended the gantry steps to the warehouse floor and Adam trailed after him. Somebody finally thought to switch off the alarm and somehow the ensuing silence seemed even louder. Work had stopped on the Warp production line and there was a cluster of white-coated men standing at one end of the room, staring down into an open drain.

'What the hell's going on here?' demanded Chalmers. He recognized Stigers, the head chemist, standing with the others and prodded him in the back. 'Where's Pinder and the guards?' he asked.

'Gone down there,' said Stigers, a thin man with wire-rimmed spectacles and shoulder-length greying hair. 'Rather them than me. It seems there was a kid in here.'

'A kid?' Chalmers looked at him blankly. 'Doing what?'

Stigers shrugged. 'When we spotted him, he was running back towards the drain. Probably came up to see if there was anything worth stealing.'

Chalmers looked around the laboratory. 'Nonsense. He was up to something. Was there anybody else with him. A man?'

'I thought I saw somebody waving to the kid,' offered another man, standing nearby. 'Shouting to him to come back.'

Chalmers nodded. He turned back to Stigers, 'Search the place.'

'Search?' Stigers eyes narrowed suspiciously. 'For what?'

Chalmers considered the options. One mention of the word 'bomb' would clear the entire warehouse in seconds. These people were just paid hands, they had no great allegiance to any cause.

'For anything that doesn't belong here,' he said. 'Come on

everybody, start looking. You men, head up to the top of the room and work towards me. You others, start from the other end. We're looking for anything that's out of place.' He turned and saw Adam sidling back towards the staircase. 'This includes you,' he snapped.

Adam looked at him uneasily. He stepped closer and lowered his voice to a conspiratorial whisper. 'But if what you said in the car is true . . .'

'Then we'd better find what's been planted and quickly,' said Chalmers, 'I'm not letting all this go up in a flash of smoke. I've expended too much time and effort on this project.'

'Maybe so, but it isn't worth dying for. I'll be outside.' Adam turned away and began to walk towards the steps.

'Fielding, come back,' said Chalmers.

Adam ignored him. He kept right on walking.

'I'm warning you,' said Chalmers. 'Don't try and walk away from this. I won't allow it.'

Adam paused for a moment and looked thoughtfully back at Chalmers. Then he shook his head and carried on walking. He reached the bottom step of the staircase and began to climb.

Chalmers made a small noise of irritation. He reached into his jacket, pulled out a 9mm automatic and shot Adam three times in the back. Adam froze halfway up the stairs. He looked back at Chalmers over his shoulder, his face a mask of shock. Then he crumpled to his knees, pitched forward onto his face and began to slide slowly down to the foot of the stairs.

If the silence had been loud before, it positively screamed now. Every head in the place had turned to look apprehensively at Chalmers. He gazed defiantly around the room and lifted the pistol so that everyone could see it.

'Mr Fielding just tried to leave the room without my permission,' he yelled. 'If anybody else would like to try, this is your perfect opportunity.' He waited for a moment but nobody took him up on the offer. 'Good,' he said. 'Now, shall we get on? We're wasting time.'

Everybody moved silently to their positions and began to search.

Will led Scally and Marianne along the endless stretch of sewer.

He was horribly aware of the beams of light, emanating from a point several hundred yards behind him, as unseen figures came in pursuit and he couldn't help but notice that the level of the water was rapidly rising, the chill surface now sloshing around his thighs. It was impossible to tell how much distance they were covering, because every view looked the same and it was exhausting work pushing against the current. He glanced at his wristwatch in the light of the torch and saw that by his reckoning, there was only five minutes to detonation. But supposing somebody had found the bomb, disarmed it.

There was a sudden deafening burst of gunfire from behind them and he grabbed Marianne and Scally and threw himself face down into the water. Beneath the roiling surface, the bullets seemed to zip and whine around them and one actually smacked into Will's leg but its power was spent, it merely stung his flesh. The shooting stopped and they struggled upward again, dashing the water out of their eyes. Luckily, Suzanne had chosen flashlights with waterproof rubber cases and they were able to continue on their way.

Another intersection loomed on their right and they scrambled around the corner, happy to be out of the line of fire for a moment. Will waded into the the new flow and turned to help Marianne around the corner. In the glow of the torch, her face looked white and drawn. She seemed close to exhaustion but she plodded gamely after him without complaining.

'We've got to keep going,' he told her. 'Sooner or later we'll see a manhole and we'll be able to climb out of here.'

She nodded but didn't seem to have the strength to reply. Will looked at Scally. 'How are you holding up?' he asked.

'OK.' Scally shook his head. 'I blew it back there,' he said. 'Pinder shouted down at me and I just froze. I couldn't help it.'

'You did fine,' Will assured him. 'Don't worry.'

'You think they'll find the bomb and get it out of there?'

'Let's hope not. There's only a few minutes to go. Hopefully, we should . . .'

He broke off in alarm as he felt something scrabbling against his legs. He looked down and saw something slick and hairy struggling in the beam of the torch. Something else plucked at the fabric of his trousers and then suddenly, Marianne was screaming, flailing at something that was clinging to the front of her jacket. Will swung the beam of the torch to illuminate the surface of the water in front of him and he saw them, hundreds of them, swimming frantically towards him. Rats. They were trying to clamber out of the water onto the only solid things available and that was the three people walking upstream.

'Jesus!' Will flailed at himself with the torch, as he felt more and more of them clinging onto his clothes. He caught a glimpse of Scally, clawing frantically at himself as scores of dark, sleek shapes swarmed all over him. Marianne was tearing at her hair and screaming like somebody possessed.

'Get down under the water,' yelled Will. 'Hold your breath and dive!' He could feel wet fur and tiny feet scrabbling around his shoulders and neck and he could wait no longer. He snatched in a breath and threw himself face down, until he was lying on the bricks at the bottom of the sewer. He felt somebody's knee bump into his ribs and he almost exhaled but he hung on grimly, aware now that one by one, the rats were loosing their hold on him, they were floating back up to the surface.

Eventually, he could hold his breath no longer. He burst back up to the surface and turned to look back downstream. The rats were swimming blindly away now, heading towards the beams of the lights that were just turning into the intersection maybe fifty yards away. Will turned back to help Marianne and Scally. A rat had become entangled in Marianne's hair and Will had to gingerly pluck it free and throw it into the water.

'You two all right?' he asked them. There was no time for anything else, the pursuers were gaining ground all the time and they were armed. Perhaps the rats would delay them a little. He grabbed Marianne's hand and struggled around to continue upstream . . .

And saw them wading towards him. The dark figures of ten or fifteen men, who had just emerged from another intersection up ahead, carrying not flashlights but kerosine lamps,

384

supported on long sticks, illuminating the sewer with a fierce, unwavering light. Thin, white-faced men in stinking rags, who had dozens of dead rats hanging from their belts. Every one of them seemed to be armed with knives, meat hooks or machetes and as they came splashing closer, Will recognized their leader, the huge red-bearded man who called himself the Rat King. He was grinning at the three figures in front of him as though he couldn't believe his luck.

'Streeters!' he yelled, and his deep voice echoed the whole length of the sewers. 'Thou art welcome!'

Then the men came running at them, knives raised for the kill.

'Oh Jesus,' Will heard Scally say. 'Will, what do we do?'

Will glanced back over his shoulders. Pinder and the two guards were close enough now to be recognized and though they looked fearsome, there was really no doubting what was the lesser of the two evils. And right now, Pinder and his men were looking distracted. They were thrashing and flailing in the water as their clothing filled with the dark, frantic scurrying of dozens of fleeing rats.

Will made his mind up. He twisted Scally around onto his back and then did the same to Marianne. He flopped onto his back, pointing his feet downstream.

'Lift off with your hands,' he urged them. 'Let the current carry you.'

'But the rats!' whispered Marianne, her voice freighted with dread.

The Subs were close now. They could hear them splashing through the water behind them. Scally lifted his body off the floor and he went speeding away like a toboggan. But Marianne hesitated, too scared of heading back that way.

'Go, go, go!' screamed Will. He pushed her hard in the back and she took off after Scally.

A shadow fell across Will and he caught a glimpse of an upraised arm wielding a machete. He pushed down hard with his arms and felt the water lifting his rump up off the brick floor. He went sliding down the tunnel towards the intersection. A thought flashed across his mind as he began to gain momentum and it was not a good one. He was now moving back in the direction of the impending explosion: but then the current took him and everything was chaos.

Suzanne lay slumped in the back seat of the car, waiting. Don Bullen was outside in the pouring rain, talking to the guards that covered the gate. She could just about hear what he was saying.

'You'd better go inside and help out. There's some kind of problem in there. Don't worry, I'll keep an eye on the gate.'

There were a couple of grunts from the two men and then the sound of their footsteps moving away towards the warehouse, splashing through the deep puddles.

The rear door opened and Bullen smiled in at her. 'Now we really are alone,' he said. He climbed in beside Suzanne and shook the rain from his jacket. Then he reached out a hand and stroked her hair.

'Looks like they're going to be in there for some time,' he said. He was still smiling, that smug, lecherous smile. 'I must say, I'm sorry to see you in such a fix, Mrs Ambrose. Lovely lady like you. Seems to me you could do with somebody on your side. Somebody who'd make sure you didn't get treated too badly.'

Suzanne's initial reaction was to slap his face hard and try to scramble away from him, but she told herself that such a move would be futile. If she was going to get out of this, she had to keep her head. So she forced herself to be compliant, submissive.

'I don't know how this happened to me,' she whispered. 'I don't honestly. I was working in the office and the next thing I know, they came in and started hitting me.' She began to sob, covering her eyes with one hand to disguise the fact that there were no tears to accompany the sounds. 'What's going to happen to me? They aren't going to hurt me any more, are they?'

Bullen hunched closer. He placed one hand on her thigh. 'Not if you're a good girl,' he whispered. 'Not if you do what you're told.' He slid the hand under her skirt and let it caress her hip for a moment, moving in what he probably imagined was a slow seductive rhythm. 'I'm an important man in this operation. I've got influence. If you were to be nice to me . . .' He leaned over and brushed her neck with his lips. 'Know what I mean?'

She dashed imaginary tears from her eyes with her sleeve and smiled up at him.

'You mean if I'm *good*?'

He grinned at her in the half-light of the car. 'I think you've got the general idea, Mrs A. And, are you? Good, that is.'

'I can be very good. When I want to be.' She reached up a hand and pulled him down to kiss her. It took every effort of willpower she possessed in order not to cry out in revulsion, particularly when he pushed his tongue into her mouth. She let him hold the kiss for several long moments, before pulling gently away from him.

'Something wrong?' he asked her.

'It's just . . .' She lifted a hand to her mouth. 'I'm very dry. If I could just have a drink first . . .'

'A drink?' He looked irritated. 'Where the hell am I going to get a drink?'

She pointed to the front seat. 'There's a drink in my handbag,' she said. 'If you could just . . .'

'You wouldn't be trying to pull something would you, Mrs Ambrose?' he asked coldly. He sat up and pulled the handbag over to him, peered into it suspiciously. 'You haven't got a weapon in here or something?'

She gave him a look of wide-eyed innocence. 'Of course not,' she said. 'But I'm so dry. I just need something to lubricate my throat. If you catch my drift.' She ran the tip of her tongue suggestively around her lips and Bullen perked up considerably.

'Oh well, I'm all for a little lubrication,' he said.

'Check for yourself. There's a drink in there. A can of cola . . .'

'Oh yeah, here it is.' Bullen's hand had found the smooth aluminium cylinder. He pulled it out and handed it to her.

'There you go, darlin'. Want me to open it for you?'

'No. I'll do that.' She took the can from him and twisted it around so that the ring pull was on the far side from her. She hooked a finger into it and snapped it back. The white plastic nozzle popped into view but in the poor light, Bullen didn't

387

even seem to notice. 'Here's lookin' at you,' he said, in a pathetic attempt at a Bogart voice.

'And here's looking at you, you arsehole!' Suzanne pressed the nozzle and squirted a copious stream of concentrated Mace into his eyes. He screamed, a sudden, high-pitched wail and flung his hands up to claw at his burning eyes. Suzanne threw an arm across her own eyes to shield herself from the vapour, up-ended the can and brought it down hard into his face, once, twice, three times. The third shot hit him in the teeth and bits of ivory pinged off the aluminium as they flew out of his mouth. He curled up into a foetal position with a moan and she grabbed a handful of hair and slammed his head against the window, cracking the glass.

Then she flung open the door and got out into the pouring rain before her own eyes began to burn. She breathed in several lungfuls of night air and raised her face to the sky, allowing the cold rain to wash it. She moved around to the front, opened the passenger door and retrieved the mobile phone that Bullen had left on the dashboard. She carried it some distance away from the car and stood for a minute, contemplating it, wondering just what to do.

In a situation like this, you normally called the police. But she didn't know how far up this thing went. Supposing she got somebody who was a part of the operation? Somebody who would move in to suppress the whole thing?

She scowled, shook her head. No, there had to be some people out there that weren't involved in it. At any rate, she had to hope there were. She punched 999 and asked for police, fire and ambulance, figuring that in all of that lot, there had to be somebody who was on the level . . .

Chapter Forty

Pinder didn't know what was happening. One moment, he was sloshing around the intersection with every expectation of unleashing another magazine full of ammunition at his quarry, the next he was being weighed down by scores of frantic, furry shapes that came swarming out of the water in front of him.

He dropped the Uzi in his panic and devoted his attention to trying to swat the ugly things off him with his flashlight. Beside him, Wilson and Tetlow were screaming and flailing about like a couple of born-again Christians who had suddenly been touched by the hand of God.

'Don't panic,' he advised them, plucking a long sinuous shape off his shoulder and throwing it against the nearest wall; but when he turned to look at them, the two men were running off around the bend, guns abandoned in their haste to get the hell out of there. Silhouetted against the wildly see-sawing glare of one of their torches, they resembled two mounds of shifting, wriggling fur. They disappeared into the tunnel but Pinder could still hear their echoing screams coming back to him.

Logic told himself to get beneath the surface of the water and he was just about to do that, when something went tobogganing past him at speed. He caught a glimpse of the boy's pale upturned face in the light of the torch, as he went skimming past on the rush of the current. Pinder made a half-hearted grab for the boy but overbalanced and went down onto his knees in the rush of water; and an instant later, somebody else came rushing towards him. A foot caught him a blow in the ribs, driving all the breath out of him and he pitched face-forward into the stinking water. His head went under the surface and he panicked for a moment, flailing his arms in an attempt to stay afloat. Then he remembered that he didn't want to be afloat. He lifted his head, upon which a couple of rats were now perching, snatched in a breath and ducked himself down again. As he went back under, he had a fleeting impression of a third figure shooting past him and a vague impression of light advancing along the tunnel. But he couldn't think about that now. He kept himself pressed down against the bricks on the bottom and one by one, the rats released their hold, floating up to the surface and away. He waited until he felt his lungs would burst then got back to his feet.

He stood there blinking owlishly in the glow of the kerosine lamps. Several people were standing there grinning at him, dirty ragged people. Even in the stink of the sewer, they smelled bad. The nearest of them, a big, red-bearded man with a crucifix tattooed on his forehead, smiled a cheery welcome.

'Greetings, Streeter,' he said. 'Thou art trespassing. I am King Rat and this is my sewer.'

Pinder suddenly registered the fact that these men were heavily armed. He noticed the dull glint of metal as the light reflected off machetes, knives and brutal-looking steel hooks.

'Er, good evening,' he said, uneasily. 'I'm sorry, I had no idea that this belonged to somebody. I, er, I'm a police officer. Those people back there, I'm chasing them. They are villains, murderers. There'll be a reward if you help me catch them.'

'Is that so, my egg?' chuckled King Rat. 'That's right neighbourly of thee, ain't it, lads?' He laughed and in the lamplight, Pinder saw something white and glistening wriggling at the back of the man's throat. 'Aye, right neighbourly. It's not often a Streeter visits us down here.' He tapped the blunt side of the machete rhythmically into the palm of his left hand and began to advance. Pinder instinctively backed away.

'Yes, a big reward,' he babbled. 'I've money waiting back down the pipe aways, more than enough for each of you.' He was looking frantically from face to face in the hope of seeing something that halfway resembled humanity, but every one of them was grinning at him like some kind of retard. One of them hawked noisily and something long and white slid out of his mouth and dropped wriggling into the water.

Pinder tried not to let his revulsion show on his face. These people were probably infected with all kinds of hideous diseases.

'Why don't you walk back with me?' he suggested. 'It's only back up here a little way. My friends will be glad to pay you . . .' He made as if to step around the intersection but a couple of the strange men fanned out to stop him. Pinder's shoulders bumped against brick and he rested there a minute, trying to conquer his steadily mounting fear.

The Rat King seemed to become fascinated by something on Pinder's face. He reached out a hand and plucked at the plastic nose protector, pulling it as far as the elastic would allow. He peered at the large hole that lay beneath.

'This man's got no nose,' he observed.

'Then how does he smell?' asked one of the others, as though he'd been supplying straight lines all his life.

The Rat King leaned forward and sniffed at Pinder. 'Terrible,' he said; and everybody laughed heartily.

'Please, don't touch that,' warned Pinder. 'It's very . . .' He broke off with a yelp as the Rat King prodded a forefinger into the hole. Pinder jerked back with an oath, smacking his head against brick. The Rat King lifted the finger to his own nose and sniffed at it. Then he sang to himself, something remembered from a long time ago.

'It's tasty, tasty, very very tasty . . .'

'Please,' said Pinder. 'If you'll just come with me, we can sort everything out. I didn't know I was trespassing. I'm a police officer, you see, just doing my job. I . . .' One of the rats hanging by its tail from King Rat's belt began to squeak and wriggle. He glanced down at it irritably.

'Wouldst thou like to see how I got my name?' he asked. Before Pinder could reply, King Rat reached down, lifted the creature to his mouth and bit its head. The small skull made a soft crunching noise as it broke beneath the man's sharp teeth and the rat's back legs kicked convulsively. A squirt of faeces pulsed across the man's hand but he didn't seem to notice. He chewed thoughtfully for a moment and something in his throat seemed to move, distending the skin, but he went right on grinning. Terrified now, Pinder tried a last, desperate ploy. It was a strange place to do it, but it had got him out of trouble many times before.

'G . . . g . . . gentlemen!' he stammered. He lifted his right arm in the air to display his hand, the fingers splayed. 'As you can see, there's nothing in my hand. Absolutely nothing. And yet . . .'

The bearded man's machete whirred as it cleaved the air, removing Pinder's hand neatly at the wrist. It fell into the water with a loud plop, leaving Pinder staring stupidly at the stump which was pumping blood down the front of his jacket.

'What hand?' asked the Rat King and his companions threw back their heads and laughed gleefully. Pinder laughed with them, not wanting to upset them, despite the fact that he was close to fainting with the shock.

'Now hold out thy other hand,' suggested the Rat King.

Pinder shook his head nervously. His whole body was shaking.

'Oh, come now, don't thee trust me?'

'Well, I . . .' Pinder screamed as one of the other men lifted a meat hook and slammed it deep into his left shoulder. He reeled back against the brick wall, gasping for breath. No hope of fainting now, he told himself, the pain of this was too intense. He was horribly aware of the steel tip grating against his collar bone. He screamed again as another hook thudded into his right thigh.

'I won't tell thee again,' said the Rat King. 'Hold out thy other hand.'

Whimpering, Pinder did as he was told. The Rat King lifted his own arm and shook hands.

'Nice to meet thee,' he said. Everybody roared with laughter, and once again, Pinder joined in, feeling that it was expected of him. He kept right on laughing till the Rat King suddenly turned the machete over and plunged it into his belly, forcing the razorsharp blade upwards from belly button to breast bone. Pinder's shirt ballooned as his guts spilled out and several men scrabbled for the tastier morsels. Pinder began to slide down the wall, numb with shock, only aware of the strength flowing out of him with his blood. The Rat King leaned over and winked playfully. He was chewing on Pinder's liver, fresh crimson flowing into his beard.

Then from up around the intersection, there came the sound of screaming. The Rat King straightened up and beckoned to his men.

'Two of thee carry yon egg back to the larder,' he said. 'We'll go after t'others.'

He splashed away around the bend with most of his men trailing after him. The two who had remained behind took Pinder under the arms and began dragging him back upriver. He was only vaguely aware of the icy water sluicing his head and face but there was no pain now and it was very dark without the glow of the kerosine lanterns, so he gave up struggling to stay alive.

His final thought was an image of the boy's upturned face as he flashed by him in the water, drifting beyond his reach for ever . . .

Will was skidding and sliding on his back through the deepening water, his impetus so great now that he could not have slowed himself if he'd wanted to. A familiar rectangle of yellow light flashed overhead and he realized with a dull shock that he was back beneath the laboratory. The bomb! Something must have gone wrong, it surely should have exploded by now. He tried to get his wristwatch around where he could see it but the action flipped him around onto his face and he saw, some distance behind him, the Subs following in pursuit, the kerosine lamps bobbing on the end of their sticks. Still, he told himself, if he and the others kept moving at this rate, the chances were they'd be out of here in a few minutes. They knew where the warehouse was now, they could always try again . . .

He came to a sudden stop as he jolted into an obstruction in the middle of the sewer. He flipped around and saw that it was human. He had run full tilt into Marianne and Scally, who had somehow managed to stop themselves and indeed, were trying to press themselves back upstream.

Crouching in the churning water, Will saw why. He had no idea where the two new Subs had come from, he could only assume that they'd appeared from one of the intersections up ahead; but he could see they were armed and that they were advancing upstream, with machetes raised and grins of pure pleasure on their filthy faces.

He shouted to the others to get behind him and pushed his way past them, the water up around his waist now, as he clawed for the baseball bat slung through one of the loops of his leather harness. His hands were freezing but he managed to claw it free and he kept it down beneath the level of the water as the first Sub closed on him, expecting an easy kill. At the last moment, he brought the bat up to shoulder height and unleashed a savage blow to the side of the man's head, knocking him sideways. His limp body went whirling back downstream.

The second man was not in such a hurry to make his move. He yelled to his friends to hurry themselves and glancing back, Will saw that they were perilously close, wading through the deep water at an almost unbelievable speed. Scally and Marianne fumbled for their own weapons, a knife and blackjack respectively and then the three of them put their backs together and waited in silent dread as the Rat King and his men closed the final distance between them . . .

Chapter Forty-One

Chalmers was still searching frantically amidst the debris of the laboratory, sweating copiously despite the fact that there was no heating in the place. Stigers must have caught the sense of panic emanating from his employer, along with the heady mingling of lavender cologne and perspiration. Stigers was sweating too, his long grey hair sticking to his face and neck, as the two men worked their way towards the middle of the room. He peered into the clutter of containers stacked around the generator.

'Would you mind telling me what we're looking for?' he asked peevishly.

'I told you,' snarled Chalmers. 'Something that . . .'

' . . . doesn't belong here,' muttered Stigers. 'Yes. But why would a boy break into the place in order to leave something? It doesn't make sense.'

'Just keep looking,' Chalmers advised him. His already reedy voice was rising steadily higher in pitch as panic overtook him. From over beyond the open drain, came the weird echoey sounds of voices shouting and screaming down in the sewer. Several men stopped what they were doing and turned to look towards the drain.

'Never mind about that!' yelled Chalmers. 'Just keep on looking!'

Stigers was leaning wearily on a petrol canister, peering down into the shadows behind it.

'This thing we're looking for,' he said quietly. 'It wouldn't be a rucksack would it?'

Chalmers stared at him for a moment, then hurried over to have a closer look. It had been packed into the dark crevice between two of the canisters.

'Pull it out of there,' he told Stigers.

'Not likely,' replied the chemist, nervously. 'But don't let me stop you, Inspector.'

Chalmers glared at the man. He pulled the pistol from his pocket and racked the slide.

'Perhaps you didn't quite understand,' he said quietly, pointing the gun at Stigers' chest. 'Pull it out.'

Stigers stared defiantly back at Chalmers for a moment. Then he probably remembered what had just happened to Adam Fielding. He turned back to the petrol canister and leaned over it to take the rucksack in both hands. He lifted it gingerly, as though afraid it might beat him. On the way up a corner of the rucksack scraped noisily against metal and Stigers winced visibly. He got it up to the top of the petrol canister and rested it there a moment. Both men could hear the loud ticking emanating from inside it.

Stigers face drained of what little colour it had left. 'It's a bomb, isn't it?' he whimpered. 'It's a fucking bomb!'

The men that were standing close enough to hear the remark reacted accordingly. There was a general stampede towards the exit. Stigers made as if to follow them, but Chalmers lifted the pistol and placed the barrel against the man's head.

'Stay right where you are,' he hissed.

'But what am I supposed to do with it?' whispered Stigers.

Chalmers looked quickly around the warehouse and made a snap decision.

'Drop it down into the sewer,' he suggested. 'Come on, man, hurry, there might not be much time.'

Stigers nodded. He looked towards the drain cover and judged the distance. Then he reached out his hands and took a firm grip on the rucksack. He lifted it from the canister and began to walk towards the drain.

The alarm clock went off with with a long shrilling clatter, that was only slightly muffled by the nylon fabric that encased it. Stigers closed his eyes and gritted his teeth, but he didn't drop the bag. He stood there, knees slightly bent, the rucksack held out in front of him like an offering. There was a long silence, while the two men waited. In the silence, there was a brief hissing noise and then the sound of liquid splashing on stone.

Chalmers looked down and saw the stream of urine running down Stigers' trouser leg and spreading out in a puddle on the concrete floor. More time passed. Nothing happened.

Stigers and Chalmers looked at each other and let out a long, slow sigh of relief.

'A dud,' said Chalmers. 'Thank God.'

And then there was a vivid flash of orange heat and, for a fraction of a second, pain beyond all imagining.

Crouched in the water, Will steeled himself for the first blow from the Rat King's machete. Then the tunnel seemed to suddenly breathe in and shudder beneath his feet. The sensation was so odd that everybody froze in position, the Subs' arms raised to strike, their three victims cowering beneath them. Will saw the explosion before he actually heard it. Everything seemed to slip into a kind of queasy slow motion.

First there was a flash of light that turned night into day. Will could see everything in excruciating detail, right down to the look of surprise on the Rat King's bearded face. Then, the roof of the tunnel some fifty yards back seemed to open as though somebody had just yanked on a huge zip set into the bricks. It broke asunder and a great oily cloud of fire came billowing out from the opening. It filled the entire width of the tunnel and came rolling across the surface of the water towards them, silhouetting the Subs who were all standing with their backs to the blaze.

A thought flashed through Will's mind, something that Roxy had said the last time he'd seen her what seemed like years ago.

I see fire rolling across water. It's like a river of fire, flowing deep beneath the ground.

Extraordinary. But there was no time to ponder on it now. Will acted from pure instinct. His arms still around Marianne and Scally, he plunged backwards into the water and allowed himself to sink to the bottom. In the panic he forgot to close his eyes. Staring up through the muck of the water, he saw black silhouettes towering over him. Then, in an instant, the silhouettes were engulfed by orange light and were sent whirling through the air like huge unwieldy birds of fire. The flames rode across the surface of the water, inches above Will's astonished gaze, and he was aware of the heat of it even beneath the surface. Now he felt the impact of the explosion, the bricks beneath his back lurching as though shaken by a giant hand. Debris hurtled down all around him, but he stayed put, not wanting to surface into that maelstrom of orange light.

Then, just as suddenly, the fire snuffed itself out, receding back up the tunnel to the collapsed roof. Will was about to scramble up out of the water, but realized that there was no need. The water was draining away from around them, leaving them lying on the curved stone floor like three stranded fish. The air was thick with smoke and a peculiar smell, like roasting meat.

They struggled upright and stared at each other, for the moment not understanding what had happened. Looking back up the tunnel, Will was able to make sense of it. A large section of the roof beneath the warehouse had collapsed, blocking the sewer; but they could hear a whooshing sound as the flood water began to build up behind the barrier of fallen rubble. Will turned and looked down the tunnel. The Subs, or rather, what was left of them, were scattered for some thirty yards down the sewer, hairless, dismembered, their clothes and skin smouldering where the flames had seared the flesh from their bones. For the first time, it occurred to Will what had happened.

Shaun's bomb had worked. They had destroyed the warehouse. He looked at Marianne and at Scally and realization dawned for them at the same instant. They hugged each other and started to laugh wildly at the wonder of it.

'We did it!' yelled Scally. 'We did it!'

There was a dull grinding noise from upstream. Will broke off the embrace for a moment, to stare suspiciously at the wall of rubble up ahead. It occurred to him how much water must be building up behind there. The pressure of it.

He got to his feet and pulled the others with him.

'We'd better get back to the outlet,' he told them.

They stared at him for a moment, uncomprehending. Then

another grinding noise made them turn their heads to look in the direction he was indicating.

'Oh no,' said Marianne. 'Come on, let's get out of here!'

They began to walk along the tunnel, but another dull, grating sound made them break into a trot. Then, exhausted as they were, they started running.

They moved past the still-twitching bodies of Subs, trying not to look too closely at their mangled limbs and flayed bones. Will tried to remember how much further it was to the outlet pipe. They came to an intersection and turned into it. There, maybe two hundred yards ahead of them was a round patch of darkness criss-crossed by a grid of steel bars.

'Yes!' cried Will. 'Keep going, we're almost there!'

And an instant later, he heard a thunderous roar, the sound of the debris being pushed aside by a torrent of raging water.

'Come on!' he screamed. 'Move it, move it!' They ran with all the speed they could muster. They were a hundred yards from the exit now and behind them they could hear the water coming with a noise like an express train. Will risked a glance over his shoulder and in the darkness, he saw a vast churning wall of water powering its way towards them, as they closed the distance to the opening.

There was an instant of deep silence and then the water was upon them, roaring like a beast ...

Will felt an impact smash into his back and then he was engulfed, thrown headlong, rolling under the water like a piece of human debris. His shoulder struck against brick but he did not know if it was floor or wall or roof that he had collided with. He'd had no time to take a breath and already his lungs ached for air, so he kicked out in what he hoped was the direction of the surface. He burst clear of the water with a gasp and saw the roof flashing by only inches from his face, but there was no sign of either of his companions. He gulped in air and dropped lower in the water, afraid of knocking his brains out on the roof. It surely couldn't be far now to the outlet.

The steel grid struck him in the chest, driving the air out of him a second time. For a moment he was spreadeagled by the power of the water as it burst through the outlet like champagne from the neck of a bottle. He struggled to work himself higher and with an almost superhuman effort, he managed to get his head above the flow. He saw somebody flailing towards him and caught a glimpse of Marianne's blonde hair trailing in the water. He reached out and grabbed her, swung her in beside him and helped to lift her head clear of the water.

'You OK?' he gasped.

She nodded, breathlessly.

'Scally?' she cried, over the roaring of the water.

He shook his head, feeling a terrible anxiety mounting in his chest; but just as suddenly, the boy surfaced beside him, laughing delightedly and flicking the water out of his hair. The force of the water was subsiding now, as it dropped down to a more manageable level. Now corpses came floating towards them, and they didn't want to stay in here a moment longer.

'Come on,' suggested Will. 'Squeeze through the gap. Marianne, you first.' She didn't protest, but pulled herself along the grille to the opening on the right-hand side of it. She pushed through and dropped down onto the river bank below. Will saw Mike and Shaun rushing to her, wrapping a blanket around her. He waited until they had led her to a safe place, then pushed Scally towards the opening.

The boy grinned and pulled himself across to the hole in the bars. He pushed through, and dropped to the river bank, where Mike and Shaun were waiting.

Now gratefully, Will started to pull himself towards the opening. Another corpse came floating towards him in the water and he put down a hand to push it away from him. His heart almost stopped when the corpse grabbed his wrist and jerked him down beneath the surface of the water.

For an instant, Will was lost in total shock. He kicked and struggled and blew bubbles into the water. Now the hand released its grip and moved to clamp around his throat. An instant later it was joined by another one, the two hands squeezing with a deadly pressure. Will opened his eyes and stared straight ahead through the veil of murky water. The scorched, half-melted face grinning at him only inches from his own had a crucifix tattooed on its forehead.

Will kicked hard and managed to surface again, feeling his back scrape against the metal bars. He lifted his own hands and tried to loosen the Rat King's grip, but the man seemed to possess a strength that was superhuman.

'What's thy hurry, Streeter?' he croaked, and opened his mouth in a feral roar. Will saw something long and glistening coming up from out of his throat, its purple mouthparts opening and closing convulsively. He tried to twist his head away but the Rat King's grip was too powerful. Now the worm was pushing out from his mouth and probing at Will's face.

Desperate, he let his hands drop to the leather harness around his waist, fumbling through the various utensils as he searched for a weapon he could use. He had lost the baseball bat back down the tunnel. His fingers closed on and identified something familiar. An old-fashioned tin opener. It wasn't much but there was no time to be picky. Will could feel a pounding in his ears and his vision was clouding with a whirling red mist.

He fumbled the tin opener out of its loop, took a firm grip on it and as hard as he could, he jabbed the point of it deep into the Rat King's belly. Will saw the expression of surprise register in the man's mad eyes. He involuntarily clamped his jaws shut on the worm and the creature began to thrash its head wildly from side to side. The hands around Will's throat relaxed their grip and with his last reserves of strength, he pushed upwards with the opener, ripping the Rat King's belly wide open. The man thrashed backwards in the water, blood and viscera spilling from his torn gut; and something even worse. Will saw them swarming in the water in a cloud, hundreds of tiny, twisting worms, writhing madly in their new unprotected environment.

With a grunt of disgust, he turned away and squeezed through the gap in the bars. He dropped the short distance to the river bank and lay for a moment, getting his breath back. Then Mike and Shaun were beside him, helping him back to his feet, draping a thick blanket around his shoulders, both of them unaware of what had just happened.

'Here, take a good swig of this,' he heard Shaun say, and the bottle of whiskey was thrust into his hands. Will raised it to his lips and took a swallow. The fiery liquid revived him a little, spread some warmth through his chilled insides.

'You fuckin' well did it,' said Mike, clapping him on the back. 'I couldn't believe it when the place went up!'

They helped him across to where Marianne and Scally were waiting for him.

'What took you so long?' asked Marianne. 'We were getting worried.'

He shook his head. 'Nothing,' he said. He was aware now of a huge orange glow in the sky beyond the ridge of the river bank. He was about to ask what it was and then he realized that it must be the warehouse.

'Come on,' he said, 'let's go and see what we've done.'

Their arms around each other, they stumbled up the slope of the river bank, away from the outlet. None of them looked back. If they had, they would have seen the body of the Rat King wedged up against the steel bars, his sightless eyes staring into the night sky. They would have noticed too the gaping wound in his stomach; and the countless quantities of tiny worms that were spilling out of it, dropping to the bank and squirming and coiling towards the river beyond . . .

Epilogue

As they drew nearer to the warehouse they could hardly believe the extent of the damage. The place was an inferno of fire, the flames spreading through the wooden floors and destroying everything in its path. The emergency services were on the scene, several fire engines parked in the courtyard, yellow jacketed firemen running madly backwards and forwards trying to organize water from the river. There were ambulances too and police cars and sirens and flashing lights.

'Looks like we started quite a party,' observed Marianne, gazing dreamily at the flames. She presented quite a picture, soaked to the skin and wrapped in a filthy blanket. But Will thought she had never looked more beautiful than she did at that moment, her eyes lit by the orange light of the fire.

They moved as close as they dared, to the chainlink perimeter fence. In the chaos, people were hardly likely to take much notice of a few Rag People but Will was nervous about being seen by any of Chalmers' men. Gazing through at the legions of shouting, running people, he suddenly recognized a face in the crowd.

Suzanne dressed in a yellow fireman's jacket, her face bruised and scratched as though she'd been in a fight, was watching grimly as a stretcher was lifted into an ambulance. Will thought he recognized the long lean figure under the white sheet as Don Bullen, but the face that stared up at the night sky was a bloody, toothless mask straight out of a wax museum. Suzanne must have sensed Will looking at her, because she turned and stared straight at him. Then she was hurrying across to the fence.

'Will, thank God, you're all right!' She was laughing with

relief. 'My God, Will, you did it! I can't believe it, you did it!' She seemed to become aware of Will's companions for the first time and she smiled uncertainly at them. 'Are you all right?' she asked him.

He smiled, nodded. 'Never felt better,' he assured her. He nodded towards the burning warehouse. 'It's quite something isn't it?' he said. 'What we did.'

'What *you* did,' she corrected him.

'You helped,' he assured her. He leaned closer to the fence, 'What happened to you? You look like you've taken a beating.'

She frowned. 'It was Chalmers. And Adam. They caught me in the office trying to go through the files.'

'What?' Will stared at her. 'Chalmers is here?'

'He was.' She nodded back at the building. 'He was in there when it went up. Adam too. The firemen say there's no chance of them walking out of there.'

Will smiled with grim satisfaction.

'And what about Bullen?' he asked. 'He looked like he'd done ten rounds with Jake La Motta.'

'Worse than that,' said Suzanne with a grin. 'He had one round with me and a can of cola.'

Will looked puzzled but she made a dismissive gesture.

'Long story,' she said. 'I'll tell you about it when we get home.'

There was a long silence. Will glanced uncertainly at Marianne, noting the worry in her eyes. 'Do me a favour,' he said quietly. 'Give us a couple of minutes alone, OK? Go on, Scally, take her a little way off up the path. I won't be a minute.'

Marianne gazed at him thoughtfully for a moment. Then she smiled and allowed Scally and the others to lead her away.

Will turned back to Suzanne. She was staring at him through the wire, a look of bewilderment on her face. 'Well, you *are* coming back, aren't you?' she reasoned. 'I mean, it's over, you've done what you set out to do. What's there to stay for?'

Will threw a glimpse over his shoulder towards Marianne and the others. 'It's not as easy as that, Suzanne. I have commitments, now. In a weird kind of way, I have a family.'

Suzanne followed his gaze for a moment. 'Those two?' she said disparagingly.

'Not just them. There's a whole tribe. Or at least, what's left of it. I've promised to help them.'

Suzanne sighed, shook her head. 'Oh Will, when are you ever going to learn? In this life, it's all about looking after Number One.'

'Maybe.' He shrugged. 'But, you know, I'm happier now than I ever was before.'

'How *can* you be?' Suzanne implored him. 'Look, at least come back and have a shower, something to eat. Your friends too, if you want.'

He raised his eyebrows, surprised by the offer. In many ways, he thought, she had changed too. 'It's kind of you,' he said. 'But we can look after ourselves. It's what we do best.' He gave her an apologetic smile. 'I'd better go. We've got to get ourselves sorted out with dry clothes and some hot food. Thanks again for your help.'

He started to move away from the wire and she pushed against it, fingers splayed, as though she imagined she could push it down.

'Will, you know where I live,' she reminded him.' If you need anything, anything at all, I'll be there for you.'

'Sure,' he said. 'Thanks. Maybe I'll take you up on that one of these days.' He lifted one hand in a brief wave and then turning, he walked quickly away to join the others.

Suzanne watched through the chainlink fencing. The other two men had walked on a distance but the woman and the boy were hanging back, waiting for him. When he reached them, he stepped in between them and put his arms around their shoulders in a protective gesture. He leaned over and kissed the woman gently on the forehead. She was pretty, Suzanne thought, in a weird kind of way.

The three of them walked away along the dirt road beside the river. Smoke from the fire was drifting low on the wind and after they'd gone a short distance, they moved into grey, appearing briefly as vague, wraithlike apparitions.

Then they were gone, leaving no sign that they had been there.

Suzanne felt a wetness on her cheek. She lifted one hand to touch at it, then stared at her fingers in dull surprise. It was only then she realized that she was crying.

Sole Survivor

Dean Koontz

The official story of flight 353 is a lie.
They say it was an accident.
It was not.
They say there were no survivors.
There was one.
She is a scientist with a secret.
A secret that will change the world.

Haunting and furiously paced, *Sole Survivor* is a classic nightmare vision from international bestselling author Dean Koontz.

'This is a book to keep you awake reading long into the night . . . Nice one, Mr Koontz' *The Times*

'A fast-paced read' *Mail on Sunday*

'A master of the thriller genre' *Washington Post*

'Koontz's art is making the reader believe the impossible . . . sit back and enjoy it' *Sunday Telegraph*

0 7472 5434 6

More Compelling Fiction from Headline Review

TWO FOR JOY

A PERCEPTIVE NOVEL OF CONTEMPORARY
FAMILY LIFE

AVRIL CAVELL

Avril Cavell casts an amused and occasionally
rueful eye over the vagaries of family life in this
engaging and absorbing novel.

'Twins, how lovely! Aren't you lucky?'

Delphine Dobson isn't so sure. Premature baby
girls seem like double the trouble to her; and
double the expense too – no joke when your
husband is an actor long on charm but short of
regular work.

And indeed life with identical twins proves
tricky. Clover and Merrie are telepathically
close and the best of friends until they are
accidentally separated. When the longed-for
reunion comes, the close and delicate balance of
their relationship has changed. With the looks
of angels and the temperaments of fiends, they
chart the stormy waters of adolescence,
bringing alternate despair and delight to their
family. Until, eventually, they reconcile the
pleasures and pains of their unique relationship
in a surprising and satisfying way.

FICTION / GENERAL 0 7472 4324 7